The First Rule

by Steven William Hannah

ISBN 9798368317694

Cover artwork by Stephen Dally (instagram: @s.dalitattoo)

For Tommye,
Thank you for giving a selfpub author a chance. Please forgive the handful of typos & two continuity errors - they have since been fixed.

The Blind Age: Book One

I hope you enjoy the story!

The First Rule

by Steven William Hannah

Steven H

Ten descended into the Inverted World, veterans all.

Two remain, and they flee for their lives.

From the oily dark of the stone tunnel at their back comes the warble of a choir, the singing voices of their dead comrades. Mournful wailing follows them, the breath of a predator upon their backs.

It wants them to sing too.

“I can hear them,” whispers Ungren, the expedition's only dwarf. He strains, forcing the words out through trembling lips. “It has me again. It's in my head. Temple.” He tugs at the half-Giant's sleeve. “Temple, help -”

Temple drags him along regardless. “Pray,” he shouts. “Sing. Focus on anything else.”

By comparison to the dwarven warrior, Temple is a wild wall of muscle, eight feet tall, adorned in a warrior's breastplate the size of a door. He is descended from Giants, blessed with their size, their strength;

and their dreams of the future.

“There is something after this, Ungren,” says Temple. “I have visions unfulfilled.”

Ungren takes a deep breath, focusing himself. “You never

mention me in these visions," he says. "I thought it unfair to ask, but now..?"

Temple grimaces; that is answer enough.

"Aye," sighs Ungren. "I thought not."

Temple stops and turns, for Ungren is barely walking now. He takes his friend by the shoulders.

"I see only moments, Ungren. I have not seen you in my dreams, but tell me, why would I abandon you?"

"Well, about that." Ungren lifts his shirt to reveal the dwarven chainmail beneath. Burned through the chain is a large handprint. Below that, a five-fingered wound upon Ungren's skin, the same hand drawn in black-burned flesh. Dark tendrils spread outward from it.

"It got you," whispers Temple. "Oh Ungren - when?"

Ungren is silent, eyes unfocused, listening out for something. "Do you hear that?"

Temple freezes, but hears nothing. "Hear what?"

"I can hear it again."

Temple bends his ear to no avail. "I hear nothing."

Ungren looks down at his chest, where the tendrils have spread over the lip of his chain shirt and began to pulse up his neck.

"It's the hand print, Temple. The bastard has left something in me. I can hear Carlan's voice." Ungren's eyes lose focus. "He's cold. He misses us."

They both flinch as the song comes again, a dozen voices clamouring in disharmony.

Temple clutches his head and curses, for his thoughts are no longer his own. Familiar voices of his fallen comrades masquerade as his own thoughts, suggesting that he make his way into the darkness and join the Choir, join his voice with theirs.

The temperature plummets, and his eyes close in shock. From the pit of his chest comes a longing, a loneliness that he has not felt for an age, as though a deep and silent ocean has opened up within him.

He feels the Choir calling to him, and the instincts instilled by training take hold. Temple prays a mantra to centre himself, and wrenches free like a man fighting sleep, arms sluggish at his sides, wrestles heavy eyelids open.

He finds Ungren wandering into the dark.

Temple lunges for the dwarf, catching him by the collar. Ungren's legs are lagging, his body slowed by the chill of the Choir, so close now. Temple drags him onwards.

Ungren whispers something, too quiet for Temple to hear. He pulls Ungren alongside him, and hears him repeat it.

"I'm all alone. It's so cold," whispers Ungren. "I'm not going to make it. It knows where I am."

"Enough," Temple spits into the darkness, shaking Ungren as he drags them surfaceward. "I have dreams unfulfilled, we *do* make it out of here. Ungren?"

Ungren's eyes have lost focus, and so Temple slaps him with a shovel-sized hand, shocking him from his stupor. "Sing, Ungren! Pray! You owe me a drink for this."

Ungren manages a nod, and together they run. For every step that Temple takes, Ungren must take four.

"I hate this thing," Ungren groans, limping alongside Temple.

"Magistry and their experiments," hisses Temple.

"The more join the Choir, the stronger it gets," whispers Ungren. "Can you feel it?"

"We should never have opened that door," says Temple.

"Had a job to do," slurs Ungren. "Reputation to uphold..."

Ungren trails off, stumbling, slowing. Temple has to stop and shake him. Ungren's eyes are glassing over, his jaw hanging slack.

"Nine Hells," says Temple, dragging Ungren along in a daze. "The Magistry can clean up their own mess, then. We'll lead the Choir to the surface. My horse is big enough for us both. We can make it to Atlan in half a day, alert the Magister there; they'll handle it."

Ungren wheezes a bitter laugh. "Think they can?"

"Not our problem."

"What if Atlan falls too?" asks Ungren, beginning to slow again, bringing them both to a stop. His face is pale, etched with the dark roots of the Choir's mark, shining with sweat and fear.

Temple grants him a second's rest, thinking out loud. "It took eight of ours with its song alone. How strong could it become if it takes all of Atlan? That's, what, fifteen thousand? Who could stop it then? How far would the song carry?"

Ungren collapses to the tunnel floor, his back against the wall, breathing hard. Temple crouches down and lifts the dwarf's horned helm from his head. Ungren's golden eyes are milky white, and he cannot find Temple.

Temple must hurry, if Ungren is to survive.

"Listen." says Temple. "We had no warning. Atlan will. Pretzia is waiting at the surface. We can outpace the monster by at least half a day. They'll have time to evacuate, time to teleport in reinforcements. There are healers there. There's time to -"

Ungren's eyes finally find his. "There's no time at all, lad," he says. "Either it takes my mind, or it stops my heart."

The dwarf clenches his jaw and raises his ancestral axe, summoning the last of his strength and planting it on the ground, fighting his way to his feet. He tests his grip on the axe.

"I heard once," says Ungren, "that those half-Giants who dream of the future; that they have to live with the knowledge of their own death."

"So they say."

"And do you know how you die, Temple?"

"In a way," he admits.

"Well," says Ungren, hefting the axe. "Then we are the same. I know exactly how I die – and it brings me great peace. Grant a dead man the grace of the Mind's Eye and answer me one last question: did you know it was going to go this way?"

Temple takes his friend by the arm. "I did not. I swear it. I do not dream in details, Ungren, only moments. I know that there are events I have yet to live through. Nothing more."

"Then tell me. Tell me what happens."

Temple realises that he is holding Ungren's entire weight for him, one arm locked upon his. Ungren's strength is all but gone.

"I fight it again," says Temple. "An attack at night, in the rain. I'm surrounded by flames. I think maybe we're in Atlan. There's a fortification of sorts. A trench. I think we win, because there's one more after that."

"One more?"

"The last one. There's snow," says Temple. "A Priestess, I think – red haired, feels like a friend, maybe. She's walking into the forest alone, carrying a warhammer with a bull's head. She is weeping, angry at me. I do not go with her – for she knows that she goes to certain death."

"You have no other dreams?"

"I do not."

"Then your path is ending shortly after mine." He laughs. "Shall I wait for you on the Black Sands?"

Temple's shoulders drop. "Put aside your pride and let me carry you."

"To die in the sunlight? Of *poison?"* he laughs. "Temple, I'm a dwarf. *Kappi.* To die in battle below the earth is what I was born for." He puts a hand on Temple's huge arm. "To die for a friend? Even better."

Temple wants to argue, but he cannot deny his friend a warrior's death. His protest is selfish; he does not want to be the last man standing. Not again.

Ungren breaks into a mad grin. "Let me die *for* something, Temple."

"It's been an honour, Ungren," he says. "I'll see that your family gets your share of the payout."

"You do that. Tell them I died the death of a true *Kappi.* Singing the battle-hymns of my forefathers."

He grips his axe and, before Temple can say goodbye, they both hear it again.

Singing. Discordant, hollow singing, echoing from the depths. Temple protects his mind with a mantra, spoken in a dominant and commanding voice, as he was trained.

The closer the Choir draws, the harder it is to distinguish his own thoughts from the Choir's song.

“Go,” grunts Ungren. “Make it count.”

“Farewell, my friend.”

“I'll see you on the Black Sands one day,” nods Ungren. “Now *run!*”

The singing is drawing nearer, louder. Through the mental malaise of the Choir's song, Ungren's booming voice breaks like thunder. He sings into the darkness, a dwarven battle hymn for courage in the face of overwhelming odds.

A song to die to.

Temple hears both songs fade as he runs, but the darkness draws on without end. The Inverted World is a trickster, as all who delve into the horrors below learn. He pushes on into the dark, able to see but a few paces in front of himself, and wonders if he has blundered into another spatial loop.

Then he sees the first of the expeditionary camps ahead, a campfire left cold and grey. Before him the darkness finally breaks. Natural light pours into the tunnel from an opening below, and Temple sees a long, deadly drop into the open air, a clouded sky, trees, and he leaps without pause into it, plummeting like a stone.

Gravity shifts, flipping him over, and Temple misses his footing and tumbles head over heel. Now he is on flat ground, running uphill as the Inverted World corrects itself, and he *leaps* as up and down switch places, caught weightless, reaching for the light.

Temple drifts across the boundary in silence, frozen in the moment of escape.

The world is finally the correct way up, and he hits the floor that had just been the ceiling.

Then he is free. Temple erupts from the cramped tunnel, stumbling for balance, falling onto the sun-drenched grass of Northern Altheim; the *real* world. The sun is setting. Birds are singing.

The horror is almost over.

His gigantic warhorse, Pretzia, waits beside the remains of their initial base camp, ears up and alert. She is saddled, fed and ready. The grass around the rocky clearing is chewed short – she has been eating well.

"Pretzia." He grabs the saddle and drags himself to his feet.

Temple can hear the Choir's song echo from the tunnel now, amplified by the acoustics of the earth. His limbs are numb, and he fumbles with the stirrups as he climbs atop Pretzia.

"Come on girl," he urges her. She moves with impressive strength, whinnying her concern for him. Temple struggles to unclasp his breastplate, to let his lungs take in the air. "I'm fine girl, I'm fine. Ride for Atlan, aye?"

Temple never hears her answer. His chest plate crunches inwards, a handprint punched through the steel. An ungodly cold presses against his heart. A black handprint burns onto his skin. He turns in shock, trying to draw his sword, but the poison is close to his heart, and his arms are frozen.

Slumped upon Pretzia's saddle, Temple's eye senses movement at the tunnel opening.

A slim humanoid form unfolds from the darkness, a body of oily smoke with long black hair, like a gown of seaweed wrapped around her frail body. Twice as tall as Temple, with a swarm of smaller shades clinging to her skirt, afraid to follow her into the dying sun light. They crouch, afraid, watching him. Their eyes are little more than dots of flickering light.

This is not right, he thinks. *This is not how I die.*

The Tall Woman watches him. Her eyes are two pale dots in the mist of her formless face, like her shades.

She is singing to him, and as the sun fades, he realises that he is singing too.

The cold spreads through his body, shivering, freezing him – but the Choir opens its long arms to him and offers warmth. Where the sunlight touches her arms, it burns with a deep hiss, and she recoils.

Ungren sings to him from the Choir, begging him to join. Temple sees the dwarf's shade, crouched behind a rock, ashamed and afraid. They are all there, the entire expedition. They are lonely without him, but none will brave the last of the sunlight to touch him.

The Choir is like ice water in his mind, and now it invades his body. The voices of his lost expedition call him home. The person called Temple is drowned; he loses himself in the noise.

She watches him, curious, caring, towering over him, staying out of the sunlight.

Ungren calls to him again.

There's no death in the Choir, he says. They will be like this forever. Safe, and warm, and together. All of them. Temple only wants to escape the crushing, heartbreaking loneliness that is choking him.

His heart is heavy with the weight of every cruelty that he has ever inflicted, for now he can feel the fear and shame of his friends, of the other victims of the Choir. He does not want to be alone ever again.

Tears escape his eyes; his friends want him to stay with them, they'll take the cold away.

The Choir finally has Temple; but it does not have Pretzia. Trained for war in the Steppe Kingdom of Thunderstone, Pretzia is not a steed that frightens easily. She breaks for the road, and surges forwards. The tall woman's grip is torn from Temple's body and mind, leaving just the poison – and the mark.

Temple feels his thoughts come to him like a rush of blood to the head. He slouches forward in the saddle with a groan, vomiting down his own armour.

No blood, he notices. No pain either. He knows that he must survive this: he has seen things that are yet to happen. He *has* to.

The sun is gone when the poison pulls Temple under the ice again, leaving him unconscious on the saddle, holding Pretzia's mane.

Minutes later, Pretzia bursts through the forest clearing and onto the road. Temple's sideways slump is a command; her training tells her to steer left, and steer she does.

Away from Atlan.

Away from the safety of civilisation and Magisterial intervention.

Towards a tiny hamlet in the North called Llantry.

At the edge of the Inverted World
where the sunlight ends
gather two dozen shades of the Choir
old and new alike
singing out of key
ashamed and afraid
children, in terror before the abyss
half dead
waiting
for the Tall Woman to lead them

Sun down
She extends a hand
in offering to the night
the pain of the moonlight is
bearable
but then all pain is bearable

she steps into a new world
her Choir follows
hesitating
the last straggler
dwarf-sized
nervous newcomer
follows dutifully along
for he does not want to be alone

Chapter One

Is there such a thing, thinks Venalia, as a *good* day for a funeral?

She wraps her arms in her cloak, and then around herself, warding away the wind and rain. She stands, as though on trial, before an unlit funeral pyre with no body atop it. Damp has claimed all; the wood of the pyre, her cloak, her dress, the faces of the many villagers gathered for the service.

Beside her, the timberman tries to encourage the kindling with a set of bellows. Embers spit and fizzle with his attempts, and spent, wet matches litter the ground. The day grows dark.

After one apologetic look at the grumbling crowd, she turns to the timberman.

“What are our chances?” she asks.

“Uh...” he mutters between bellow-blows. “Well -”

She hears what he will not say. “It's not happening, is it?”

“Very sorry, Lady Venalia.”

“Don't apologise for the weather,” she sighs, patting him on the shoulder.

He puts the bellows down, but will not meet her eyes. “I could cut dry wood for tomorrow?”

“I'd like to be gone by tomorrow.” She looks around, aware of the eyes burning into her back.

It is clearly not punishment enough, she thinks, that her first duty as a Priestess should the burning of her adoptive father, Marius. It seems that she must also deal with gossiping villagers and wet timber.

"I'll bet Father Marius is laughing at us from the Black Sands," she muses.

The timberman flashes a polite smile. Without the order to stop, he continues with his futile effort. She wonders if it is fear or duty that are driving him. Venalia signals for him to stop, and he nods his thanks and leans back, catching his breath.

The change of tactic catches the attention of the restless crowd. To glance their way and see their judging eyes might be enough to break her spirit.

Venalia had imagined that her return would be a firm lesson to Llantry: a well dressed, well educated Priestess returns home from six years of study. Here to mourn her adoptive father, the villagers would marvel at her poise and elegance, the grace with which she performs the ceremony that is breaking her heart. They would ask her about the wonders of Whitehallow, about the Temple States. None would dare mistreat her, not with the death of Marius on her shoulders.

And yet;

Nobody has asked her anything, neither do they seem to care which of the Gods has chosen her. None will give her anything except a polite nod of sympathy for Father Marius.

Llantry holds an image of her that is stained too deep to undo. The villagers stare, and in doing so, undo the last six years of strength that she has built. She is an embarrassed, ashamed child again, and Llantry will never see her any other way.

Shuffling her hood over her red locks, Venalia turns her head so that her face is hidden from them. She cannot think beneath their stupefied gazing.

"Will there be a fire, then?" asks a child from the crowd.

It immediately earns a *SHUSH* from the parent, but the words are out now; damned children, thinks Venalia, they have a knack for speaking the truth at the worst possible moments.

"Probably?" she tries.

"*Probably?*" shouts one of the older women. "Lass, I'm *probably* freezing to death here. Can you set *me* on fire, at least?"

This brings laughter, and Venalia groans internally. She wishes she could calm them with a half-truth, but now that she has graduated, it is forbidden.

The third rule of the Priesthood: no lying, except to save a life. If a Priestess starts to play with the truth, then the people cannot trust what she says. Venalia is only a few weeks beyond her graduation, and already she longs for the soothing simplicity of a white lie.

"I won't tell you that the sun is going to shine," she offers. "Neither weather nor flame are domains of the Mind's Eye, and so -"

The eyes of the crowd all dart to something behind her, and she whips around with dread bubbling in her stomach. She sees the last person that she wants to see, and today of all days. She prayed that he would miss this.

He wears the expensive wolf furs that his father was known for. The copper-crystalline circlet of his office nestles atop his long black hair, framing a red face that always looks out of breath. Looking at him, Venalia can only think about all the times Gregor would invite every child in Llantry to his birthday, whilst setting aside a letter for her telling her not to come.

He stops atop the burial mound with his two guards.

Venalia has not seen Gregor de Llantry, the Burroughmaster, since the day that she left for Whitehallow, six years ago.

Six years since Gregor's elder sister, Anabel de Llantry, went missing; since the search parties, and the questions, and the panic. The blame. The interrogations.

Venalia remembers Gregor's father breaking down in the village square, begging Marius for the help of the Gods, bargaining for the return of his daughter. Amidst the chaos, she had quietly departed for Whitehallow.

Venalia has played out a discussion with Gregor in her own head, several times, dressing him down in front of everybody; but now that he is here, it feels foolish. Her tutors at Whitehallow spent years teaching her to maintain her composure, for both spellcasting and societal matters; she is expected to behave, and

Venalia supposes that this may as well be the first real test of it.

"Either I am early," bellows the young Burroughmaster, "or the funeral is running late?"

She bows, curt and professional, refusing to break his gaze. "Burroughmaster."

"Venalia," he draws up before her and looks at her boots, her soaked green dress, with a raised eyebrow. "I heard you were back."

Leave it behind, she tells herself; do your job, and be out of here at sunrise.

"I'm here to bury Father Marius, at his own behest," she says. "I don't expect I'll stay long."

"I see," he says, shifting onto a grassy clump so that he reaches her height. "You're not here to take his place, then?"

"No," she says. "No, I am not."

They both seem to breathe a sigh of relief at that. She remains aloof and polite – for the sake of old Marius' memory.

Gregor says nothing, leaving only cold air between them. She reflects that nobody in Whitehallow ever taught her to how to fix an awkward silence either; though they did teach her the list of *proper conversational topics* for leaders and officials.

Family is the first topic that she recalls.

"I was saddened to hear that your father had passed in my absence," she says, voice clipped with professional courtesy.

Gregor drops his gaze, clasping his hands behind his back. "A sad day for all of Llantry." He puffs his chest out. "His name is survived by myself; and by Evelyn, of course."

Evelyn de Llantry. The youngest sister.

"I hope your sister is well?" says Venalia.

"She is – she apologises for her absence here; alas, she does not like funerals. She has seen too many of them. We are, of course, saddened to lose such a wonderful priest." He motions to the pyre, where Marius' body should rest. "Speaking of which," he takes on an accusing tone, "where is the old joker?"

Venalia looks at her wringing hands like a scolded child.

"In his bed."

"Why is he there?"

"He hasn't been moved yet."

Laughter. "Are we to have a funeral without him?"

"I thought I might ensure that the pyre would actually light first. I don't -" want him to get wet, she almost says. She lets the unfinished sentence hang, and Gregor pounces.

"Seems like a slight oversight for a Priestess, no? Is this your first funeral?"

Venalia tries not to react. He is correct. It *is* her first, and for Marius no less, and here she is making a mess of it.

The timberman saves her from having to respond. "We're having some issues with the wood. All my fault, sir, my apologies."

Gregor looks over at him, and smirks. "If only there were somebody here who could dry the wood with, say, a prayer? I recall that Marius once extinguished a burning building with nothing but a song."

"I am not Marius," she says. "The Mind's Eye has no power over flame."

Gregor gives a smug nod, and looks at the crowd. "Perhaps you should not be burning him, then? A shovel may be more fitting – we have plenty, if you'd like one?"

Murmurs of laughter from the crowd; Venalia's face turns red as she fights to keep her composure.

"Marius asked that I burn his body, given the domains of his Goddess."

"He *asked* you?" he raises his eyebrows.

"In the letter asking me to conduct this very funeral, yes. He said he'd be at home -" her voice breaks.

Home. She has not been home in a very long time. She coughs to cover it up, giving her time to regain her composure. The child in her wants to burst into tears, and hope that Gregor takes pity on her. The Priestess in her refuses to break, especially not for *him*.

Tears or not, Gregor backs off a little. "Well, I think that I speak for everybody when I say that *it has been a long week*," he waves to the crowd, and they nod along, "and anything that keeps me and my people from the tavern is a hard sell, am I right?" He laughs for the crowd, and they laugh with him. Someone whistles. "How long will this take?"

Venalia has been waiting for the obvious bait, and tries not to let it show on her face. The laughter is too familiar. She is a child again, mocked for her red hair, her freckles, for the way she speaks. Inward and unseen, her temper flares. Curses go unsaid; she sticks to her training and breathes through the anger.

Let them laugh, she thinks. She will be leaving soon enough. Gregor can keep his illiterate backwater, while she moves on to bigger, better things. Granted, she has no idea what those things might be yet, but Priestesses are in high demand across the continent.

Venalia lets her righteous indignation swell, and uses it to sharpen her voice.

"The funeral will commence shortly," she announces to the crowd, grabbing their attention. "If any of you have such a *lack of respect* for Father Marius and his memory, then feel free to go to the tavern. Go," she urges them. "Have fun. Go and drink in his absence, and complain about the weather while he rots in his bed." The crowd bristles at the accusation, but she rounds on them further. "Marius gave Llantry the best years of his life. We like to talk about how tough we are in the North, and here you are shivering in some rain. So go on; leave, those who want to. I won't judge you." Nobody moves. She lowers her voice and layers it with sympathy, stepping towards the crowd. "I am not a Magister. I cannot command fire to burst forth from my hands, nor can I command the sun to shine. My talents lie elsewhere." She turns back to Gregor. "I am no wizard, Burroughmaster. My God is the Mind's Eye."

"The God of knowledge, secrets and scholars," he says. "Then perhaps you can pray to him," he looks at the crowd, "and ask *him* for a way to get this fire going?"

There's a burst of chuckling from the crowd. Now she has to force the smile.

"I *could* do that, Burroughmaster," she takes the tone of a teacher, "but prayer is no simple thing. We do not pray for assistance unless we have no other choice. To even ask a favour of the Mind's Eye, I have to offer something first. Hidden knowledge, or a secret of some kind. Father Marius wouldn't have wanted me wasting my limited supply of secrets." She pats the timberman on the back. "Not when the help of our kind timberman and some dry wood will suffice. Unless you would like to tell me one of *your* secrets, Burroughmaster? I could trade that?"

The crowd chuckles, and she smiles; she can feel them coming to her side. Remain polite, she tells herself, and resist the temptation to put him in his place. Let the public theatre play out for what it is.

"I have no secrets worth telling," he gives her a look – a warning. "I am retiring to my estate. Have someone send a runner for me when the funeral is actually *starting* this time?" With another warning glance, Gregor turns and marches off, followed by his two guards, their chainmail jangling as they descend the stone steps back to Llantry.

Still the petty child that he always was, thinks Venalia. He has not changed at all since she last saw him: still just a middle manager, a tiny and petty king.

In Whitehallow she met so many little Gregors – the world, she wrote in one distressed letter to Marius, seems to be full of them. Little emperors, and emperors of what, exactly? This place? Llantry resembles a grey watercolour painting of a village, left to gather dust. At Whitehallow, she learned that Llantry is not even *on* most maps, given how small it is. Just a raised wall of earth and blunt wooden stakes surrounding a damp village of thatched longhouses. Most of Llantry is mud.

The crowd are waiting in awkward silence now. She has them, but not for long. A bleak wind whips across the gathering, and the crowd bristles. She can sense their resolve running like ink on wet paper. She'll be left to burn old Marius by herself, if she cannot fix this.

"Venalia?" whispers the timberman. "I hate to ask, but, uh, *is* there anything you can do to help?"

Maybe," she says, and turns, looking across Llantry. She lifts the green hood of her cloak, trying not to shiver for the sake of appearances. There has to be something.

In her head comes Marius, telling her to *think, lass. The Gods should not need to help us sweep the floor*.

She wishes again that she could lie. This was easy, she thinks, when it was all just a part of her training at Whitehallow. When she and her peers made a joke of the oath of honesty that they were all sworn to.

Does this dress suit me, Venalia?

That depends, are we following the third rule today?

She must think of something soon. It is only noon and already the sun is setting. The days are short, this far North. Here, it starts snowing in autumn. Daylight lasts but a few hours. Come the snow, the villagers will bed down for winter in the warmth of their houses. At least in Whitehallow the tropical winter evenings were a time to see friends and eat on balconies. The crystalline lanterns shone all night, lining the streets like soldiers.

Lamps, she thinks; Llantry is always behind the curve on technology. “Do we still have old alchemical lamps here?” she asks the timberman. “We could douse the pyre in lamp oil.”

The timberman's eyes light up. “Aye, Priestess, that would do it.”

“So fuel then? How much do we have?”

He chews his lip. “Mm, not much... and Gregor will likely want to save it for the coming snows, but -”

“We don't need much. Go grab some fuel, timberman. I'll see to Marius,” she turns to the crowd, triumphant. “The funeral will proceed. Thank you for your patience. I'll need six strong men?”

A handful of young men raise their heads and step forward, eager to be a part of the proceedings, eager to be considered strong. Venalia recognises none of the volunteers; no help from those who grew up with her. She swallows it with bitter acceptance, forcing a smile. She is forbidden to lie, but it would also be frowned upon to tell them what she truly thinks of them. It is her pride that fights her training.

Venalia leads them down the mound, into the village where she grew up. Llantry has lain buried in her memories for six years, a corpse that has only decayed with time.

Marius raised her as best he could, but there are some things an old Priest cannot teach a young woman. It made her an easy target for the children's cruelty. Venalia remembers the girls being the worst, Anabel de Llantry in particular. Being Gregor's older sister put her next in line as Burroughmaster, and that sense of entitlement and superiority bled into every game the children played.

Anabel never lost a bet. Anabel made the rules, was always right, organised every game. She led the children in strangely specific attacks on Venalia, for the most infuriating of reason. Laughing at her for not knowing how to shave her legs, of all things. *Legs*, she despairs, in Llantry. As if anybody here *cares,* our skirts go to our ankles and we wear thick wool stockings. It is *freezing*.

They used to tell her that even the barn doors weren't as flat as her chest, then mock her for stuffing a dress with fabric to try and fit in. They filled her favourite book with dead bugs, so that they'd all fall out when she tried to read in bed. She screamed the first time it happened, trying to hide the bugs amongst the folds of her bedsheets before Marius came to check on her; she remembers the shame of him finding them.

Worse, was his sympathy; she had not wanted to burden him. She had not wanted him to think that she was weak. She cried only out of shame; that he might see her torment and feel responsible.

The same girls who laughed along with Anabel are mothers now, staring back at her from the crowd. She tries not to let it bother her. She is not doing this for them. She is doing this because Marius asked her to. After everything that he did for her, it is the very least that she can do.

Were it up to her, she would have never come back to Llantry.

Miles away, hanging limp from the saddle, Temple's eyelids creak open. Pretzia has slowed to a canter in the darkness of the evening forest. His memory gradually returns, as he struggles upright in the saddle, rubbing his eyes.

Pain, in sickening waves, overwhelms him. Blotches on his vision, swaying colours. He curses, and clings to Pretzia as he waits for it to pass. Sensing his distress, Pretzia stops.

When the pain has slowed to an ebb, Temple looks down

at his breastplate, and finds the hole where the tall woman punched through it.

He finds a black handprint burned onto his abdomen. Pulsing black veins spread from the wound, creeping further with every beat of his heart.

He recalls Ungren's dying moments, and then his song. Ungren had the mark, and Ungren is part of the Choir now. Temple quiets his mind, awaiting the dreadful sensation of the voices amongst his thoughts, but -

Nothing. Not yet.

He wonders how much of Ungren remains, if he is aware of what is happening; he wonders if the soul is trapped, unable to pass on, or if the Choir only keeps echoes of its victims. Either option is horrifying to consider. Dying comes natural, but being unable to cross the Black Sands and find peace is a crime against the soul itself.

It must be thousands of years old, his analytical mind informs him, and he regrets giving it any thought. It serves only to frighten him.

Temple notes a tide of numbness rising through his body, as though he is being lowered into ice water. Again it comes; he is assailed by strange thoughts and ideas that are not his own, memories that are not his, in languages that he does not speak.

Temple *knows* that he survives this. He has *seen* it – but he is not sure *how*. Were it not for his dreams of the future, he would be in a panic. Instead there is only the low and constant fear, creeping up on him, that his time is *soon*. Two of his visions remain unfulfilled, after which there is no future to see.

Such is the lot of a half-Giant.

“Onwards to Atlan, girl,” he groans as he pats Pretzia. She whinnies and starts off, but his grip on the reins is failing as the numbness spreads. “Pretzia.” He leans by her ear. “If I black out, keep on. Reach Atlan. Night falling. Can't be far.” He looks around, bleary eyed. “Though, I do not recall this road.” He struggles with a length of leather strap, tying it around Pretzia's saddle. The other end, he ties around his breastplate straps. Should he fall unconscious, Pretzia will drag him to Atlan.

Night grows colder, and the bird calls settle; calls that Temple recognises. Scaled falcons, with their distinctive wooping cry; the same bird calls that woke him years ago, when he was on campaign in the Northern wilderness. Their unit had a scout, a Steppe nomad with an animal familiar, a scaled falcon that obeyed his commands. She kept watch over the Steppe as they travelled, and so Temple knows the bird's call well.

It is not a call that is heard near Atlan.

“Pretzia,” he whispers. “Pretzia, I don't think we're heading South.”

He looks up to the stars, and curses. Amenemi, the water moon, hangs over his path. He is travelling North – away from Atlan, away from safety. Temple tries to speak, to tell Pretzia to turn, but his tongue is numb, swelling to fill his mouth. He tries to right Pretzia, to turn her around, but his hands will not obey his commands. The numbness spreads across his chest, and Temple slumps from the saddle again. He hits the ground shoulder first, crumpled in a heap.

Pretzia, trained for such eventualities, slows down to avoid hurting him too much, and carries on regardless. Temple's breastplate clatters over rocks on the muddied road, slick with rain. Eyes closed, Temple is dragged North through the night. His breathing is haggard, his lungs drowning in poison. He is unconscious when they finally pass a road sign, telling them that they are only three miles from Llantry.

The Tall Woman stalks the trees

her shades remember the feel of roads

they are at home here

at home in the darkness

where none can see

nor judge

Her shades follow as ducklings, trying

and failing

to sing any song but hers

to pull away from each other
but never enough to break from the song itself
Bound together in harmony

The Tall Woman stops
waits
perfectly still
reaching for the sky
hand above the canopies
she calls to the singers there
and soon
a bird alights on her outstretched hand
the panicked flapping of small wings
the bird is gone
only a shade remains

Its song joins the Choir
Now, she can sing like a bird
Now she can see what the bird has seen
Remember all that the bird remembers

the mountain ranges and rivers of the North
where swamp
turns to Steppe
turns to sweeping seas of grass
the world stretched out before her

Little wing takes flight

and she sees
a half-Giant man dragged by a horse
an armoured snow angel in the mud
Temple.
she knows his name from the minds of his comrades
knows that he is strong
a talented warrior
but most impressive of all
Temple has dreams of things yet to come

if Temple sings with her
then she will have his dreams too
she will have his mind
and all of its strange gifts

on stilt-thin legs she strides
North
towards a village that the birds know
mud and thatched huts
surrounded by a wall of earth
and wooden spikes
two hundred hearts for beating
two hundred mouths for singing

Chapter Two

Venalia is glad to finally be doing something useful. She leads the six strong men – cattle herders and shepherds – to Marius' house.

Tall lamps light her way in the dark, blazing flames protecting by glass bulbs, fuelled by the same oils that she will use to burn Marius. Puddles muddy the hem of her dress as she traipses the dirt road. Behind her march the pallbearers, carrying a pallet between them.

She stands before Marius' house, a tombstone of its own. Through the window she sees the warm glow of the fireplace, and her heart skips. She had been so confident on the way here, but this is her first sight of home in six years.

This was her favourite place to be, for as long as she could remember. Safety; home and hearth. It feels hollow. The music is missing. Marius was always playing one of his many instruments when she came home; tonight, there is just the howl of the wind, singing alone.

His spirit will have long since began the journey across the Black Sands. There will be no malevolence in her old home, no restless spirit to exorcise – yet she is terrified to enter.

She takes a breath to steady her voice. “Who lit the fire?” she asks the men.

“Ol' Bell the Blacksmith, mos' likely,” says one. “He says he'd care for the house. T'was he that found auld Marius.”

"Gods be good," she whispers. Bell is perhaps the only person in Llantry that she will be grateful to see. "I'll need a bit of time alone."

The men nod, and move under an awning to get out of the wind and the rain, huddled in a circle to share a few puffs of a pipe.

Venalia stands by the door, hesitating. She puts her hand on the door, tempted to knock out of politeness, and takes a breath. She holds her sigil, the symbol of the Mind's Eye, for strength, knowing already that strength is simply not the domain of her God. Nor is bravery. These things she must find for herself. Her God deals in curiosity, and answers, and that is what finally moves her: curiosity.

Dropping her hand, she strides through the door with authority granted by her station. The air is warm, the fire crackling, the candles lit, the kettle whistling over the flames. She knows the kettle by sound alone, for it served as her alarm clock for many years.

By the fire sits a hunched, cloaked figure, bent like a question mark, with a hood and a leather blindfold obscuring most of his face. A crooked arm with a leather-gloved hand is raking the coals of the fire to expose the cherry-red embers.

"Venalia?" he rasps, his voice a thin, papery whisper. He looks up, but not with his eyes; Bell has been blind since before Venalia ever knew him. He wears the blindfold as a courtesy to those with weak stomachs. Even with it on, Venalia can see the lumps and twisted skin on his cheeks, where his scars begin. "Why, is that really you, Venalia?"

"Bell?"

He stands at her approach, and she falls into his open arms. Under his cloak is a misshapen body hidden under bundles of clothing, ruined and twisted by a lifetime of battle wounds and badly healed injuries.

"You've grown," he says, holding her as he laughs. "Tall. Skinny, too. Who did this to you?"

She laughs, despite herself. "I'd ask you the same."

Bell certainly feels older, weaker. His shoulders sit at different heights, his hips are twisted to one side – one knee will not bend at all, and his muscles creak and groan when he moves. Nonetheless, he is a massive figure of a man, once a sought-after blacksmith to kings and lords, with impressive strength. He smells like soot and iron, befitting a blacksmith, and she can feel the heat of the furnace radiating from his chest.

He takes her shoulders and sits her on the chair – on Marius' chair – and kneels before her, taking her hands in his. Though his eyes are hidden, Venalia can see the sadness in his sagging body.

"Last we met, you were a child."

I'm a child still. "I wish it were under better circumstances."

"As do I. As do I," he says, creaking as he takes a chair beside the fire. "What a loss for Llantry."

"A loss for us all," she whispers.

"Often were the nights that we would drink together," says Bell. "Marius would read me some of your letters. Imagine my surprise, to hear that you had been chosen by the Mind's Eye. Imagine our pride."

She laughs, rolling her eyes. "I'm sure you'd rather I wore the sigil of the Forge."

"You were never drawn to that life," he says. "But to books? To knowledge? You were always a scholar. The Mind's Eye was the obvious path."

"Marius was always certain that I would walk with the White Wrath."

"He knew your temper," nods Bell.

Venalia remembers; Marius put up with a lot from her as she struggled into adolescence. For a long time since leaving, she has wanted to apologise.

"How was he?" she asks. "At the end?"

Did he say anything?

Anything about me?

"He was Marius," laughs Bell. "Till the very end, he was Marius. He made us drinks, before he told me the news," says Bell, waving his hands as he tells the story. "Fancy glasses, fruit, exotic spirits from Sarantja. Filled a few pipes for us too. We sat on the crest of the wall in our cloaks and watched the stars come out, charted the movement of Tunga, then Amenemi." Bell takes a deep breath. "Then he told me that he was going to die."

"Yeah," she says.

Venalia knows how to comfort those in grief. She passed exams on it, studied it from books; but now that it is her own private grief, she has nothing to offer; only fears, things that she wants to lay to rest, the questions that have played over in her mind throughout the entire journey home. "Was he scared?" she asks, voice shaking.

"Not for himself, no," says Bell. "Just for you."

Venalia sets her jaw, determined not to let the tears come. She is, she tells herself, a professional – tears are not becoming of a Priestess. She is grateful, right now, that Bell cannot see her; though she is certain that he can hear her struggling to breathe through her tightening chest.

"He read me your last letter," Bell continues, "about how you didn't know which path to take, what to do with your future after your ordaining. He wanted to answer it then, but alas, his next letter would have to be the one that brought you home." She remembers opening it, excited to read his advice, only to have the smile fall from her face. Bell hears her sorrow, and lowers his voice. "If he had been able to bring you home in time for a goodbye, Venalia, he would have."

"I was halfway across the continent," she whispers her excuse to herself. "Two days by airship, then two by carriage. He was given three days."

"He asked me to give you this." Bell pulls an envelope from inside his cloak. She recognises Marius' handwriting, and her name, and takes it. Bell stands up as she stares down at the letter. "I will be waiting at the pyre, with everybody else. Marius is in his bed." Bell puts one heavy hand on her shoulder before he leaves. "Take all the time that you need."

He stretches a hand out and walks towards the door till he finds it, and wind whistles through the old house, whipping the fire into a roar before the door slams shut.

For a few moments, Venalia sits at peace with herself, building up the strength required for her task. She takes the letter – it smells of Marius, like old pine oil and evergreen – and puts it inside her dress pocket. She wipes her eyes; Marius would not want her getting emotional. He always told her to temper her heart, and engage her mind – and so she tries to.

She takes the kettle from the flame, and pours herself a cup, testing the aroma before drinking: Sarantja Orange, obviously, her favourite. Marius would have the fire lit and the tea ready every morning for getting up – and here, he has done it one last time. A little goodbye.

It dawns upon her that she has not heard his voice in six years – and never will again. Venalia pauses, trying to hold back the tears, but she is alone here – there is nobody to judge a moment of weakness. She buries her face in her hands, and lets the dam burst, sobbing like a child until she can breathe again, relieving a little of the pressure from her chest.

There she remains, until the wave subsides, and she can breathe once more.

Venalia crosses the room and eases into his old rocking chair, next to his lute, his sitar, his harmonicas, his panpipes, all stacked in the corner. His sermons were about performance, about celebration, about joy and appreciation in all things. He had an infectious laugh, and a smile like summer sunshine. He embodied his flower-draped Goddess, the Wakened World, lady of life, love and the arts.

Her eyes fall upon his bedroom door, and she knows that he would scold her for procrastinating in her duties. Those poor boys are waiting on her in the rain, after all. Venalia rises, determined now, and opens the door to his bedroom.

The crack in the door first reveals the shape in Marius' bed, and she pauses in fear. It is not Venalia, but the Priestess, that forces her to walk in. The professional. Even so, she avoids looking at his face.

Letting herself down slowly onto the bed, she hesitates before resting a hand on his arm, still and grey. Finally, she looks at his face, and regrets it. His eyes are open, as is his mouth. He stares at nothing, still and lifeless, lips pulled tight against toothless gums. She reaches up and closes his eyelids, shuts his mouth.

"Oh Marius," she whispers, and finds his sigil around his neck, on the usual chain. The symbol of the Wakened World: a silver mandala, the flower of life. She gives it a squeeze, and looks skywards. "You'd better take good care of him," she tells any listening Gods. “This one is special.”

When she was young, she was beset by nightmares. Marius would tuck her in, just a tiny child in a huge bed of her own, and kiss her forehead to banish the fear. It worked whenever he did it. Now she can return the favour. Venalia folds his hands over his chest, and then leans down, kissing him on the forehead.

Venalia has a thought, and checks what he is wearing. As expected, he has dressed in his best vestments for his own funeral.

“Of course you did,” she laughs to dispel her nerves, a trick that he taught her. She does not know if she can do this without running it past him first, and so she tells him. “Right. Listen up old fella. We're going to burn you as per your instructions. That is,” she rolls her eyes, “if Gregor doesn't throw a fit beforehand. Speaking of which, I see that Gregor is the Burroughmaster now, too? Hope he's doing right by everybody. Hope he's better than he was when I knew him. Having met him earlier, I don't hold out much hope for that statement. Hope he never gave *you* any trouble.” She looks at Marius, who looks to be asleep now, and gives him a knowing smile. “He hates that I'm back. I'm his equal and he hates it.”

She plays with her own deity's sigil, a stylised human face with a third eye blazing open from the forehead.

“Maybe,” she admits to herself, “I just remind him of Anabel. I maintain that she ran away. Who wouldn't want out of here? Anabel was due to become Burroughmaster. That means she'd be trapped here forever. I think I'd just take my chances marrying a passing merchant,” she laughs, and it sounds forced even to her. Venalia pats Marius' chest. She takes a shuddering breath. She wants to leave, but it does not feel finished. There is more yet to say, and the questions are bubbling up inside her, straining to escape. She lets them loose like doves from the cage.

“I've got so many things that I wanted to ask you. Like: what the hell do I *do* now that I'm ordained? My tutors said I could do anything, but I don't know what I *want* to do. The Mind's Eye wants me to find my own path, of course. He chose me as a Priestess, so now I've got *that* to live up to. Gods, Marius, I've got so many big decisions to make.”

He remains silent, of course, but already she feels better for voicing it aloud.

“You know, I'm glad that I left Llantry. Anabel's

disappearance was - well, it was just bad timing, right? I can't imagine how bad it must have been here. I'm sorry to have left at such a bad time. But you were right to push me to go to Whitehallow. I knew it was the right call. I *did* miss you, even if I didn't miss Llantry. I'd have written home more, but I was just so busy with my studies and - I'm just -" she stops, catching herself. "I'm just sorry that I couldn't be here for you to -"

To die.

She stops short of saying it, and pats his chest, swallowing her grief. "I'll miss you, you old charmer," she whispers, and leans across, taking his cold hand. "Thank you for everything. For raising me. I should have thanked you for that while you were alive. You knew, I think. I hope you knew that I was grateful; that you were loved. I know that I was."

She stands up and looks at him. Marius, of course, says nothing, and she laughs, wiping tears from her freckled cheeks. "I hope you equipped me well enough to go it alone." Venalia takes his hand, squeezing it, and lets out a deep sigh. "Anyway, let's get you onto that pyre and send you skywards, before you really start to smell."

She walks outside, into the rain, her head held high.

"Boys!" she shouts on her pallbearers. "He's ready. Bring him out."

Atop the grassy mound where the villagers wait, Marius is placed on the pyre with a cheer. The villagers are huddled around smaller fires, waiting, whilst the timberman sits atop a keg with a lamp stamped upon it, reeking of oil. He gives her a nod and passes her a lit torch.

She wrinkles her nose. "Gods above, I can smell that oil from the square. How much did you use?"

"Well, it poured out a lot faster than I expected, so, uh, the whole keg."

"Gods above, man," she laughs, "we want to burn him, not vaporise him."

"Sorry Venalia. The top came off. At least we know it will

work. Good luck; maybe throw the torch from a distance?"

Venalia nods, and prepares herself for the ceremony by warming up her vocal cords. She once had to sit exams on funeral ceremony, like any other Priestess. She can recite the rites by heart – but now she wonders if the standard words are enough for Marius.

They see torch-flames in the darkness at the bottom of the mound; Gregor is approaching from the village, his bodyguards and younger sister Evelyn in tow. Venalia fights a scowl. This isn't *for* him. Most of Llantry has turned out by now, huddled together in the dark and the rain.

She takes her hood down and raises her hands to the sky, demanding attention. Aloft, she brandishes a blazing torch.

"Let us begin," she shouts, and the crowd turn to her. "I will speak of Marius de Aria – then I will sing of him to the Gods."

She lowers her arms and lets the crackling fire speak for a spell, before she begins.

"If his face and accent did not make it obvious, Marius de Aria was not from Llantry," she says. "He wasn't even from the Herdsman's Moot. No, he hailed all the way from the vinyards of Sarantja where, as a young man, he played music in taverns for money. He found faith in the Wakened World through his music, in bringing joy to others, and that was what would define his long life. Marius bore witness to many great wonders. He lived through the Age of Fear – was there, when the Devourer was struck down, and the Scar closed. He saw Atlan rebuilt after the plague, saw Sunstone restored, witnessed the unification of Whitehallow's temple cities. He lived a long and wonderful life."

She looks around, and sees that Gregor and his younger sister Evelyn have now joined the crowd. Gregor sniffs the air, and mutters something to his sister. She promptly elbows him in the ribs. They can smell the oil too. She speeds up the service.

"When it came time for him to retire," she continues, "he retired to Llantry. You all know and remember him for his jokes, his music, his stories. Those of us lucky enough to know him closely, however, will remember him for his wisdom, and for his bottomless love of all creation."

She raises the torch, and Gregor looks at her in alarm. He can smell the fuel too. Venalia holds the torch ready, and now she must sing, for the Celestial language of Gods and angels cannot be expressed in anything less.

She opens her mouth, and something between a trumpet blast and an operatic voice comes out. What she says, in the Celestial tongue, is: *I begrudge not fate for a friend lost, but thank it for his rest at the end of a long journey.* What the villagers hear is an aria, the kind to lift flames to in a cathedral. Her voice carries high, silences the world around, in harmony with the wind and the rustle of trees.

Nobody will understand it, she knows; but this is not for them.

Her voice strains to hold the notes. The air vibrates, and Venalia feels akin to a single particle of air in the mouth of a vast trumpet.

"Walk the Black Sands in peace," she sings in the Celestial harmonic.

She looks Gregor in the eye, enjoying the glimmer of fear on his face, as she finishes the ceremony.

"May you find what you seek," she sings.

He paces towards her, about to say something -

Venalia tosses the torch into the pyre.

They may have overestimated the amount of fuel required, she realises, as a pillar of flame erupts in the night sky, and a fireball briefly consumes her, throwing her and Gregor backwards onto the grass. When the flames abate, Venalia struggles to her feet, brushing ashes from herself. A quick glance confirms that nobody is harmed. The pyre blazes, consuming Marius' body.

Nervous laughter breaks across the crowd as they collect themselves. Some cheer in awe, over a scattering of applause. She checks that her eyebrows are intact, and breathes a sigh of relief.

Some mutter prayers, holding aloft sigils of the All-Faith. The tension breaks as the flames settle down to a small inferno, and she laughs with them. Then she sees Gregor, lying on the ground, cursing loudly as his guards and sister lift him to his feet. He bats them away.

She watches the sparks soar skywards.

"Uh oh," says the timberman as Gregor begins pacing across the turf, fists clenched. "Uh, ma'am, I think -"

"Sorry for the explosion, Burroughmaster," she says, still laughing. "Slight miscalculation."

"It was entirely my fault, sir," shouts the timberman, but Gregor barges straight past him. He doesn't humour her for a second, jabbing his finger at her chest.

"How much lamp fuel was that?"

The third rule: tell no lies. "Most of a keg, I think."

"You wasted most of a keg of lamp fuel on a *funeral pyre*?"

He spits the words at her, and her temper flares to match. "It was an accident, Gregor, nobody was hurt – and it's not a *waste* if it's for something. Marius deserved a send off like that."

"And how are we to light the streets at night, hm? When the snows come? Which they will, I assure you, and very soon. Or did you forget about winter, too, whilst you studied in the tropics of Whitehallow?"

She bites her tongue. He has a point. "My apologies. How much is a keg of lamp fuel?"

"It's not a matter of cost, Priestess," he hisses. "I don't want your money. It's an issue of whether or not any traders will even visit Llantry before the snows come; and if none do, you can explain to the children why they are about to spend four months of the year stuck inside their homes, in the pitch black, feeling their way about during the long, freezing nights."

She becomes aware of everybody looking at her, and realises from the energy in the crowd that none are on her side. Things have shifted, she is a child again, being singled out before a crowd. Even the timberman has slunk away, unwilling to bear Gregor's wrath.

"Should it come to it," she says, "I will travel to Atlan myself for fuel."

"Well good luck dragging a keg on your own for the sixty mile journey." He rounds on the timberman, who is trying to join the crowd. "Gods above, man, were you trying to destroy the village?"

He looks at his hands. “Sorry sir, I -”

“Leave him out of this,” says Venalia, stepping in front of Gregor. “It was my fault. My doing, my idea, my plan. My fault. I'll make the journey for more fuel.”

“No need,” says Gregor, lowering his voice. “I'll send one of my guards. The sooner you leave Llantry, the better.”

“Agreed,” she says quietly, and folds her arms.

There's an awkward, heavy pause, as the two size one another up. Both are about to speak. Venalia can see it burning in him.

Go on, she thinks. Bring up Anabel. Ask me why I didn't join the searches. Ask me why I left.

“Brother?” comes a tired girl's voice from the crowd. “I hear the tavern calling your name. Come hither.”

Evelyn, Gregor's younger sister, marches forward and stands between the two of them. When Venalia last saw Evelyn, she was on the edge of womanhood. Now, she's as tall as Gregor and, by Venalia's eyes at least, already more mature. Pale faced and raven haired, she has the same emerald-green eyes as all of her family.

“Evelyn,” sighs Gregor. “Don't give me orders.”

“I didn't.” says Evelyn, lowering her voice. “I'm advising you to do something else before you cause a scene in front of the entire village. We both know how *that* goes.”

Gregor scoffs, playing it off – but Venalia can see that the quip got to him. She is immediately curious as to what he did in front of the entire village; never has Venalia been able to resist the pull of a scandal.

He looks around, and forces a laugh. “This is beneath me.” Gregor turns and signals to his guards, marching away, but stops after a few steps, turning back to Venalia. “Once you're done here, I assume you *are* to leave?”

“My intention was to spend the night at home, then leave at first light.”

“Of course. Did Marius – did he give any indication as to an inheritance, or -?”

She lets him hang on the question a little longer. How *dare* he? Marius is not yet ashes and Gregor wants to know who will have his house.

"He did not," she says. "Though he did leave me a letter. I assume that it will have more details."

"Yes, well, do keep me informed. If he fails to name an inheritor – and I understand Marius bore no sons or daughters – then it falls to the domain of the Burroughmaster and -"

"I know," she says. "I'll ensure that Marius' affairs are in order before leaving."

"Good," he says, and turns to the crowd. "This cold, hard week is over, then. I'll see you all for a drink."

The invitation quite explicitly does not include Venalia. The crowd begins to disperse, and follow him down the slope back to the village. Bell the blacksmith is led to her, hanging onto the arm of an elderly woman. He finds Venalia's hands.

"A good service, Priestess. Even I was in awe of the flames."

Venalia laughs. "Thank you, Bell."

The procession continues, and the silhouettes that pass offer a routine of curtseys or bows, passing on warm wishes and thanks, blessings and prayers. She receives her first thanks for doing the work of a Priestess, and cannot help but smile. She wonders if Marius intended for her to feel this, to be the first real work she would do as a Priestess.

When most are gone, it is Gregor's younger sister Evelyn who remains, walking back against the flow of bodies. She folds her arms, left alone with Venalia in front of the burning body, their faces lit by the flames.

"Venalia," she smiles. "A wonderful service for a wonderful man – and my apologies for my brother. He is still learning how a Burroughmaster behaves."

"Evelyn," she manages a weak smile. "I'm used to dealing with Gregor. You'll have to forgive me some unfamiliarity with yourself, though; I don't think that you and I spoke much, back in the day."

"We spoke a little," she says. "About my sister, Anabel,

mostly."

"I -" Venalia is caught off guard. "Yes. Probably."

"You weren't at her funeral, were you?"

"I mean -" *it's not a funeral without a body,* is what Venalia wants to say. They never *found* Anabel de Llantry.

"It's alright," says Evelyn, shrugging. "It was a long time ago. You had left for Whitehallow, I believe."

"It *was* a long time ago," says Venalia. She *doesn't* say: your sister was a horrid bully, far worse than your brother. She made my life hell, and I would not trust myself not to tell everybody exactly what I thought of her at the funeral. Nor did I care to search for her, given that I did not care if she vanished. "I had different priorities back then. I had to get to Whitehallow before their student intake closed for another year."

Not a lie. She did. The third rule remains intact.

"Well, it seems that you made the .most of your time away," says Evelyn, taking on a much more politically polite tone than her brother ever mastered. "Congratulations on your Priesthood, by the way – do you mind if I ask you some things?"

"Oh thank you," says Venalia. Despite being a head taller than Evelyn, she feels somewhat intimidated by the girl. "Ask away – what do you want to know?"

"Just about the world. You've been all around the place, right?"

"Well... I've been to Whitehallow?" laughs Venalia.

"That's a lot further afield than I've ever been."

"Well, it needn't stay that way," says Venalia. "You must be aged to take a profession by now, get out of this place, no?"

"Oh I wouldn't leave. Not until Gregor has, you know, grown into his role a little more."

Venalia declines to comment. "Have you taken a profession then?"

"Apprentice blacksmith," says Evelyn, smiling. "Bell says that I'm pretty good – I can take over when he finally retires."

"You're working with Bell?" she almost shouts. "That's

amazing; he's wonderful, really, not just as a blacksmith. He used to visit us all the time, spend his nights drinking and telling old war stories. You know, the funny ones. Not the terrible ones."

Evelyn laughs. "Aye, he speaks about you a lot. He used to tell me about the letters that you wrote."

"Oh Gods above, I hope not," she laughs. Some of those letters were quite personal.

"He built some instruments for Marius, I believe?"

"Ah, the steel drums? Beautiful work."

"And I think he's been working on something for you – something Marius commissioned before he passed. You'll have to come by and visit the forge before you leave."

Venalia feels her heart lift. "Well, of course I'll come and visit."

"I'm sure he'd love to see you properly - or rather, to hear you, I guess?" They both laugh. "I'll let him know you'll pop by. It was him that brought you to Llantry, wasn't it?"

Venalia never tires of telling the story; she feels like a princess in a children's tale.

"He did," she tries to play it down, but tells it like the anecdote it has become. "Found me as a baby, amongst the wreckage of a cart, ambushed by bandits on the road to Llantry. They'd burned everything, including my parents, apparently. He heard me crying when he stopped to search for survivors. I was encased between their bodies."

"God's above," whispers Evelyn. "Well. That makes us both orphans."

Harsh, thinks Venalia, and true – but there is no real sorrow to her statement. It is something that binds them together; children, alone in the world.

Evelyn breaks into a smile. "I'm so grateful for Bell's time. He's a wonderful teacher. Offered me the apprenticeship so that I could, in his words, do something useful with my Draconic blood."

"Of course; your Draconic bloodline, your mother was the Magistress. Though I don't remember her ever doing much in the way of magic?"

“Aye. The Draconic blood of our line isn't *that* strong, but it makes the heat of the forge far more bearable.” To demonstrate, Evelyn rolls her sleeve and rests her hands in the bright red flames of the pyre. “Bell says it's useful enough to give me an advantage. He forges in temperatures that would make most mortals pass out. It's like working in a sauna. He must be used to it – or have a little Draconic himself.”

“Weren't you ever tempted to study magic? Pursue the arcane arts yourself? Your bloodline is a rare gift.”

“Magic?” laughs Evelyn. “No, no thank you. Would be nice to keep me slim, though.”

Venalia gives a genuine laugh. The one real benefit to being a spellcaster of any kind is the energy that your body expends when casting, demanding a rich and often excessive diet just to maintain a healthy weight.

“It has its upsides,” she admits. “I could teach you a simple Light spell? It's the first thing we learn – and it's *very* useful for midnight runs to the privy; or the fridge.”

Evelyn chuckles, waving her away. “Oh, I get enough exercise in the forge, but thank you.”

“I'm surprised Gregor didn't pursue magic, he always struck me as the type who might take to it.”

“He preferred horses and swords,” says Evelyn. “Anabel was the special one, she had the knack and the brain for it.” Evelyn drifts away into memory. “She was the best of us three, really. When she vanished, it all fell apart pretty quick. Mother kind of, faded away. Gregor had a few months to learn how to run the place, and then father died. It's been us two on our own for a while now.”

“Must be tough,” says Venalia. *Not Anabel again.*

“We got used to it. What I'm trying to say is, don't hold it against him? He has a lot on his plate.”

“Not to worry. I'll be out of Llantry before the sun rises tomorrow. Gregor need not worry about me ever again.”

“What are you going to do, then? Priests of the Mind's Eye usually become teachers, right? Or scholars? What about you?”

Venalia opens and closes her mouth a few times, laughing

at herself. “Uh, I'm actually not sure. I'd like to see some of Altheim? Explore my options. Atlan is first. Then, I'll get the Emerald Express somewhere. South, maybe? Sorenheim, or Mul? I don't know. I like the heat, and the ocean. I guess I'm not sure what kind of Priestess I'd like to be. Yet.”

“I'm sure you'll figure it out,” says Evelyn. “You were always a smart one, I remember that much.”

“Thank you, Evelyn.”

“Gods keep you, Priestess,” smiles Evelyn. “Oh, before I forget, could I ask a favour?”

“Of course,” says Venalia.

“Could you ask your God about my sister?”

Venalia's smile freezes to her face, and she lets it melt slowly. “I'm sorry?”

“We never found Anabel – never found a body, or anything, you know? You commune with the Mind's Eye? Mysteries and secrets, aye? Could you ask him if Anabel is dead? Or where her body is, anything like that? Father stuck to the old faith. Never trusted the new Gods to answer a straight question.”

“It's -” not that easy, she thinks. The truth never is. The truth, she will never tell a soul, is that she was quite happy for Anabel to go missing. But she cannot lie. The third rule forbids her. Gods above, she thinks, this is *hard*. “It's not as simple as asking the Mind's Eye,” she says, aware that she has been frozen, quiet, for a while. “He only knows what his Priests and worshippers know, and I must exchange a secret for a favour. If nobody knows what happened to Anabel, then The Mind's Eye won't either.”

And whilst that is the truth, it is not the *whole* truth.

The whole truth is that Venalia was awoken by the cries of the Burroughmaster. Anabel's bed was empty, they could not identify her tracks amongst the others. The first, frantic search had begun; and upon a sodden path of mud, far from the noise of the village,

Venalia had spotted a bright red bow.

Anabel's bow. Clean, pristine upon the mud.

The only one like it in the entire village; indicating that she was moving North past the smithy when she dropped it. An important clue for anybody searching, one that must be reported immediately.

Venalia did not report it immediately. She put it in her pocket and, when Bell was distracted, tossed it into his crucible. The trail turned to ash with the bow.

Anabel was never found.

The truth is that she didn't care if Anabel vanished, if she was abducted or killed or spirited away. She was glad, if anything. Venalia had harboured such a hatred for her, that she was glad she was gone. Never since has she spoken of it – except to the Mind's Eye, whom she stood before in Whitehallow, who saw into her heart and read her deepest secrets.

All mortals carry secret, quiet guilt; but the weight of Venalia's sin, and her ability to hide it, even from herself, was enough to impress the God of Secrets.

"Could you try?" asks Evelyn, snapping her out of her daze.

"In truth, I could," says Venalia, wincing. "But I'm sorry – the Mind's Eye isn't omniscient. If nobody knows the answer to a question, then neither does he."

"Isn't that what his Priests are for?" asks Evelyn, raising an eyebrow. "He sends you to find the answers to questions like this? To solve mysteries?"

"Much bigger questions, perhaps, yes," says Venalia. "This is..." she waves her hands, sighing. "Local. Personal. Of little interest to a God. I have no secrets to exchange for a favour at the moment anyway."

Technically true.

"Oh," Evelyn's face drops, and Venalia's heart breaks a little. "That's alright."

"I'm sorry, Evelyn," she says, trying to be polite. "It's just that praying to a God is a really big deal, and we try not to do it if we don't have to."

"I see," she nods, sad but seemingly satisfied. "Well, I'll see you before you leave tomorrow, I'm sure. Pop by to see what Bell has made for you, aye?"

"I will."

"Oh, and Venalia? Gregor may not realise it, but his anger and grief are the same. You and Anabel left his life on the same day. You have returned. She has not. Allow him some resentment."

Venalia is taken aback by the girl's wisdom. Evelyn leaves with a polite curtsey, arms still folded in the howling rain. Venalia is left standing on the mound herself in the rain. Somehow she has managed to isolate herself from the village *again*. She swears under her breath, but refuses to leave the pyre.

As the wind dies down, Venalia watches Marius burn away to nothing. His silhouette becomes part of the kindling. She hears the workers come in from the fields, rows of torches in procession, footsteps in the dark. The fire pops and hisses beside her. All around her stretches the expanse of night, beneath a wild spray of stars. She can hear drunken laughter echo from open windows, and she finds herself both glad to be away from it, and also longing to be included in the merriment. All introverts suffer a quiet pride in their isolation, Marius had once said.

She pulls her cloak in; watches over Marius as the night rolls in. The fire keeps her warm, sizzling as the rain begins to fall harder and faster.

Venalia takes out the letter that Marius left for her, and reads it by the pyre light.

Ven,

Sorry I couldn't hang around a little longer, lass. I know you came as fast as you could. Your last few letters home left me a little worried for you, so I thought I'd better leave you with some last bits of advice, from an old priest, to a young one.

You're going to have more options than you can count, when you are first ordained. A priest is many things to the people of Altheim. Warrior, hunter, healer, sage, scientist, scholar, musician... but there is only enough time in a human life to follow one path to its end.

If you're feeling angry, there's always the Purifiers, but I've never seen you as the fire and brimstone purging type, honestly, and he who battles demons too often falls foul to their tricks.

Perhaps you need some time to decide. If so, then I bequeath unto you my house and title in Llantry. You are welcome to become their Priestess if you so choose. We both know that they could do with some knowledge and learning, even if only for a little while. See if you can't get some of them literate.

That said, I know that you did not enjoy living here. I know that life was not easy for you. I hope you don't hold any grudges. They are simple people, but that does not mean that they are stupid, or wicked. One way or another I would dearly like for you to leave the pain of this place behind you – but there is good here, a simple honesty to a hard life that has many lessons for you, if you want it.

When the time comes, I will be there to walk with you across the Black Sands.

Till then, farewell, and may the Gods be with you, child

All of my love

Father Marius de Aria

She smiles inwardly and presses the letter to her chest, holds it against her cheek. Of course Marius knew that she was going to struggle with a direction upon her ordaining. Of course he prepared accordingly.

Ven remembers that there is tea waiting at home, and food in the larder. It has been a long day of travel, and she is beginning to feel light headed. A Priest, he used to tell her, should always be working on a full stomach, just in case they need to cast something.

There is nothing left on the pyre but sputtering flames; his body is long gone. As she walks home, leaving the pyre to burn its last, Venalia thinks about all the things that she could do with her life now.

Tomorrow, she decides, she will set out a plan for her future , and leave Llantry forever. This chapter of her life is over, and that is how she would like to keep it.

The Priestess leaves the pyre and steps, blind and uncertain, into the rest of her life.

Stars overhead
the clouds blown aside by howling winter winds
and the shades of the Choir fade into the darkness
the first she has seen
in millennia
long aeons
strange centuries
for a mind to live

shades cover the ground
invisible amongst the trees
following the Tall Woman
She shivers
they all shiver
huddling for warmth
They march to a song
staccato
off-beat
grasping and feeling
with hands
whilst the Tall Woman
grasps, feels
for the mind of Temple
for the mark she left upon him

They would all feel better if Temple joined them
Temple would feel better too

They would feel better if everybody joined them
Everybody would feel better too

hoof prints on the road
amber glow on the horizon
they flinch as though the sun is rising

not the sun
a bonfire
funeral pyre
a candle
drawing them like a moth

Llantry, isolated

cold and alone

the shades
the Tall Woman
would feel better if Llantry joined them
Llantry would feel better too

Chapter Three

Temple opens his eyes to the sound of a man's voice. A young human kneels over him, a concerned face cast in torchlight. He cannot be older than seventeen – barely a hair on his face. He wears a yellow gambeson over a chain shirt, both too large for him, that bear the sigil of a bull's head. Behind him are the stars, the moons, and the dark branches of the forest.

"Gods 'bove big man, I thought ye dead," says the boy. "Can ye stand?"

Temple tries to ask where he is, but his voice is but a croaking gasp. He swivels his eyes down and sees that his hands and palms are riddled with black veins.

"Right. I'm gon try get ye back on ye horse." The young man tries to grab Temple by the arm and heave, but to no avail. He sighs. "Gods man, ye weigh near a horse-worth. This willn't work."

Temple's arms are totally numb. He realises with a start that he is no longer attached to Pretzia. He tries to look around, but in the dark he cannot see her shape.

"Ye horse?" asks the man. "Aye, she's a right size of a beast. Bolted North when I cut ye free."

Temple groans, but the words still will not come. It is unlike Pretzia to leave his side, but for all her training she is but a beast, sensitive to danger.

The man pulls a waterskin from his belt and offers it to Temple. He tries to shake his head. He does not know if he can swallow with his numb throat. The water may just drown him.

"Ye need t'drink, big man." The boy looks frightened, and starts thinking out loud. "May be I run for help? Rest my cloak over ye, leave ye here?"

Temple tries to shake his head again. If he is left here, the Choir will claim him. Every time the wind whistles through the trees, he thinks that he can hear it again.

This is neither where nor how he dies. The water will not kill him. Temple looks pointedly at the water skin, and the man nods, tipping a few drops into Temple's mouth. His throat spasms and he coughs, but it clears his voice a little.

"Danger," he manages. "Danger. Coming."

"Danger?"

Temple forces a nod. "Run."

"Ain't leavin ye, big man, come on. Yer in luck, we have a Priestess staying t'night– she'll help ye."

The words mean something to Temple. A dream, recurring – a vision of the future that he shared with Ungren. One of the two visions yet to pass. A Priestess he is yet to meet.

"Red?"

"Eh?"

"Hair," he clarifies. "Red?"

"The Priestess? Aye. Red hair, right 'nough. Ye ken her?"

Temple shakes his head. "Not yet."

The man gives him a look of sympathy. "That's the spirit! We'll get ye safe. Say, what did this to ye?"

As if in answer, a voice finds them over the wind. It carries the singing, the horrible singing of the Choir. Temple swears he hears Ungren's final war hymn amongst the distant murmur. The sounds of the forest die away.

"Run," he urges the boy. "Now."

He is shaking. "Say, what's that? Ye hear that?"

"Monster," he manages, as simple and straight forward as he can. "Pray."

The boy looks at his own horse, then at Temple, and at the rope on his horse. They lock eyes; same idea.

“Do it,” whispers Temple. “Tie me.”

The guard starts murmuring a prayer to the All Faith under his breath, as he retrieves a length of hempen rope from his saddle and ties it around Temple's boot.

“Ye sure?”

“I'm tough,” he rasps.

“A'right.” He puts his hand on his horse, and stops. His jaw goes slack, and Temple curses.

“Boy!” he wheezes. “Boy, *move!*”

The poor lad is blinking and whispering, trying to fight the singing in his head. Temple forces out a loud, violent bark, and the boy snaps out of it, jumps on the horse and kicks the beast into a gallop.

Temple grits his teeth as the sudden jolt knocks the wind from him. Numb all over, he cannot tense his muscles to soften the blows. The ride beats the hell out of his bones and his skull, but he is merely grateful that he does not have to hear his dead comrades sing to him any longer.

Venalia lights the fire in Marius' house – in *her* house – and peruses the bookshelf. Marius barely read these books, she remembers, and it only now dawns on her that he got them for her.

Venalia tries to find one that she has not read yet. When she was young, she would take notes while she read, and try to figure out who the murderer was after every chapter.

She settles for an old favourite, anything comforting to busy her mind, and nurses her tea until the fire goes down. When her eyes start to drift shut, she retires to her childhood bedroom.

It has been left exactly as she remembers it. She finally changes out of her robes and dress after three days of travelling in them and makes a mental note to find a bath as soon as she gets to Atlan.

The bed is a little too small, but she sinks into it

gratefully, clutching the feather pillows, and thinks of more pleasant memories. She thinks of reading her books beneath the shade of Whitehallow's titanic oak, the towering symbol of the All-Faith on the far Eastern coast of Altheim around which the temple-city is built.

There, the sun is always pure white, the sky clear and blue, the streets flanked by rivers of deep blue water; every wall covered in plants, murals, colour; the days tropical and long, the nights warm and short.

Here, everything is wood and mud, and it smells of farm animals and dung. She wonders how many of her classmates in Whitehallow noticed the smell and refrained from saying anything. She wonders how long it took to wear off, and feels another pang of embarrassment.

She banishes it and tries to remember the smell of her bedroom in the dormitories, and sleep finally finds her.

Ungren is lost
alone
terrified
he follows the sound of song
till he is no longer alone

to lose the song
is to feel a tug on the soul
painful, sharp
a leash, keeping one close

Ungren begins to love the song
if only for its modest warmth
a candle in a snowstorm

Ungren begins to love the song
because if he admits that he cannot stand it
then he will have no other choice
but to abandon his mind completely

The door to Venalia's house bursts open, loud enough to shock her wide awake. She throws the covers back out of instinct, grabbing her robes and wrapping them around herself, jamming her awkward long arms into the sleeves.

Practice and training tell her to form the shape of a spell in her head, as though forming a complex matrix out of numerous parts. It is a spell of protection, of shielding, the first line of defence that every priest learns. She holds off on flexing her cerebral muscles and casting the spell, saving her energy in case she is mistaken.

And just as well.

“Priestess!” comes a young man's voice. “Priestess, we need ye!”

She rolls her eyes and drops the spell. Unless Gregor has gone off the deep end and intends to kill her, then this may actually be important.

“Let me get dressed,” she shouts back.

“Quick as you please, ma'am. We've a wounded man.”

“Heavens above,” she hisses. Venalia throws her dress and cloak on, dons her leather boots, and tosses her Priestess' satchel over her shoulder before storming out with her hands on her hips, her hair a wild mess that she barely contains with a hastily made braid.

The guards look like children being forced to talk in front of a crowd, staring at the floor. She remembers her training from Whitehallow:

People will not follow if you do not lead.

“Apologies m'lady, we was fear't to wake you but -”

“Talk and walk,” she waves for them to move, heading for the door. “Where are we going? Come on.”

They follow like lost lambs, out into the blistering wind and the frozen night, pitch black under a starry sky. Adrenaline makes her shiver; she talks faster than she'd like to.

“The guardhouse, m'lady. Young Agnir was on the road -”

“Ah, I remember Agnir. Nice lad. Why was he on the road

this late? In the dark, no less?"

"Emergency supply run."

"Let me guess: Atlan, for lamp fuel?"

"Aye.""

"Of course it is. Go on."

"Well, young Agnir met a half-Giant fella being dragged by a great big horse, says the poor fella was near dead. Said something was chasing him."

"*Something?* Specifics, please. Bandits? Scarlings?"

"Ask Agnir, ma'am, he weren't making much sense to us. The man's horse bolted. Us in Llantry got the horse first, then Agnir turned up with the rider a bit later, dragging him."

"*Dragging* him?"

"Half Giant, ma'am. Agnir couldn't move him. Says he's paralysed or something. Poison, he thinks."

She picks up the pace. "In the future, try to start with things like that. Maybe something from the Wildlands got him then, some venomous predator? Though half Giants tend to be pretty hardy to things like poison and venom. How badly hurt is he? Did you check the usual places for bites and stings?"

"I don't rightly know, ma'am, apologies. Agnir just shouted at us to fetch you."

Venalia stumbles into yet another puddle and curses loudly. "Gods above! Why aren't the lamps lit? It's pitch black! I can barely see."

"Well, uh, the fuel -"

"Oh," she pauses in embarrassment. "Alright. Well. Let me cast a Light, come on."

She knows how to create light, how to rapidly heal a wounded body, and how to momentarily shield herself from harm. The three requisite spells that all priests learn before graduating. It covers almost every eventuality that she might encounter. Light is the easiest by far, and does not burn much energy.

Ven lifts a hand and lets out a deep breath, centring herself. Casting anything always feels, to her, like painting a detailed picture, with invisible paint, whilst holding a conversation. Think about three things at once, and try to focus on all of them. Light, at least, is an easy painting.

She forms the geometric patterns in her head and applies a nameless intention to it. Light blooms soft from her fingertips, the deep gold of sunlight, and she illuminates the road before them.

The guards step back in brief awe, as if they have forgotten that she *can* cast spells.

“Faster,” she says to them, jogging now. “Sounds as though this man has little time.”

“Aye ma'am,” says the guard. “One other thing, m'lady?”

“Hm?”

“Agnir said that he was asking about ye. About the colour of yer hair.”

“What? What was he saying?”

“Just seemed to know ye, m'lady.”

She nods, notes the facts, and makes a mental reminder to check in with Agnir about what he heard. Facts, during times like these, get distorted far too easily. Nevertheless, despite her scepticism, the question puts her on edge.

Time for that later, she tells herself. There is a problem at hand to be dealt with – and she'll find no answers if the man dies. One thing at a time;

if only her heart would listen to her and stop trying to jump up her throat.

Venalia goes down the checklist of requirements as they jog down the muddy path, against the wind the whole time.

She will have to cast, most likely, on a starved stomach of tea and a light dinner. Not good. Were she richer, she might commission a staff or pendant laced with crystalline, into which she could pour energy to store it. She might spend a fair sum of money on a custom mixture of high energy liquids to drink before casting a powerful spell – if she *knew* any powerful spells.

Always beware a caster with a bottle or a staff, her tutors told her. She has neither, and so she must make do with the budget, home-made equivalent that caused so many hangovers during her time at Whitehallow.

"You," she turns to one of the guards. "Get the tavernkeeper out of bed. I need a mixture made up of ten parts, so remember this. One part water, two parts honey, two parts rum, the dark stuff with molasses, not the white stuff. Then five parts fruit juice, the more acidic the better. In fact, tell them to dump in as much fruit juice as they can. I need sugar. Then a handful of salt. Bring it to the guardhouse, time is of the essence. As much as they can spare, aye? I'll pay them later."

"Aye ma'am," he says. No hesitation. She could get used to this; she feels like a real professional.

The guardhouse looms in the dark. Outside stand a few guards, in their chainmail and yellow heraldry, tending to an exhausted warhorse.

"God's above, that's a *horse,*" she whispers.

The mare stands at least eight feet tall at the shoulder, ten including its broad head, where bright amber eyes swivel in alarm. Not fear, Venalia notes, for it is not afraid. It is concerned, trained to ignore fear and think clearly. Chestnut and white, with a soldiers saddle: this is a war horse. A bloody big one, but a war horse nonetheless.

A saddlebag has been removed and splayed open on the ground, revealing all manner of weaponry, tools, camping equipment, and a few pouches that jingle when they move. The guards are poring over everything, marvelling, and she walks straight past them. This is an issue for later.

Venalia drops her Light and pushes through the door without knocking. First, she smells blood, and something *else.* Something that she recognises, but from where? She tries to place it; Whitehallow, she thinks, her studies. *Magic.* Not the loud, bright magic of the Gods, no; that smells to her like fresh grass and the ocean. This is the arcane. chaos given form. It smells like polished brass and rust.

The scene is a mess. Bloodied rags litter the floor around a table being used as a makeshift bed. The Burroughmaster, Gregor, presides over four guards with tired black rings under their eyes. They crowd around a wounded, Giant man, unconscious on the table, clad in Northern winter furs. He looks as though he has been hit by a landslide, covered in bruises and cuts. His breastplate is battered too, with a hole punched straight through it.

Not just a hole, she notes as she approaches; a handprint.

Gregor and his men are trying to help, pawing at the half-Giant like panicked animals, making things worse. Time slows. Venalia's blood rushes to her head. Details stand out, the scene starts speaking to her.

First, the half-Giant is not moving; that is her first cause for alarm. Amateurs clawing at a wound should illicit a scream. Her training kicks in and she pushes through, ignoring their protests.

“Venalia?” shouts Gregor, pointing to her. “Who - what is *she* doing here?”

A guard steps up. “We thought she might be useful sir -”

“I did not request her presence,” he shouts down the guard. “No order was given for -”

“Out of my way,” she pushes the guards aside, dropping her satchel from her shoulder. “What have you given him?”

“Venalia,” begins Gregor, and she hears the indignation in his voice. This is his show, his village, and here *she* is to take charge. How very dare she? “Priestess. May I ask that -”

She silences him with a look. His face drops into a dark scowl, and he stands down. This is her domain now. He steps back and raises his hands, a storm brewing in his eyes, and watches.

“You,” she repeats the question at the nervous guard, all whilst checking his breathing, his pulse. “What did you *give* him?”

“A little booze for any pain he might be in,” says the first guard. “It's what we usually do?”

“Great.” She sighs in frustration. “Thin his blood so he bleeds out faster. Never do that again.”

“He isn't bleeding -”

“He isn't bleeding *externally,* but *something* punched through that armour so he's probably bleeding into his own chest. All of you step back. Give me space until I ask you to do something.”

“Are you gonna use magic?” asks Agnir.

"Only if I have to," she says.

She rummages in her bag for her medical kit, the standard one that all priests carry. Healing with magic is entirely possible, but if the body is not prepared for the sudden rush of energy, it can do as much harm as good. Knitting a bone back together only works if the bone is set properly first, for example. Not only that, but if she passes out from magical exhaustion, then she is no use to anybody.

Never *start* with magic, she was taught.

As she lays out her tools, she examines the half-Giant man – no, she thinks, the half-Giant *soldier*. Short cut black hair, greying at the sides on a head twice as big as hers. No telling his age, half-Giants age fast, but he's old for a soldier. Crow feet, laugh-lines; this is an old man in a profession where growing old is not guaranteed – and where he would be a huge and obvious target. He must be well decorated, yet his tarnished steel breastplate bears no insignia, no identification. A mercenary, she wonders?

His breathing is shallow and wheezing. It sounds wet. Damage to the lungs, perhaps – or fluid filling them. She turns her attention to the wound.

"It's not bleeding," she thinks out loud, producing Light from her fingertip and peering into the wound through his breastplate. "It's a handprint. Burned into the skin. Help me get this off."

She unclasps the breastplate, lifting it gently. His gambeson and undershirt are drenched with sweat that has yet to dry. Fever? She feels his head. Boiling. All signs say infection, the guards say poison or venom.

One of the guards produces a knife and they cut the Giant out of his shirt. As soon as Venalia cuts it away she sees the problem.

Black veins have spread across his body, densest around the handprint, greying his skin, reaching up for his neck.

"Magic," she sighs. "But he's fighting it. Cold burn, no bleeding. Agnir? Where's Agnir?"

Agnir pushes forward. "Ma'am?"

"He was like this when you found him?"

“Seems worse now, ma'am, but he had that same wound, aye.”

“Did he say what did it?”

“No, ma'am, not in as many words. Told us to run though.”

“Well? Run from what?”

“Don't rightly know, Priestess. I just heard it singing from a long way off.”

“Singing?”

“Singing, ma'am.”

“Let me think.” Nothing. “I'm coming up blank. Right. You two, take some knives and *gently* cut off his breeches. Look for puncture marks, bites, stings, you know? Or a big handprint, I guess. Could be more than one of these.”

Two guards jump to the task. Before long, the half-Giant lies nearly naked on the table. Professional decorum dictates that Venalia does not react, but in a purely medical capacity, he is an impressively built warrior. This mountain of muscle is easily four times the weight of any man in this room. Barely any fat – probably from weeks on the road, or at war. His beard and unwashed hair tell her that he hasn't had a bath or a shave in at least three weeks. Looks like he hasn't eaten much in that time, either.

No sooner have they gotten his clothes off, than Venalia shouts for them to stop. She checks his breathing. His body is going yellow and purple, blotched and bruised.

His breathing has stopped.

“Oh no,” she whispers. “No, no, no -”

“What?” shouts Gregor.

“He's dying. His blood is congealing, all of it at once, look at the bruising. I need to use magic.”

“Gods above,” whispers Gregor. “What could have done this?”

“Someone go and hurry up the guard with the mixture, I'll pass out without it.”

The guards scatter to help, leaving her alone with Gregor.

She barely notices him, for she is enraptured by the handprint. It seems to be pulsing now, filled with some kind of black, oily poison. Something swirls beneath his skin like smoke through water. The only reason he is alive, she is sure, is his size. Most of the mortal races have remarkably similar physiology – if he was a normal man, it would have overwhelmed him hours ago.

She whispers a prayer over him, placing a hand on his heart, feeling for the beat. She prays to the Wakened World, Goddess of Life and Love, the Goddess Marius was sworn to; she sings her prayer softly in the Celestial tongue, and as she does, Gregor lifts his eyes and watches. Could he understand her, Gregor would hear her bidding the soldier to hold a little longer, for he is almost home safe.

Venalia focuses on his heart beat. It's there – weak, and slow, but there. She pushes a little bit of energy into his heart and helps it to beat. It won't do much good to pump his blood, however, if his blood is killing him, but it might buy him a little more time.

What is she trying to treat here?

“Knowledge is everything,” she murmurs, remembering lessons from Whitehallow. “I need to speak with him.”

Gregor, watching in silence, steps back. “What?”

“Something I was taught in Whitehallow.” As she drops her spell and explains, she lifts her medical kit and begins picking out vials and powders. “He's heading for the Black Sands, and I'm *not* asking the Open Door to let him back in. There's only one way I can think of to find out what happened to him, and that is to ask him.” She gives Gregor a fearful look, and he returns it. Whatever hatred is between them, they're both way out of their depth here.

Venalia drops some water into a vial with four different powders in it, shakes it till it turns blue and starts fizzing, and then forces open the half-Giant's mouth and dumps the whole thing in. She holds his nose and mouth shut with both hands as he coughs and splutters. He swallows.

“This might be messy,” she whispers. “Step back.”

Gregor doesn't even hesitate.

The half-Giant's body seizes violently, and Venalia fumbles a wooden suppressor into his mouth before he bites his tongue in half. His jaw breaks the wooden rod, and every muscle in his body tenses; then he flops down, completely still.

"Come on," she whispers, and feels for his heartbeat.

He sits straight up, like something from the grave. Venalia tries to leap away, but the soldier is far too fast. Supercharged with the mixture she gave him, he has about thirty seconds of consciousness before his heart stops. He grabs her arm – grip like steel. His eyes are wide and red, terrified – but he is strangely calm. She can almost hear his heart pounding.

"Unhand her -" begins Gregor, going for his sword.

"It's alright, Gregor," she shouts. Venalia is on her tiptoes, arm held aloft by the huge man. "My name is Venalia, I'm a Priestess, you've been wounded and poisoned, I'm trying to save you; you have about twenty seconds to tell me what did this, otherwise you're going to die."

The half-Giant looks at her intently. He has to force the words out, as though his throat is full of dirt.

"I know you," he manages.

"You're delirious," she says. "Please, you have to tell me what did this to you."

"Magisterial experiment," he wheezes. "Inverted World. Singing. It's not far behind me."

"What isn't?"

"This isn't how I die. It attacks tomorrow, not tonight," he says. He seems confused. "You'll be crying, in the last one. With a hammer. So, not yet."

Then his heart stops, and he thuds back to the table. Venalia drops onto the floor and curses.

"Well that was pointless," she whispers. "Was he talking in the future tense, by the way, did anybody notice that?"

The door slams open and the guards rush in with a huge glass mason jar, filled with a brown and pink fluid that smells like the fairground, all hot sugar and alcohol.

"Sorry ma'am, fast as I could!"

No time for anything else. No time to process what he said. All other options exhausted.

Now is the time for magic.

She grabs the jar and, with the grace of a student who is used to drinking competitions, props it up on one elbow and gets almost half of it down her throat before spluttering and stumbling away. The guards watch, impressed. Even Gregor raises an eyebrow in surprise.

The sugar hits her like a hammer blow to the skull. The world is trembling, alight with colour. She has done this a hundred times before; on rabbits and rats, on cuts and bruises. The alcohol is an easy source of energy; it is also a source for the courage she is going to need to do this.

She puts her hands on the soldier's bare skin, where the black handprint is etched into the flesh, and takes a breath, centring herself in the headspace required for magic.

The bubbling well inside of her surges up at her command, and she shapes it into a very specific mental sculpture. The shape speaks of wellness, healing, repair, renewal, rejuvenation; all things that the body can do to itself. A sunlit field of flowers blooms in her mind, the golden mandala of life.

Heal, she thinks, and the dam bursts open.

She feels it suffuse his body. The two of them become one living thing. His wound begins to knit back together, erasing the handprint. The black veins recede. His heart starts to beat with fierce power. His body gently glows as Light floods his veins, purging whatever was in them.

Light, thinks Venalia. Damn it; Light is inefficient. All of her magic should be to Heal. If you can *see* Healing, it is wasted energy. Light is the framework from which she learns most new spells, and it is easy to forget to take the Light out once you have mastered it.

She focuses on the primary shapes and lets the healing speak for itself. To her, it feels like music is blaring in her ears, a symphony to the senses. She can hear and feel everything that is happening to him.

She hears singing, and it is not hers. Something foreign to his body is in there, hiding from her gaze. His blood begins to flow properly, his organs strain and squeeze the venom out of him. Venalia is fairly certain that he is vomiting, given that the guards are reacting to something with disgust. She closes her eyes to focus.

Blood flushes his veins clear. He breathes deep, and clear.

The blood is absorbed back into his body, clean and free of venom. The singing fades, and his brain begins to cool down, free of the fever that has gripped it. She takes her hands away and a wave of nausea and dizziness overwhelms her. She skirts the edge of total depletion.

Venalia looks down at him, exhausted, breathing heavy, and admires her own handiwork. His handprint wound is now a scar over fresh, pink skin. Blood flushes his body until the bruises and mottling are gone. He is breathing. Pulse is strong and steady.

Good, she thinks, for she can barely stand. She motions to the guards to bring her the rest of the sugar mixture, while she is able.

The guards passes her the mix, staring at the soldier. "Is he..?"

"He'll live," she smiles, taking sips of the mixture to stay conscious. She sits on the side of the table to take the weight off of her feet. "I think. Now, Agnir? Where is Agnir?"

The young man steps forward, takes his helm off, and raises a hand. Young Agnir is just as she remembers him. Unable to meet her eyes, quiet spoken. He is as thin as an urchin, chain mail hanging off of his bony shoulders. His sword, safe in its scabbard, looks like it has never been drawn.

"Agnir, I understand that you were the one that found him?"

"Aye, Priestess," he nods.

"I need to know what he said to you. Not in your own words, now – what *he* said."

Agnir opens his mouth and then shuts it again. He looks over at Gregor, as though asking permission.

Gregor steps forward. "Why do you need to know that, Priestess?"

She holds his stare. "Because whatever hurt him is like nothing I was trained for, to speak plainly. I'd like to fill in that gap in my knowledge, especially since the injured gentleman on the table told me, though unreliably I'll admit, that whatever hurt him is coming *here*."

Agnir goes to answer again, and the guards all stand up,

panicked, fearful suddenly. What Venalia speaks of is *danger,* and Gregor can hear their fearful murmurs. He holds his hand up to silence them.

"The words of a drugged and delirious man, Priestess. I have a different theory. This gentleman was riding a horse carrying the brand of the Redwood Company, yet his armour bears no such marks. We will be sending word to their Atlan offices to make them aware of this interesting development."

"What? Why?"

"I suspect your *gentleman* is guilty of stealing that horse; or desertion from the Redwood Company. Maybe both. He has a fair amount of coin and weaponry on him."

"Well perhaps those things belong to him," she laughs. "You're not seriously going to accuse an unconscious man, who was riding a horse, of having stolen that horse, are you?"

"A man, I would not accuse," says Gregor. "A half-Giant, however..."

Venalia has to squint and make sure that she is not imagining things. She stares right at Gregor, but finds herself fighting a truly horrific hangover that announces its presence and gets rapidly worse. After-effect of magical strain.

"What?" she finally asks, pinching her nose and breathing through the pain. "Are – are you serious? His accent isn't from the Steppe, he sounds like he's from Caladan. You heard him, right?"

"His horse is branded and his armour is not. Come on, Venalia," he scoffs. "You grew up here – you know what half-Giants are like. There's no way that's *his* horse."

She narrows her eyes. "He tells you that something is coming after him, something dangerous, and you're worried about whether or not he stole the horse?"

"A fine horse it is too," smiles Gregor, "as you've likely seen for yourself. And a trained war horse, definitely from the Steppe. Worth a lot of money, more than a soldier could afford. Very prestigious, a horse like that."

"Oh, I see," she whispers, seeing the pieces fall into place. Is he really that petty, she wonders? Is that *all* this is going to come to?

She does not say aloud that she knows Gregor wants the horse – nor does she accuse him of any kind of corruption, or a crime. To do so would be to invoke a challenge that Gregor could meet, and this is his village and these are his men. She'd lose, Gods on her side or not.

She meets Gregor's eyes, and sees that he understands the impasse. He has her cornered. Venalia has to fight to believe that somebody could be so short-sighted, but her long-standing dislike of Gregor blunts the surprise.

“No matter, the issue of his innocence is not urgent. I'll stay here until he wakes, then, and I can ask him about this monster that's chasing him.”

“You have no legal right to do so,” says Gregor, and Venalia's heart surges into a panic once more. “Therefore I refuse your request.”

“What? Why would you do that? Gregor, he was talking about the thing that *did this to him* -”

Gregor ignores her, and signals to his guards, who don their shields and face Venalia.

“The Lady Priestess is done with her good work here. Escort her back to her bed. See to it that she is not disturbed.” He fixes her with a stern glare, full of meaning. “She'll need a good night's sleep. She has a long journey ahead of her, when *she leaves in the morning.*”

Her face flushes bright red, and the temper that Marius always teased her for rises to the surface. The embarrassment turns to anger, enough for her to push away the guard who puts a hand on her shoulder.

“Unhand me. I have the right to question any prisoner, and stand in for him as legal representative if required,” states Venalia. “I am the Priestess -”

“No, no,” sighs Gregor, hands clasped behind his back. “You are *a* Priestess. One. Of many. Not *Llantry's* Priestess. We burned him earlier today.”

“Actually,” she takes a deep breath. This one needs to be delivered in a single go. “The Accords of the First Saint, enshrined in the shared law of the Temple-States of Whitehallow and the Magisterial Republic of Caladan, declare that any prisoner has the right to a priest of their chosen faith, be it a druid, priest, paladin, or otherwise -”

“Yes, my lady, yes,” he smiles like a teacher dealing with an uppity child. “But he must *request* your attention. I expect that he will not.”

She throws her hands up. “He's unconscious!”

“Still. He did not ask for a Priestess.”

“That's against the spirit of the law!”

“But precisely within the *wording* of the law, Venalia. Rest assured that when his guilt is discovered, we will have a fair hearing -”

Venalia explodes. “When his guilt is discovered? Our laws assume innocence until proven otherwise.”

“Those are Altheim's laws. We are in Llantry.”

“Llantry is part of Altheim, you idiot!”

“Now now, Venalia,” he smirks, knowing fine well that he has won. He still knows how to draw out the worst in her. “This is no way for a Lady of the Faith to conduct herself.”

“Llantry,” she takes a breath, slows down. “Llantry obeys the same continental laws as everybody else. I *am* going to talk to him.”

Gregor shakes his head. “I forbid it.”

“You can't stop me,” she says, and the mood takes on an edge that was absent previously. Venalia can feel her heart in her chest, knows that she is shaking.

The guards look at one another, then at Gregor. Venalia does not turn around, but she knows that some of them have their hands on their swords.

“Can't I?” asks Gregor, goading her.

She takes a deep breath. She was hoping that it would not come to this. If she stops and thinks about it, she will not do it – she knows it is foolish, hot headed, rash, all of the things that Marius told her *not* to be; but Marius also told her to battle injustice wherever she found it.

She took an oath, to adhere to three rules.

The third rule:

Do not lie.

The second rule:

Never let evil take root.

She has a duty to investigate the beast that attacked this man. She has a duty to oppose this obvious corruption.

All this for a horse, too, she despairs.

Venalia raises her hands to let them know that she isn't pulling a blade, and lifts Marius' letter from her robes, handing it to Gregor. He snatches it, and begins scanning the lines. She knows what it says: that she has the right to inherit Marius' title and home. She draws herself to full height, and produces her sigil from beneath her dress, letting them all see it.

"I accept the offer given by the late Marius de Aria. I will not be leaving in the morning. I will take his place as the serving Priestess of Llantry. I will also inherit his property."

Gregor's eye twitches. He has not looked up from the paper yet, though he finished reading it long ago – the stalling tactic of a sore loser, scrambling for options.

"Which," she continues, "grants me the right to speak with any prisoner, of war or otherwise, and parley in assured safety on behalf of Llantry in the event of a siege, as stated in the Accords. You see, Burroughmaster, following the War of Storms, power in Altheim is *shared* between the Magistry and the All-Faith. Which makes us equals, now that I am the Priestess of Llantry."

She takes the paper back, delicately, and Gregor looks at her as though she has just spat in his face. To his credit, he drops the look quickly, and gives her a warm, forced smile. He knows, at least, when he has been outmanoeuvred.

"What wonderful news," he gives a sickly sweet smile. "Well then, the prisoner can wait until the morning. We'll see that he's well looked after, and send a runner as soon as he wakes."

Venalia wants to press it, to wait here for him to wake, but she knows that with everything the half-Giant has endured, he is going to need sleep. Waking him now would be not only difficult, but probably harmful.

"I'll need a full inventory of his belongings, then," says Venalia. "I'm sure I saw some pouches full of precious stones out there, just cut open – and some very exquisite looking weaponry. If the prisoner *did* steal it, then the Redwood Company will want to know that we found it. It must be entered into evidence for his eventual trial, if there ever is one."

"Of course," he smiles.

"They wouldn't want to hear that it had all been lost, somehow."

"Indeed."

She steps closer to him again. "And they would most certainly want to hear about the state he was in when we found him – and the state that I last saw him in, when he was *perfectly healthy*, healed by my own hands."

Gregor sneers at the accusation. "What a vile assumption to make, Priestess," he seems genuinely taken aback. "That I would hurt a prisoner, indeed."

Venalia meets his eyes. "If anything happens to that prisoner during the night, anybody involved in the arrest would be suspect to murder; a crime of the third degree."

"Priestess, I don't appreciate the implication. We were trying to save his life when you arrived."

"You were failing, badly. I think you ought to know better than to give a wounded man alcohol. Your father was a soldier and your mother was a Magistress – you know enough about infection and blood loss, surely, to avoid a mistake like that? To know that a blackened handprint that smells of the arcane *might* require the attention of a Priestess? Yet no attempt was made to reach me, your men had to take matters into their own hands."

"We did what we thought best," he says, drawing himself up to his full height. "But if you wish to make allegations of a legal nature, I would be more than happy to meet you in Atlan for a more thorough discussion before the moot?"

"I didn't make any allegations," she cuts him off, her voice flat. "I'm simply sharing the observed facts, Burroughmaster. I'll be here at first light to question the prisoner. If the doors are not open, I will exercise my right to force an entry. Make sure this man has a bed, food, water."

She nods to the guards, and they look at Gregor. He sighs and gives them the signal, and finally they put the half-Giant soldier on a stretcher and begin dragging him towards the cell block.

The two who remain are looking around, lost.

"You two," says Gregor. "Go and catalogue the prisoner's belongings, and stable his horse. Agnir?"

"Yes sir?" he pips up from the back.

"Get the prisoner some food and water, and some buckets. How does it work with half-Giants, would a trough be better?"

Agnir laughs, nodding as he leaves.

The door slams shut, and Gregor and Venalia are left alone. A decade of untouched resentment fills the air between them. Rain batters the window. Gregor folds his arms. She can feel his anger, fermenting under the surface, as he speaks.

"I do hope you've thought your decision through, Priestess."

"I have," she says. Technically not a lie – though it feels like one. "And between you and I? I find your decision not to call for me - when a man was injured - highly suspect."

"Llantry has no Priest or Priestess. I had no duty to call for anybody."

"Llantry has a Priestess now," she reminds him. "You knew I was here. You know who I am and what I can do. You *chose* not to."

He holds up his hands. "Honestly? I just didn't want to have to speak to you."

"You know Gregor, that's a really childish reason to let a man die – but I would prefer that to *malice,* which is what would be required for you to let him die so that you can rob him."

It hits him, she can see his eyes react, though he keeps his face as still as stone. When it starts to break with anger, she is taken aback – not by the rage itself, but by the immaturity of it. This, she realises, is the reaction of a brat, throwing his toys out of the pram.

"Well, I hope you enjoy your time as the Priestess of Llantry, because that is how you shall remain," he growls, stepping closer to her now that they are alone. "Or did you forget, Venalia, that to be relieved of their duty, a Priest must have permission from their counterpart? That's me. So perhaps I'll keep you here forever."

"We both know you don't want me here. When this business is concluded, I'll resign my post and leave."

"If I allow you to."

She steps back. "Neither of us want me to be here, Gregor. Even you wouldn't do that just to spite me." Venalia looks, and finds no bravado. "Gods above, you would?"

"I might, Priestess. If that's the game that we're playing, then I'd wager that I play it better than you. This is *my* town that you're playing politics in."

"It's *our* town now."

"It was never *yours,"* he barks. "You hate this place, these people. My sister went missing and you just *left*. You hate us. You can't *stand* it here. And remember," he hisses, "that whatever the big city, whatever Whitehallow, taught you? It only *works* in the city. Out here? We're right on the edge of the old empire, one day from the Wild Lands. Our ways and traditions have endured dragons, Venalia, they have endured the Magistry and the All-Faith, the War of Storms, the Age of Fear, the Devourer; our ways are older than the forests, older than the Druids of Sunstone. Out here, our tradition *is* our law. The decree of the Burroughmaster is the law. Me; I am the law."

"No," she manages, emboldened by her desperation. "No, Burroughmaster. Out here, *we* are the law. You and I – and I intend to see that very law followed, to the letter."

He slams his hand on the table, and Venalia jumps, almost casting her shield spell out of instinct.

"Damn it, why?" he asks, angered and confused. It's a genuine question, she realises. He doesn't understand her at all. "Why are you being like this? We could have been rid of one another in *hours."*

"Because I took an oath," she shouts back. "Second rule of the Priesthood: never let evil take root. In myself or in others. To rip corruption out, and let it rot in the light of day. That's why, Gregor. Goodnight."

He realises the implication, what she is saying about him,

and before he can respond with his anger, she turns and leaves. Ven is painfully aware that his eyes follow her out of the door and into the cold, where the rain whips itself into a frenzy at her return. She wraps her arms and her robes around herself and runs home, Lightless, going purely by memory. Venalia stumbles through the door in soaked clothes and slams it shut behind her, breathing hard.

"What am I doing?" she asks the room, trying to calm herself. "Oh Gods above, what am I *doing?*"

She drops to the floor and shuffles closer to what remains of the fire, holding herself, trying to contain the panic. It all seems so big, despite being so *stupid*.

So what if Gregor wants the man's horse? Who cares, it's just a horse. Why is she putting her life on hold, her life that was *just* about to start? She was one night away from finally leaving this place forever. Instead, she has tied herself to a rock and cast it into the ocean.

Venalia starts building the fire again, anything to distract herself. Surely, she thinks, Gregor wouldn't force her to stay here.

Imagine, says a little voice in her head. Imagine that the half-Giant really *is* a horse thief, a simple criminal, and he is put to death. He doesn't know anything of interest. He's delirious and asking weird questions, declaring the end of days. Then he's charged, tried, executed, and Venalia is bound to stay in Llantry forever, until Gregor sees fit to release her, spending all of that time playing Priestess to the worst people in the world, in its most boring corner, in a place that she cannot stand.

"Come on Venalia," she mumbles to herself. "That's not going to happen." She blows on the fire till it sparks to life, and Venalia sits in front of it, head in her hands, lost and alone in the world again. "Oh what have I done?"

No breaks in the wall
the Tall Woman stalks the trees
far from the torchlight of the guards
if she sings too soon
they will stay
they will not sing with her

the woods are not safe
her shades huddle close
the denizens of the forest
know to avoid the song

the dead walk freely in places
but the dead pay her no mind
pay her song no mind

Llantry is isolated
no easy escape to the North
East
or West
the road South is open
and the road South
is hers

Dawn blazes
burns their skin
her Choir retreats

crouched in the dark corners of the woods
waiting for nightfall

Chapter Four

Sunlight brings sanity. Window shutters clatter in the wind, snapping Venalia awake. The fire is burned down and ash coats the fireplace. She groans and stands from her chair, cracking joints and stretching.

She closes the window, but not before she beholds a grey and windy morning, storm clouds rolling in as an avalanche might. She can see down the length of Llantry's main street, all the way to the central shrine to the All-Faith, and the village's only clock.

No monster.

She breathes in the country air, and tries to force her tired brain to think. After a while of trying and failing, she sits down at Marius' desk – *her desk* – and pulls some parchment from a drawer. Dipping a quill into an inkwell built into the desk, she begins writing out her thoughts, trying to put them on paper to make better sense of them.

Her immediate future hinges, she concludes, upon whether or not the prisoner is innocent. If the horse is his, then he is being wrongfully detained. Once he is released, Venalia will be in a much stronger position, able to hold Gregor's behaviour over him and secure her release.

Knowledge, after all, is power.

Ven lists her legal rights to conversation with the prisoner, straightened the arguments in her head. Should she be confronted, she will be ready. Even the thought makes her stomach curdle.

Whilst they are in Llantry, Gregor has her politically outclassed. Even if they appear equal on paper, he controls the flow of information, the distribution of food and water, the protection and orders of the guard; but worse, Venalia realises, he controls the guards. They're *his*. If it comes to it, a handful of decently trained guards could take her down with ease. She completed her four weeks in the Champion's Hall, like all acolytes, but she's no warrior.

A well aimed javelin or arrow will cripple or kill her. Concentrating on a spell whilst injured is next to impossible for all but a trained War-Priest. She has options; to Shield herself, or blind her attackers with Light. Some priests carry a weapon; Venalia does not. She was taught to grapple, but has not practised since she learned.

No, a Priestess of the Mind's Eye is not a force for the battlefield. There are Priests who can paralyse a foe, blast them apart with Celestial fire, summon bolts of lightning, command the forces of nature, channel the terrifying presence of an angel; but not Venalia. Her strength lies in knowledge, research, facts, and secrets.

She has to outmanoeuvre Gregor in a fight that she *can* win.

Venalia raids the larder and stokes a fire, making herself a generous bowl of porridge and honey. She has a pounding headache coming on, partly from the rum hangover, mostly from the sugar crash. Over breakfast, she begins recording her intentions - another learned trick from her Whitehallow days. Protection and reference material, in the event that she is accused of something heinous.

As is her custom, Venalia then takes a moment, and prays. It is no simple or easy task: it feels like trying to force oneself to sleep.

It takes minutes of blank-eyed breathing, repeating her mantras, counting her heartbeats, before she is ready. Only when she is totally quiet and still can she feel her own soul, the silent watcher that resides in all mortals.

It is from here that she prays, not in words but in feelings, the shapes of thoughts that precede the thoughts themselves. It is here, opening her heart and soul to the world and abandoning her ego, that she is able to sense the eyes of her God upon her.

There is a part of her that watches herself. Then, further back still, there is something larger than she has words for, and it watches her watching herself. When first she felt the Mind's Eye upon her, the reaction was terror. She woke herself and tried to block out the presence.

Only later, with training, did she come to understand that there is no secret, no shame so deep, that the Gods do not understand. Mortals are flawed, inherently prone to sin; there is no judgement from the Gods, if one comes to them with an open heart.

Venalia can feel the Mind's Eye watching her now.

He can see her fear and trepidation.

She need not endure this alone.

The offer is there, if only she reaches out and touches it.

Venalia does not want to go all the way and touch the mind of her God, not today. There is extreme stress and effort involved in doing so. Today she need only dip a toe in, enough to make a connection without the spiritual turmoil of actually touching the divine, of breaching the Celestial barrier and leaving her body.

Venalia lets one fingertip of her astral soul brush the edge of the divine.

Light.

Light.

Now she can smell old books and parchment, wet ink and hot wax, the smell of Whitehallow's libraries, with their incense and tea leaves. She lets it pull her in that terrifying inward spiral that feels like a void without end.

Infinite information-space, a library of impossible size where all truths are recorded. She feels her mind expand to fill this space, expanding to an impossible size.

Keeping her soul firmly in reality, she feels for her body, and lets the Light of this place pour into it through her forehead, her third eye.

Her body breathes on its own, whilst her mind explores outer and inner spaces of infinite size and scale. With the vaguest of self-awareness, she speaks the most basic, most common, of prayers in Celestial, a noise like an organ buzzing from her throat as she attempts to mimic the cries of angels with a mortal mouth.

I seek the Scholar's Blessing, she says. *As I face adversity, I ask only that you guide my eyes to falsehood and truth alike, and that you grant me the wisdom to know one from the other.*

There comes a moment akin to the applause of a parent. Joy spreads through her like fire. She feels a swell of pride rise in her stomach, up her throat, into her mouth, where she bursts into pleasant laughter. She opens her eyes as cold clarity washes through her brain, unclouding her thoughts briefly. It feels like home – like an embrace from someone that understands her.

She feels her energy return, unable to decide if she feels nervous or excited, and opens her eyes to find the world a little less threatening. This is the job of a Priestess. Venalia leaves *her* home and makes for the guardhouse, hands tucked inside the sleeves of her robes to hide their shaking.

Venalia pushes into the blustering gale and throws her shoulders back as she reaches the guardhouse, breathing deep and grateful in the morning chill. Outside stands a single guardsman, struggling to light his pipe in the howling wind. He sees her and straightens up.

“Uh -” he begins.

“At ease, man,” she smiles, feigning confidence, and walks straight past him, into the guardhouse. He does not even try to stop her.

Inside, a guard lies asleep at the desk, a puddle of drool forming under his open mouth. She recognises him from the night's events, and leaves him to his slumber. Venalia heads for the door to the cells, and when she opens it, finds herself staring at yet another guard. Inches from one another's face.

The two of them jump in surprise.

“My apologies,” she says, laughing.

“Lady Priestess,” blurts the guard. Another one from last night. He has some parchment rolled in his arms, and immediately

Venalia reads shame, panic, in his expression. He tries to barge past her, but she moves to intercept him, freezing him in place with a polite smile.

"What a night, eh?" she puts a hand on his arm. "Do you still keep a kettle over your fire for a tired Priestess?"

"Uh -" he looks around for help, but finds none. "Uh, sure, Priestess. Shall I pour you a mug?"

"Please," she says, and closes the door to the cells. She can hear something huge moving around, and assumes it to be the half-Giant. If he is alive, then he can wait – she wants to know why the guard looks so ashamed; and what is written on those scrolls of parchment? Why not send for the Priestess immediately?

The guard clatters to the fireplace, loudly stomping his feet, trying to make enough noise to wake his companion. Venalia watches him wrestle with his options: he tries to set down the scrolls somewhere out of sight, making a great show of finding the kettle.

When he sets the scrolls down, Venalia tiptoes over and puts a hand upon them, baiting his reaction. He looks at her, then the scrolls, and flaps his mouth a few times.

"Interesting," she says, slowly rolling the parchment open. "What's your name, guardsman? I don't recognise you."

He looks at the kettle, trying to act disinterested. "Uh, Corryn, m'lady."

"Your accent; not from Llantry, are you?"

He shuffles his feet. "Atlan, m'lady."

"Can you read, Corryn?" she asks. He looks at her, lips pursed. The kettle whistles, demanding attention.

"Read, m'lady?" he asks, and licks his dry lips. Venalia doesn't need to push him any further to know that he is defensive, probably lying, hiding something; but she wants to know what he'll give up willingly.

"Yes, Corryn. Read. Interpret the written word. You're familiar with the concept?"

He winces. "Uh, a little, yes. I can read a bit, aye. Not much. Places and numbers, really."

The kettle is screaming. Venalia nods to it, and Corryn turns to take it off the fire. Corryn's hands are shake as he pours. The tin cup rattles against the kettle spout, ringing like an alarm bell.

Whilst he is distracted, Venalia scans the parchment.

Confess...

theft of the horse...

desertion of my duties...

death penalty...

bail of two thousand crowns...

payable in the exchange of goods and chattel, livestock...

valuation of the horse and equipment at two thousand crowns...

Oh Gregor, she thinks to herself. You *snake.*

This is blackmail, clear and simple – and now she has the scrolls to prove it. *Your money or your life.*

There is a blotchy signature on the contract.

“Did he sign it?” she asks, keeping her voice aloof and uninterested, eyes on the scroll.

“Uh...” Corryn tries to pass her the mug of tea, and she extends a palm, keeping him at arms length. “Uh, yes he did.”

“Oh yes,” she stifles a laugh, seeing what the prisoner has written. “I see that he's – well he's written *something.”*

“What?” asks Corryn, looking at the scribbles on the line. “Is that not his signature?”

“This is not a name, Corryn, it's a bunch of swear words in old Druidic,” she whispers, “that instructs you to take the scroll to the privy and use it to clean yourself. Sorry Corryn. Gregor should really have sent somebody who can read Druidic; it's not your fault.”

He flaps, looks at the tea, and looks at the scroll again. “Uh, the Burroughmaster never – he didn't, uh -”

“Now, now,” she puts a hand on his chainmail, gently pushing him back. “Keep that tea away from these scrolls now,

Corryn. Wouldn't want to spill it and destroy any *evidence* now, would we?"

"Evidence?" He looks at the mug in his hand, and at the scrolls. She can see him trying to work out if it's worth the risk, and sees him remember that she is a Priestess. He doesn't know exactly what she is capable of, and the thought is enough to scare him.

"I'll take this," she smiles, plucking the cup from him. Her hands are stable now, no more shaking. She stuffs the scrolls inside her robes. "And I'll take these, too."

"Uh, ma'am? The Burroughmaster'll want to know what happened to those scrolls, am I to -"

"Tell him the truth," she finishes for him. "Tell him that Priestess Venalia wanted to study them, as she suspects both foul play and conspiracy to extort an innocent man. Understand?"

Corryn nods, relieved not to be taking any blame himself. "The Burroughmaster will have my hide if I don't report this immediately."

"Then report it immediately," she pats his shoulder. "And if the Burroughmaster wishes to come down here and face me, he is free to do so. Although - Corryn?"

"Yes ma'am?"

She drops her polite smile. "Despite what the Burroughmaster tells you, you are under no compulsion to take his side if he has broken the law. Tell Gregor that if he does come down here, he will be facing the Priestess, not Venalia."

Corryn looks at the door, at Venalia, and then nods and leaves at a brisk walk. Venalia watches him go, leaving the still sleeping guard at the desk, and smiles.

Caught red-handed, she thinks; not very smart, Gregor.

She whispers some thanks to the Mind's Eye and heads for the cells, alone now, finally back in control of her own destiny.

Venalia opens the door, to speak with the prisoner.

The walls flake with plaster, lit by a single flickering alchemical lamp that pops and hisses as it burns through its fuel.

There are two cells, and only the furthest one is occupied, nestled in the furthest reach of the hall where the light is least and the stone is coldest.

Venalia hears heavy breathing coming from the cell. The hairs on her neck stand up as she approaches. There is a beast within the cage, shaped like a large man. He is the same thing that she saw lying on the table, wounded and unconscious; only now that he is in motion, he seems so much more frightening.

The breathing comes from his exercise; he is performing push ups in a handstand, with his legs against the upper walls of the cell. His feet almost touch the top of the ceiling. Sweat and dirt stain his body, visible because the guards have obviously not seen fit to dress him beyond his underclothes.

He barely acknowledges her presence, and continues to train. There's a pail of water in the cell with him, and another empty bucket in the corner. At least, she thinks, they've seen to the most basic of his needs.

She decides to start there, too.

“Have you been fed?”

He stops mid push-up, and lowers himself to the ground, rising from his low crouch and sitting on the cell's bed. It looks like a man sitting on a child's chair. He is breathing heavily, dripping with sweat, but seems strangely at peace. Upon his abdomen sits a pink handprint of fresh skin. Venalia cannot, no matter how hard she tries, picture him smiling. His eyes are dark and deep set, his brow thick, his skin riddled with scars.

“I have,” he says. His voice sounds much clearer now than it did on the operating table. It's deep, with the long vowels and drawling accent of Caladan. “Thank you. You're the Priestess.”

“I am. My name is Venalia.”

“Of the Mind's Eye,” he nods, pointing to her sigil. “Secrets and knowledge. Of course.”

He speaks with the wisdom of age, as her teachers in Whitehallow did. She has a hundred questions and limited time. To her mind, Gregor is storming towards the cells right now, his guards at his back.

“Who are you?” she asks, going for the broadest strokes possible. “Tell me your story.”

"You seem to be in a rush," he notes, taking his time. "You keep checking the doorway. Why?"

"The Burroughmaster: Gregor de Llantry." She pulls the scroll from her robes to demonstrate. "The man who wanted you to sign these. He's on his way. We don't have much time."

"You aren't allowed to speak with me?"

"He doesn't approve," she says. "So the faster you answer the questions, the more likely it is that I can get you out of here."

"Getting out of here is no challenge," he says and *there it is.* A smile, confident; the kind of confidence that comes with being as tall as two men and as heavy as four.

"You intend to break out? I mean – these are lead and steel bars, they're strong, impervious to magic."

"But not to raw power," he says. "The bars are held by old, cracked stone. I don't need to break the bars; only what holds them."

"There are better ways to get out of this cell," she offers.

"Such as?"

"Such as helping me clear your name of any wrongdoing. That way you won't have to flee with a bounty on your head."

"Preferable," he admits. "Okay. My name is Temple."

"Just Temple?"

"Just Temple."

"Okay then, Temple: what happened to you?"

"I'm the last surviving member of a Redwood Company expedition. Went into the Inverted World, on behalf of the Magistry. Woke something up. It took most of us. Rest were picked off as we fled for the surface. It wounded me as I escaped."

"What was it?"

"Some old Magisterial creation. Pre-Dragonfall. A collection of shades, or spirits. Kind of thing that used to crawl out of the Scar. Looks like a real tall woman, all shadow, little white eyes. Hair like she's underwater. She sings, the song gets in your head. Makes you want to sing too. Takes you. Most of my team wandered into the darkness. Then we heard them singing to us.

Took to calling it the Choir. Sure you can imagine why."

"Oh," says Venalia. She can feel her heartbeat speeding up. This is the kind of thing that she has studied, but never expected to face.

Her first job should be mildly unpleasant – some undead, maybe, or a feral wolf terrorizing the cattle, something that she could handle with a few armed men and a Shield spell. This calls for a High Priest, with a team of other Priests, and usually a detachment of soldiers. Magisterial artillery. Airship support.

Her throat cracks dry. The threat of Gregor finding her talking with the prisoner seems petty now. This is far beyond her.

"You, uh, said that it was coming after you?"

He nods, points to the handprint on his stomach. "Think she can track this. Sorry. I was aiming for Atlan. Pretzia brought me here instead."

"Pretzia? That's your horse?"

"It is."

"Well, if we can prove that Pretzia is yours, we can get you released. Do you have papers?"

"No," he shrugs, "not that it matters. You'll let me out anyway."

"Because the Choir is far more important, and we're going to need your help," she says. "Right?"

"Indeed."

"Will it be bad?" She scolds the worried child that she hears.

Temple nods. "I expect that it will."

She rubs the bridge of her nose. "What do we do?"

"See to the defences," he says. "It comes for us tonight, after sunset."

Venalia steps towards the bar. "You're talking in the future tense, again; you did that when I was treating you, too. You said: it doesn't attack tonight. How can you *know* that? What are you?"

"I know that it attacks tonight for two reasons," he holds

up his fingers. “Firstly, because it's been inside my head. I know how it thinks. In a way.”

“I felt something singing, when I healed you. That was the Choir?”

“Likely. It's driven by fear. Loneliness. Hunger. Cold. It won't risk it during the day. It hates sunlight. Avoids direct confrontation. It'll attack at night.”

“Okay. What's the other reason?”

“Because, like some half-Giants, my ancestral blood gives me dreams of my future.”

She tries to maintain her composure, but she may as well have unearthed a bar of gold in the privy. “You're a seer?” she whispers. “A real one?”

“Yes.”

“And you said you knew me, didn't you? To the guardsman?”

“Priestess with red hair. You.”

“Did you see me in your visions?”

“In a dream.”

Venalia leans against the wall, trying to take everything in. She knows the stories about half-Giants, rare though they are. The Giants saw in both directions at once – past and future were, are, will be the same to them. That gift lives on in Temple.

She does not have enough time in one life to ask him everything that she wants to.

She takes the leap, asks the big question on her mind. “Have you -”

“Stop,” he holds up his hand, already weary of her question. “You're about to ask me what happens next.”

He is correct. “How did you know that? Did you dream of this moment?”

“No,” he laughs. “You're predictable. Everybody wants to know their fate,” he shakes his head. “Till they hear it. Are you sure that you want me to tell you, Priestess?”

“I've studied Divination, sir. I know how this works. If you tell me, it changes things. Which means there's little harm in asking."

"No," he says. "That's how *your* Divination works. Magic and Gods can see into many futures. Possible futures. I see only one – mine. And it does not change. Trying to stop it only brings it to be. I dream of what *will* happen. To me. In flashes."

She is silent for a while. For a Priestess of knowledge and secrets, this is an irresistible pull. It takes Venalia a moment to process it.

"Can I ask you other questions, then?"

"If you'd like," he leans back. "Maybe this is how it goes."

She marshals her thoughts, gets them straight.

"This monster; it attacks tonight?" she asks.

"It does."

"Do we survive?"

"Tonight? Yes. Tonight, there is an attack. Then, sometime afterwards, you and I part ways. It's snowing, which it won't be today, so I can assume that we do not die tonight."

"Does Llantry survive this?"

"I don't think so."

Venalia grips the bars of his cell. "What? You don't *think* so?" Temple shrugs in answer. "Well, what -" she stops, finds her courage, and asks. "What happens to me?"

"We part ways. I see the village empty. It seems that you have failed. You walk into the woods with a warhammer. You are in tears. That is the last time that you appear in my dreams."

Venalia slides down the wall until she is seated. The fight has been roundly knocked out of her in one breath.

It occurs to her that he could be lying. This might be some long game, some con – but what reason has he to lie?

"So that's it?" she asks. "This monster comes for Llantry, and we lose?"

"I believe so," he says, holding up his hands. "Do not be quick to despair. I only see things, Priestess. I do not know the context, nor the details. Perhaps the village is empty because we evacuate it?"

Her heart leaps. "Of course! Should we do that?"

"Absolutely. The Choir grows in power the more people that join it. How many people live in Llantry?"

"About two hundred, I think."

"Evacuate. Today, preferably. Before it gets dark."

"How much have you seen? Do you know where it attacks from?"

"No details. Flashes. Images. I know it comes at night, and I know that we face it from the walls. There's fire, too. Trench on fire. Choir doesn't like the flames, we found."

"Okay, that sounds like something we can manage. How do I fight this thing?"

He raises his eyesbrows. "Priestess; a team of well trained mercenaries could not handle this. I doubt that you can. You don't fight this. You *survive* this."

"Do I?" she asks. "Survive?"

He hesitates, and Venalia feels rush of vertigo, as though the world is falling past her.

Temple, to his credit, does not mince his words.

"The feeling, in my dream, is that you go to certain death."

Certain death.

"And you don't see me again?" she asks.

"No."

Her first, second and third instincts all tell her to run, to escape this place and this fate. Dread fills her head with imagined ends, her mind lost to the singing dead. Death is terrifying; but to lose her free will, to be a slave to a monster's song, is a nightmare without end.

There is nothing keeping her here but duty and legal technicalities; she *could* run. She should.

They are not your people, she thinks, and hates herself for it.

You owe them nothing.

Then speaks the Priestess, who took an oath, and reminds her of the first rule:

A Priestess must never, under any circumstances, give up on her people.

She cannot leave her new flock to such a fate, no matter if it is already written.

And it is already written.

The Priestess knows that she must stay, but the girl who has yet to see her twentieth summer breaks down in the face of those words:

Certain death.

Her composure lost, she buries her head in her arms and cries, knees curled to her chest.

This was not how the day was supposed to go. This is not what she had in mind when she graduated, when she returned home to bury Marius, when she rose this morning.

Venalia takes a deep breath and forces herself lift her head.

A Priestess cannot simply give up because she feels frightened. Nobody in the village is better equipped to deal with this than her; except, perhaps, the half-Giant soldier in front of her.

"You good?" he asks her. It sounds alien – she cannot imagine for a second that he cares, so flat is his voice. His body language says relaxed, and Venalia wonders if his cold confidence comes from knowing that he will survive.

"I've only just come back to Llantry," she explains from her seat on the concrete. "I've only just graduated. I came home to bury my father. And you're telling me that over the next few days, I lose everything else too? My life? No, Mr. Temple. I'm not good."

"I'm sorry," he says, though it does not sound genuine. "I can only tell you what I've seen, Priestess."

She gives him a curious look. "Why do you stay here?"

"Your guards put me here."

"No, I mean; you said that we part ways in a few days. Why do you stay till then? What keeps you here?"

"I'm not heartless."

"What?"

He thinks on this before answering. "We cannot change the future. But I have a heart, and I cannot, in good conscience, allow you to go through this alone."

Venalia remains silent. The words keep playing over in her head.

"Me? You stay here for me?"

"So it seems."

"Why?"

"Sympathy. I know what it's like to face death alone."

Because that is what she is doing. No doubt. The path is set. She wanders into the woods alone to die.

"Why would you tell me this?" she whispers, and she can see that he will not meet her red eyes.

"I'm not given to lying," he says. "Sure a Priestess understands that. You asked about your fate. I did warn you. You worship knowledge, no?"

She sighs, and closes her eyes. He is right.

"How do you do it?" she asks. "How do you live, knowing what has yet to come? Because I've only known you a few minutes and already I want to put you in a box and make sure you never tell me anything ever again."

"Many have tried. I simply do not understand their hardship. I have never lived any other way. This is all I know."

"Does it comfort you?"

"Makes me unbeatable in a fight."

"How so?"

"I'm sure to survive any fight that I get into. No need to hold back."

"Maybe that's *why* you survive every fight?"

"Perhaps."

She tries to silence her mind, clamouring as it is. Her own imminent death has overtaken her stream of thought.

"How do I do this?" she asks. "How do you do it? Do *you* know when you'll die?"

"Maybe. In a way." He nods, unmoved by the question. "I dream of days ahead. After I live it, it's gone. No more dream. There are much less of them, now."

"They run out, at some point?"

"So it would seem."

"And that's when you die."

"Seems so," he says.

She mulls it over. "So I can't change the future? I can't just leave Llantry?"

"That's the problem, Priestess." He stands and walks over to the bars, sitting cross legged opposite her. "You could. Easy."

"But I don't?"

"Won't," he corrects her.

"Why not?"

"Only you know the answer to that."

"The first rule," she sighs. "It's the one that gets Priests and Priestesses killed all the time. We can never, under any circumstances, give up on our people."

"There it is then," he folds his arms. "You *could* flee. But you don't."

"Damn it," she deflates. "It makes sense. I couldn't abandon these people, knowing what's coming for them. If nothing else, I can try to save as many as possible. Gods above, Temple, what a way to start the day." She breaks into cynical laughter, throwing her hands up. "You know, I was nervous coming here because I might have to contend with the law? The *law*, of all things. Words on paper."

"The law is more than just words on paper," says Temple.

"I know, I know," she concedes. "It's still less terrifying

than, than, *certain death.*"

Venalia feels herself buckle under the impossible weight of the task set before her. She wishes to flee. She knows that she won't, but Gods above, she wishes that she could. For now, all she can do is breathe deeply, and try to stop the panic from overtaking her.

"Priestess?" asks Temple, noticing her sorrow, her silence. She looks up in answer. "We have work to do."

"I know, I know," she whispers, annoyed that she has to be reminded of the basics. He looks up, and gives her the slightest hint of a smile. "You know," she says, "when I was trying to heal you, I looked at you and thought 'wow, he seems old for a soldier,' and Marius always told me that I should respect any old person in a dangerous profession."

"Because they have survived it?"

"Exactly - but you haven't survived because of talent or skill, have you? You've survived because you know that you can't die. Is that a paradox?"

"I still need to focus. I still have to fight."

"Do you? What if you stopped? Would you lose your next fight?"

"I wouldn't stop. That's the point – and I won't lose my next fight."

"Do you know what your next fight is?"

"Oh, I don't need to be a seer to know that. I believe it happens in a few moments. Outside this very cell."

Venalia raises her eyebrows. "Against me? No, that doesn't feel right. Against – oh."

Gregor is standing in the doorway, watching them. Silhouetted behind him, Venalia can see the guards. They have shields and batons at the ready, and two of them have bows with arrows already nocked.

"Priestess," says Gregor. "Step away from the prisoner."

"Oh no," she whispers. "Gregor, look, I know you aren't going to listen to me – but you absolutely *will* come to regret the decision that you're about to make."

“Well you're correct about the first thing,” says Gregor. “Tell the prisoner to sign the scroll. Properly, this time. Then he may leave, and there will be no further action.”

“The scroll that forfeits his horse, equipment and money?” Venalia glances at Temple, who is standing up with a kind of weary acceptance. He shakes his head. “He will not,” she relays.

“Then he will be charged.”

“Not under my watch. What are your guards going to do with those weapons?”

“They're here for my protection,” he says. “Stand aside.”

“Why?”

“So that I may persuade the prisoner of his best interests.”

Venalia counts two men with bows. She hears their chainmail rattling; they are terrified.

“Bows,” she says. “So you can shoot the prisoner without a fight if it comes to it?”

“We have to assume that he's dangerous until proven otherwise.”

She looks at Temple, who shrugs, arms still folded.

“I *am* dangerous,” he says. “Those archers aren't. Shaking like dogs.” The guards look at one another, doubt streaking from their forehead in beads of sweat. Temple puts his hands on the bars. “When I rip the floor from the ground and charge, they'll all be crushed anyway. Few arrows won't stop me.”

“See?” Gregor looks at Venalia. “He's threatening my guards.”

“No threat,” says Temple, slow and steady. “Won't be me that starts anything. Priestess, step back. Let him talk.”

She steps back after a moment's hesitation, and allows Gregor to look through the bars at Temple, hands hooked in his belt, head tilted back. A boy's idea of intimidation.

“We can do this the easy way, or the hard way,” says Gregor.

“Hard way,” says Temple.

“If you will not cooperate, you will stand trial without

representation. We will seize your belongings as evidence in the meantime."

"No," says Temple. "You won't."

Gregor stumbles in his thought process. He blinks a few times. "Excuse me?"

"There's an aberration on the road," says Temple. "From the Inverted World. Coming this way. Took nine of my ten-strong unit. Redwood Company, well trained. It's coming for Llantry. Tonight."

Gregor is at a loss for words. Like Venalia, he did not expect to be hit with this kind of thing today. He clearly had other plans, though Venalia is at a loss for what they were.

"Release me," says Temple, "and I will help."

"I'm sorry?" asks Gregor. "Is this – what?" He turns to Venalia. "This is obvious nonsense. You believe this?"

Venalia clears her throat. "He's telling the truth, Burroughmaster, I swear by my Gods. You saw the wound!"

"And I am not signing a thing," says Temple, putting his hands on the bars. Gregor is within his grasp, but he does not make a move. "There's but one horse thief in this room, Burroughmaster."

Gregor, bewildered, opens his mouth a few times before he manages to find the words.

"Guards, open the door," he says. "The prisoner will learn some manners."

"It doesn't go well for you," says Venalia. She wants to add that it doesn't go well for any of them, in the long run; a part of her wonders if Gregor might bear some responsibility for the destruction of Llantry, should that come to pass. "Trust me. You lose this fight."

"Why are you on his side?" he turns on her. "Aiding a criminal now, Priestess? An accusation was made against my character, I have a right to defend myself."

Gregor draws a silver-and-steel warhammer from beneath his cape, the haft inlaid with dark purple crystalline. It was his father's once, Venalia knows; he called it Minotaur.

The head of the warhammer is shaped like the head of a charging bull, with two great horns. The crystalline inlaid along the handle once held a powerful magical charge, but now is dull and empty. Gregor grasps it, sweaty-palmed, crossed over his chest. She can hear him breathing.

"Listen to me," she says, stepping close to him. She drops her voice to an absolute whisper, so that only he may hear. "Please. For all our sakes. Your men are terrified. Facing a mercenary four times their size. You'll lose this fight, and then *we'll* lose Llantry. We are about to have our own little Age of Fear, and I absolutely *cannot* do this without you, Gregor."

Gregor's hand squeezes the warhammer, but young Corryn steps forward. "Sir?" Everyone is silent. Venalia's heart swells. "Sir, they're telling the truth – about the monster. Agnir heard it, sir, he told us all about it."

"Gregor," she whispers. "*Please*. For your people."

She steps back, and sees an expression on his face that she has not seen in a long time.

Fear. Dread. He swallows, and they all hear it.

She sees the thoughts racing across his face. The tiny problems of wealth and winter seem to pale when faced with an imminent, existential threat. His mask drops, however briefly, and she sees that he too is a scared child.

Venalia pleads with her eyes, begs with her heart – and to her surprise, he seems to settle on a decision. Stepping back, Gregor motions for his guards.

"Stand down – and open the cell. Prisoner, what is your name?"

"Temple."

"Then Temple, you are a prisoner no more. Do not leave Llantry until the case against you is resolved. We'll be keeping a close eye on you," he looks at his men, checking that they remain at his side. "Priestess, I am placing him in your care. See to it that he is fed and clothed. If this threat is as severe as you say it is, then we will need all the help we can get."

She nods, and mouths a silent 'thank you' to Gregor. He does not return or acknowledge the gesture.

Corryn steps forward and opens the cell. Temple does not move.

"The rest of you," says Gregor, "attend to your tasks. I have business to see to. Priestess, you have an hour to make your charge presentable. We will speak then, once Mr. Temple is dressed and fed. We will have his horse stabled at my estate. What is the horses name?"

"Pretzia," says Temple.

"Come by in an hour and you may retrieve her. Your equipment is in her saddlebags."

"As is all of his money and other belongings," says Venalia, "right? It will all be there?"

"Of course," scowls Gregor, as though this was ever in question.

"Then, uh, thank you, Burroughmaster," she bows a little. Positive reinforcement. Play the game.

Gregor turns and follows his men out. She can feel the relief coming from each of them. When they are gone, Venalia turns to Temple, still standing in the cell.

"I don't trust him at all," she says.

"Nor do I."

"I thought there was going to be a fight?" she asks, coy.

"There almost was. It will happen as it is supposed to. Do not overthink it."

"Easy for you to say," she sighs. "Okay, come on, I'll feed you. Marius should have some old robes or some curtains that I can stitch together – and we have a blacksmith who can repair your breastplate – I have to go and see him anyway."

Temple gives the kind of bow that shows respect, without necessarily granting her authority over him.

"Lead the way, Priestess."

Chapter Five

Heads turn as they walk through the village of Llantry. Venalia lifts her head like royalty, pacing her kingdom with a Giant bodyguard. For now, Temple is draped in a huge canvas that is usually reserved for protecting timber from rainfall.

"What happened to my other clothes?" he asks.

"We had to cut them off."

"Fair. Thank you again. For saving my life."

"Just doing my job," she smiles. "You had some very unusual wounds. That was the Choir? The handprint?"

"Yes."

"What *did* it do to you?"

Temple grumbles, recalls the pain. "Felt like a spell."

"Smelled like one, too," she says.

"A charm, maybe. Like mind control. Wasn't expecting it. Felt like I was afraid, desperate. Lonely. Cold. I felt what it felt."

"You were a part of it?"

He nods. "The song is a connection. So is its touch."

"So we shouldn't get close to it," she says. "How did you escape its song? You said that anybody who heard it would fall under its control."

“Gradual effect,” he explains. “You hear the song, you get lost in it; next you know, you've lost five minutes, don't know where you are.” He sees the worry in her eyes. “Praying or singing helped.”

“Praying I can do,” she gives a dark laugh. “So how can we hurt it?”

“Fire. Fire, and light.”

Venalia's eyes alight with a memory. “You said we start a great fire tonight.”

“We do.”

“Fire and light.” She folds her arms, deep in the strategic state of mind. “I can cast Light?”

“Wouldn't be enough,” he gives her a kind but dismissive pat on the back, and hesitates when he sees the first cinders of her temper. “Right idea though,” he adds. “Flame is better.”

“Flame it is. Anything else?”

“Yes. Silvered weapons. Steel did not work.”

“Ah,” she flashes a smile. “I've to go and see the blacksmith; I'll ask him what he can do.”

“You know him?”

“I do - he was the one who found me as a child.”

Temple looks at her, as though from far away. “You mentioned an adoptive parent,” he says. “You're an orphan?”

“I am.” She raises an eyebrow, “and *you* are very blunt, Mr. Temple; and very *forward.”*

“Is that a problem?”

“Not at all,” she glances up at him. “I'm sworn to honesty. I find your approach refreshing.”

“Permit me another question,” he says, and lowers his voice. “One orphan to another?”

Oh. “Of course.”

“What happened?”

”Bell the Blacksmith found me as a baby, in the burned

ruins of a cart. An ambush, probably. I was between the burned bodies of a man and a woman. He thinks they were my parents."

Temple says nothing; just nods.

"I've no memory of them," she adds.

"Did they name you?"

"No, Marius did. Venalia is Celestial, it means 'little angel'; which is ironic because it must have been hell raising me," she says, and Temple lets out a chuckle.

"He spoke Celestial?"

"He was a Priest of the Wakened World. We burned him only yesterday."

"He chose a name fitting for a Priestess," says Temple, "though not for a woman of the Steppe."

Venalia has only ever heard it as an insult; her hair, her height, her temper. Hallmarks of a *woman of the Steppe*. A barbarian, out of place in the library.

"I'm not really a woman of the Steppe," she says.

"Your hair says otherwise."

"It does?"

"Only passes from the mother," he nods. "Your height, too. Tall. For a human."

"Are you from the Steppe?" she asks.

"Why would you assume so? Because I am half-Giant?"

Venalia rolls her eyes. "No. You wrote Steppe curse words on the scroll? In Druidic?"

"Ah," he concedes. "Fair – but no. I was raised in Whitehallow. Moved to Caladan later."

"Whitehallow? Really?"

He nods. "Temple of the Champion. That's what my mother wrote on my forehead. When she abandoned me. Apparently. Just *Temple*."

"Like an address? As in, *deliver this baby to a temple?*"

"Yes."

Venalia has nothing, save for the obvious.

"I trained in Whitehallow," she says.

"I know," he pats her back again, hand like a shovel. "You're a Priestess. You all train in Whitehallow. Is that where *you* learned Steppe curses?"

"I can swear like a sailor in ten languages," she smiles. "Thought it would make me more fun at parties."

"Did it?"

Venalia sighs. "No. But if *did* pay off today."

Venalia's spirits lift – but they drop a second later.

Little victories, in the face of certain death;

but certain death nonetheless.

She stops walking. Her heart beats behind her eyeballs, mouth dry, vision blurred at the edges -

"Stop that," orders Temple, and kneels to head-height, turning her around. He puts his hands on her shoulders. "Stop that right now."

She focuses on him, and tries to breathe. "Temple; *certain death?*"

"Death is always certain," he says. "You understand?"

"Of course."

"Then stop this despair."

"But you said I couldn't change it," she mumbles, unable to meet his eyes. "Certain death leaves little room for interpretation."

Venalia feels her heart racing again; *oh,* she thinks, *to be lost in an interesting conversation again, to be free of this burden.*

"You walk into the woods," says Temple. "Hammer in your hands. To certain death. I am not there to see what happens next. Perhaps I simply abandon you. Never see you again. Do not think me above such things. It is not *set*."

"I just -" *don't want to die. I'm too young, my life is only beginning.*

"Venalia," he claps her shoulders hard enough to jolt her. "I do not see you die. But know this: give in to despair, and you *will* seal your own fate."

"I know," she whispers, and as the wind picks up she finds her centre. This is just another test, she thinks, just another exam, another challenge. "I know. Fear only begets fear."

"Correct," says Temple, and begins walking again. "Good."

By the time Venalia catches him up with his long, slow stride, they have reached her house.

Temple takes up most of the living room, sat on the floor in front of a roaring fire whilst Venalia brings him piles of food from the pantry. Keeping busy distracts her mind from the

certain death

that looms dark and heavy at her back.

After going through half the pantry, Temple raises his hand for her to stop bringing him things. She feels like the mother of an extremely large baby.

"How much do you eat?" she asks.

"A lot. Can go a long time without. If required."

"Don't suppose you'd mind doing that? So that I can eat?" she laughs.

He nods, eyes closed. "I shall fast."

"I mean -" she was only joking, but in all honesty, she cannot imagine trying to feed him for any longer than that. "Well. Alright."

Temple watches her from across the room, thinking in silence.

"Yes?" she prompts him with a smirk.

"Thought you'd ask more questions."

"Why's that?"

"Priestess of the Mind's Eye. Secrets. Knowledge."

"I am – but, well, you're a seer and you're a mercenary, and I feel like you've got a much better handle on this situation than I do. I'm following your lead. Don't want to annoy you with questions."

She sits on the rocking chair, pawing through the chest of clothes and capes that Marius left her. Her stitching is a matter of personal pride, and Temple is an interesting challenge. It takes almost six of Marius's shirts to make one for Temple.

"Your questions annoy people?" asks Temple.

"Oh all the time," she smiles. "I mean, I ask them anyway."

"So ask," he says, putting an entire chicken leg in his mouth, bones and all, and crunching it to pieces. When she looks out of curiosity, she sees that his teeth are like gravestones; no incisors or canine teeth, just molars.

"What was your mission?" she asks.

"Magister paid us to delve down. Into the Inverted World. Big money to go down there."

She laughs, shaking her head. "*No* amount of money would get me down there."

"Wise," he nods, continues. "Ten man team. Magisters, priests, warriors, scouts, scholars. A stalker who knew the tunnels. Me and Ungren," he stops, presses his hand to his heart in a full fist, "were hired as muscle. We were to find an old Magisterial outpost. "

"Down there?"

"Pre-Dragonfall," he says, and sees Venalia's eyes widen. "Magistry built it to hide from their Draconic masters. Whilst they plotted to overthrow them."

"Over two thousand years old, then," she whispers.

"A long time, down there," he says, grave and quiet. "Long time to drift. The Inverted World moves. Shifts. Our scholar was an expert on that drift. Believed he had the approximate location of the outpost."

"Was he right?"

"Almost. He got us close enough that our scout found it."

“And why did they want you to find it?”

“Not for us to know. Some arcane advance in psionics. Neural stuff. Not my wheelhouse.”

Venalia is on the edge of her seat. “Did you find anything?”

“Yes,” he says, and Venalia watches him drift away. “We opened the door, and shone our light. The shadows opened their eyes. Then the singing.”

Temple is there again.

The dark bursts open like a spider nest, and shades swarm them

His sword does nothing

He turns to Ungren, sees him break and run

Follows him

Sees their expedition drowning in the thick black mist, and

then

They start singing too

A shiver courses through Venalia., and she finds herself looking out the window, trying to guess how many hours of daylight remain.

Temple shakes off the memories, and continues. “Ungren and I escaped – but he was marked. He did not make it.”

She meets his eyes, burdened and heavy. “I'm so sorry, Temple.”

“We knew the risks,” he waves her away.

“You knew you'd survive, I assume?” she asks. “Being a seer? Right?”

“Knew I'd escape,” he says, and drops his head. “Didn't know I'd be leaving them behind.”

“Are they..?” she begins, morbidly curious. Temple

motions for her to ask. “Are they part of it now?”

“Perhaps. It has their voices. It knows what they know.”

“It mimics them?”

“I hope so. Otherwise, it truly has them.”

“And if we hurt it,” she asks, feeling her heart race, “do we hurt them?”

“Yes.”

Venalia sits back in her chair, taking a breath. “God's above,” she says, lacking anything else to give.

“We knew the risks,” he repeats, though he does not sound convinced.

She gives him a guarded look, and they both know what she is thinking; that Temple might not have the heart to slay his own comrades, to elicit cries of pain from them.

“I owe them a good death,” he says, reading her face. “I will not hesitate.” He lifts the plate of food and tips it into his mouth, holding the clean plate up. “Thank you. I am finished.”

“The food or the questions?”

“Both.”

“Well, good timing,” she says, presenting her finished project: a long white shirt, made of many other smaller shirts.

“It's a shirt,” he states, taking it in his huge hands.

“Not just a shirt,” she smiles.

He eases one arm into it, then another. Venalia was worried that it would be too tight but, owing to her skill, it is loose and comfortable. Temple fastens the shirt closed with pegs, arranging it with a sash to hang from his waist.

It resembles a kilt.

He admires Venalia's handiwork in the mirror. “Just like the men of the Steppe wear.”

“You look like one of the cattle herders now,” she smiles. “You'll fit right in.”

“I doubt that. But, thank you.”

"Now that you're dressed, we should get moving. Daylight is fading, and the sooner Bell can get started on your silvered weapon, the better."

"Indeed."

"Then -" she stops; Temple whips his head up, like a guard dog sensing an intruder. "Temple?"

"Shh," he bats her away, listening intently. "Bastard. I knew it."

He barges through the door into the rain, and Venalia rushes after him, wrapping her cloak around herself.

She hears it now:

Hoof beats, whinnying, the sound of a horse angered. She runs after Temple in his new kilt, and together they see a crowd gathered in the square.

Venalia curses under her breath; the spectacle has attracted a crowd.

Gregor is seated atop Pretzia, a warhorse far too big for him, who does not recognise his authority. He clings to the saddle, blurting instructions like a child, driving spurs into Pretzia's side.

He has enough time to look around, to see Venalia, to know that he has been caught – and then Pretzia rears in fury. For a moment, Pretzia and Gregor resemble a coat of arms.

Then Pretzia tosses him from the saddle. He hits the wet mud with a slap, hard enough that he stops moving. Venalia's schadenfreude comes to an abrupt stop at the same time that Gregor's body does. She rushes to his side, but Pretzia is trained to fight, trained for war. The warhorse stamps the ground twice to warn Venalia, then turns, and rears up over Gregor with her hooves like warhammers, ready to dash his skull to paste.

"Temple!" she shouts.

Temple barks something – a command in the Steppe language, something old and archaic. Pretzia stops, balancing on her hoofs, and -

- stays there, frozen. Temple approaches, hand raised to her nose, and Pretzia snorts. She shuffles back on her hind legs as the village – and Venalia – look on in awe. Temple puts his hand to her muzzle and whispers in her ear, stroking her mane.

Once Pretzia is calmed, he leads her away from the road. “Easy girl,” he rubs her ears, down her neck. “Easy. I'm here.”

He gives Venalia a *look*.

All clear.

The rain is lashing down as Venalia runs to Gregor's side, shooing curious villagers away. She can see on Gregor's face what she felt at the funeral. He turns his face from them, unable to meet their eyes.

If the villagers knew that this was an attempt to flee Llantry, to leave them to their fate and save himself, they'd have him hanged.

Venalia knows that she could cast him down for this. She could turn the table on him for everything that he ever did to her; but looking at him, soaked and close to tears, muddied and humiliated, she cannot bring herself to inflict anything upon him but kindness.

“Come on, Burroughmaster,” she kneels beside him and extends a hand, keeping her voice low. “That must have hurt.”

“I'm fine!” He pushes her away. Venalia stumbles, almost tumbling into the mud herself. Gregor lunges to his feet, slipping in the mud, arms flailing. Venalia keeps her distance, but his ill-balanced limp elicits whispers and gasps from the crowd.

She paces after him. “Gregor let me help you,” she says, quiet enough that only he can hear.

“I don't need your help,” he says, his voice breaking.

“Stop it,” she hisses, and puts her hand on his shoulder, and raises her voice so that the villagers hear her. “That was incredibly brave of you, Burroughmaster -”

Gregor throws her hand off, wraps his soaking cloak around himself, and storms into the mist. Venalia sighs, tries with all of her might not to roll her eyes, and rushes after him. Temple raises his eyebrows as she runs past, and in answer she can only shake her head.

“Follow me,” she tells Temple. “Stable Pretzia at his estate, then hang around. I have things to settle. I might need you.”

Temple nods, leading Pretzia away, distracting the crowd who come forward to lay their hands on the magnificent beast.

Venalia hitches her dress, cursing her profession's dress code, and slogs through the mud after Gregor. She reaches the iron gate to his estate as he barges through it, and though she shouts after him, her pleas are ignored. Gregor storms up the short, muddy path to his longhouse, splintering the old rotten wood as he slams the door shut in Venalia's face before she can follow.

Instinct tells her to angrily chap the door, and then burst through it, but she forces herself to wait. He has a warhammer called Minotaur in there, and he is emotionally volatile. She looks around for help, and finds only rain and mud.

Venalia steps back and takes a deep breath.

Standing in the garden of the de Llantry estate (in reality no more than a brick-walled garden around a longhouse), soaked by the rain, Venalia allows herself a sigh of frustration.

There is more going on than meets the eye here, she thinks; there must be. Gregor's cowardice alone does not explain his reaction.

Perhaps the estate itself can.

Venalia walks the grounds of the longhouse, bundled in her cloak to keep the rain out, leaving puddles where she steps. Gardens once cared for have fallen to weeds and slugs. Brickwork flakes, the windows need cleaned, the gutters are overgrown with moss.

At the end of her circuit, she finds herself once more at the front door. This time, it opens under her grasp, and she eases herself into the closest thing Llantry has to a Great Hall.

She steps into a room with four fireplaces, only one of which is burning. Gregor sits beside it, having removed all of his clothing save for his undershirt and breeches. Upon the floor lies a breastplate, stamped with the de Llantry crest - a bull's head. On the table rests Minotaur, the once-magical warhammer, dulled and rusted.

Gregor inhabits his little corner like a house spider, no more than a visitor. The great table, built for banquets, boasts a thick layer of dust. It is swept clean in a single corner, where Gregor must eat his meals.

He looks up at her with a tired scowl. “Leave me to the crows, woman.”

She motions towards the warhammer, Minotaur, and his breastplate. “Were you expecting a fight?” He does not answer; instead he runs his hands through his long hair, pulling at his hair, grimacing. She presses him. “I'm curious what your plan was. Flee to Atlan? The Choir attacks from that direction, you'd run right into it.”

“I know.”

“To the North, then?”

“Into the Steppe?” he gives a grim laugh. “I'd not last a day. Something would eat me. Most likely the half-Giants, which would be fitting.”

“East?”

“Into the forest? Where the Scarlings have been breeding? We haven't hunted them in too long. Their attacks have shut the roads from the East to all but armoured convoys.”

“West, then?”

“Into the mountains – there's worse there than Scarlings.”

“So where were you going?”

“Away,” he looks at the floor, defeated. “I hadn't thought about where. I just have to get out of this place.”

“Oh believe me, Gregor, of all people; I know the feeling.”

“No, you don't!” he snaps, driving her back. “You *did* leave this place. You got to walk away from the hard work and the hard living. You gave this up so that you could live easy in the sunshine with your books. Well, the rest of us had to stay here, Ven, we had to endure – and me? I never even *had* a choice. This was forced upon me, while you ran off to the edge of the world. Right as Anabel went missing, right as things got hard, you vanished.”

And then came back, it goes unsaid. *Unlike Anabel.*

He spits on the floor. “Well, not all of us have the luxury of running away. This place *is* my life, Venalia. Llantry is *my* family, *my* responsibility, and -”

Gregor stumbles over his words, the rage catching in his throat. He puts his hand in front of his mouth as though only now realising what he is saying.

“I cannot protect my people.”

“Perhaps not,” she concedes, and he stares into the fire in answer.

She looks up at the heads of great elks on the wall, of bears, of eight-eyed Scarlings with three mouths, slain by better de Llantry's in better times.

Once, this place was a bulwark of Northern strength, living on the border of the Deadlands before they were restored and renamed. Llantry has faced more than one existential threat in its time – but that was when it was younger, and stronger.

“Gregor, how did this happen?” she gestures around the great hall, unkempt and covered in dust. Those same mounted heads look down in disappointment at Gregor.

He collapses back into his chair. “Things have been getting worse since Anabel went missing.”

Since Venalia left for Whitehallow. Since she found Anabel's ribbon, said nothing, and burned it because she hated her. Venalia feels the locked box in her chest rattling, eager to be opened, and instead opts to chain it shut and bury it.

“How so?” she asks.

“Family fell apart,” says Gregor. “Mother went first, drank herself sick. Went to sleep one night and didn't wake up. Father followed shortly after. They couldn't keep going, living with the uncertainty. The lack of closure.”

Venalia gives an understanding nod, but her stomach is tying itself in knots, heaping the blame for this upon her already weak shoulders.

Gregor takes a shuddering breath. “It's just me and Evelyn now, and she won't take the position of Burroughmaster. I've no wife, no children. The pastures are suffering under the rains, ever since Sunstone was restored. Scarlings take our livestock in the night. Merchants won't risk the roads, and even if they did, we've little money.” He looks up from his hands, and she realises now that he is absolutely exhausted. “Venalia, I don't have Anabel's gift for magic. I do not have Evelyn's intelligence. The herdsmen keep it a secret, but I've overheard them speaking about taking their herds South to warmer climates. Llantry was already dying when I took over. Alas, that it should breathe its last under my watch...”

“And now,” she finishes his thought, “this horror crawls

up from the Inverted World to finish us off."

He finally meets her eyes. "I know you think me a coward and a failure, but try to understand. There are more than sixty villages in the Moot that pay tribute to Atlan, to the Broadhelms, and do you know which one is the smallest? The poorest?"

"Llantry."

"Little Llantry. Little Llantry, where little ladies are liable to get lost," he sneers. "That's the rhyme they teach their children, Ven, about my sister. My family. That's our legacy. Everybody knows to avoid this place. So when I turn up to Atlan with our pathetic tithe and taxes every year, riding on a plough-horse with mud on my boots and cloak, do you know what the other Burroughmasters do, Venalia?" he spits again. "They laugh; oh, never to my face, no, but they laugh behind their hands. Whisper to one another. Poor little Llantry, with its poor, *little* Burroughmaster."

He turns and points out the window, jabbing his finger like an accusation. "This place is my only family, Venalia, it is *everything* to me."

Venalia shakes her head. "So you try to blackmail a man out of his horse and his money?"

"Imagine it!" He throws his hands out. "Next time that I ride to Atlan, it could be atop a prize warhorse, worth more than the village. A host of guards with exquisite weaponry, adorned in polished armour. Imagine that. Imagine making Llantry worthy of respect."

"By robbing somebody?"

"We saved his *life*, woman; the least he can do is pay us back."

"I saved his life," she whispers.

"And we have nothing to show for it – I have to put Llantry first."

Venalia laughs in disbelief. "You were about to flee and leave us all to die!"

Gregor leans his elbows upon his knees and covers his face once more. She folds her arms, waiting for him to continue. He stands up from the chair, paces back and forward, picking up his warhammer, Minotaur, and swinging it back and forth. It seems to calm him a little.

She leans against the arm of the chair, searching for common ground; like it or not, this is the game that she must play.

“You know, when Temple told me what was coming, my first instinct was to run. Get out of Llantry, leave it to its fate.”

“Why didn't you?”

“Duty,” she gives a sad smile. “One of the rules that I'm bound to follow under my oath as a Priestess. The first rule. Don't give up on your people.”

“My people?” he laughs. “My family name is spent, my bloodline burnt out. My people do not want me. I have to work with what is given.”

“Come on now -” she begins, and he flourishes the warhammer and slams it onto the table, startling her. He leaves it there, pacing the room in an impotent rage.

“I go to the Moot, and I am mocked, Llantry is mocked. People in the capital pretend to have forgotten my family name. I come home, and I lie to the people. I tell them that the others wish us well, that they are envious of what we have. I just *lie.*”

“At least you *can* lie,” she offers.

“It helps little,” he says. “Tell me honestly then: do you think that we can survive this?”

A Priestess is many things, Venalia was always told. At times a warrior, at times a nurse. At times a teacher, at times a student. Judge and jury; sometimes executioner. Today, she must be Gregor's friend; there is no other way. She cannot simply give up on him. The first rule forbids it.

“You asked me if I think we can survive the coming attack?” she stands up from her chair.

“Do you?”

“No,” she says.

He stares at her for a moment, dumbfound. “Uh -”

“I think that, with floundering, cowardly leadership, the people are scattered and lost. I think that this monster bolsters its ranks with hundreds of men, women and children from Llantry.

Then it goes for Atlan, and suddenly the capital city of the Herdsman's Moot is under siege; and it is all because the Burroughmaster of Llantry was too weak to act, too scared to lead. A country falls into chaos, because Gregor de Llantry just *gave up*."

He opens his mouth to retort, but stops himself. Gregor looks at the warhammer, and picks a speck of dirt from it.

They both look at Minotaur, the hammer. The crystalline woven into the handle has long since lost its glow, its magical charge. It is, until somebody charges it, simply a hammer. Venalia makes a mental note to charge it for him, at least a little, when she has a moment to breathe and magic to spare.

"I think that you could change that story," she tells him. "I think that you've forgotten what your family stood for. What's the motto of your house?"

"Stand tall, stand fast," he mumbles.

Venalia puts her hand on the table, where Minotaur is. "Then that is what you must do. This was your father's hammer, yes?"

"And his father's before him," says Gregor.

"They were great men," she begins, and Gregor raises his hand to stop her.

"They were great husbands; little more than bodyguards to the women who carry our Draconic bloodline. That died with Anabel too; we've no Magistress now."

"No magic," says Venalia, and a horrible guilt comes over her.

"Llantry died with Anabel," he says, and sags into a chair, despondent, gesturing to the mess around him. "What Magistress in all of Altheim would marry me for this?"

Venalia wants to sit, to let the weight of responsibility overwhelm her; for this was her doing. It should crush her, to hear that her childish grudge has brought her home so low, but Marius would tell her to let that guilt be what drives her.

Venalia feels the first embers of defiance; maybe they *are* doomed, maybe this *is* hopeless, but fates be damned, she got Llantry into this mess, and fate has presented her a chance to save it.

"For better or for worse, Gregor, you are the Burroughmaster of Llantry," she says, standing over him, "and you are going to restore the name of your family before this is over."

He looks up from his shame. "How?"

"With my help. I don't know exactly what the next couple of days will bring, but as your sworn Priestess, I am honour-bound to see this through; to *any* end. If we're going to fail, we'll do it together."

"Why would you risk your life for this place? You've always hated it here. You couldn't wait to leave. Why do this?"

Tell him, she feels her soul urge her. *Tell him how you threw Anabel's bow in the fire out of spite, how you indirectly caused all of this.*

"Because," she mirrors Temple's reassuring tone, "I have a heart; and I cannot, in good conscience, let you face these next few days alone."

Gregor takes his time to think this over, before he nods in agreement. "What do we have to do?"

Venalia drags a chair over and sits opposite him. "A lot. To start, you've just embarrassed yourself in front of your people, so we need to take action immediately."

"You have a plan?"

"Well, I know a guy who might, and I told him to stable his horse here. Let's see if he's there?" She cups her hands to her mouth, hoping her voice carries through the walls to the stable. "Temple!"

They wait until they hear the stomping of feet, and then the door opens and Temple squeezes into the house, taking up most of one corner of the great hall by himself.

Venalia watches his eyes, and once Temple has sized up Gregor and noted the exits and windows, his eyes fall upon the hammer, Minotaur, and linger there for a moment.

"Yes?" he grumbles, sitting cross legged on the floor for comfort.

"Temple," says Venalia, putting the warhammer out of her mind, "tell the Burroughmaster what we need to do to survive tonight."

Temple folds his arms. "Gather everything flammable that you can. How many fighting men do you have?"

"Trained?" asks Gregor. "Twelve. If we raise a levy then we have about a hundred men of fighting age – but little to arm them with, asides farm tools and kitchen implements."

"Good," says Temple. "We don't need fighters. We need workers. Levy the men: they're digging a ditch. Four to six feet deep. Within arrow-shot of the Southern wall. Every shovel you have. Set up flaming braziers, ready for archers. Best archers on that wall. We lure it into the pit, and light it up. You have till the sun sets."

"Right," says Gregor, hesitating. "Uh, what do I tell them?"

Her training *has* covered this:

"You tell them what the people of Altheim have been hearing since the Titans put us here: there's a monster coming, and it's time to band together. That's the truth, and it'll get them moving."

"I can do that. Okay." He exhales, long and slow. " I'll get dressed -"

"Bathed first," Venalia cuts in. "You stink of mud and drink. Be presentable."

"Yes, Priestess," he sighs, his body language that of a defeated man.

"Good man," says Temple. "You're learning. Now; get a message to Atlan - can you do that?"

Gregor looks around, uneasy, pretending to think. "Hmm, a message, well -"

"Gods above, Gregor," she groans. "What now?"

"Our sending relay -"

"It's arcane," she realises, pinching the bridge of her nose. "It requires somebody with Draconic blood. You need training in the arcane arts to use it. Like your mother."

Or Anabel.

"We have nobody capable of using a sending relay," says Gregor. "I sold it."

"You *sold* it?" asks Venalia, standing from her chair, raising her voice. "And nobody thought that this might be a huge oversight? Didn't Marius check on these things?"

"Marius, uh... may not have known about this," mutters Gregor.

"You kept this from him? You've got no way to communicate with the capital, and you just hushed it up?" She can hear herself getting louder, angrier, and forces herself to calm down.

"This is bad," says Temple, making a pointed look at Venalia. "We cannot hold forever. Victory requires heavy weaponry; airships, canons, battle-mages. A military response; not peasants with pitch forks."

"Why don't we send a runner?" asks Gregor. "Two days to Atlan on foot, one by horse – on Pretzia, I could perhaps make it?"

"You aren't getting away that easily," says Venalia. "Nor is there any guarantee that anybody would make it through."

As they talk, Venalia can see the horrible pieces of the puzzle falling together. This is why it goes so badly: mismanagement and corruption.

"The other directions?" suggests Temple. "Ride East, and follow the Horn to Atlan? Three days on Pretzia."

"Not that simple," says Venalia. Temple has only just joined; he does not know how bad it is. "They haven't kept the Scarlings under control. The only clear route is South, and guess where the Choir is?"

"Couldn't we send all of my men?" asks Gregor. "Twelve runners, one for each of the cardinal directions?"

Temple is staring, simmering. "There's nothing for days. If you had kept the roads clear, the woods safe, it *might* be an option."

"So send them all South?" tries Gregor. "Surely some of them would make it?"

Temple is shaking his head. "Say we do. Choir gets one of them; now it knows what he knows. Goes after the rest – and it *will* catch them. It's fast. Not to mention, Pretzia can just about handle the singing. She's a trained warhorse. Your drafting ponies won't last a minute."

"Oh Gods above," whispers Gregor, putting his hands over his face.

"It can do that?" asks Venalia.

"Seems so," says Temple. "The words they sing? Either it eats their memories, or -"

Or it truly has them, soul and all. He does not say it – but Venalia hears it.

Gregor has gone pale. "Help isn't coming, is it?"

Venalia's little puzzle is complete. This is how she falls: trying to save Llantry, with every possible card in the deck stacked against her. All because Gregor has neglected his duties.

All because the true Burroughmaster of Llantry went missing, and the only clue to her location was destroyed.

She wants to slap him for putting her in this position, but deep in her soul she knows that she has inflicted this upon herself; finally, she has to pay the price for her sins.

Temple shakes his head. "Help is not coming."

"Oh Gods," says Gregor, clasping his hands before his face. "There are herds on the hill right now, shepherds with them."

"Get them down immediately," says Temple.

"They won't leave their herds -"

"Then they'll perish," says Temple.

Gregor sags, leaning over the warhammer on the table. "What do we do?"

"*You* need to get those shepherds home," says Temple. He motions to Venalia. "*We* need to see the blacksmith."

"Bell?" asks Gregor. "Blind Bell? My sister works with him."

"He's *blind?*"

"Yes," says Gregor.

"Is he good?"

"The best," says Venalia.

"I hope so," says Temple. "I need him to forge me a weapon capable of killing this thing."

"A weapon?" asks Gregor. "You said that this thing took apart your team of mercenaries. What use is a weapon?"

"A lance," says Temple. "One sized for me. Delivered at a full charge, from Pretzia? Similar power to a cannon shot."

Venalia folds her arms, thinking aloud. "How will you get that close? The singing will stop you, surely?"

"I will require protection," says Temple, motioning towards Venalia's holy symbol. "A prayer? A blessing?"

"Of course," she says, ever the professional. "Leave it with me."

In truth, her prayers and protections are only as powerful as her faith. Venalia can protect herself, but if Temple does not *believe* then prayer is merely a genre of poetry.

Gregor speaks up. "Are you sure this will work?"

"No," says Temple.

"No?"

"I am sure of very few things, Burroughmaster."

"We'd better get started while it remains light," says Venalia, motioning for Temple that it is time to leave, and leaving Gregor with his instructions: "You handle the workers, Burroughmaster; the trench and the braziers." She sees the weight on his shoulders, his nerves. "Hold your head high, Gregor. Tell them the truth."

"Of course," says Gregor, taking a deep breath. Venalia turns to leave, when he calls her name: "Venalia?"

"Yes?"

"I am not sure what your Gods teach about forgiveness – but for what it's worth, I am sorry to have pulled us all into this mess."

Venalia softens, and offers him an olive branch. "Forgiveness is the domain of the Light Within, Goddess of light, redemption, and righteous, purifying fire – and she tells us that to seek redemption, is to deserve it."

Gregor has the look of a dog that has been kicked. Venalia leaves him staring at the warhammer, deep in thought. She turns and leaves with Temple, feeling altogether confused about Gregor. She wants to slap him to death, hug him, punch him, look after him, shout at him; she wants him to fail, and she wants nothing more than to see him succeed.

Gregor, she thinks, is *her* test. Breaking him, crushing him, deposing him, would be all too easy. The hard thing – but the *right* thing, she is sure, is to save him. Restore him. Redeem him. Maybe that is what causes her to fail.

What if he cannot be helped?

She shakes these thoughts from her head as they approach the blacksmith on the Northern outskirts of Llantry, soaked by soft rainfall. Temple takes a breath as if to launch into a long speech.

"You remember the vision of which I spoke?" he asks. "Of you and I, parting ways?"

"I walk into the woods, to certain death," she says, and puts the pieces together, remembering how Temple looked at Minotaur. "With a warhammer. It's Gregor's hammer, isn't it?"

"Unmistakable."

"Do you know why I have it?"

"No."

Venalia lets out a deep, shuddering breath, and Temple graces her with a change of subject.

"You did well, back there," he says.

"Thank you," she tries to show a little grace with a sarcastic half-curtsey.

"A lesser woman would have crushed him."

"I did; the best way that I know how. By forcing him to confront himself, and be better."

"Very pious."

"It's called atonement, actually, when you do it that way," she looks up at Temple. "Whitehallow did teach me *some* things of use."

"Can you smite an enemy with divine light?"

"Well, not this early on my path, no, I'd have to exchange a secret or -"

"Didn't teach you enough then. We need a lance."

Venalia tries not to take it personally. "You think it'll work?"

"Very few things on this plane can survive a lance blow from Pretzia. Very few. We need it before sunset. Can your blind man manage that?"

"Yes. He smithed for kings and Magisters, once. Which always made me wonder why he chose to settle down in Llantry, of all places."

"Peace," says Temple. His tone tells her that he has experience with the matter.

Chapter Six

Venalia smells the iron, hears the clanging, feels the hot air on her face. Bell's forge sits atop a mound at the North gate, open to the world. His home and shop are well built, but the forge is the centrepiece to a cavern of canvas. Billowing smoke flies skyward with every hammer-blow.

Outside sits a rain-soaked A-board upon which is written: *Blacksmythery*. The Sarantjan spelling; Venalia remembers the day that Marius painted it for Bell.

Often are the days that Venalia would sit near the forge for heat, reading her books, watching the horizon. The best view in Llantry, she used to joke, totally wasted on a blind man. Distant, ancient peaks that line the horizon like sawteeth, tipped with snow, set against the first stars of a winter afternoon.

Evelyn de Llantry scurries between forge and shop, red faced from heat and effort, carrying bags of coal in each hand.

Temple casts his eye across it. "It's not much of a forge."

"Bell doesn't care for aesthetics, I assume," she waves him away. "Make no mistake: he's the wealthiest person in Llantry."

"Wouldn't be hard."

Evelyn spots them and turns to the forge, where Bell stands obscured by clouds of steam and smoke.

"Bell, visitors!" she shouts, and then walks to meet them on the mound, dropping her coal-bags and kneeling into a curtsey.

"Lady Priestess. Sir."

"Oh, no need for that," laughs Venalia. "Temple, this is Evelyn de Llantry. Gregor's younger sister."

Temple folds his arms. His silence is impatient, and it reminds her that nobody else in Llantry knows what is coming.

"We need to speak with Bell," says Venalia.

"Am I detecting some urgency?" asks Evelyn.

"Aye," she says, deciding upon honesty. "Gregor is about to break the news, but you and Bell will hear it from me."

"Ah," she seems to have expected this. "Something *is* wrong, then?"

Interesting. "You had an inkling something was going to happen?"

"Bell did," she says. "He was talking about a shift in the air. Said something felt off."

"Soldier's instinct," says Temple.

"Fine," says Venalia. "I'll tell the two of you together then, where is he?"

"Follow me," she jogs up the mound. "Bell? Bell we have visitors. *Bell?* I swear he's deaf as well."

Evelyn leads them into the forge, forcing Temple to duck under the tarpaulin and crouch on the wood-chipped ground around the forge. He starts warming his hands over the crucible, eyeing the half-finished weaponry left in various states of completion. Hilts and blades and handles and heads, glistening steel. No silver.

"Where is he?" asks Venalia.

Bell is a part of the scenery, until he moves.

He is called Big Bell for good reason: despite his age, he stands as tall as the tent, stooped and bent under it. Beneath his leather apron and ash-stained shirt is the body of a warrior, spine curved like a country road, head sagging forward like an old dinosaur. His eyebrows lift from behind the blindfold.

"I have been waiting to hear that voice," says Bell, his voice a dry rasp.

"Hello again, Bell," says Venalia.

His face breaks into a broad smile and takes a deep breath, stopping his work and turning around. He grins, barely any teeth left, and comes to her, taking her hands in his. "Marius went well, didn't he? I heard the wind howl as the flame was lit. A good funeral."

"He went well," she sighs, embracing him – for a moment, she is truly home. "It's a relief to see you, Bell. How have things been?"

Bell motions for her to follow, and he grasps a length of rope that runs around the forge.

"Things have been quiet, my girl. The way I like them. Evelyn!" She scurries over to him. "See to two cups of tea, Venalia takes the same as I do – and..." he trails off, pointing in the general direction of Temple. "And whatever our large friend here would like."

"Water is fine," says Temple, and Bell gasps upon hearing his voice.

Bell cocks his head, listening, screwing his face as he thinks.

"Oh, that's not a Llantry accent; Caladan?"

Temple nods, and then realises that Bell cannot see him. "Correct."

"I've an ear for accents," he says, wagging a finger. "What's your name?"

"Temple."

"A man's name," he says, "but you're no man. Half-Giant, I'd say, and..."

He steps closer to Temple, who eyes him warily. Bell sniffs a few times, and recoils.

"You've been *below,"* he rasps, and he cracks and snaps upright, and leans his ear towards Temple, two old friends sharing a secret. "Why are you *here*?"

"The Inverted World. You smell it?"

Bell scans him up and down, sniffing the air around him, but does not answer.

"Well," says Venalia, "that's what we've come to speak to you about."

Bell connects the dots, and he shrinks back to the stooped hunchback he was at first, pointing a gnarled hand at Temple. "What manner of horror have you brought upon us?"

"I was pursued here," says Temple. "By a creation of the Magistry. Thousands of years old."

"Always the Magistry." Bell shakes his head as Evelyn hands him a cup of tea. "Yet, I infer that you intend to stop it? That *is* why you are here?"

"Yes," says Venalia. "We need a weapon that can kill it."

"Weapons." Bell grins. "Weapons I can do – and if this beast is from the world below, you'll want silver?"

"Yes. A lance," says Temple.

"Bold choice," says Bell. "I assume you have a suitable horse?"

"A Steppe charger, thoroughbred. If any horse can do it, she can."

"That may actually work," says Bell. "What are we dealing with? A construct of some sort?"

"An aberration, we think," says Temple. As he and Bell put their heads together, Venalia sees their own professionalism shine through. These two are soldiers, already talking in codes and tactics. "It defies classification. Looks undead. Has a small army of shades."

"This thing is Pre-Dragonfall?" asks Bell, almost to himself.

"Pre-Dragonfall," says Temple. "At least two thousand years old."

"What could live so long?" asks Bell. "And what has two millennia in the deepest dark below the earth done to it?"

"It sings into the mind," says Temple. "Impervious to most weapons. But fire, it fears. Fire, and silver."

"It's afraid of light?" offers Venalia, but neither pays her suggestion much attention.

Bell considers all that he has heard, and then nods. "How long do I have?"

Venalia looks to the sun and holds her thumb against the horizon, measuring the daylight left. "Two hours."

"I see," says Bell. "Evelyn?"

She appears at his side like an apparition, having faded into the smoke. "Yes?"

"Fetch the scrap silver – start heating it. I will prepare a mould." He waves his hand at Temple. "How long would you like the lance?"

"A haft twenty feet long," says Temple. "With a vamplate for the grip, if you can."

"I have a few that could be easily modified."

"How much do we owe you for materials?" asks Venalia.

Bell waves her away. "No money, girl, no money. Just make it work."

Venalia glances at Temple. "We will."

But we will not. We do not. Somehow, this fails.

Like hell it does, she thinks. Venalia did not study for six years, did not bare her soul to the God of Secrets, so that she could perish a meaningless end.

Bell drinks all of his steaming hot tea in one gulp. "We have no time to lose, then," he reaches for the rope, and guides himself to his workbench. "When it is done, Evelyn will need to know where to find you. We may be cutting it close."

"By the Southern gate," says Temple, turning to young Evelyn. "If you see fire, I won't be far. You cannot miss me."

Venalia notes how certain he sounds; but of course he does. He knows exactly where he will be tonight. He has seen it – there are flames.

Bell paws about for her, until she offers her hands and he takes them. "I wish that you were here under better circumstances. When this is over, you and I have some catching up to do."

"Bell," whispers Evelyn. "The gift?"

"Oh of course," he cries, throwing up his hands. "I have

been swept up in the drama. Evelyn, fetch it for me."

Evelyn disappears, and returns with a steel breastplate, the most important part of a full suit of armour. Upon it is etched the sigil of the Mind's Eye: a human face with a third eye on their forehead, emitting the light of knowledge, and allowing wisdom in.

Venalia can only blink, for no words come to her.

"Marius paid for this commission," says Bell, "before his death." He taps it, and it rings beautifully. He brings it to her, head bowed. Venalia is shocked at how light it feels, with velvet trim around the neck and arms. The inside is thickly padded for comfort, contouring around her torso as he helps her into it.

"This is beautiful work," she whispers, silent with wonder and gratitude.

"It's made of a steel alloy, mixed with a fibrous wax produced by Giant wasps in Caladan. All the money in Llantry couldn't buy this, my girl. It has a shape designed to bounce instead of bend. It'll turn a rifle shot at anything less than point-blank, stop any non-magical blow from a humanoid. Just try to get hit here, if you have to get hit at all."

He taps the armour again, and Venalia laughs out of embarrassment. She does not know what to say, but her training tells her that grace is what to aim for.

"I'm honoured," she says. "Thank you. So much."

"Thank Marius," says Bell. "He perhaps did not know how badly you would need this."

"Gods be good, Bell," she says, and kisses his cheek. He flinches like he always does, but pulls her into an embrace.

" Gods be good, Priestess."

She steps back, bows, touches his hands to her forehead, and turns to leave. Behind them erupts the clang of hammer and steel, and the rushing air of the bellows sends sparks heavenward.

From the top of the mound, renewed by the fresh, cold air, Temple fixes his eyes on the setting sun, and lets out a long held breath. Clouds pile above, filtering golden rays, impatient and churning.

Beyond lies the Steppe, rolling plains of long grass, swaying in waves with the wind. Venalia thinks that if she could paint a picture that said 'freedom', it would look much like this.

“I've never been,” says Venalia. “To the Steppe, I mean. I used to see it almost every day.”

“Nor have I,” says Temple. “People assume a half-Giant must have been – but not once.”

They spend a moment taking it in, the last of the winter daylight before a long night of pain. Venalia's eyes glaze over, and she finds herself fixated on the anticipation of pain, of horror.

“I don't like the look of those clouds,” she says, desperate to occupy her mind.

“It rains heavily tonight,” says Temple, and then reads her concerned expression. “Storm won't put the flames out. Don't worry.”

“I know,” she says. “I've seen the fuel go up in worse rain than this. I was thinking of what else might go wrong.”

“Fret not. I know we both survive tonight.”

“Does Llantry?” she asks.

Temple shrugs in answer. “Focus on what we *can* control. We will check the walls.” He points to the distant palisades. “The archers must find their range. The trench must be deep. The Choir is led by a tall woman. Tall indeed. It is her that we must focus on.”

Two hours till night. Venalia feels the wind rising with her worries. She falls back to her training: that action is what overcomes anxiety. She busies herself with tactical preparations:

“If you want me to protect you when you charge this thing,” she says, “then I need to know how you survived it. How did you protect your mind?”

“Songs. Didn't matter which. Not a reliable tactic, but the only one that we had. Ungren sang dwarven battle hymns.” Temple is gone again, somewhere else. “When last I heard the Choir, it was singing his hymn.”

“God's above,” she whispers. “Did you try prayer?” Temple shakes his head, turning away from her. “Why not?”

"Prayer does not come easily to me, Priestess; not *genuine* prayer."

"You don't have a good relationship with the Gods?" she intones it with understanding.

"I don't have *any* relationship with them."

"But you grew up in a temple -"

He reads the puzzling look on her face. "I know that you follow the God of secrets and knowledge, Venalia, but please – I am not a puzzle to be solved."

"Sorry." She scolds herself. Often has she been told those very words.

Temple leads them off the mound. "Anything that focuses the mind. Prayer will work if it is genuine. Have the people pray to whatever gods they wish – but have them pray."

"They'll pray to the Minotaur, then." Venalia motions to the statue of the Minotaur as they pass it, opposite the small shrine to the All-Faith.

Even during these hard times, the Minotaur's statue boasts offerings of wool, meat, fruit, pipe leaf, and carvings of his likeness. The shrine of the All-Faith has not been kept clean since Marius passed.

"This far North, the people have their old Gods," she says. "Whitehallow send Priests here because they have to, by law. Marius took the post to retire early; he thought it would be an easy gig."

"Before he adopted you, I imagine that it was," says Temple, and Venalia hears the rare sound of his laughter.

She matches his laughter. "I complicated his life somewhat, yes."

Temple looks at the Minotaur. "If it gives them confidence, so be it. The Choir preys on insecurity. On fear."

"Is that why you survived it?"

He gives a sad, defeated chuckle, this time to himself, and turns, dropping to one knee and looking her in the eye.

"You think that I feel no fear? Venalia, I am just as afraid as you. The future is a frightening place. Whether you can see it, or not."

"But you know you survive."

"Until you and I part. Then – no more visions, remember? I dread it, Venalia. Every day is numbered. Always has been. Do not presume that I feel no fear. I have lived my entire life in fear."

As have I, she wants to say - but she has to stop and consider if her life, tough though it has been, can hold a candle to the curse of knowledge that rests upon Temple's shoulders.

"So," she turns to him. "When the time comes to charge the Choir head on, who are *you* going to be praying to, Temple?"

"I have no idea," he admits.

"Well, you tell me when you find the answer."

Temple is deep in thought, eyeing the long road through Llantry, playing out the coming battle in his head.

"*Can* you protect me?" he asks. "With a prayer?"

"I can give your mind some measure of protection, aye. I'll need to ask my God first, of course."

They pass through the village centre in silence. The hiss of rain has been replaced with the rush of work. Shovels and carts are ran back and forward, stakes and fuel, pitch and oil, arrows and crates for the barricade. None stop to gawk at Temple this time.

Temple breaks their silence. "What do you intend to do after this?"

"After tonight?"

"After Llantry."

She flashes him a bemused, questioning look. "Well, I think I'll take Gregor's warhammer and walk into the woods to certain death. Right?"

"No," he says. "If you had never met me, what *would* you have wanted to do?"

She thinks in silence. "Truth be told, I had hoped that coming home to bury Marius would help me figure that out."

"You don't know?"

"Never really have. A scholar maybe – I like solving

puzzles."

"You also like commanding people."

"I do," she admits. "It suits me."

"You did a fine job healing my wounds; and you saved me from a potent toxin. Not many fledgeling Priests could have done that."

"I do like healing, but... there's not a whole lot of mystery and inquiry to be done. Those who worship the Wakened World tend to see to that kind of thing."

"What about freelance work?"

"As a Priestess? You mean, perform exorcisms and put the dead back in their graves? That sort of thing?"

"Sure. Perhaps mercenary work? Priests are highly sought after amongst free companies."

"I don't know if I've told you this," she breaks into a cynical laugh, "but I don't know any offensive spells."

"None at all?"

"I have my Light, Heal, and my Shield spell. Asides that, it's whatever I can manage on my own. I don't even have a weapon."

"You'd be paid handsomely just for the healing," he says. "You'd get to travel, learn more as you go?"

"I don't know if the soldier's life is for me," she admits. "I'm a bit soft in that regard."

"Private investigator? Make your fortune while you solve mysteries."

"That does sound appealing," she says. "But enough about me, what about you?"

"What would I have done next?"

"Yeah."

"I'd have gone to Atlan. Got paid," he sighs. "Paid my friends' widows. Their children."

"And then?"

"See what other work there is," he says, and they both sense that his answer is unsatisfactory. Venalia enjoys these moments with Temple; even when he unknowingly lies to himself, he quickly corrects it. He is as much a truthseeker as she is. "In truth, I'm not sure. The great Steppe calls loudly to me of late. When we stood atop the smith's mound, and I saw the horizon? I felt something stir."

"You want to go home?"

"The Steppe isn't my home."

"But it's in your blood," she says. "It'll keep calling."

"It's in yours too," he gives her a knowing look.

"Perhaps," she says. "We're both strangers here, aren't we?"

"Orphans." Temple nods, and though the two differ wildly in size and history, they see the wild open plains in one another, the longing to be under the endless sky, a common bond between unlikely friends.

They reach the Southern gate, where people rush past them with barrels, wood, tools, wheelbarrows. Temple stops and takes a breath to steady himself. He is shaking just like she is, though he hides it well.

"You *are* afraid," she says.

"Of course."

"Good," she says, holding up her own trembling hands. "That makes me feel less of a coward."

When Temple next speaks, he is distant, mourning.

"I am not afraid of the fight," he explains. "I expect that tonight I will hear Ungren's last hymn again. My brothers-in-arms will beg me to join them. I will feel the isolation, the cold, that they feel. If our plan works, I will hear them burn."

"We'll endure it together," she says, hushed now, in the caring voice that a Priestess must learn to foster, and speak to the person behind the walls. "I will not let you go through this alone."

Temple gives her a wry smile. "That's my line."

She grins. "I know. I used it on Gregor too."

"Very good, Priestess." He nods his approval. "Very good."

Venalia wants to keep talking, for in Temple's steady nature and blunt observations, she finds comfort;

but the hour grows late, and the day dark.

"I need to pray," she says. "If you want to charge the Choir, then you'll need to shield your mind. I can ask the Mind's Eye for such a blessing, and confer it to you."

"Good; I'll busy myself with this," says Temple, and motions to the scurrying workers at the gates. "Be here before sundown."

"I will."

Temple gives her a nod, and joins two men rolling a barrel of oil, picking it up under one arm. Wherever he goes, the people gravitate; they want to be near him, to earn his approval with their hard work. More impressive, thinks Venalia, is that Temple takes the time to *give* his approval. A mere nod, a look, and the men redouble their efforts.

Venalia heads home, against the flow of the crowd.

She feels herself shaking as she closes the door – not with fear for what the night may bring, but in anticipation of her prayer. Little pleas for help and strength are easy enough – but a real prayer, the act of communing with a God, is a terrifying and humbling prospect, akin to diving out of an airship.

A temple would be best, sanctified and protected, where so many prayers have slid through the Celestial membrane over time that the barriers are weaker, more familiar. In lieu of a temple, she will use a shrine, in a place of comfort.

Venalia kindles the fire, and begins assembling her shrine. Normal prayer will not suffice. A face to face meeting with the divine requires that she fall deep into communion, a state that requires absolute safety and peace of mind.

She moves with efficiency, assembling books of history and wisdom into a small pyramid. Atop it she places an inkwell and a quill, sheaves of parchment, and begins writing her intentions.

Kneeling in front of her little shrine of books, Venalia takes her holy sigil from her neck, the steel face with its third eye blazing open, and takes the quill in the other, resting it on the paper.

As she writes, she removes her focus from *what* she is writing, and allows her hand to take over.

Her eyes drift out of focus.

The words turn into long, untangled shapes on the page.

Her breathing slows, a dying tide, to a stop.

Then her heart, it beats like a ringing bell.

Venalia is silent, and in the absence of noise she becomes aware of another presence. A watcher, part of her, that follows everything that she does. It sees only the truth.

As though holding a hand to a mirror, the illusion shatters.

Venalia is the watcher. She always was.

She sinks through the layers of herself, down into the deep, dark wild.

First, the surface of herself, the mask of her ego, the personality that she puts on before she steps outside.

Then the thinker that is always in dialogue with her, always doubting and checking and worrying.

Deeper still, she passes the familiar growling of the beast, the idiot animal that governs hunger, lust, rage, jealousy; familiar, and well tamed.

Then Venalia passes into the deepest parts of her mind, where words lose their meaning and the abstract senses rule. Here live the formless intentions that will become thoughts, the impulses with no name that are on the verge of becoming.

Here she waits.

Silence and peace surround her in the calm waters of her soul. Time slows, and Venalia senses a feeling that has no matching word in any mortal language: a sense of connection, a subtle awareness of something watching her, simultaneously part of her, and part of everything else.

She has arrived in the mindspace required for prayer.

From here, she can begin her journey to the Celestial membrane, and touch the all-knowing Mind's Eye, the part of the universe that knows itself, to whom she has pledged a lifetime of service.

Currents of thought flow, pulling her in conflicting directions. The draw of the Mind's Eye is the most familiar to her. His influence feels like denouement, the revelation of an answer long sought.

Ah, yes.

She dives, beset by the rustling of a million pages. Snippets of secrets and whispers abound, leaking from the infinite bookshelves of the endless library.

This is the domain of the Mind's Eye, where all information is born, lives, dies. Here are written all names, all events, everything that could be;

should be;

might be;

is.

Then come the angels.

Self-repeating geometries, filled with their own reflections. Little infinities, fragments of eternity that fill her perception in every direction. She feels her soul bared before them, naked and afraid.

They ignore her. The sensation of warm light pulls her downwards. So far from her body, she has no sense of mortal time.

She feels resistance, like that of one magnet repelling another. Physical strength means nothing here. She pushes with her essence, her spirit.

It bends and stretches, a membrane pulled tight against her soul, and then -

Breakthrough.

A flare of love, patience, intention. Understanding.

Her soul burns incandescent, a bright star in the deep.

Above her:

the watcher of watchers.

Akin to standing at the base of a mountain, one that stretches to the heavens.

The Mind's Eye is a star watching over his angels, pure light, a blazing eye in the swirling fractal clouds of secrets above her. A kaleidoscope of consciousness. Curiosity summons her forward with a sense of recognition, the way that she might recognise a cat after a few meetings on the street.

She need not *ask*. Her intent is bared along with the rest of her soul. There is no hiding here.

Around her flash images of Llantry, of a tall dark shadow reaching over the palisade, of flames, and a half-Giant charging on horseback, a silver-tipped lance in his hand.

Another image, this time of Anabel de Llantry. Venalia, only eight years old, is in tears, struggling to climb the gate and get the shoe that Anabel has torn from her and lodged there. New shoes, bought from a trader as he passed through, a gift from Marius.

Then she sees Temple's vision.

She stands weeping in the snow. She grabs the warhammer, Minotaur. She goes to certain death. For people who never accepted her, nor liked her.

But she does it anyway.

Pride swells in the Mind's Eye, and it considers her intent.

She needs a prayer of protection.

The Mind's Eye grants it:

She expands with the implanting of knowledge, swelling to such a size that she loses herself.

Venalia is thrown back into her body with such violent velocity that, when her bloodshot eyes slam open again, she vomits on the floor.

Heaving chest, she crumples to her hands and knees, vomit and saliva hanging from her chin, coughing and weeping, her body seized by tremors.

There is a reason that Priests do not pray too often.

As she recovers, she notes the alien sensation of a new memory in her head. She has a prayer in there, the geometric blueprint for a spell – but not the one that she asked for.

Instead, the Mind's Eye has given her a spell to paralyse an enemy, a *Hold* spell. It sets her will against another's, holding them in place for as long as she can dominate their mind.

"What am I supposed to do with this?" she asks the shrine. "I need a prayer of protection."

Venalia curses as she wipes the sweat and vomit away. She slicks her red locks back, and twists them into a braid around her head, fastens her sigil around her neck, and squeezes herself into the breastplate.

She drinks as much water as she can stomach and wolfs down some of her trail rations, dissolved in milk to form a paste. Easy energy. She huddles by the fire, sweat-soaked, shaking like an addict deep in withdrawal.

A mental inventory confirms that she is still there, that she is not innately changed by the meddling of a God in her mind. After some minutes in silence, Venalia takes a deep breath, and the shaking begins to subside.

A knock at the door shakes her from her daze, and when she calls to enter, it is Temple that ducks in. Behind him, the light is low in the sky. She wonders how long she was out.

"Venalia?" he asks, eyes avoiding her. "Are you decent?"

"Of course I'm decent," she feigns offence. "I'm just recovering."

"Did it work?" he asks, closing the door behind him.

"To a degree," she says.

"Meaning?"

"Meaning that I asked for a spell of protection, and I was given *Hold* instead."

Temple furrows his brow. "Why?"

"The Gods often give us what we need, rather than what we want."

"I think we *need* a spell of protection," he sighs. "No matter. This must be how it goes."

"I can teach you a prayer?" she offers.

"Will it do anything?"

"That depends – will you put your whole trust, your entire soul, in the hands of the Gods?"

Temple's face does not move, and that is answer enough. "I shall sing Ungren's battle hymn."

"Very well."

Temple glances at the setting sun. "It's almost time. Are you ready?"

"I don't see that I've much choice."

"New spell going to be of any use?"

"Well, it's a Hold spell. I can lock somebody in place for as long as I can mentally overpower them. Does that sound like it will help us against the Choir?"

"Sounds exactly like the Choir, actually," says Temple. "A battle of minds would not be my first choice. It could backfire."

"Probably. I've never cast it before."

"Can you practice?"

"If we had a few hours to let me recover, sure."

"A few *hours?*"

"It's a powerful spell, it'll take a lot more effort than a Light or a Shield."

"Then we improvise," he says. "You Hold the Choir whilst I charge. I can better aim the lance blow if she is immobilised."

"What if I can't Hold it?"

"Then we burn her."

A shadow falls across Llantry as the sun dips and hides behind the hills. Temple cocks his head, massive hand cupped around his ear. His expression snaps from concentration to fear, and Venalia's heart skips.

"What?" she asks him. "What is it?"

"I can hear it."

Chapter Seven

The Tall Woman changes her song
as the sun
blazing light of judgement
finally goes down

She sings
and all join
locked in bitter harmony

they burn the night air
metallic taste of the arcane

song growing louder
shades growing bolder

now to the march

Temple bursts onto the street, Venalia following close behind. They nearly slip on the mud, holding onto one another for balance. The clouds burst, and a torrent of rain drenches the village.

"The gates," he shouts. "Organise a prayer or song. Keep their minds busy. Civilians to the Northern wall, as far from the singing as possible."

"Where are you going?"

"For Pretzia, and the lance. Hit it with the flames. Then open the gates. Give me a clear charge and I'll finish it."

He thunders off in the opposite direction, and Venalia begins to trudge her way to the gates, slogging through the mud, dress hitched high.

"To the Northern wall!" she shouts, shepherding scared villagers. "Get to the Northern wall! Guardsmen to their posts, man your positions! The monster is coming!"

Villagers stream past her, and she walks in the opposite direction. One of the guards – young Corryn, his chainmail trailing to his knees – waves to get her attention.

"M'Lady," he struggles, out of breath. "We're all set to go, the ditch is dug -"

"Where is Gregor?" she asks him. "Where is the Burroughmaster?"

"At the trenches," he says, and they share a look of surprise.

"Good," she says. "Make sure everybody is safe at the North gate, and keep the streets clear for Temple and his horse, do you understand?"

"Yes, Priestess."

"Good man. Go!" she slaps his arm and struggles through the mud to the Southern gate.

At the gate burns four braziers, elevated just above the palisades on rickety platforms. Four men stand atop the platforms, bows at the ready. The gate itself is open, logs and beams lying nearby ready to close it shut.

“Archers!” she shouts, and they turn from their posts. “Be ready to loose, at my command!”

She hears a chorus of replies to the affirmative, and barges out of the gate, into the no-man's-land where the trench is dug.

Gregor and two of his men are rolling the last of the barrels into a trench that impresses her. The people of Llantry are many things, but they are not work-shy. They have produced, in a few hours, a long trench filled with whatever barrels of oil and pitch can be spared, firewood and timber, with the fiercer, spear-like planks facing outwards.

It is also the first time since her arrival that she has seen Gregor behave like a leader.

“Burroughmaster,” she approaches him. He's sweating, red in the face. “Good job – now I need you to go to the Northern wall with everyone. Look after your people. They need to pray, or sing, when the fighting starts.”

He turns to the two men as they finish their work. “You heard the Priestess.” They salute and rush off over the mud, but Gregor remains. “I won't abandon the walls, Venalia. Not whilst my people are still out there.”

Venalia searches the hills in the evening twilight. “Who's still missing?”

“Agnir went up into the hills to bring the shepherds home – that's his torch,” Gregor points to an orange light in the distance, across the pastures and rolling hills, flickering in and out of view. “He is leading them down.”

“If he isn't fast -”

“He knew the risks,” says Gregor. “We couldn't leave people up there.”

“Come on Agnir,” she whispers. “You're almost home, lad.”

“Was, uh – was that the right decision?” he asks, nervous.

She hears his need for approval, but now is hardly the time.

"It was *a* decision."

"Well you told me to start acting like a leader."

She sees – and cannot quite believe it – resolve in his eyes.

"And you are. Now stay close to me. This may get very, very unpleasant. If I start praying, pray with me, aye?"

"Understood."

They return through the gates together and join the archers atop the wooden platforms.

Her heart swells as she sees Agnir emerge from the low mist of night on his horse, with the shepherds jogging behind him, soaked and breathless. They are close enough to see the exhaustion on their faces, their mouths hanging slack.

Venalia hears the sizzle of rain on the flaming braziers. She hears the wind through the trees, whistling, howling, and the constant drum of the rain.

Then, over the top of it, Venalia hears singing.

"Faster, lads!" shouts Gregor. Agnir raises the burning torch and shouts something to the shepherds. They pick up the pace till one of them stumbles in the mud, and his friends stop to help him up.

The singing is more than just noise on the wind now.

A melody

itching at the

inside of her head

insisting upon itself

repeating

clouding her thoughts

She wonders where Temple is. She wonders why she didn't prepare some mixtures to replenish her energy.

A horse whinnies in terror, and Venalia rushes to the gate to see Agnir's horse rear in panic, throwing him onto the mud.

The shepherds do not help him. They are standing still, jaws slack, eyes glassed over.

"No, no, no," she whispers. "It has them." She grabs Gregor by the shoulders. "Start singing with the men! Anything, just sing with them! Drown it out."

He looks confused, irritable, itching at his eyes. "I, uh, what?"

"Just *sing* man!"

"My thoughts aren't my own," he whispers in alarm, looking at his hands.

She gives him a satisfying slap across the jaw, and he shakes it off. "Get it together man, and start praying! I need to go!"

"What? Where are you going?"

"To get *them*. Hold off with the arrows until I return!"

Gregor riles the men into a scattered, weak song, struggling to find his voice. Once others join him, they all sing louder together – an old shepherds song, equal parts tragedy and comedy, about a man who falls in love with the moon.

She drops down into the mud and begins walking towards the gate. Before she was trembling, nervous, dreading this moment. Now that the moment is upon her, the choices are to either act, or die.

She chooses to act, and the fear, the mirage of self-doubt, dissipates.

The Mind's Eye once looked into her soul, saw her bare, and asked for her Priesthood. It saw what she should have known all this time:

She is born to this.

Venalia asks the Mind's Eye to watch over her, and breaks into a run. She struggles not to slip in the mud as she draws closer to the shepherds. Agnir's horse bolts into the darkness.

Agnir is motionless on the ground, surrounded by listless shepherds. One by one they begin to turn towards the misty treeline by the road, as though someone is calling their names.

The closer she gets, the louder she hears it: a pleasant song, like those sung by her mother *hold on, I never knew my mother* to put her to sleep.

Then come the discordant undertones, faint, hard to hear, like the sound of sharp steel slicing across warm flesh *I've never heard that, I don't know what that sounds like.*

It fascinates her, and it takes a moment for her to realise that she is a couple of steps towards the treeline, steps that she does not remember taking.

She shakes her head, slaps herself across the cheek, and shouts a curse to the heavens to drown out the music.

A little voice tells her that she is out of her depth. Trained experts faced this, and lost.

She acts, and the doubt retreats.

"Shepherds, *move!* Listen to my voice!"

The shepherds do not hear her. They wander still for the trees.

Walk with them

No, thinks Venalia, I am not some untrained child – my mind is a fortress. I have training.

Lonely girl

child

missing out again

never with the crowd

birthday by yourself again

you'll never be

alone

with

us

Venalia snaps herself back out of it, but now she is on the ground. More lost time. Closer to the treeline. Dark night. Heavy rain. Her clothes, her cloak, are soaked in rain and mud.

Moments of awareness blur together. On, then off again.

Shepherds wander around her, open-eyed and awestruck,

like sleepwalkers.

Venalia is overcome, overwhelmed;

but the Priestess that graduated Whitehallow rests below the surface, and the training is instinctive.

A prayer, a mantra, rises from her memory unbidden, and she clings to it like a drowning sailor to a raft. Venalia whispers the prayer aloud, remembering her voice, remembering herself.

The shepherds need her.

"Listen to me!" she cries. "Block it out! You have to pray -"

She is gone again. Sinking under the surface of her own thoughts, unable to think.

You would be better served with us

part of something

we are many

great minds

scholars

thousands of years old

think of what you might learn

Venalia comes back to herself praying, clutching the sigil of the Mind's Eye.

She is in the dark, amongst the trees now. Things are moving nearby, dark shapes.

The singing is much louder out here.

She covers her ears, battling to focus, and looks around in panic; she keeps losing time, losing track of where she is.

She cannot remember what is happening.

The shepherds stand still, heads bowed, chanting.

There are others, here. Humanoid. Crouched, afraid, shy. She can see the tiny lights where their eyes should be. They beckon to her, obscured silhouettes of people that she does not know.

They sing to her.

She screams for them to shut up, to leave her alone, but she can feel their voices in her head, blurring who she is from who *they* are and merging the two together.

Where is Temple? She screams his name; is he among them now?

This is how it happens

child

how it must happen

Venalia is frozen, winded, surrounded by the lost and enraptured.

Pray, comes a voice, and she is relieved to hear that it is the voice of Marius, her own memories, her own training.

Pray hard, Priestess.

Pray loud.

The shades beckon to her, surrounding the shepherds. Some of them are moving, arms open, to embrace the shadows amongst the dark trees.

It is afraid of light.

She *knows* that it is afraid of light.

Surrounded on all sides by the thralls of the Choir, with the piercing, bass-low discordant singing, Venalia scrambles for a fallen tree and leaps atop the trunk, standing above the shepherds.

Concentrating on a spell is difficult, even in ideal conditions.

Concentrating on a spell whilst the Choir's song assaults her mind, itches at her skull, and scatters her thoughts like wild birds; that is much, much harder;

but far from impossible.

Venalia breathes deep and forgoes the usual focus – this is not the time for subtlety.

She touches the divinity within herself, the spark of her soul that is always shining.

From that place, Venalia casts a spell of Light from the palms of her hands.

It cuts the song short. The shades screech and duck behind the trees, shielding themselves. Great beams of white-gold, the screaming of the sun, push the shades back.

It lifts her spirits – and the shepherds, briefly relieved of the song and therefore of the Choir's hold, look around in confusion. She directs the Light beam as a weapon, keeping the Choir shades pinned behind cover – but the shades are many, and start creeping out when her back is turned.

"To me, to me!" she orders the shepherds. "Follow my voice."

They flock to her like lost cattle, and under the umbrella of her divine light she shepherds them back, away from the trees.

The Choir shades stalk after them, clambering over the trees and mounds as she backs up. Behind them, the same height as the trees, she sees the unfolding silhouette of an impossibly tall woman, her limbs drifting like smoke on the wind.

She looks like an ink spill, two white dots where her eyes should be, and she follows Venalia.

Together with the shepherds, Venalia stumbles out of the woods, breathless and shouting orders to drown out the Choir.

Keeping the Light spell active whilst shouting *and* running is hard, but this is why she was trained.

Someone shouts her name from the walls, Gregor's voice among them, calling for her to come back, to run. She knows that the Choir is directly behind her, she can feel it. She hears individual voices, different languages, all trying to reach into her mind.

It feels weaker, as though divided.

"Go!" she shouts to the shepherds, turning around to face their pursuer. The shepherds run past her, helping one another through the mud.

She finds Agnir, motionless on the mud at her feet, right where his horse dumped him.

Venalia spins around and holds her Light on the shades of the Choir, keeping them back. Wherever the Light falls, they scatter; but she cannot cover all of them at once, and they are working their way forward.

They have managed to flank her, surrounding her in the dark where her Light does not fall. A shade emerges, reaching for Agnir.

The first rule – never give up on your people.

She turns her Light on the shade and it hisses, recoiling. The other shades scatter to avoid the beam, but they are everywhere.

"Agnir, get up," she whispers, kicking him. He does not move. "Agnir!"

Nothing.

The clammy, cold touch of a shade finds her cheek. Clumsy fingers dig into her skin and she panics, screaming. Other hands are upon her now, pulling her to the ground, pawing at her. Their very touch sends her into convulsions, her temperature plummeting.

Venalia is dragged on to her back. The shades are caressing Agnir, cooing and singing over him.

Venalia thrashes and screams in blind panic as the Tall Woman emerges from the forest, her hair drifting over the treetops.

The voice splits her thoughts in two.

she is cold

You are cold

she is afraid

You are afraid

she is alone

You are alone

she will sing with us

You will sing with us

"Like Hell I will," she shouts back. Venalia feels her

mother's anger rising in her stomach. The Tall Woman reaches for her, the same awful handprint from Temple's skin. No more time. “Agnir,” she screams, “if you can hear me: close your eyes.”

She takes a deep breath and tenses every muscle in her body, straining with concentration. From every inch of skin, unfiltered Light erupts, a silent detonation across the plains.

For a moment, Venalia is the brightest star in the sky.

She is the dawning morning sun, a frozen flash of lightning. Light blows the shades and the Tall Woman back.

Then it fades, and she struggles upwards, dropping to one knee from the effort. Exhaustion is close. Her head is swimming.

Agnir is unconscious.

Cursing in the Steppe tongue, Venalia grabs him by the armpits and starts to drag him back across the field. She hears her name shouted from the gates – she must be close.

Agnir sits up, bewildered, but he is not himself. He reaches for *them* with his hand outstretched. She follows his gesture, and sees the shades regrouping. The Tall Woman strides across the clearing.

“Come on Agnir,” she groans, struggling to stand. “Run, man! Go!”

“Priestess?” Agnir shakes his head, rubbing his eyes. He jumps to his feet and grabs her, putting her arm around his shoulder.

The Choir starts singing.

Agnir almost loses himself again before Venalia grabs his hand and runs with him, both of them stumbling over the mud.

“Block it out!” she cries over the rain.

They are almost back inside.

The trench lies before them, the burning braziers of the archers, ready to fire. Behind Venalia stands a dark shape in the rain, a hole shaped like a tall woman, an absence in space.

“Prepare arrows!” she shouts as they make it back through the gate.

The guards do not respond. They are awestruck by the

Choir. Their eyes are unfocused, their bows lying wet on the ground where they have dropped them.

Temple is nowhere to be seen.

Venalia stifles a scream of frustration.

"Agnir, keep praying, go and find Temple!" she orders him. He squeezes his hands over his ears and runs off, nodding.

Venalia grabs one of the bows and leaps to the top of the platform. She prays, loudly, a single mantra over, and over.

My eyes are blind; I trust the mind.

My eyes are blind; I trust the mind.

The Choir looms over the trench of oil barrels, singing loud as thunder, shaking her ribs, the wall, the air. It towers over the trees, over the palisade. It blocks the night sky, where dark rain falls in sheets.

Her spirits soar, as behind her comes the marching of hundreds of feet. Help has arrived, she thinks – but when she turns, she sees only the villagers of Llantry, dumbstruck and awe-bound by the song, marching towards the Choir to join it. She feels her stomach sink.

"I'll do it myself then," she mutters.

She grabs an arrow from the bucket of pitch, lights it on the brazier, and lifts the bow.

It has been a year since she last used one.

Venalia lines up the shot, aiming for the trench, as the Choir approaches. She looses the arrow, but the wet string shudders with a damp twang. The arrow tumbles uselessly over the wall. Cursing loudly, she lights another arrow, only to fail again.

The guards around her are dazed, useless; one of them sleepwalks over the palisade and tumbles head first towards the ground, landing flat in the mud. He begins to drag himself towards the Choir.

Behind her marches all of Llantry, Gregor amongst them, blank eyed.

A village sings together, and all she can do is repeat her mantra.

My eyes are blind; I trust the mind.

The song crashes upon her like waves upon a harbour wall.

The Tall Woman stands on the other side of the trench, arms stretched out to greet the villagers, a mother to her children.

This, she thinks, is not playing out as Temple said it would. He saw fire – he said that they survive tonight.

But Llantry, perhaps, does not.

The plan has failed.

The Priestess must act.

Face rigid with effort, sweat pouring from her forehead, Venalia lights another arrow, and leaps from the platform, straight over the wall. She drops for a few seconds, bending her knees on impact and tumbling into the mud.

She fights her way to her feet, and sprints for the trench. There, shining in the firelight, is the line of pitch leading to the barrels.

The fuse; though she has no idea how quickly it may burn.

This close, the Tall Woman resembles the memory of a woman, a silhouette under the water, flowing like seaweed, moving in slow, stuttering motions, and always singing.

She forces herself to look at the Choir dead on, into the hole in reality, into those two tiny white pin points of light that are its eyes.

It extends a hand, then another, warping space around it. The hand is familiar; Venalia remembers the wound on Temple's abdomen. She is about to endure the same fate, and she does not expect that anybody will save her.

Time is up.

The Choir's song is loud enough that Venalia feels her nose begin to bleed. The song hits a high pitched note, a crescendo. The sound feels like a physical force, driving her to her knees.

Why delay the inevitable?

It asks,

and Venalia screams back:

"When you get to the Nine Hells, you tell them who sent you!"

She plunges the burning arrow into the fuse oil. The fire licks along the trench in a second and there is a brief moment, as though the world has to take a breath for what is about to come.

Night turns to day.

An explosion like a small sun. The faces of the shades, the Tall Woman, close enough to her own that she can see their open mouths.

They are screaming.

Her instincts take hold, and she puts the last of her energy into her Shield spell. Divine light blossoms in a sphere around her just as the blast wave hits. She is blown clear of the trench, robes aflame, quickly extinguished by the slurry of mud and rain.

Where she rolls and comes to a stop, her body is spent.

The rain cools her smoking robes. Venalia has never been so grateful for the cold embrace of mud. Hands grab her and lift her up, aching and bruised, but alive, exhausted from the effort of the spell.

Her vision is blurred, but she hears the worried cries break out around her; Llantry's people, confused and lost, returned to their senses. She smells burnt flesh, charred, rotten and riddled with some strange magic that she cannot place. A hot metallic burn.

The taint of the Inverted World, she thinks. Bell could smell it on Temple, after all. Like the arcane, but rotten. Mouldy.

She clears her eyes, catching her breath, jostled by bewildered villagers. The Choir is nowhere to be seen; it has fled Llantry, back into the night, burned and wounded.

Through the rain comes Temple, barging through the crowd, shouting her name. She laughs out of relief, out of joy, and lets herself fall into his arms.

Venalia dreams of the sun over Whitehallow. She dreams of Anabel's red bow drifting on the wind and chases it, like a child to a butterfly, but never quite able to catch it before it lands in the crucible.

She dreams of songs in the darkness, of soot and flame and fire. She dreams that she herself is adrift on the wind, falling into the blacksmith's crucible, burning, she

awakens without opening her eyes.

Wrapped in blankets, safe. Warm. Home.

Delicately, she moves her aching arms and stretches under the covers, finding that somebody has removed her clothes. She smells still of burnt oil, remembers the fire; panics, checks her hair – but it seems to all be there, along with her eyebrows.

She breathes a sigh of relief.

"Morning," comes the booming voice of Temple, trying to whisper and failing. She opens her eyes and finds him sitting in the corner of the room, like a huge piece of furniture.

Venalia groans and tries to focus on him, vision blurred. She *may* be looking at a wardrobe. She cannot tell.

"Temple?"

"Good morning, Priestess."

It is, in fact, the wardrobe. Temple sits to her side.

"Am I in bad shape?" she asks.

"No. Your robes need to be cleaned and repaired. It's good that you were wearing that breastplate. Seems your Shield spell protected you from the blast, too. There was shrapnel."

"And the others?"

Temple takes a second to answer. "No deaths. Casualties, but no deaths."

She did not lose anybody – a great victory, all things considered. That feeling of elation fades quickly; for this only ends one way. The Choir asked her why she delays the inevitable, and that statement is burned like a black handprint upon the inside of her mind.

Win the battle. Lose the war.

Temple ducks out the door, and she hears the fire roaring in the living room. He returns with a bowl of oats and fruit, layered in honey and thick cream. “Eat. You spent much of yourself last night. There's eggs for after.”

“You're giving me dessert first?” she laughs. “Do I seem like a dessert first kind of person?”

“Yes.”

“Lucky guess,” she makes a scene of taking the bowl, but in truth her body feels depleted and it smells like heaven.

The painted walls of her childhood bedroom are a sanctuary. Marius went to great pains to get the paint, even let her pick the colour. Here, at least for a while, she can recover. She eats, feels her body's gratitude, and when the bowl lies empty Temple brings her tea, water, milk, and then a plate of eggs and toast.

Her mind is hard to settle at the best of times, and errant thoughts peck at her peace like crows. She finds a place in her mind, a temple of cool running water, and bathes her soul in it. Another trick that Marius taught her, learned from his time at war.

Peace, if only for a moment, and she lets out a breath that she did not realise she was holding.

Only when she looks his way with her eyebrows raised, does Temple speak.

“People are talking about what you did.”

“What did I do?” she asks. “I'm not sure I remember most of it. Feels like a dream.”

“They're saying that you ran into the dark. Into the forest. Alone. That you came back with everybody alive. Shepherds are saying how you saved them. Agnir told everyone; about how you lit up the very night – how you set the oil aflame yourself, even though you were in the way of the blast. How you faced down the Tall Woman without any help.”

“I did?” she muses. It feels like a different woman did all of those things. She does not know if she could do them again. She wonders how she ever regained control of her mind. “Temple, I think it had me for a bit.”

“It does that,” he nods. “Me and my team. We would lose time. Others would have to stop us walking into the dark. You don't notice it. Then it has you.”

It was in her head – she was briefly a part of it. She heard its voice.

“It's female, whatever it is.”

“It sounded like my comrades to me,” he says. “Begging me to join them. Using military language.”

“Interesting.”

“I think it can read us,” he says.

“Aye, it knew things about me,” she says. “Things it shouldn't know. Gods above, what a horrible thing.”

“It's a predator.”

“I'm not sure how I got out of there alive,” she admits. “It had us surrounded, exhausted – why didn't it strike?”

“It isn't here to kill. It's here to feed,” he says. “It only feeds when it knows it's safe.”

“*Feed?*”

“Never seen it. Only heard it,” he whispers. “It lures prey into the dark first, *then* it does – well, whatever it does. Sounds like digestion. Smells like hot acid. Bile. Leaves nothing of them.”

“Maybe it's vulnerable when it feeds?”

“Now you're thinking like a soldier,” he smiles.

“I'm trying to think like a Priestess,” she waves him away. “So it fled? The fire worked?”

“It did.”

She remembers the fire; the archers failing, the population of Llantry making for the gate with loose jaws and wide eyes, all singing softly in the rain. Only now does she remember the plan, and how badly it actually turned out.

Where was the horseback charge?

Where was the silver lance?

“Where were *you*?” she asks, and the break in her voice betrays her feelings. “We had a plan – if I hadn't lit the fire I think we'd have lost.”

“The lance did not find me,” he says. “Wanted to let you get your strength back first. Before we discussed this.”

A chill runs up her spine. “Why? What happened?”

“Bell made the lance in time. He sent Evelyn to bring it to me at the gates.” Temple shuffles in closer to Venalia, lowering his voice. “Evelyn has not returned.”

“What?” she sits up, covers held close, her heart pounding again. “What do you mean?”

“Nobody has seen her since last night – that's what the village is currently concerned with. Evelyn de Llantry is missing.”

Venalia's heart drops into her stomach. Her skin prickles cold, hairs rising.

“Oh,” she takes this in, processing it, covers held up around her chin to hide her panic. “Right.”

Her mind races.

Choir attacks, everyone has their brain scrambled, Evelyn isn't here. Why? Maybe she got confused? Lost? Maybe she was hurt and somebody is caring for her but hasn't reported in yet?

Perhaps she was so afraid of the Choir that she fled North? Maybe she will return shortly. There is far too much that Venalia does not know, far too much up in the air. Maybe there is a vital clue to finding her, and a child finds it and throws it in a fire out of spite. Maybe she is never found.

Venalia fights to keep her focus on her breathing, on clear lines of thought, but she can feel her grip on it slipping.

She needs to know things, put the timeline and the facts together – the longer that somebody is missing, she was taught, the lower the chance that they'll turn up alive. She thinks this, and then immediately has to block it from her mind, lest she lose control.

“You're going to go and look for her,” says Temple, watching her. “Aren't you?”

“Of course I am,” she says.

“Priestess, the Choir may return tonight. We should prepare.”

“*May* return?”

“I have not seen tonight. I do not know what happens.”

“Do you know if we ever see Evelyn again?”

“My visions do not feature her, no.”

Venalia curses; she cannot endanger the entire village to chase one girl – but that one girl is everything to her. Gregor has lost a sister because of her already.

This is what the Mind's Eye saw, when her soul was laid bare before him. Guilt. A wound that will not heal until she can redeem herself for her part in Anabel's fate. A sin that requires penance.

No amount of meditation will give her peace from this. Venalia needs to move, needs to act. Sitting in bed wondering what might happen is helping nobody, especially not herself.

“We need to prepare another defence,” says Temple. “This time, we'll have the lance.”

“Did you find the lance, then?” she asks. Temple shakes his head. “Right. Well, maybe you should go and find it. Ask around; the people like you, you make them feel safe. Someone has to have seen it, it must be massive. Probably trampled under some mud.”

“What are you going to do?”

Lose my mind in solitude, thank you.

“I'm going to draw a bath and get dressed. Then I'm going to find Evelyn de Llantry.”

“As you wish, Priestess.”

Temple stands to leave, and Venalia fights to maintain her composure until he is gone – but then he stops, and she has to fight her own mind a moment longer.

She wants to burst into tears and beat her hands against the wall, and she wants to do it *alone.*

Temple sees her anguish. “Are you alright, Priestess?”

How does she say it? How could he understand?

Last night was a triumph in every way. She was tested, as she knew she would be one day, and she passed. Her courage prevailed, she threw herself into danger knowing that she might not survive, she stared into the abyss and set a bomb off in its face. Everybody survived, she's a *hero;*

but Evelyn is missing, just like her sister before her.

Another missing De Llantry girl on her conscience. Venalia winces at the ache in her head and her heart, at the weight of the sin built up within her. She buries her face in her hands so that Temple will not see.

"I'm fine," she groans. "I'm – aye, I'm fine."

"Battle is chaos, Priestess. These things happen," he says, and lowers his booming voice. "We should never blame ourselves."

Venalia casts around, looking for the words, but Temple does not see, does not know. "It's not that -"

"It's alright," he returns to the bedside and kneels beside it. "You did everything correctly. Sometimes we lose people. Surviving last night with one person missing; Venalia, that is a *triumph*."

"It's not -" she begins, but the pressure in her throat and her chest is too much, and a sob escapes her mouth before she can catch it. She puts her hand over her mouth. "It's not that."

"What do you mean?"

That I let one of Gregor's sisters vanish already.

She wonders if Temple will understand. He is a warrior, a mercenary, he has to have made decisions that he wasn't proud of; done things that stop him from sleeping?

She has been silent for long enough that Temple prompts her. "Venalia?"

"It's not that," she repeats, quietly now. She pushes the sorrow down, as she always has. The shame has become a familiar old friend, always with her. The guilt is pressing on her chest like it always has.

He must understand.

Surely.

"Evelyn's sister went missing, too. Years ago."

"Anabel," says Temple. He remembers. "I am told that Gregor keeps a beacon lit atop his house for her, every night."

Ah, she thinks. The lamp oil anger makes more sense now.

"Does he?" she asks, but her heart can take no more of

this. She looks out the window, to the pale light of winter, harsh and unforgiving, looking for an escape of any kind.

There is none to be found. No running from this any longer.

Hands shaking. Heart pounding.

Venalia closes her eyes, and confesses.

“It was my fault that his sister went missing,” she says.

“You were fighting a predator from the world below, Venalia,” he says. “It wasn't your fault.”

“Not Evelyn.” She plays with a thread on her pillow. “Anabel.”

“What?”

She wipes her eyes and forces it out of her aching throat. “His sister, Anabel; she had the strongest Draconic blood of the three. The makings of a powerful Magistress, due to leave for Yorostadt in a year. She made my life a living hell.”

Temple watches, silent.

“She did such horrible things to me, but when I tried to tell the adults, she'd put on another act and fool them all. Marius believed me, but he couldn't do much. He taught me to read and he kept me supplied with books, never forced me to go anywhere I didn't want to. He taught me about the faith. My chance to get out of Llantry.”

“Whitehallow,” says Temple.

“When I turned thirteen I was eligible, and Marius had arranged a cart for me to go to Atlan, paid for my ticket aboard the Emerald Rail, bought me clothes and supplies and all sorts.” Venalia closes her eyes. There is a door in her mind that remains locked, and behind it waits the perfectly preserved memory of that day. Now, voice shaking, she recounts it.

“I hadn't been able to sleep, I was so nervous about Whitehallow. I was on my way to go and wait with Bell, by the Northern gate. It was raining, just like today. I heard Anabel's father shouting her name. He was running up and down the square barefoot, looking for her.

Temple shifts in his unease, unsure of where Venalia is

going.

Shoulders sinking, Venalia wipes her eyes clear and breathes. “There in the mud, fresh and unmarked, was the red bow that Anabel always wore in her hair. I'd never seen her without a bow of some sort. It was just laying there.”

“It had been dropped recently,” says Temple, leaning forward. “What did you do?”

Venalia looks away from him, sagging into herself. “I threw it in a crucible fire, so that nobody would ever find it.”

She is terrified to look back, to see his reaction. Temple's face is hard to read at the best of times, but she senses his eyes widen.

“Venalia,” whispers Temple, like a disappointed father.

“Oh, I *hated* her, Temple,” she breaks down, tears flowing freely. “I really, really hated her, so much that I wanted her to just vanish, and I'd never done anything bad to *anybody* before.” She hangs her head, wiping her eyes. “I told myself that she probably left, right? She went North – she had problems in the family, you know? She hated Llantry as much as I did – I thought maybe she'd left to go to Yorostadt early, or to Caladan to find a Magister who'd take her as an apprentice, or something? I think that I was trying to justify it.”

She trails off, and with the vault of memories open they begin to spill out unabated. Venalia stares into space as she speaks them out loud, trying to stop them from overwhelming her. The dam has burst, and there is no containing it now.

“I remember hearing Gregor – Gods above, he was so young – shouting himself hoarse, screaming his sister's name. Evelyn was old enough that I knew she'd remember it. Gregor's father took his men into the forest to search. I heard later that Marius himself had led searches all around the village, up into the hills. At night he enchanted their torches to burn all night, so they could keep searching. By that time, of course, I'd left. I was on my way to Atlan. I assumed – I think – that they'd find her. She was doing it for attention, I was sure.” Her voice falls to a whisper. “I thought she just wanted to steal the limelight from me one last time.”

When Temple finally speaks, he does so very carefully. “Do you still think that?”

"No," she admits. "She was just a child. So was I. Marius wrote to me once I reached Whitehallow. When he told me that Anabel had never returned, I knew that it was my doing. I buried that secret deep, deep down, and I kept it there. That's what led me to the Mind's Eye, in the end. He saw this awful secret. My ability to live with it was what he saw in me. That's what I am, Temple. A horrible little keeper of secrets. A stupid, jealous child."

It sounds so shameful when she says it aloud, and she finds that all of the hatred that had once been directed at Anabel has turned, soured, upon her own cowardly self.

Temple sits on the floor, thinking. "Do you intend to tell Gregor this?"

"I should, shouldn't I? It was a long time ago."

"He may not see it that way."

"No. No, he may not. Worse, I keep wondering if maybe that's why we fail here?"

"What do you mean?"

"If we'd found Anabel de Llantry, the family wouldn't have fallen apart. Maybe Anabel would be in charge today, a strong Magistress, and Llantry would have kept the lands surrounding it secure. We'd be able to get a message South to Atlan for aid. Gregor has ruined Llantry – but he wouldn't have had to, if Anabel hadn't vanished." She finally speaks the truth that has been welling up inside her since she met Temple, and she feels her cheeks run wet with anger. "Temple. Perhaps the reason that Llantry falls, is that a long time ago I did something terrible."

Temple shakes his head. "If my visions, my gift, has taught me anything – it is that very rarely do things ever work out as we intend, in the long run."

"Nobody gets away with anything," she echoes one of the teachings of the Light Within, Goddess of purity, fire, and redemption. "Sooner or later, I'm going to have to pay for that sin, Temple. I worry that Llantry might have to pay for it too."

"Perhaps," says Temple, and stands up. "Or perhaps, you have been given a chance to make things right." She manages a nod as he leaves. "Make yourself presentable. I will find the lance. We each have a part to play, Priestess."

Chapter Eight

The last of the bubbling water splashes into the wood and copper tub. It was always the right size for Marius, but slightly too small for Venalia's long legs. She takes a look over her body, now that she is disrobed. Blood and bruises cover her arms and legs, cuts run along her torso; everything smells of smoke, fire, blood, and sweat.

Venalia winces as she tests a toe, then a foot, before finally stepping in and sinking into the near-boiling water. Days of stress and worry, fear and anger, all drift away with the steam. Venalia allows herself a smile, finally, and closes her eyes.

She spends as long as she can bear the heat. In a place of such peace, allowed her privacy and relaxation, Venalia begins to heal herself. It is something that anybody able to cast a Heal spell can do; but healing oneself is a tricky business, requiring peace and concentration.

The same energy that she once used to heal Temple now courses in her. Her bruises fade with every passing minute, until finally she can move without pain. By the time Venalia steps out of the bath to dry herself, she is pristine once more. She wraps her hair in a towel whilst she examines the clothes that she has scraped together from Marius' wardrobe.

Venalia ends up dressing herself in the garb she imagines a mercenary Priestess might wear. A poor one. Donated underclothes. Dirty, old riding boots. A small set of men's breeches. She settles for tucking an oversized shirt into a belt. She can run and move her feet far easier in these clothes – though they do not afford the immediate recognition as a Priestess that her robe or cloak does.

Her dress-robe and cloak lie half-burned on the couch, awaiting repair.

With her hair drying in a single long braid around her head, Venalia lifts her sigil onto her neck, and then struggles into her breastplate. One half of it is blackened with soot, and she takes the time to rub it clean, allowing the engraved symbol of the Mind's Eye to shine through.

She throws her surviving green hooded cape over her shoulders, and brushes herself down. Venalia likes what she sees in the window's reflection; all that's missing is a sword at her side, and she will look like a real mercenary.

Is that what you want to be, lass?

Her soul still has no answer.

Venalia checks everything from her satchel; her medicines and books, her ink and quill.

As ready to face the world as she can be, Venalia breathes deep and steps out into the cold air.

Llantry is in turmoil.

Ash coats the walls of every house, the reek of smoke trapped in the thatched roofs. From the crater at the South gate rises a blotchy pillar of smoke still. Worse, winter has brought the first frost, and the rain has frozen, turning the mud into a thick sludge. Shoeless children cling to their mother's necks as they pick through the village, shouting Evelyn's name in a broken chant.

As soon as people notice Venalia, they start to gravitate towards her. They seem nervous at first – and as usual it is the children who disregard etiquette to ask her the awkward questions.

“Did the monster take Mrs. Evelyn?” asks a young boy.

Venalia has no answer for him.

More join the crowd now.

“Wha' 'appened, Priestess?” asks his mother. “Is yonder

beast dead? We ain't find no corpse."

Hopeful but fearful faces line the gathering – it is evident that few of these people have slept at all. Venalia wants to tell them that it is safe, that she has this under control, but she cannot lie.

"It isn't gone, no," she says, and the crowd deflate, and so she tries to rally them. "But we hurt it, badly – and now we know much more about how it hunts. We had no weapons and we weren't ready, and we still beat it, right? We need to prepare for the next attack, and this time, we'll kill it."

"How?" asks one of the shepherds, old and bearded.

"We have a weapon, crafted by Blind Bell. A lance. Temple is going to use it to kill the monster."

"The Giant," says one of the children. "The Giant is going to kill the monster?"

"Yes. Until he does," says Venalia, "we all need to rebuild, and you have to keep praying, keep your mind busy."

"Aye," says a shepherd, rolling his eyes. "Yon Priestess bids us pray. Marius ne'er asked us pray to his God, ken."

"I'm not asking you to pray to mine," she sighs. "Pray to the old Gods, to the Minotaur, to the spirits of the earth, pray to the four winds and Lady Altheim if you so choose; just *pray."*

She sees them trying to find a flaw in her argument, something to be angry about, but even they struggle.

"It took Lady Evelyn, then?" asks the same old shepherd, who is turning out to be a real mixed blessing. The rest of the crowd follow his lead. If Venalia wins him, she wins the crowd.

"I'm not sure. I was just about to start the investigation. Incidentally – did any of you see her last night?"

A small, stout woman beside the shepherd – his wife, judging by her body language – speaks up.

"Sure, I couldnae tell ye *what* I saw'd last night, lass. All sorts a' madness, all manner a' it. I've not seen such madness since the Age a' Fear, and I'd rather nah see it again, truth be told. Sure Atlan is sending help by now?"

"Aye," the shepherd nods, as does the crowd. "Where's the airships? Time was, being under the Magistry meant that ye got protected. No offence, Priestess."

This, she groans, coming from the same people who want to consider themselves outwith the Magistry's influence.

"None taken," she sighs. "And I'd love to tell you some high tale about treachery or honour; but the horrible truth is that help is not coming."

No reaction. She would have accepted some complaints and arguing and eye-rolling, but *no reaction* is much worse. It means that they're processing what it means.

"We on our own?" asks the shepherd. Bursts of whispering break out across the crowd. "Nine Hells, wha' are we staying here fer?"

"Aye," shouts his wife. "We can lead our herds to Atlan in a few days. We's bin talking 'bout it fer a while -"

She is hushed by her husband, but the idea is out in the wild now.

"You can't flee," says Venalia. "I know that many of you *want* to, but you heard what happened to the shepherds last night. If you are out in the open when this thing comes for you, there is no fight to be had. I assure you – if you try to flee Atlan, it will take you. No matter your number, or strength."

"So that's it?" asks the shepherd. "We's just to sit and wait for our end?"

"Not quite," she says. "I don't know if any of you noticed, but we have a half-Giant on our side, with a warhorse to match."

"He weren't much help last night," says the shepherd.

"That's because Evelyn was supposed to bring him a weapon that can kill the beast," she explains. "It never reached him." Now they're quiet, she notes. Now they're listening. "So our priority, right now, is to find Evelyn de Llantry, find the lance that she was carrying, and get it to Temple. If all of us pitch in, this'll be done quick. If we can get it sorted before nightfall, we have a chance. I'm not asking anybody to fight – this is for Temple, and me. Do you all understand?"

There's a rumbling of agreement from the crowd.

"Then go," she says. "There's no time to waste."

Her tone marks the end of the conversation, but as the crowd disperses the old shepherd remains, alone, leaning on his crook.

"Something else?" she asks him once they are alone.

"Wanted to thank ye fer getting me boys out of yonder woods last night. I don't like strangers in me head. You did good."

She gives a nod, one survivor to another. "Just doing my job."

"Nah, it ain't yer job," he shakes his head. "It's Gregor de Llantry's feckin job – an' I reckon that ye ain't heard how he's takin' this."

Oh no. "How *is* he taking this?"

"He ain't snapped yet, some'ow," he grimaces. "Just locked himsel' in his estate. Ain't no way fer a man to act."

"No, it isn't," she admits, glad that nobody is listening. "He's got a lot to deal with. Please, you have to give me time to get him straightened out."

"Ain't no time, Priestess. Between you and I, we're willing to take our herds and risk a run to Atlan, owin' in no small part to his behaviour."

"If you take the herds, Llantry dies," she says. "This is your home."

He smiles. "Home is where me wife and children sleep. Ain't no home if we're all taken by some forsaken aberration."

Maybe this is it, she thinks. This is why Llantry is emptied, in Temple's vision. The shepherds leave, and everyone follows them. They are taken by the Choir during their journey, and there's nothing she can do about it.

"Please, I'm not trying to manipulate you here," she begs. "You'll *all* die trying to reach Atlan. Let us fight it on our terms."

"Join us," he says. "If ye know it'll come fer us, then ye can use us as bait."

"Two of us can't protect hundreds of you. Not at night. We need our walls to funnel it into a trap."

"Those walls is Gregor de Llantry's walls. They ain't protecting nobody while he's in charge."

Venalia bites her lip, testing out arguments in her head till she finds a reason for the shepherds to stay. "What if his leadership was no longer an issue?"

He gives her a sideways look, the expression of a schemer. "Go on."

"The men listen to you, right? They'll stay if you ask them too?"

"They may do, aye."

"Then tell them to stay. I'll speak to Gregor, and see to it that he steps up."

"Stepping up ain't the issue -"

"I wasn't finished. He'll step up, I'm sure – but until then, you listen to and take orders from *me*, or Temple, ok?"

He mulls it over. "I'll run it past the lads. Ye sure that yoursel' and the Giant lad can kill it?"

Of course not, she thinks. The only clue to her future is that she walks into the woods in tears, alone, to die.

"Nothing is certain," she says. It is technically true, keeping the third rule intact.

He hums and haws, and then shrugs. "Priestess? We want him *gone*."

"Who would you put in as his replacement?"

"Yonder sister that just went a-missing," he says. "She'd listen to sense, I reckon; get Llantry on track again. She picked a hellish time to go missing."

"Aye," says Venalia, thoughts springing forth in her mind. "Very inconvenient."

"Good luck, Priestess," says the shepherd, walking away. "Ye've got an impossible job."

"Aye," she whispers. "I know."

Venalia makes her way to Gregor's estate. Llantry will not survive the night at this rate; but if it is going to survive after this at all, it needs a Burroughmaster who inspires the trust of his people.

When the shepherds start making plans to leave, something is badly wrong. She knows that Gregor has allowed Llantry to fall to pieces, but she was unaware that it was *this* bad.

She hears a crowd roar in the distance, as though in shock or surprise, and she picks up the pace, wondering if it might be Evelyn that they've found. It takes Venalia a few minutes to navigate towards it, threading through the crowd of people. Children first, then the elderly, all come to see what the commotion is about.

She catches snippets as she passes by. Some whisper her name, her title – others, asking about last night. They ask where they were, what happened to them, if the Gods are with them. Venalia touches them on the shoulder as she passes, smiling, trying to answer their questions with a single, confident look. There are too many to stop and talk to; and all they really want, she knows, is to see that she is in control of everything.

The crowd is thickest near the Burroughmaster's estate, crowded into the garden. Outside the main door, two of Gregor's guard are waiting. They are telling people to stay back, to keep the noise down. They exchange nervous glances – and Venalia finally sees why.

Some of the window shutters are riddled with crossbow bolts – from the *inside*. There's a throwing knife embedded in a guard's shield, plus a few choice bruises.

Venalia keeps pushing forwards, curious and angry now. She can hear, over the whispering of the watching crowd, a man roaring and shouting, throwing heavy things around inside the house.

Temple appears, standing up from the back of the crowd. He sidles up next to her and puts a hand on her shoulder, stopping her shortly before the door. He holds her where she is, and nods to the guards. They see her, and relax a little.

"Priestess," says Temple, voice low, steering her away from the crowd. "We need to talk."

"What happened? Is Gregor in there?"

"There is an expression amongst mercenaries," says Temple, separating her from the throng now. "When a soldier loses their nerve and begins to see enemies everywhere. We call it *war-*

struck. Combat stress. That's what I am seeing here."

"Gregor has gone off the deep end, hasn't he?" she asks, though she knows the answer.

"Listen," whispers Temple, "if you can hold his attention out here, I'm going to go in through the stables, like last time. He won't even hear me – I'll choke him out, we can put him in the cells until he calms down, but first -"

"Wait wait wait," she waves her hands. "What *happened?"*

"He thinks that the villagers took Evelyn, and now they're coming for him."

"Why?"

"No idea."

Venalia tries to see it from his eyes, remembering the plotting shepherds. "Enemies everywhere," she whispers. "It's just him now."

"Bad place to be."

She nods. "No wonder he's going berserk."

"I've heard bits and pieces. He thinks that there's a conspiracy against his family."

"I can hardly blame him," she says. "Everything they've endured? There might be."

"He told us he'd kill the next person he saw. In self defence, he said."

Venalia looks at the guards, waiting for the word. She sees their hands trembling, and sees in their faces the urge to be anywhere else. They are not trained for this; she sympathises with them on that.

"If Gregor is unable to lead," says Temple, "then the people will turn to you."

"I know," she sighs. "I just had a chat with one of the old shepherds, one that people listen to. They want to evacuate."

"They'll die."

"I told them that, Temple."

"You have to stop them from evacuating."

"I'm trying to. For the duration of this crisis, I've told them to listen to us instead."

"Smart – but they should listen to you, not me."

"Why me? You're an experienced soldier, you're a natural leader."

"I've never *led* anything," he shrugs. "I'm just a soldier who knows he won't die. I can command other soldiers. I cannot command *people*. You're the Priestess of Llantry. Remember? Of equal standing to the Burroughmaster."

"That was a power move to save *your* life -"

"There's no Magister. You're next in line. For what it's worth, I think most of the guard will back you. They certainly hold no love for their Burroughmaster. He attacked them when they tried to calm him down, bloodied a few lips and noses too."

Venalia wants to feel smug. She wishes that she could relish this development, that she could revel in Gregor's suffering; but Temple is right. That hatred has done nothing but poison her over the years.

"Poor lad," she says, and comes to her decision. "Right. Temple; you only come in if I shout your name."

"You're going in?"

"I might be the one person that he *knows* isn't plotting against him."

"Venalia..." begins Temple, giving her a questioning look. "You two have bad blood. Is this wise?"

"Well I know that I don't die here," she shrugs. "Besides, he knows exactly where I was when Evelyn went missing, he *knows* that I'm not plotting against him."

Temple considers her point, then nods. "So be it."

"Tell the guards to stand down – and get everybody away from here. I'm sure there are things needing done in the village. These people should be looking for Evelyn – and the lance. Where's Bell? Find Bell."

Temple nods and, before he leaves, kneels beside her. "At least take a weapon?"

She silences him with a look, and he accepts it and backs

down. Temple turns to the crowd and begins to address them, whilst Venalia leaves them behind and makes for the door. The guards let her pass with curious but grateful expressions, tipping their helms to her.

Venalia feels bare without her robe, without the clothes telling the world that she is a Priestess, but the engraved breastplate does a good job of announcing her station. In the breeches, she feels much more capable of *moving,* like she could grapple and roll in her new outfit, making up in mobility what she lacks in grace.

Next to the door, she hears clattering coming from within.

"Gregor?" she announces herself.

Silence. Then a strained *click-clack* – she knows the sound of a lever-drawn crossbow being loaded.

"Who is it?" comes the voice of Gregor. He sounds exhausted – or drunk. When dealing with somebody who is a danger to themselves, to others, you cannot allow them to take control of the situation.

She is not entirely sure that she agrees with the sentiment, but she has to trust her training and so she does not ask permission, but tells him exactly what she is going to do.

"It's Venalia. We need to talk. I'm coming in. *Don't* shoot me."

"Just you!" shouts Gregor.

"Just me," she says.

Venalia prepares a Shield spell, and opens the door.

The main room of the long-house is a mess. Little sunlight gets in through the boarded shutters, shafts of light creeping through bolt-holes. A dozen alchemical fuel lamps cast flickering shadows – lamps for which Venalia was sure there was no fuel left. Tomes and scrolls cover the length of Gregor's table. He has been reading all night, evidenced by the empty bottles of Sarantja Blue Gin clattering against her feet.

He stands at the far end of the room, crossbow raised.

Venalia keeps the Shield spell ready in her mind and, before crossing the threshold, checks for any traps or tripwires. It remains a product of her training – to enter any dangerous room with your eyes first.

She keeps her hands raised in surrender, and steps through, kicking the door shut behind her, sealing off the world outside.

Gregor is trembling. His shirt is drenched in sweat, and he reeks of drink and smoke. His eyes are red, and wild, and the crossbow rattles in his hands.

"Gregor," she says, "I'm going to put my hands down. You'd *better* not shoot me, I swear."

He nods, and she pulls a seat out and sits across from him, crossing her legs.

"Venalia," he begins, and his voice cracks. "Evelyn is -"

"I know," she says softly. "I know. I'm so sorry."

"Ask him," he motions to her breastplate, to the Mind's Eye's symbol, with the crossbow. "That's why you're here, right? You're going to ask your God for me?"

"Gregor," she closes her eyes, shaking her head. "The Mind's Eye can't help us find somebody if nobody knows where she is."

"Then ask the Open Door," he says. "Ask if she's crossed the Black Sands, so that I can at least grieve."

"I don't talk to the Open Door," she shrugs. "I'm not hers. I am not a servant of death, just knowledge and secrets."

Gregor looks around in desperation – she can see it in him, that he *wants* to be angry at something, that he needs something to break, but there's nothing that he can do. So much pent up frustration and power - and absolutely no use for it.

He throws the crossbow down, causing Venalia to flinch, and pulls at his hair, teeth clenched.

"Gods above, Gregor, don't throw a loaded weapon -"

"Where are my sisters?" he screams, squeezing his own skull. "Where are they? Where *are* they?" He is in tears, and she wants to join him in his grief; but her job is to be the rock that others can tie themselves to in turbulent times. "I can't do this again, Venalia, I can't do this again, not again, not again -"

"Gregor, Gregor," she stands up and crosses the room,

taking his hands and clasping hers around them. “Breathe, man. I'm going to find her, okay? I'm going to find her.” Her heart scolds her for bending the third rule; but she is determined that she will. It does not feel like a lie.

Gregor nods, breathing deeply, and sits himself down, eyes closed. He weeps silently, one hand hiding his face from her.

She clasps her hands, and takes the opportunity to look at the books that Gregor has spread across the table. Family lineage, arcane tomes, ancient records, writings old enough that some of them are in Old Draconic, others written in the Druidic runes of the Steppe.

“When did you last see her?” she asks him.

“With Blind Bell,” he manages. “Making a spear – or a lance? For Temple.”

“And where did Bell last – well, not *see her,* you know what I mean.”

“Bell says that she took the lance to find Temple. That was the last he saw of her. Then the Choir's song reached the far end of town.”

“Did nobody notice her wandering away?”

“Nobody,” he sighs in defeat. “I didn't even see her last night. It felt cold, and then; I remember little.”

Venalia frowns. “The gates were all closed. She must still be within the village.”

“Exactly,” he says. “It was the villagers that took her. I'm sure of it.”

“Gregor, come on - who would want to hurt Evelyn?”

“I don't know,” he admits.

“And how would they get to *her,* without also getting close to the Choir themselves? Everyone was affected by it.”

“Except for you,” he says, aiming every word at her.

“Oh God's above,” she throws her hands up. “Really? Except for me?” she repeats, her temper flaring. How *dare* he. “That's right. So. Gregor. Let me ask you a question. What was I doing when Evelyn vanished?”

"What were you doing when Anabel vanished?" he asks. It comes out of nowhere, and hits her hard enough to knock her off track and give him an opening. "You were running off to Whitehallow to play Priestess."

"And now I'm back, and thank the Gods that one of us is capable of protecting this place, Gregor, because you're busy firing crossbows at your own men."

"What *were* you doing when Evelyn vanished?"

"I was throwing myself in harm's way, to save *you*, and *your* village, and *your* people!" she jabs her finger at him.

He screws his face up, trying to summon some acidic remark, but it fizzles out. They both know that he just wants somebody to shout at, and so he goes for the worst thing that he can think of.

"You've always hated our family – you hated Anabel. You're the only one who would have taken Evelyn."

She sighs, rolling her eyes. "I won't pretend that I didn't hate Anabel, but Evelyn? She is a kind young thing, why would I ever want to harm her?"

He scowls in confusion. "To hurt me."

"If I wanted to hurt you, Gregor, I'd hurt *you*. If for some reason my God allowed me to, I'd gladly trap you in a memory of mine, so that you could understand exactly *why* I hate you – but I will not, because it goes against the oath, it goes against my own code, and because we aren't *stupid children* any more."

"Well," he shrugs, brooding in his corner. "Somebody wants to hurt my family – of that much, I am sure."

"The Choir wants to hurt every family in Llantry," she tries to be reasonable. "Evelyn put herself at risk to help us defeat it. If she was taken, most likely it was while she was trying to find Temple with the lance."

"No, no," he whispers, growing distant now, shrinking away from her. "Nobody could get out the gates. She's still here somewhere. This is personal."

"My family were destroyed too. It was bad luck. Being in the wrong place at the wrong time. It wasn't some grand conspiracy, sometimes these things just happen. Sometimes bandits burn your parents bodies to ash, and sometimes people go missing during a fight. Let me find her."

He is shaking his head, and when he finally gets the words out, Venalia sees the first flickers of madness in him.

"I think I've found a conspiracy," he whispers.

"Gregor listen," she sighs, rubbing the bridge of her nose between two fingers. "I like a good theory more than most, I *love* conspiracies – but we can't act upon something without proof."

"What if I have proof?"

She stops herself. The Priestess in her wants to put him in a cell for his own safety – but if there *is* a conspiracy, if somebody is acting against him, then her duty is to unveil it. He does, she reasons, have a fair amount of enemies with sufficient motive.

"Go on then," she says. "Show me your proof."

"Venalia. Priestess. I believe that my family is suffering from a blood curse," he says, and he rushes for the books, flicking over pages. Out of begrudging curiosity, she joins him. "Look at this; going back generations upon generations, my family line has had something *haunting* it. Since the Dragonfall, no less."

She looks at the yellowed, ancient family trees in the parchment. "For twenty-two hundred years? How so?"

"Each generation there are... gaps. Look: ten generations ago, almost three hundred years, the modern records begin. Read the entry."

Venalia tries to parse the writing, which switches between Draconic and the common tongue.

"Five children," she manages. "Three boys, two girls. Male eldest. I don't see the issue."

"How many lines go on?"

"Four," she sees. "Oh. Oh, hold on. No death recorded."

"No death, but they vanish from the record," says Gregor, jabbing his finger at the page.

"Right. So they were a subject of shame, perhaps? Cut off?"

"Read what it says in Draconic below."

Venalia's Draconic is school-learned, but the root of many modern words are found in Draconic, making reverse-translation somewhat intuitive.

The word sounds like *astray*.

“This is the root word of stray,” she says. “I think. They went missing?”

“Not missing,” says Gregor, and leads her to a dictionary of old Draconic. “Look, there's the word there. *Aberare*. Ab-er-ar-ay. To go astray.”

“Go astray,” she whispers. “What does it mean?”

It happens every generation, too; Gregor is correct.

She feels a cold breath on her neck, the hint of something. Her instincts are never wrong here – the connections, the little details, the names and dates; something is hiding from her.

She sits down and begins poring over the books. This is her own talent, something she was good at before her Priesthood and her magic. The truth hides between the columns and numbers, disguised behind words and turns of phrase, but somewhere there will be stories that do not match, and within those twisting lines she will find the truth.

There are one or two gaps in every generation. A child – or two, sometimes – who is not listed as dead. *Aberare*, it says. Astray.

“So they went on to become Magisters?” she suggests. “Maybe they were sent to Yorostadt to learn the arcane arts, and that's what it means?”

“If they became Magisters, there'd be a continuation of the line. Magisters *always* have children, it's the law. Preserving the bloodlines.”

“Maybe they were sent to the military? Maybe they died there?”

“They aren't listed as dead, the military would have killed-in-action listings, they were *astray*. Astray how?”

“Well, isn't it listed?” she asks, and an idea strikes her. “Wait. Wait. I have a theory.”

“Go on.”

"I know you might not like this, but in times long past, things like pregnancy out of wedlock were a much bigger deal; to have a daughter fall pregnant before marriage was enough of a shame that they were often sent to live with other relatives, to raise the child as their own. It happens a lot more as you go further back in our histories. They went astray, you know? Off the ethical path, in our ancestors eyes? Maybe -?"

"There are men sent away as well," he says. "Were they pregnant?"

She sighs, admitting defeat. There goes one theory. "Well," she begins, and he cuts her off, pointing to their names again.

"Read what's written , Priestess," he is pleading now, his voice growing louder. "They didn't die – they went astray. What does that mean? Did my ancestor make a deal with some ancient Fey? Is every seventh child promised to some demon?" He slams his fist next to the book and she jumps. "Where are they being sent? By what? To whom?"

"It's..." she looks, and frowns. "It's a root word. Wait. Its meaning has changed over time."

"What?"

"How old is that dictionary?"

Gregor flips to the front of it. "It was published in – I don't know how to read this."

Venalia slides over. Usually, dates are written in relation to their time pre- and post-Dragonfall. This one is old enough to have been published during the reign of the Dragon Emperor Karak, the Red Terror, over two thousand, two hundred years ago.

"This book is ancient," she sighs. "The root words have changed. I knew *Aberare* sounded familiar, Gregor, it's the root word of Aberrant. As in *aberration*."

The word brings a shock of realisation from Gregor. Snippets of information, tales and stories, rush to her.

Draconic bloodlines. *Aberrant* bloodlines.

Magic came from the Old Gods of the earth, and their druids were the first priests.

Then came the dragons, from another world, led by

Karak, a red dragon half the size of a city.

Karak sealed off the Gods by solidifying the Celestial membrane, starving them of the worship of mortals.

Dragons ruled Altheim for thousands of years, uncontested, demanding constant sacrifice, endless wars of vanity, and mindless worship.

But mortals would not be so easily conquered.

For dragons are phenomenal and unstoppable on a battlefield, but they make for terrible rulers – and even worse politicians. They chose loyal subjects from amongst the mortals who served them well, and granted them a gift. An infusion of Draconic blood, granting those mortals a connection to the arcane. They created magicians that did not rely upon any God.

The Magistry.

After centuries of planning, the mortals of the Magistry enacted the mother of all coups, and exterminated Dragonkind in a single night of coordinated slaughter.

Poison, traps, magic, and silver; the Dragonfall.

Having grown fat and lazy, the Dragons were taken completely off-guard by their own servants.

There are no dragons left now, and the Magistry rule from Caladan, the arcane city built atop the remains of Karak's hoard, having turned his body into Brokenscale Keep as one final insult to the last creature that thought it could conquer Altheim.

Dragonblood flows, however diluted, in Gregor; and in his sisters, too, and all of their ancestors. It is why they rule. Common knowledge, taught to children.

Less commonly known is the risk of a Draconic bloodline.

Aberrant blood. Aberrations. Sometimes, the Draconic blood comes through a little *strong*. The results are unusual and frightening; Venalia has seen some paintings during a class, and little else.

The blood causes the growth of scales, useless tiny wings, fangs, reptilian eyes, growths across the body, causing great pain and complications for the Aberrant. Enough to create a mutated outcast. Then the dragonbreath; fire, lightning, frost, steam, acid, depending on the blood. The rage. The desire to control. Dragons were proud, violent creatures that believed they were designed by the universe to rule all creation.

For a long time, Aberrant children were left on mountainsides to die.

That's what the rune means. Aberrant. Astray.

It runs in the bloodline. She can see it, trace it down the lines.

"These children didn't go missing, Gregor," she realises. "They were-"

"Aberrant," says Gregor. "They were quietly disposed of, right? Probably thrown in a sack of rocks and taken to the river."

"Surely not," she whispers, turning the pages to follow the line. "That was stopped a few hundred years ago; they built places for them, I think."

"Places? Venalia -"

She sees the joy of a breakthrough in his eyes, and she feels it too. "They must have been sent away to those places?"

"That's it, then?"

He seems so excited, but Venalia sees no connection to Anabel, no connection to Evelyn.

"Your family seems to have a fairly strong Aberrant bloodline; one every generation or two. But Gregor – neither Anabel nor Evelyn were Aberrant. Were they?"

"No," he deflates, and sits back on his chair. "They were not. And I've no scales, Venalia, if that's what you next thought to ask. No wings, no eyes that can see in the dark. Swords cut me just fine. I cannot breathe fire, nor acid, nor anything else you care to name. I'm human. Mortal. Thank you."

"No offence meant," she shrugs, and tries to keep pulling on the string that interests her most. "Was Anabel... you know?"

Gregor shoots her a scowl, but he is softening. "She never gave me any reason to believe that she was Aberrant. Nor did Evelyn, for that matter. Our branch of the family tree was clean."

"To your knowledge," she points out, and he sours.

"It is *clean*," he repeats.

"Well, then, why would they vanish? Your Aberrant ancestors were sent away, sure – but Anabel wasn't Aberrant."

He rubs his eyes, frustrated. "I don't know, it just feels like a connection. Maybe someone else found this information? What if somebody has a grudge against us, or wants to protect Llantry from Aberrant bloodlines?"

All possible – but she sees no connection to either sister's case.

She shakes her head, and says as delicately as she can:

"Gregor, I think maybe you *want* there to be a conspiracy."

He looks away, tries to summon some anger, and comes back empty handed. Gregor deflates before her eyes.

"I know," he says. "I know that I'm grasping at the wind. This doesn't explain where Evelyn is. Does it?"

"Even if she were secretly Aberrant, and wanted to leave, I don't think she'd pick now to do it. You need her right now – she wouldn't abandon her brother."

"Then the alternative explanation must be true. That she's with the Choir now."

Venalia nods. "I'm sorry, Gregor."

His anger was easier to witness than his sorrow, for his grief seems bottomless, and Venalia can see herself in that endless, lonely tunnel with him, mourning for something that will never grant any closure.

"I should have protected them," he says. "My own sisters, in my own village. Can you -" He stops, and gives in. Gregor curls in the seat, and holds himself.

"Can I do what?" she asks.

"Can you find her?" he whispers.

She's dead, Venalia wants to say. Worse, perhaps – but her code will not let her. To tell the truth is one thing, to destroy hope another.

"If I cannot find your sister, Gregor, then I will find out what happened to her."

"I know that she's gone, Venalia, I mean: can you find me something to bury?"

Probably not.

"I will try," she says.

He nods. "I'm sorry. Sorry for all of *this,"* he gestures to the mess around him. "This would be much simpler if somebody just wanted to hurt us. I'll take Scarlings and raiders over something from the Inverted World, next time."

There will not be a next time.

His people have lost faith in him, his support is non-existent. He rules now by the polite unwillingness of the people to throw out the last of a once-great line. That goodwill is fading fast in the face of annihilation.

"Gregor," she changes the subject, and stands as tall as she can. "I won't stop until I know what has become of Evelyn, for better or for worse. The first rule forbids me from giving up on my people."

The two meet eyes with a look that they have not shared before. Respect. Concern. Gregor looks away, agitated.

"If you cannot find her -" he begins.

"Then I will deliver justice upon whatever, or whoever, has done this."

Gregor replies with a firm nod. "Is there anything I can do?"

Lead your people.

There is no way for her to wrap this up and make it hurt less. The best practice in all situations, as a Priestess, is to tell the truth – or, at the least, to not lie. Gregor needs to know that his position is tenuous at best, if only so that it will shock him into action.

"The people are worried that you aren't fit to lead," she delivers the line like a doctor reading a diagnosis, polite and detached. "Many are planning an exodus. I believe that they have been for some time."

"The people are right," he gives a dark laugh. "Look at Temple! He has the respect of the people, and he did it without trying to rob anybody of their bloody horse. He got it by virtue of being big, he hasn't even had to do anything." Gregor sits forward, putting his elbows on the table, trying not to look at her. "Look at you," he sighs. "You've been here two days, and already it's obvious that I've got no idea what I'm doing. The people listen when *you* speak."

Venalia raises her eyebrows, surprised to hear Gregor admit any of this. Were she a worse person, she would agree. She would encourage Gregor to step down. She would jail him, after a public trial. She would humiliate him, make him apologise for a decade of bullying.

But to see him now, broken and beaten by nothing more than awful, random chance? There is no honour in defeating an already-beaten man – and if her intention is to leave Llantry again, then she cannot leave them leaderless.

The right path is usually the hardest one, she thinks, and with a heavy sigh she puts a hand on his shoulder.

"You may have lost their trust," she admits. "Maybe even their respect." Gregor nods along, agreeing in his depression, till she blind sides him with kindness. "But those people need their leader, not some outsider. They need *you,* you who knows each of their names, their children's names, you who knows Llantry, who loves his home and his people. Your bloodline continues out there, Gregor; with the people whom you've sworn to serve. Who else can lead them? Temple is just a soldier. Me? I'm just a girl with a curious God and a temper. These are *your* people. Lead them."

Gregor looks up, taken aback, and manages a laugh. "Perhaps this is all a bad dream," he says. "That would certainly explain why you are standing before me, trying to... *help* me?"

"I'm trying to help Llantry," she laughs, "don't flatter yourself. But you do need to go out there and take charge."

"But -"

"Lead them through this. *Then,* you can rest. Then you can grieve."

He looks at the floor in shame. "Is that what I do?"

"What do you mean?"

"Well, your Giant tells you the future, doesn't he?"

"In a way."

"So answer me: is that what happens? Do I stand up, triumph, lead my people?" He stands up, his tired eyes pleading with her. "Are we going to make it through this, Venalia?"

She takes a deep breath; no lying, says the third rule. "Honestly? I don't know for certain."

"Well - does *Llantry* make it through this?"

"Perhaps?" she offers him.

"It's pointless," he storms away, throwing his hands up. "It's all for nothing!"

His insistence upon giving up finally breaks her temper, and her blood surges with her mother's rage.

"It isn't *pointless*, Gregor, it's your *duty*!" she shouts, and he backs away in surprise. "You think I'm here laying my life down because I want to be? Do you think I'm walking to my own death for fun?"

"No?" he whispers, and she sees tears well in his eyes.

"No, I do it because it is my *duty* to the people – because the title of Priestess means something, *Burroughmaster!"*

"These people don't want me," he wails, jabbing a finger outside. "They hate me, everyone hates me! You're the only one on my side, and even you hate me."

"Well now you know how I felt," she jabs his chest, cornering him. "All those years growing up on my own, with you and your awful sister making every step of the way more difficult than it ever needed to be." He is taken aback, and looks genuinely hurt. She wants to apologise, but she can't turn it off now, the floodgates are open. "You were right - I was glad to leave, and I didn't really care that Anabel vanished, but maybe she would have done a better job. And if she hadn't vanished then maybe we'd survive this after all. So *when* we fail, it'll ultimately be my fault, not yours. Spare me with your woe-is-me nonsense, Gregor, you had every chance to do this properly - but it's my fault that we fail."

"Your -" he stops, and the pieces begin to fall into place. "What? Your fault? Why, what do you do?"

Oh Gods, she thinks.

Well, I've come this far.

"Now what I do," she says, and drops her head. "What I did. The day that Anabel vanished."

"What?"

"I found her bow. The red one."

"What? Where?"

"By the Northern gate, you know, on the way to Bell's?"

Gregor is aghast. "And you told nobody?"

She winces with the pain of it. "I burned it so that nobody would know where to look."

Venalia prepares the Shield spell, watching him with one eye. She waits for Gregor to strike her, to grab the crossbow, she is ready for a *fight*. What she gets is far worse.

Gregor shies away, wounded, and folds his arms.

"Gods above, Venalia," he whispers.

There's a long silence as he walks to the end of the table, and picks up the crossbow. He sits it on the table, watching her. She is not sure what to say – this isn't what she had expected.

"Gregor, I was a lonely child, full of hate," she pleads. "I'm so, so sorry -"

"Doesn't matter now," he is absent mindedly running his hand over the crossbow. "We all die anyway."

"We don't know that."

"No, no, that seems accurate. No way out, besieged by a monster that we cannot kill," he lets out a manic, private chuckle. "You know we used up almost all of our flammables last night. To wound it, you said. We can't repeat that. Not enough material, unless we light the whole village aflame. Either way we lose Llantry, don't we?"

"We might still find the lance," she says, but even to herself it seems like the hollow bravado of a teenager. "Then Temple and I can kill it."

"Maybe you don't," he shrugs. "Maybe you can't."

"Well at least I'll *try*. Look," she says, the anger turning to sorrow now, as it always does in time. “If we are destined to fail here, then I want you to know that it is my sin, my failure all those years ago, that brought us here.”

“Because if Anabel were alive, she'd be a much better leader?”

“Yes?” she shrugs. “And Llantry would have kept the countryside clear around it, the Scarlings, the undead. Instead, it fell to you, and here we are. No way out.”

“So I am to blame?”

“We have to share the blame,” she says. “That's the point. You're the Burroughmaster, I'm the Priestess. We're supposed to work together.”

“Yeah,” he says, laughing. “That's not going to happen. If Llantry died with Anabel, then let it die. Tell the shepherds to leave, if that is what they want. They've never given me a chance, why should I give them one?”

“Oh Gregor come on,” she says. “Don't give in.”

“Don't give in?” he barks another, final, dark laugh. “The only thing that I had to fight for is gone. Evelyn is *gone*. When people in Llantry vanish, they don't come back.”

“Then we are set upon the road to failure,” she whispers. “The future will come as it is meant to, and Llantry will fall. All because we cannot put our past aside.”

“All because you put your grudge before the life of a promising young woman.”

“And I was wrong!” she explodes. “It was a *mistake* - and here you are, doing the same thing.” She sighs, and stands up. “Well, you can roll over if you want. If we are going to die, at least I can ensure that I die on my terms, doing everything that I can. I can die *for* something.”

“For people that you always hated?” he asks, thinking it rhetorical.

“No,” she says. “I'll die for my God, for my oath, for the memory of Marius, and what we stand for. Give up if you so wish. The first rule forbids me that luxury.”

She turns and leaves, frustrated and upset, but more determined than ever.

"We'll end up in the same place anyway," he shouts after her.

She ignores him.

This, she thinks, is most definitely how Llantry falls.

Chapter Nine

Outside, Llantry has fallen calm again. Temple has dispersed the crowd, as has the cold and the snow. The streets are busy – but busy with working people, busy with industry. Walls need repaired, braziers stoked, cattle fed. Work, she was taught, keeps people occupied during a crisis. Stops the mind from racing.

Temple stands at the bottom of the pathway from Gregor's longhouse, waiting on her.

He raises an eyebrow in question.

"Llantry falls after all," she answers, pacing North as Temple strides to keep up. "Evelyn is dead or missing. Vanished sometime last night whilst trying to find you. She had the lance. I have to assume that the Choir got her. She's gone."

"We'll know if the Choir got her," says Temple.

"How?"

"We will hear her sing."

"God's above," she sighs, rubbing her eyes.

"Why was he screaming?"

"Thinks there's a conspiracy against his family."

"Why?"

"Because they have a somewhat Aberrant bloodline."

"The Draconic, murderous type of Aberrant bloodline?"

“Nobody knew about it until today,” says Venalia. “It's possibly why Anabel, his elder sister, left? Maybe? But I doubt it has anything to do with Evelyn's disappearance. It's not an answer, to put it bluntly. Just another breadcrumb.”

“Nothing to do with the Choir either,” says Temple. “Will he lead his people?”

“No. He's not going to work with me.”

“Why not?”

“Because I told him what happened with Anabel's bow.”

Temple rubs his eyes and shakes his head. “Good timing.”

She lifts her shoulders and drops them. “Well, you know Temple, maybe this is how it all happens.”

She feels strangely at peace with it. The talk with Gregor felt like a confession, and now that she has said it aloud, the weight upon her soul is gone. She feels lighter than she has in an age, unburdened for the first time.

“So what now?” asks Temple.

“We need to find that lance,” she says. “The lance was with Evelyn last. She was sent to find you, and she didn't. That's where she vanished. Find the lance, find the girl. That's my thinking. Start with Bell and try to pickup her trail.”

“May I suggest that we make a brief stop at the inn?”

“The inn? Why, are you hungry?”

“No – I'm an old soldier. I know an exhausted leader when I see one. I'm getting you a drink.”

“Temple I really don't have time to -”

He raises a finger, motioning for silence. To her surprise, she obeys. “We have time. Trust *me* on that. I heard you shouting. You are starting to crack. Time to blow off some steam.”

The first words of a retort form on her lips. Instead, she sighs and, in doing so, admits defeat. That her anger bubbles so close to the surface is a good indication that Temple is correct.

He leads her through throngs of people to the inn, and as she walks she realises how *annoyed* she feels, how ready she is to snap and break something. This is no mindset for a Priestess, she hears Marius say; save your rage for those who really deserve it, not those who are trying to help.

Venalia strides into the tavern, struck by the mellow atmosphere. There are clusters of villagers, men and women, old and young, whispering and drinking in small huddles. She picks up pieces of their conversation: they are planning their escape. These are people who have lost friends and family to the dangers of the Steppe, to Scarlings. They have seen the dead rise and be put back down again. These people lived through the Age of Fear, and they know when the game is up.

Those people look up at her as she passes, and fall silent. She recognises some from her childhood. Some of them were in her schoolgroup, familiar faces. They say nothing to her, but the audience of dark-rimmed eyes speak volumes.

They want her to save them.

It strikes Venalia that these people are enduring what she is, all of the same fear and doubt. The difference, of course, is that they cannot summon the gifts of a God to protect them; instead, they must trust in somebody else. If nothing else, she thinks, that is one thing that she has done right. The people trust her.

She rests her elbows on the bar, but the barmaid is busy cleaning plates in a bucket. Venalia has grown used to the polite bar staff of Whitehallow, to full sentences and good manners. Finally, the barmaid shoots her a look that is a question.

Venalia answers. “I'm going to need as much of that fruit and rum mix as you can make. Put them in sealed jars for me, please? I think I might need them.”

“Of course, m'lady, I'll fetch what I can.”

Temple shuffles next to her, kneeling by the bar. “And eight pints of ale, m'lady.”

The barmaid laughs. “Would sir like those in a bucket?”

“Yes,” says Temple, straight-faced.

“I'll see what I can do. Nothing lighter for yourself, Priestess?”

Temple jabs her in the ribs, and she admits defeat. “Fine, I'll have a glass of wine, white please, Sarantja-anything, if you've got it.”

"We don't."

"Just white, then," she laughs, fishing in her new breeches for her purse. "How much do I owe you?"

"Let me see how much of your caster's mixture I can make first, and -"

A chair is scraped back, and a weathered herdsman stands up.

"The Priestess will pay for nothing today," he says, and approaches the bar. He reeks of alcohol, the hard medicinal stuff that is popular in Llantry, and slams down a handful of crowns. Far too little. As Venalia begins to politely decline his charity, others stand up.

"Brought our boys home," mumbles a woman, joining him at the bar. "Only right. She don't pay for nothing."

"Aye," shouts another. "Aye, get the girl anything she wants. Old Marius would have said the same."

"Woulda done the same too," comes an echo.

The older women put their hands on Venalia's shoulders as she turns to thank them, giving her the kind affirmations that only a grandmother can. They pile upon her their fear and their rage and their doubt, and they tell her - without saying it aloud – that they are trusting her, with their lives, not to fail.

Venalia sees the smile on Temple's face, and for a moment she sees Marius. She has done well. If this is her only job, the only work she ever does as a Priestess, then at least she can say that she gave a good account of herself. A feeling of warmth washes over her, the kind of pure and unashamed pride that one feels no need to fight. It is earned, like rest after a hard day's work.

She realises that she has not said a thing, and that there may be tears if she tries to, and so she stands tall and tries to embody what a Priestess looks like in her head. Then, with a smile, she pushes the coins towards the barmaid.

The barmaid takes the coins and dumps a few sealed jars of the her mixture on the table, packing them into the satchel for Venalia, cushioned by hempen cloth so as to avoid smashing them. Then she serves eight ales in a bucket to Temple, and some wine in a ram's horn to Venalia.

She counts the crowns on the table, and as the townsfolk return to their seats, gives Venalia a look.

There is more money than they need – by a large margin.

"It's yours if you want it, Priestess," she whispers. "Might be the only payment you get for all this."

She almost does – but she can feel Marius at her side, judging. This is a test, and she is confident that she knows the answer.

"Keep it," says Venalia, smiling. "Buy everybody in here a drink, something fancy that you don't often break out. We've plenty of reasons to drink."

She turns to their table, throwing the satchel over her shoulder: four flasks of her mixture, more than enough for even a protracted fight. Which, the pessimist in her brain informs her, there certainly will be in the near future.

She takes a drink, and tries to douse the anxiety. Llantry's wine tastes like paint thinner, a world away from the full-bodied flutes served in Whitehallow.

Temple sits on the floor next to her table, in a corner lit by a lantern. Above the table is a map of the Herdsman's Moot, from Llantry and Atlan to Elmholm on the South-Eastern coast, and their border with the much sunnier Vinyard Confederacy, home to the finest wineries in the world, and its capital city of Sarantja. Venalia misses good wine, however briefly.

Temple lifts his bucket in a toast, and she laughs and meets it with her rams-horn of wine.

"Here's to the future?" she suggests.

"I'll drink to that," he pours the bucket into his open mouth as some of the villagers watch on.

Venalia sips her wine, reminded of warm nights by the waters in Whitehallow with her friends. She can almost hear the music.

"Look, I'm relaxing," she rolls her eyes back in her head. "Happy?"

Temple gives her a knowing look. "Make the most of these moments."

She returns to her more serious demeanour, with an aim to distract her mind from anything about Evelyn, or the Choir, or the Tall Woman. "Can I ask you something?"

"Of course."

"What do *you* want to do after this?"

He shrugs. "I'm not sure. We've discussed this."

"No, I mean – what do you *want* to do?"

"Well," he says, "I'd take another job, I guess."

"That's all?" she sits up aghast. "A life changing experience like this, and you just go back to work?"

"I'm afraid that's how life works, Priestess. Every job I take turns out to be life changing."

"The life of a mercenary, eh?"

"Indeed. What about you?"

It catches her off guard, and she struggles to keep her mind from going to the future, the future she *knows* comes to pass, the one in which she *goes to certain death.*

She takes a breath and whispers a prayer to calm herself, sips the wine to buy some time, relaxing back into the bench. "Well -"

Temple raises a hand to stop her. "Assume, for a moment, that you know nothing of the future. What do you do next?"

"I don't know," she has to admit. "You remember I was going to come home after graduation and ask Marius? Maybe try some things? Priests of the Mind's Eye are well sought after in research, scholarship, education. I could live a very comfortable life, if I so wished."

"And is that what you wish?"

"What, comfort?" she thinks long on this one. Too often has she soaked in the bath and dreamt up fantasies of comfort and wealth, a handsome husband and enough money that she need never work; of being a lady of just enough repute to command respect, but not so much as to require responsibilities. But a daydream is just that. Real life is muddy, after all – and messy. Comfort seems wonderful, but it is so very boring. "No, I don't think I ever wanted comfort, not really. Momentary comfort, yes –

but a comfortable life? No."

"Wise answer."

"It reminds me of something Marius told me."

Temple takes another swig from his bucket. Already his eyes are misty from the alcohol, and she feels her own brain growing fuzzy.

"Mhm," he prompts her.

"Well, when I was young, I asked him; I remember my exact words: *Marius, I don't think I'm like other people Am I normal?* And he burst out laughing, and that made me relax. He laughed for a good while, slapped his thighs, wiped away a tear – he always overreacted to jokes, and it made it funnier. Soon, I was laughing too. So eventually, he says, *Venalia? You are most definitely not like other people – thank the Gods.* And he said that it meant I was just a little weird, like him, and that he had always known that."

She feels a ramble coming on, the kind of wine-induced rant that her friends in Whitehallow know all too well, but Temple's eyes are deep and old and full of patience, and they tell her to continue.

"He told me that my parents were probably smart, creative, types. And do you know, he told me right then and there; *listen child, there's a good side and a bad side to this. Good side,* he said, *is that you're either gonna be something really special or something really awful. Bad side,* he said, and he's laughing the whole time, *is that you're never gonna feel comfortable with either.* And do you know? He was right – I've never really felt comfortable my entire life, not around people, teachers, children. But then; I've never expected to. Why should I? Marius made sure that I knew not to."

Temple raises his glass, ignoring the tears in Venalia's eyes. Temple is old enough to know when somebody is somewhere else – and when to let them stay there for a while.

"To Marius," he says. "He sounded very wise indeed."

"He was," she raises her glass and takes another drink, wiping her eyes absent-mindedly. She becomes self aware again, and bursts into laughter. "Sorry, I got carried away there. You were asking about what career I might go into. Like it matters."

Temple laughs. “Well, you listed all the boring ones. A Priestess of the Mind's Eye could enter into some other, less savoury industries.”

“You mean spying?” she gasps in feigned shock. “Aye, we're well represented in espionage, I hear. Secrets and forbidden knowledge are our domain, after all - but spies also have to be good at *acting,* Temple, and whilst I reckon I can turn my hand to most things, I assure you: I am not a good actress.”

“Is the life of a Priestess not an act?” he muses.

Venalia waves her wine glass at him. “Excuse me, I am trying to have a good time here, and you are hitting me with very deep and complex questions. Give me solemn Temple back, please, until the wine wears off.”

He holds his hands up in surrender. “Well – what other paths are there for a Priestess?”

“Good question,” she says, putting her rams-horn wine glass in a table slot. “There's always the life of errantry. Travel the roads, preach the good word, help those who cannot help themselves. Battle demons, smite the undead and the unholy, tussle with warlocks atop tall buildings while it rains, all of that. It sounds very cinematic, but most Priests just aren't cut out for that kind of life. It involves a lot of fighting, usually. We lose a lot of good people that way.”

“Sounds like mercenary work.”

“They're probably very similar.”

“Do *you* think you're cut out for that line of work?”

“What, mercenary life?”

“Errantry. A Priestess who travels.”

“I mean – I think I can do anything that I set my mind to,” she says, quickly adding, “except acting. The thing is, demons and warlocks are powerful and terrifying, and an errant Priestess will *inevitably* face one of those things.”

“You've already proven that you can triumph. Are warlocks and demons more frightening than the Choir?”

“Yes,” she says, falling quiet. “When Priests confront a warlock, we aim to have a five-to-one advantage in numbers, at *least.* Doing it alone? No, I don't think I'd like to do that for a living. Those who do have to be... a bit mad, I think."

"You mean like the Purifiers?"

Venalia would swear that every time she hears the name of the All-Faith's aggressive militant sect of demon hunters, she hears the sound of flames, screaming, and steel.

"Yeah," she says. "Like them."

"I've worked alongside Purifiers before."

"Aye?"

"Terrifying. No mercy for their enemies. I'm glad they're on our side."

"As am I." She takes another drink of wine. "No, that kind of life isn't for me. I want to help people, I guess. I want to learn – I want to see this beautiful continent, and I want to answer some great big question before I die. When my soul goes to the Mind's Eye, I'd like to have given him something back."

"A noble life," nods Temple. In the time that she has spoken, Temple has drank most of his bucket. "Could I suggest a path, Priestess?"

"Of course."

"There are mercenaries who do not fight for money. A company needs healers, spies, scouts, administrators, paymasters. The fighter has five others behind him, feeding and clothing him, making his armour and weapons, guiding him. You'd see the world, make your fortune, and you wouldn't have to lift a sword. You may have to get good at healing."

"That's one idea," she shrugs and drinks the rest of her wine. Her head is foggier, but the thoughts of her imminent confrontation with death creep back in. "Between you and I, Temple, I don't think it's a good use of my time; to dwell on these things when this situation needs my full attention. We should get back to work."

"You need to remember what it feels like," he drinks the last of his ale. "To think of the future, without knowing what it holds. Do not assume that anything is final, nor set in stone."

"I suppose." She deflects, lowering her voice. "You said that you haven't had any visions of the future beyond our goodbye. You still haven't?"

He shakes his head. “Nothing.”

She drops her voice to a bare whisper. “So then, presumably, you die after that?”

Temple sits his empty mugs down, and lowers his voice so that only she can hear. “It would seem that my journey comes to an end too, yes.”

“And you're just good with that?”

“No,” he laughs. “No, I'd like to keep living.”

She leans in as a spy might, whispering. “So let's try to change it.”

“We cannot.”

“We can try. What do we do tonight?”

“I'm not sure. My one remaining vision is of us separating.”

“Anything else you can tell me? Is that today? Tonight? Tomorrow?”

“I do not know. It is snowing, when you leave. We are beside evergreen trees, on a road. I am atop Pretzia.”

“Snowing,” she whispers. Something is itching at the inside of her mind. A clue, a path to follow. Footprints in the snow, she thinks, and stands up. “Temple, are you any good at tracking?”

“As a matter of fact, I am.”

“Then follow me, I have an idea.”

They finish their drinks and leave the inn, waving at the others as they do so.

No sooner are they outside than Venalia comes to an abrupt stop.

Llantry is coated in a fine dusting of snow, and more falls from the sky, melting on her skin, cast down from a grey and rolling sky.

Temple curses.

"How many hours of daylight left?" she asks, trying to find the sun. "Six?"

"Thereabouts."

"Do we fall out and abandon one another today?"

"It certainly doesn't feel that way."

"And the Choir won't attack during the day anyway?"

"No. It hates the light."

"Then we have time," she says.

"What are you thinking?"

"Temple – if Evelyn de Llantry isn't *in* the village, then she must have left the village last night. There'll be tracks in the mud. I had to wade through it, there'll be footprints everywhere. Nobody else left the village. The ground will have frozen, so if she *did* leave then the frozen mud will show us. Could you take a walk around Llantry's walls? Look for footprints before the snow covers them?"

"As you wish."

"And I'll try to find that lance," she says. "If it comes here tonight, we need to have the lance. Then you and I kill it together. Are you with me?"

"Better than sitting here waiting to die. Perhaps we go our separate ways tomorrow?"

"Maybe you're really mean to me and we fall out over something else? Maybe your dream occurs after we've beaten it?"

"Perhaps, Priestess," he smiles. "Maybe you leave to find Evelyn de Llantry, wandering into the woods to follow a lead?"

"Perhaps, perhaps," she says, and for the first time, she feels a little optimism. "Let us see to our mission then, Temple. Good luck."

Temple gives her a single massive pat on the back, and he sets off across the village.

For the first time since the beginning of the nightmare, Venalia feels her spirit return, and she sets out to find the lance, starting with the man who made it.

Venalia steps over the same patch of mud, hardening in the frost now, where she once found Anabel de Llantry's red bow. She walks up the steps to Bell's forge, ducking under the tarpaulin to where she once burned that same bow. The inside of the forge is cold and silent. Where once was fire, now there is only cold metal, and stone.

Bell sits on a stool near the crucible, his limbs hidden beneath his long apron and leather coat. Gnarled old hands, wrapped in gloves and furs, strain over the crucible for the residual heat in its embers.

He cocks his blindfolded head. "Priestess?"

"Bell," she whispers, and drags a stool over, sitting across from him. The last of the crucible's heat is in the stones, and she rests her hands on it to warm them. Nearby she sees the broken mould of the silver spearhead, shattered on the ground where the hammer broke it open. The lance is nowhere to be seen.

She is unsure of what to say.

"How are you?" she tries.

His reply is weak and soft, a far cry from his usual power. "I have not felt this way since the Age of Fear, Venalia. You must forgive me for my failure. I was not prepared."

"Oh Bell," she reaches out, but he shies away as though out of shame. "The Choir is a monster – this wasn't your fault."

Bell takes a great shuddering breath. "I should have told her to remain here. She would have been safe here."

Venalia gives a patient nod that he will not see, and pushes as much as she feels is justifiable.

"Can you tell me what you remember from last night?"

"She was right here," he says, disappearing into memory. "The rain was battering the tarpaulin, the forge was roaring. I shattered the mould of the spearhead, I quenched it. I bound the head to the shaft, and drove the nails through it. Evelyn shouted in triumph. She told me it was perfect – that she would take it to Mr. Temple immediately."

"By herself?"

“Far too heavy for her to carry. She has the eyes, but not the strength. I have the strength, but not the eyes.”

“You went together?”

“We did. Then I remember...” Bell is gone for a moment. His muscles twitch as he relives the moment that the Choir took his mind. “I was a soldier again. Young. From the dark of my own memory crawled old horrors. I felt alone, cut off from the world. Cold.”

“Cold,” repeats Venalia, remembering the Choir's fingers in her head, the words it spoke. “Cold and alone.”

“Yes. Yes, exactly. By the time the song faded, I was lost, alone, confused. I thought that the Choir had made me apart of it. I had moved, and neither the lance nor Evelyn were within my reach. I called for help until somebody found me. That was the last that I saw of Evelyn.”

“Oh Bell,” she says. “None of us are immune to the song. It did the same thing to me. There was nothing more that you could have done.”

Bell remains silent, wringing his hands beneath his cloak, working up to ask: “Have you found her?”

“Not yet,” says Venalia. “We will. I'm trying to retrace her footsteps. Do you remember where you were, when the Choir's song reached you?”

“I remember a crowd – Evelyn was afraid, I think; she wanted us to avoid the crowd. She said they were sleepwalking to the South gate. She could hear it as well, the song. We could hear her brother leading people in a song, trying to protect their minds. That's the last I remember of her. We weren't far from here.”

“At any point,” she continues, “did you hear *her* voice in the Choir?”

“Evelyn?” he asks, shocked. “No, no I'm certain I would have recognised her voice. She sings all the time when she's working.”

Present tense, notes Venalia. He still thinks that she's alive. That gives her a little bit of hope.

“The lance could not have gone far,” Venalia reasons. “If she was alone, then she'd have dropped it. We really should have stumbled over it on the way here."

"She could have dragged it – she's a strong lass, it's not impossible."

"We'd find a track then," says Venalia, and curses upon a realisation. "Unless the marching villagers destroyed any evidence when they all went South. Damn it all."

"If you find her -" he begins, and cuts himself off. She can hear the pain in his voice.

"You'll be the first to know," she says. "And I *will* find her, Bell. One way or another. If you hear anything, will you leave a message at my house – well, at Marius' house."

"It's yours now, girl," says Bell. "That house is where our Priest lives, that's the rule. You're our Priestess. It's your house."

"It'll always be his, in my mind."

Bell stands up, and without a word, uses his forge's guide rope to feel his way over to a chest in the corner. Opening a complex lock, he produces a crystal bottle of amber liquid, and two small glasses.

"This is long overdue," he says, working his way back to her. Venalia rises to help him, and he raises a gnarled hand to keep her sitting. "I do not mind admitting that I miss him," says Bell. "This is what I'd drink with Marius. It's an orange liqueur from -"

"Sarantja," she says, laughing. "Always missing home, he was."

"Llantry became his home, in the end."

"I am glad that old Marius does not have to see these dark days come upon us," she stands up, patting Bell on the shoulder. He feels warm, as usual – the heat of the forge burns in his bones, he once told her. Venalia pours two glasses, and passes one to Bell. "A toast?"

"How about a toast to dark days?" he offers. "For I have lived through many. Remember, Venalia, that your very life was borne out of a particularly dark day. Your parents were murdered for no reason – but in return, Llantry got you. Marius, a daughter. Me, a niece of sorts."

"Not sure it's a fair trade," she laughs, but her heart swells. To hear Bell think of her as a niece makes him a brother to

Marius.

"You were born from ash, and flame, and death," he says, raising the glass. "A few weeks old. None of my caravan heard you – they didn't want to stop. But I swore that I could hear the crying of a child."

"Everything was burned," she says, telling what she knows of the story.

"Not everything," says Bell. "Not you."

"Thanks to my parents – or, I suppose, the people we *think* were my parents."

"I trust that they were. No other love would lead two people to shield you between their bodies." Bell takes the glass from Venalia, and raises it. "Your parents passed through flame in order to save your life. I hear that last night, you did the same thing for Llantry."

"It's my job," she dismisses him.

"You owe this village nothing," he says. "But you did it anyway. Something of your mother and father obviously lives on in you, Priestess."

Venalia has never been one to take a complement well, but a Priestess must always act with grace, and so she raises her glass and clinks it against his. "I will find Evelyn, Bell. I swear on my oath."

"I trust the Gods to make that call," he smiles. "I'll pray for your safety – and for the return of my apprentice. Gods be with you, Venalia."

"And with you," she throws the shot down her throat and savours the sweet orange flavour before the heartburn kicks in.

Standing, she embraces Bell, a child again for just a moment, and leaves the forge behind.

Temple is waiting outside the forge, snow gathering upon his makeshift kilt. His face, hard to read as always, tells nothing.

"Find anything?" she asks.

"Not quite," he says. "I want you to come and see."

She follows him to the Eastern gate, which the guards have kept open at Temple's request. They nod as he approaches, and leave the two alone.

Banks of earth separate the dirt road from the flat and tended fields on either side, a scene dusted in snow. Beyond are the woods, evergreen, wrapped in mist and darkness. Though a winter sun fights through the snowfall, the forest has kept for itself a portion of the night's darkness.

Huddled in cloaks against the snow and wind, the guards hold Venalia's gaze. There is respect there that was missing previously. Temple raises his hand, and the guards salute them both.

Temple walks her along the outside of the wooden palisade, atop the raised earth wall. Outside of the wall, Venalia feels the false veil of safety shatter. Snow muffles all sound, but the forest whispers, dark and wild, on the other side of the field.

"Look," he says, drawing her attention to a deep set of footprints. Venalia tests her own boots against it, and finds that they are almost the same size.

"A young woman's boots!" she says, casting around, re-enacting the scene. "And handprints. She jumped the wall? Landed here, stumbled on to her hands. Facing East, into the trees?"

"My thoughts exactly," says Temple. "One problem. The Choir was in the South. Why go East?"

"Maybe the Choir got to her," says Venalia, putting the story together. "She clambers the gates, limber young woman like her would have little problem – there are platforms on the inside. It's a steep drop, but I managed it myself. It's possible."

"Why East?" repeats Temple. "Was she under the Choir's control or not?"

"Bell certainly thought so."

She trails off, looking into the Eastern wood.

The Elderwood has grown upon Llantry's Eastern edge since she can ever remember: the forest that children do not play in. When an animal wanders into the woods, it is considered lost. Dead. When Gregor's father searched the woods for Anabel, all those years ago, he took his entire guard and Marius with him, all armed and on horseback.

"You think she went into the forest?"

"There are a few indications that she may have. Nothing concrete."

Temple sees the look in her eyes, the excitement, and shakes his head.

"Venalia," he says. "We are not entering the forest."

She deflates. "Do you think there's any chance she's alive?"

"Do *you?"*

Venalia looks long into the trees, and knows the answer. As a child, her nightmares took her there. Bad things happen in the Elderwood.

There is but a small chance that Evelyn is in there, a smaller chance still that she is alive.

"Venalia?" asks Temple. "Even if she made it. Winter will have killed her."

Venalia curses. "I know."

"Priestess?" asks Temple. "This is a hopeless endeavour."

"I know," she repeats.

"Shall we return to the village and search for the lance?"

The first rule of the Priesthood: never, under any circumstances, give up on your people. That – and her soul will not let another de Llantry girl vanish under her watch.

"No," she says. "I have to try and find her. Dead or alive. Saddle Pretzia and prepare yourself – we're going to follow the trail into the Elderwood, and see if Evelyn de Llantry was there."

"Priestess?" he asks, and she can see that he doubts her. "There is an immediate threat to your people – and without the lance, we cannot fight it."

Venalia simmers, though she knows that Temple is correct.

Maybe this is it, she thinks.

Maybe this is what they fall out over – she has to make a decision about Evelyn, and she makes the wrong call. The Elderwood beckons her into its jagged teeth.

Snow settles on her shoulders.

This is just as Temple described, though she is not holding Minotaur, or crying.

"I cannot fail to follow up a lead like this," she says. "Temple, Evelyn was *here.*"

"She was running away," he says. "Terrified. Not a satisfying answer. These things usually aren't."

"Evelyn wouldn't run," she says.

"Wouldn't she?" asks Temple. "You know her that well?"

"We grew up together," says Venalia, and winces. "No. We grew up in the same village. I barely know her, in truth. But I think that she's a strong young woman, too brave to just run, not when Bell was in trouble, too. This story doesn't hold together."

Temple stands at his full, considerable height. "You are sure that this isn't personal?"

It stings because it is true, and she feigns surprise. "What?"

"Priestess. I think that you seek redemption for your own sins."

Of course I do. "Whether I do, or not, is of no real consequence. Either way, my oath dictates that I have to *try*. I will go myself if needs be, but -"

"You aren't going alone," says Temple, shaking his head. "This already looks too familiar. Don't pick up any warhammers that you find."

Venalia sighs, relieved. "You'll come with me?"

"Yes. Come. We'll saddle Pretzia. The quicker we do this, the quicker we can prepare for tonight. We'll have the villagers and the guards keep searching for the lance."

Venalia nods, grateful to have him. Nevertheless, she can tell that Temple is growing annoyed at her insistence on her oath.

"You'd rather we fought for Llantry first," she says.

"Focused our efforts."

"Of course," he says. "I'm a soldier. Basic tactics. Concentrate resources and manpower for effect. Evelyn seemed a nice girl. It's a shame. But any battle has casualties."

"If you think that we should change our priorities, I'm willing to listen to your argument?"

Temple stops and turns on her, outside the gates where winter winds wrap them in flurries of ice. Behind her, the Elderwood lies silent, an evergreen cemetery.

"Are you sure?" he asks.

"Of course," she straightens up. "Tell me what you think."

"Evelyn is not important. We need the lance. Tonight we could end the Choir. You have a Hold spell prepared. Forests full of Scarlings are dangerous. Deathtraps, even for a company of well-prepared soldiers, let alone a fledgeling Priestess and – well, me. I suspect that you are underestimating the dangers. This is your first time. It is not my first time."

"I'm well aware of the dangers," she protests. "I also know that since I haven't grabbed a warhammer and stormed into the forest myself in tears, that this is *not* the end for either of us. If we go in, I know that we come back out."

"Unless it happens in there. Maybe we separate in the forest, and *that* is where I die."

"Ah," she catches his slip, pointing like an accuser. "So that's it. You're afraid to die."

"There are things far worse than death," he says. "Have you seen a Scarling before? Do you know what they can do?"

"Well -"

"No, you do not. Nobody does. Each one is unique; and dangerous."

"You said that you win every fight you have," she says. "If there's a fight to be had in that forest, then we win that too."

"I said that I *survive* every fight," says Temple, angry now. "I don't *win,* otherwise I would have prevented the deaths of my friends."

Venalia eases off, unwilling to press upon such a raw

wound. “Sorry. We've both lost people,” she says. “I know that Evelyn is not your priority. I would ask that you help me here anyway. If we find a body, then the closure might stop Gregor from completely losing his mind. I'm trying to save Llantry here, in my own way.”

“Priestess..” he trails off, realising that she is not going to relent.

“I'll go in myself if I have to.”

“I can't let you do that.”

“Then we're locked into this, like you say we are. Any other questions?”

He sighs deeply, and sags. “This is how it happens, then.”

And so they make for Gregor's estate, to saddle Pretzia, and prepare.

Venalia wonders as they walk, if each and every decision she makes drives them closer and closer to something awful. Does the future come about because she is too stubborn to admit defeat?

Is this a test of some kind?

At some point she walks into the woods with Gregor's hammer, in tears. To certain death.

But until her hands close around the haft of Minotaur, she is invulnerable, and that gives her great confidence.

Chapter Ten

Temple sees to Pretzia, clipping her saddle and barding on, brushing her down, calming her with deep humming from his chest. Pretzia's presence puts Venalia at ease. The loyalty of animals has a texture different to that of mortals, but Temple's horse shares his authoritative and protective aura; she even has a trustworthy face.

Venalia finds that neither her body nor mind will settle, trembling in anticipation of action. She revises her training, a calming practice to ease the anxiety.

First year class, forty students. Title: Fieldwork and Survival. How to start a fire, find shelter, set a snare, purify water. Useful in an emergency.

Second year class, thirty students. Title: Tracking and Evasion. How to be on either side of the hide-and-seek equation. Fun class, lots of hiding in the woods. Learning about tracking, navigation, cartography, scents, wind-direction, how to hide in plain sight, urban evasion.

Third year class. Twelve of them in a study group. Title: Pro-active Management of Dangerous Creatures. Hunting, by any other name, but hunting the kinds of beasts that sometimes take mortal lives. Wolves, rock eagles, bullet worms. Dangerous and fascinating. Venalia watched a bullet worm cut in half on a cold steel table. The tutor had them count the victims by the pieces of jewellery they found, for the bullet worm cannot digest gold or silver. More than a few people had gone for a drink afterwards, to purge the memories, but Venalia had relished the glimpse into the macabre.

Fourth year. Last year before specialisation. One-to-one training. Title: Combat with non-humanoids. How to fight. How to face the undead, the aberrations and monsters that have always plagued Altheim; somehow worse now, after the closing of the Scar, the act that ended the Age of Fear.

How to fight something with eight arms and no face, how to fight something with no physical body, how to fight things that can only be seen when you have your eyes closed.

All of her training has to be thrown out when Scarlings and aberrations come into play. No longer can one track footprints and scents through forests; now, you might have to track a monster that lives in the memories of victims and passes onto new ones through ritualistic torture. There is no almanac of Scarling creatures. There is no encyclopedia to memorise, no guide to tracking something like the Choir.

There are rules, however, that each creature must abide by. There is always a preferred method of attack, the way that it likes to stalk or choose its prey. There is always a vulnerability, something that it will avoid if it can. It is on these topics that Venalia dwells, whilst Temple finishes packing the saddlebags.

"Priestess?" he asks her. "It's not like you to stay quiet."

"How many Scarlings have you fought?" she asks.

"Fought? One."

"Well, how many have you met?"

"Two."

"Obviously you survived those encounters, though?"

"Of course," he turns like a teacher, lesson at the ready. "You want to hear the stories."

"Of course."

He is busy fastening the breastplate around his abdomen, over his shirt. The hand-shaped hole remains in the steel, bloodless, where the Choir struck him.

It triggers a memory, another meandering thought-wander, this time a reliving of the moment that the Tall Woman almost did the same thing to her. She can remember the song in her head, the aching cold, the weight of isolation that she felt near the Choir.

Still she is not certain who stood in the rain that night. Of all the curious things that she has encountered, has learned, this is the greatest mystery of them all; and it is a mystery entirely of her self. Venalia watches herself charge head first into danger, throw herself in harms way again and again. She does not yet know if she can be that woman again, on command.

She is not yet sure how she did it in the first place.

Temple rescues her from a thought-pit of self doubt when he begins his Scarling stories.

"The first," he begins, checking Pretzia's hooves. "Was in the Southern tropics, near Mul. During the Age of Fear. The Scar was open. I rode past a woman, injured, crying for help. When I slowed, I saw that something with a great many mouths was impersonating the sounds of a woman in agony. I spurred Pretzia, and did not look back."

"That was a Scarling? What did it look like?"

"A puddle of mouths," says Temple. "Hard to describe."

Venalia thinks better than to ask, for her own imagination is putting her hair on edge with vivid mental images of such a beast.

"The second was in an underpass," he continues, "a mine through a mountain. Old *Kappi* trade route to Byore. Long defunct. Friend of mine knew the road. Ungren."

He stops preparing Pretzia and holds his fist to his heart, before continuing. "Something that watched us for the entire journey. We found its trails. Slime on the ground. Never saw it. Ungren did. I heard him scream, clutch his eyes – and when I managed to lower his hands, his eyes were gone. Not *removed,* Venalia. No blood. Just gone. He says the beast looked like a swarm of eyes, lurking in the dark. Twist was, he could see what it could see. His eyes were a part of it now. So he knew that it had followed us out of there. We set a trap, and I fought it blindfolded. Ungren could see me through its eyes, and told me when to swing."

"Gods above," she whispers. "How did you beat it?"

"It had a physical body. At the time, I carried a greatsword inscribed with silver. It was a cowardly creature, in the end; unable to fight when it could not first blind me. I cut it in half with a single swing. We got his eyes back," he says, strangely cheerful. "Bless the healers of the Wakened World. They made him almost anew."

It takes Venalia a moment to word her question. "How do you be that person?"

"I do not follow. A warrior?"

She sighs. "Perhaps your visions give you the confidence, and you will not understand, but I find myself wondering if I can replicate what I did last night."

"Ah," says Temple. "That was your first time. Right."

"Is this normal?"

"Absolutely," he says. "Some people freeze. You did not freeze. Some people panic. You did not panic."

"I mean, I panicked a bit."

"It did not overcome you."

"So am I a veteran now?" she laughs.

Temple shows a rare, good-natured smile. "You are – but you will learn quickly that every battle is your first battle. That said; there is a reason that veterans are valued."

"Because they've seen battle without freezing or panicking."

"Exactly." Temple finishes preparing Pretzia. "And the longer you live, the more you learn. So when we enter the forest, you follow my lead. Do as I say. Do not question my judgement. Do you understand?"

"Absolutely."

From his saddlebags he pulls what Venalia would consider a large battle-axe. For Temple, it is a one-handed weapon. He swings it a few times in practice.

"It'll do," he says. "I have a selection of smaller weapons in here, things that I recovered on our escape from the Inverted World. What weapons are you trained with?"

"Uh -" she wishes that she sounded more confident. "I've been trained with shortswords, staves, spears, uh -"

"You have not killed before, no?"

"Well, no -"

"Take this." Temple passes her a shortsword the length of her forearm, a stubby weapon for short thrusts. He hands her a scabbard to clip to her belt, and she rests it against her hip. "Use it if required. Otherwise, should trouble find us, use your Shield spell and stay next to me. Understood?"

"Yes," she says, fighting her instinct to add *sir* to the end of it, as she did during her training.

"Come on then," he says, offering his hand like a stepladder for her to use. "Up you come."

It gives him no strain to lift her. She probably weighs less than some weapons he has used.

Temple secures the axe by its head, hanging from his kilt sash, and leaps into the saddle. Venalia holds on to the edges of his armour.

Pretzia whinnies at Temple's command, and with the reins in his hand he guides them out. The villagers watch as Pretzia saunters past, crunching the icy mud under hoof. Children run alongside as Temple ups the pace, wrapping a huge shawl around his shoulders to keep the snow off. Venalia pulls her cape around herself. Up atop Pretzia, the snow seems heavier, thicker somehow. It clings to her clothing, to her red hair.

A figure waves to them on the road, clad in winter furs, with the bull-headed warhammer resting on his shoulder. At his back stand a number of guards, spears resting on the ground, shields on their arms.

"Burroughmaster," says Temple, pulling Pretzia to a stop.

"You have a lead?" he asks. "My guards tell me that you found something in the fields."

It is Venalia, embarrassed to be peeking out from behind Temple's massive arms, who answers.

"We have some tracks, Burroughmaster," she says, "but they lead into the Elderwood. We would not risk all of Llantry's warriors pursuing it."

"I want to help," he says, nodding at his warhammer. "You'll need backup, going into the woods."

"Stay. Defend Llantry," she says.

Gregor hesitates, and looks at the warhammer, then to her shortsword. "Well, you would do better to carry a silvered, enchanted hammer, than a paltry sword."

Oh no.

No.

"Gregor, you can't -"

"You should take this," he steps forwards and offers the warhammer up to Temple.

Temple raises a hand, declining it. "Burroughmaster," he begins. "We are honoured -"

"I insist," he says. "If you are pursuing my sister, then I will not see you fail. Venalia could charge the weapon, even a little, and it would help a great deal should you come under attack. It has a command word, which summons a charging bull of force -"

"Gregor," she meets his eyes, and shakes her head. "I *cannot* take Minotaur. If I do, terrible things may happen. Do you understand?"

He looks between her and Temple, and walks up, motioning for her to lean down. He brings his mouth to her ear, so that only they may hear.

"Are you leaving?" he asks her, and she can hear his terror.

"Of course not," she hisses. "But in Temple's vision, I have Minotaur. If I avoid taking it, then I make sure that this doesn't end badly. Understand?"

"Ah," he sees sense, and steps back, relieved. "In that case, I may as well hide this blasted thing forever."

"Keep it close," she says. "If you want to be of use, have your men and the villagers scour Llantry for the lance. Bell made it, but it never reached Temple. We'll need it before nightfall."

"As you say, Priestess. We'll find it."

She gives him a nod, and Gregor raises his warhammer in a farewell as the gates creak open for them. Before them, the guards raise their shields. Venalia spares one last look back to see the curious children of Llantry pulled back inside by their parents.

"Good luck, Priestess!" shouts Gregor from atop the gate.

Then the gates shut, and they set out.

Pastures turn to slopes, to frozen muddy paths, to evergreen forests. The snow-dusted pines of Llantry's countryside are home to singing maidens tempting men to their death; snow-spirits who'll freeze the blood in your brain; beasts with trees growing out their backs, who pose as the landscape until they're ready to take their prey.

Venalia shudders in her cloak. Beneath it she wears her thick shirt and plaid riding breeches, her breastplate over the top. It is a style that makes her feel equal parts scoundrel and professional. Utilitarian with some flair. There was a teacher at Whitehallow, a Priestess of the Champion, who explained in no delicate terms to the girls in the class that dresses are lovely, wonderful, comfortable things to wear; but that when trying to ride a horse, when trying to shift your weight in a sword fight, when running to the aid of some poor hurt soul, trousers and sensible shoes will win out every single time.

Context, she had told them, is everything. Do not wear trousers to consult with the local Magister. Do not wear a dress during a dawn raid on a cult. Compromise.

Pretzia walks them at a brisk trot through the low forest branches. Snowfall muffles everything. The birds are silent. The path falls away, leading into unkempt forest hidden under the snow. Without care, the path has become overgrown and hard to find.

"There is little to follow out here," says Temple, his voice low. "What I'm seeing could be tracks. Could be animals. Nothing obvious."

"I see no animals," she whispers.

"They're here. They can sense something is wrong," he whispers back. It still sounds deafening in the silence. "It could be us. It could be something else. Be on your guard; and if I shout *Shield,* you cast it, no questions. Around both of us, if you can."

She nods, and keeps her eyes peeled. It sets her nerves on edge, to watch out for something that could look like anything.

Venalia has a keen eye; and sure enough, her sight darts to every swaying branch and flickering shadow. A Scarling, however, does not move in a predictable manner. It might be invisible, for all she knows. She whispers a prayer to stop her pounding heart from deafening her, and tries to focus.

So far, the bold Priestess of last night has not shown her face; Venalia is shivering with adrenaline.

Temple casts his eyes around. “On a path this unkempt, a track should be obvious.”

“Perhaps she wasn't on the path?”

“Perhaps she couldn't find it,” says Temple. “It would have been dark. We cannot scour the entire forest...”

Temple trails off, and tugs the reins. Pretzia stops suddenly, blowing a burst of hot air out her nostrils. Venalia peers over Pretzia's mane, and feels her gut curdle. Through the soft visual fuzz of the snowfall, there is a shape, unmistakable. A building of some sort, a house, more of a mansion, two stories high.

“What is that?” she asks.

“Do you know of anybody who lives out here?” he whispers.

She shakes her head. “But perhaps Evelyn took shelter here?”

“Maybe. Or this could be the lair of some beast.”

“The Choir?” asks Venalia.

“The Choir did not have an above-ground lair. It already has one in the untouched dark, below the earth. There are other things out here that would take residence in a house of stone. I am certain.”

Something about this does not feel right. “Temple, I lived in Llantry my entire life. I had no idea this was here. Could it be a trap? An illusion?”

“Possibly,” he says, and breathes deeply. “Taste that on the air?”

She extends her tongue and breathes in. Copper, so faint it is barely there, but definitely copper.

“Magic,” she says. “Arcana. We have to go in, don't we?”

“No. We should return.”

“We came this far. We should at least check inside.”

“You think Evelyn is in there?”

“She could be?”

“Is it worth the risk?”

“Yes.”

“Fine. Be silent, and follow me.”

He dismounts Pretzia and drops to the ground like another snowflake, silent.

“I don't like this,” he says, and reaches into the saddlebag. He draws a torch that reeks of pitch, and a wicker match that he lights with a flint and steel. The torch bursts into flame at his touch, warming them both. Snowflakes sizzle as they hit the open flame. He hefts the battleaxe from his kilt sash and holds it ready in one hand, the torch in his other.

“Fire is good. Stay close,” he says. “Always know the closest escape route. If anything goes wrong, get to Pretzia. Do not wait on me.”

“Alright,” she says, and climbs down from the saddle. She wants to add more to the discussion, but this is Temple's domain.

Temple rubs Pretzia's flank, whispering assurances to her, telling her to stay put. He nods to Venalia, and she joins him as they move towards the mansion house. The trees here are snow-covered stumps as they stalk forwards, cut down an age ago.

They kneel at the edge of the clearing.

“No tracks of any kind,” says Temple. “See the doors?”

The building looms above them, a memory of a Magisterial estate house. It seems to have fallen from the sky in the middle of nowhere. She sees no roads or walls, no sign of habitation. The windows are gone, their edges overgrown with fungus.

Venalia walks across the clearing, slow and deliberate, and tests the snow outside the windows. Glass, she notes, crunching beneath the snow.

Something blew the windows out, from the inside.

She continues round the building, where Temple meets her.

The door, which rests atop a dozen stone steps, is ajar. It is half-broken off its hinge, showing them the ruined interior, and another set of once-luxurious stairs with red carpet. She'd expect some sign – one of Evelyn's earrings, perhaps, a spray of blood, a handprint, anything.

Nothing leaps to her attention.

Temple's foot falls upon something solid, covered by the snow, and he stops moving entirely. In a profession where traps and tripwires are not uncommon, Temple is trained to freeze at such sounds.

After a pause, Temple prods the snow with his axe and they both hear the distinctive sound: wood.

He scrapes the snow away, and they see the words written below, revealing what was once a large signpost:

De Witt's Home for Orphaned Children

"Orphanage," whispers Temple.

"I had no idea this was here," she says. "How old do you think it is?"

"No idea," he says. "The wood is rotten, though, grown through with fungus. Look," he points at the lice and insects burrowing into it. "So. That old, at least."

"It's written in the common tongue," she notes. "No strange spellings, no Druidic runes. Proper use of an apostrophe. This is less than fifty years old. Llantry was using Druidic grammar till Marius arrived. Which is to say, no grammar at all."

"Any idea who De Witt is?"

"Sounds like a Magisterial name, but not one that I recognise. De Witt is the family name – the use of '*de*' for '*of*' comes from the Vinyard Confederacy, but it tells us very little. Gregor's name is De Llantry. Marius had the surname De Aria, because his hometown was called Aria. I know of no town called Witt, but those are the conventions."

"Could be anyone then."

They both look up at the mansion, as a long, low groan echoes from its stonework.

"Do you hear that?" asks Temple.

Then follows the rapid click-clack of legs upon stone. Dozens of them.

"Oh, Nine Hells," hisses Temple, and pushes Venalia behind him.

From the upper windows comes crawling creatures, dog-sized and grey as stone. Six legs adjoin a body like a wasp nest, legs straight, like stilts. Their heads resemble human faces, as though inverted and covered in wet cement, mouth stretched open in a noiseless scream.

Scuttling down the walls, the crawlers come fast, flanking then surrounding them. Temple backs them into the clearing, keeping his back to Venalia's.

"Pack tactics," says Venalia. "What do we do?"

"Draw your sword!" he orders.

"What are they?" she asks, fumbling her sword from its scabbard. It shakes in her hand.

Temple throws his lit torch on the ground in front of him. "Scarlings, I think, we – *Shield!*"

Venalia freezes – and the Priestess takes over. The shape of the spell comes without a thought, and divine light ripples around them in a sphere.

The Shield is hit by three streams of acid, one from each side. It hisses and bubbles on the ground where it slides off the Shield. She hesitates to drop the spell, and another spray of acid hits it.

"They're coordinating," she says, waiting for an order.

"Shield down, stay close," he says, and opens his lungs. "Pretzia!"

His horse bursts from the forest, a warrior herself. Pretzia is not here to rescue them; Pretzia is here to fight. Temple barks an order, and Pretzia slams her hooves down upon the closest of the crawlers. It explodes under her weight in a sick spray of blue foam and viscera, cracked like a clay pot.

The crawlers charge them – all but one, that makes an awful belching sound, rearing up on its legs. It sprays a stream boiling, foamy acid at Temple

Too far away for her to Shield him.

"Temple!" she shouts in warning, and he spins on his heel.

Temple is far faster than a man his size has the right to be. He rolls under the spray, coming up with the battle-axe raised high. With a warriors' roar he throws it over-hand. The axe splits the crawler down the middle, spilling its boiling blood across the snow.

Temple's skin is smoking in places, black dots spreading across his face. He curses and wipes his skin on his sleeve as he sprints for the axe – but Venalia is closer.

She runs for the axe, but the remaining four crawlers are upon her, brandishing their front legs, the shell peeled back to reveal barbs dripping with venom.

Venalia wants to flee, to cower, but Temple needs a few seconds to get the axe and come to her side. Pretzia is charging from her flank, but will not arrive in time.

She is on her own.

The crawler rushes for her legs, barbs raised.

The Priestess steps back into a duellist's stance. Muscle memory takes over, and she holds her shortsword with two hands by her cheek, aiming the point, turning her body side on to minimise herself as a target.

The crawler rears up, bringing it to chest height, where it brandishes its stings. Venalia lunges with a roar, and jams the short blade into the creature's shell where it meets the head, sinking it to the hilt.

Locked together now, the creature rasps from its oddly human mouth. Venalia cannot get the sword free. The crawler coils one of its stingers, and she feels it impact her chest with a cold shock.

It finds only the steel of her breastplate.

Venalia wrenches the sword from the creature's neck and stumbles backwards as it thrashes its barbs, searching blind for her skin. It collapses, thrashing, boiling its head in its own acidic blood.

The other three crawlers advance as one; she cannot fight three of them. Barbs raised, jaws unhinged from grey screaming faces, acid boiling in their throats. She hears herself making the panicked noises of a child.

They are upon her when, from her flanks, come Temple and Pretzia. A crawler's barbs catch on Pretzia's barding, before it is mashed to pieces beneath her plated hooves.

Temple swings the axe like an artist. The first blow comes up from the ground, striking a crawler and carrying it into the air, dashing it against a tree trunk on the other side of the clearing. It screeches as it flies past Venalia.

A spray of acid comes his way, and Temple pirouettes with his own momentum, spinning under it and landing on his knee, the axe having bisected the offending crawler.

The last one leaps for him, barbs raised, and Temple jabs it in the chest with his axe, driving it over and onto its back. The haft of the axe is longer than the crawler's arms, and so he stands above it, pinning it to the ground.

"Priestess," he says, catching his breath. "If you'd like to study one of these things, now is -"

Pretzia whinnies a war cry and smashes her hoof upon the creature again, and again, and again. Temple, his eyes closed, sighs.

"I cannot fault her training."

Venalia is yet to say a thing. She stands under the falling snow as the earth around her boils from the spilled blood of these creatures.

Hyperventilating. Shaking. Her eyes are pinpricks, focused on the creatures and their bubbling remains.

Temple is at her side. He reaches into her satchel for her, recognising the vacant stare of a post-combat adrenaline crash. He hands her one of her mixtures and she drinks it without question.

When it is done, she closes her eyes, begins to breathe, and then sits down on the tree stump.

"You good?" he asks.

She struggles to place the shortsword in its scabbard. Temple grants her the time without a word, and after calming herself, she manages it. Venalia holds out her trembling hands. With every breath, she steadies them a little more.

“I'm good,” she says. The black spots on his face bring her to her feet in a panic. “Gods above, Temple, you're hurt!”

“Just a little acid, I'm fine.”

“Let me Heal you before that scars permanently.”

“Don't knock yourself out,” he says. Though the fight is over, she sees his eyes remain alert. Temple drops to one knee, offering a bared forearm upon which she lays her hands.

She cannot find the centre required to cast, so violent is the shaking in her hands.

“Scarlings,” says Temple, distracting her. “You did well.”

“Thanks. So did you.”

He laughs. “Was that your first kill?”

“Did I kill it?”

Temple looks over at the crawler. Its head has long since fallen from its body, the tissue corroded by the acid. “I think you killed it.”

“I mean, how many other insects have I killed in my life, right?”

“They are not insects. Those are Scarlings. Aberrations.”

That word again. Another word for *things gone wrong*.

“Okay,” she takes a breath, her hands and her mind calmer now. “Ready?”

He nods, and she forms the shapes of a Heal spell in her mind, layering shapes upon frequencies until it begins to sing. She harmonises with the song she feels within Temple. As they hum together, she begins to pass energy into his body. Acid-burned skin begins to knit itself back together, and in this state she can feel the hundred tiny burns across his body that he has received.

When she releases her hold, her head feels remarkably clear.

“You good?” asks Temple.

“I am,” she says.

“Drink another mixture anyway.”

She does not argue, but takes another bottle from her bag and tips it into her mouth. Fruit, alcohol, sugar. Atop an adrenaline rush. She finds herself shaking again – this time with impatient energy.

“Now I'm good,” she says, looking at the slaughtered crawlers.

“Then we shall return to Llantry?” asks Temple.

She looks up at him, her excitement snapping to anger. “Return?”

“To Llantry.”

“But Evelyn might be here!”

His eyebrows tell her that he is, if nothing else, impressed by her commitment.

“There could be more of them inside?” he says. “Evelyn would not have survived them.”

“Then we find proof of death.”

“You are sure?”

Venalia fights the urge to throw up, and stands. Queasy, unsteady, she holds onto Temple for a moment before she can continue.

“I am sure,” she says, and begins walking towards the door.

Temple stands on the opposite side of the door, his axe ready. The metal of the blade is cracked by the crawler's acid, just like her shortsword. It trembles in her hand still, despite having tasted blood.

“Venalia?”

It snaps her to attention. “Temple?”

“Look at the stairs.”

Once wooden frame on stone, all that remains is a blackened skeleton of the stairwell. The stonework is blackened and cracked.

“What do you think did that?” she asks.

“I do not know,” he says. “Nothing mundane. Smells arcane. Casters?”

“Do you think they're still here?”

“Always assume the worst. Do you feel that? The hairs on your neck standing up?”

“Aye.”

“Always trust that feeling,” he says, and begins walking towards the doors. “Assume danger. Always assume danger.”

Temple holds his axe ready as he approaches. Venalia readies her new spell, Hold, and tries to keep the shapes in her mind as she follows Temple's flaming torch.

He enters first with axe, side-stepping in and spinning to clear both sides of the wall. In comparison to his graceful, well-practised technique, Venalia shuffles through the door. She has one eye half-shut in concentration.

“Venalia,” hisses Temple.

“What?” she manages.

“Were you not taught to check for tripwires? Traps?”

She curses. Of course she is trained to look out for traps; but she was concentrating on her Hold spell, and trying to keep it ready. This is the kind of thing a Priestess should really be able to do: concentrate on a spell, and still act out their training properly.

“Sorry,” she whispers, bowing her head.

“Follow my lead,” he says, and they begin to clear the building.

The atrium is overgrown with weeds and fungi. Spores hang heavy in the air, caught in light beams from broken skylights.

Doors lead to the East and West wings of the ground floor, symmetrical with the upper level. The doors to each wing have been blown off the hinges and lie rotting on the grassy carpet.

“Something exploded in here,” she says. “A long time ago. Probably the same thing that burned into the wood and stone.”

“Aye,” mutters Temple, and uses the axe to pry a rotten door from the forested carpet. Centipedes and beetles swarm out as he lifts it. Venalia recoils and lifts one foot off the ground, stifles a scream, and freezes in shame. She lowers her foot, apologising.

"Insects?" asks Temple.

"I know, I know. It's a thing. Bad memories."

She expects disappointment or condescension, but he merely shrugs and laughs to himself.

"We all have something."

"Yeah? What's yours?"

"Deep water," he tells her. "Never been on a boat."

"Really? You seem so well travelled."

"I am. Roads, horses, airships. Never boats. Hate boats."

"No worse than insects," she concedes.

Temple looks under the door, and heaves it up with two hands, turning it over.

East Wing, Lower: Children's Rooms

"What do the others say?" asks Venalia. Together, they turn the doors over:

Common Rooms - Kitchen

Classrooms

Research - Basement

Venalia lets out a tense sigh at the last one.

"Yeah, I was afraid it would say something like that," she complains. "Common rooms, classrooms, children's rooms. Great. Fine. Then the we get *Research Basement*. You know, I read a book like this once?"

"You talk when you're nervous," whispers Temple. "Control it."

She nods, but everything is an effort to hide her trembling. Her heart is pounding in her ears despite years of training for this.

Venalia runs her hands through her hair, giving up on the spell she was trying to hold. She feels herself unravelling, feels the fear getting the better of her. Her heart is beating faster, running away from her.

Temple kneels down, meeting her at head height.

“Venalia?”

She winces. “I know, I know. Sorry. I'm trying to calm down.”

“Venalia, breathe,” he orders her. “Three seconds in. Three seconds out.”

She obeys, feels her body relax as she focuses on the counting. Thirty seconds and ten breaths later, and her mind starts to slow down.

“Good?” he asks, seeing the relief on her face. “Every time you need to take a rest, you tell me. Yes?”

“We really don't have time for that,” she protests. “Sorry, I'm supposed to be trained, and -”

“Focus, Priestess.”

“I know. I know.”

She casts her gaze around the atrium, trying to be useful, taking note of the stranger details. She looks for what is there; she looks for what is *not* there.

“There are no lights,” she notes.

“Shattered,” says Temple. “Probably by whatever exploded here.”

“Magic?”

“You tell me.”

Venalia looks at the light fittings, and finds shards of crystalline on the ground nearby, drained and grey, just like the dull neon crystalline on Gregor's warhammer. Magical, at one time. Defunct now.

“Lady Altheim is reclaiming this place”, she says, leading Temple's attention to the fungus in the walls, the skittering insects making their home among the wreckage. Fungal blooms break through the wallpaper, drawing her eye. It has ripped the wooden walls apart, burst out of the seams, staining a bright, vivid blue, fading to grey at the edges, like a map of ocean coral. "Look at this."

"What is it?"

"I think I recognise this kind of mushroom," she answers, trawling through her memories of classes and botany. "These can tell us something, at least. Watch."

Venalia casts a spell of Light from her hand, illuminating the atrium and casting long shadows against the stairs. When the light dissipates, the mushrooms are swelling, growing in size.

Feeding.

"Muskaria Arcanum," she turns to Temple, grinning, massively impressed with herself. "They grow in basements in Whitehallow all the time. They're all over Altheim, barely anybody notices them."

"What *are* they?"

"Fungus that feeds off of magical energy. They feed off of the latent wild magic in the world. They were once used for making potions for Magisters, to restore their energy," she explains, tapping the satchel of sugar-drinks that she carries. "Over their life they build up a huge deposit of arcane energies."

"They are not used any more?"

"Well, they're almost lethally toxic, so if you get the balance wrong with your base and your acid then you'll die in agony; plus they cause hallucinations, waking dreams, sleepless nights, personality changes -"

"Ah," nods Temple. "So their presence here means, what? Somebody cast magic nearby?"

"The opposite. This tells me that the Choir hasn't been here, at the very least."

Temple is attentive now. "How so?"

"It's a Magisterial construct. Arcane in nature. When it's close, I can taste the copper."

"As can I," he nods.

"Muskaria Arcanum feeds off of that same energy. If the

Choir had passed by here, these mushrooms would have been swollen and blue when we found them. See what my little Light spell did to them?"

"You got all of that information from a mushroom in the wall?"

"I'm a Priestess of Knowledge," she grins. "Knowing weird and specific stuff like this is my calling." The smile fades. "Tells us little else, though. No sign of Evelyn. Shame. I'd like to take a look around. This place is full of mystery."

"It isn't going anywhere," he says. "Investigate it later. Let us return to Llantry."

She looks around the atrium again, thinking. This place is unknown to her, despite spending most of her life in Llantry. She cannot help but feel drawn to investigate it.

Did Evelyn pass through here?

Did Anabel?

"There's more to this place than meets the eye," she muses. "I'm sure of it."

"We don't have time to waste, Venalia." Temple points outside, where the sky is dark grey through the thick snowfall. A storm is rolling in, shortening the sun's reign.

"This isn't just about the Choir, Temple," she says. "Or even Evelyn. Something has been happening to Llantry for generations. Children going missing. Children being sent away. It's connected, I just don't know how. I *have* to look about, Temple."

He grimaces, obviously debating if he should make it an order. He sees the pleading in her face, and relents.

"Be quick," he sighs.

"Thank you," she whispers.

The tension around the place leans in heavy as the two of them ascend the stairs, starting at the top.

She heads first to the classrooms of the Upper East Wing.

Wooden hallways, blackened and burned through. On the

walls are yellow, rotten parchments, peeling like scabs. Tapestries displaying the alphabet in common, then the alphabet in Druidic runes.

Stranger is the tapestry of an alphabet that Venalia recognises. Draconic – the language of the Magistry, of arcane magic, the magic gifted to mortals by Draconic blood.

The Draconic blood that makes some children Aberrant.

"Now why would an orphanage be teaching Draconic?" she asks the wind.

Because they are teaching orphans of the Magistry. Maybe not even orphans, she reasons. Perhaps this is where Gregor's ancestors were all sent, one generation after another, when their Aberrant blood presented itself.

"This is all related, isn't it?" she asks Temple.

"I couldn't say, Priestess," he sighs.

There are lessons on the chalkboard, weathered by time but still readable. It throws her back to Whitehallow, to the scrape of chalk on slate and the sun through the window.

She misses it, she realises, but that ship has sailed. The next time she is in a classroom, it should be to teach.

Returning to the atrium, Venalia heads for the Upper Western Wing: the common rooms and kitchen.

"The stove dates the place," she says. "Modern coal-fired model. The place might be hundreds of years old, but that stove says the last fifty years."

"There are no knives," says Temple. "Only blunt cutlery. Look."

Impressive observation, she thinks. "That's alarming."

At the back of the kitchen is a heavy iron door with a lever to open it. Out of curiosity, Venalia cranks the lever against the rust. Her wiry arms bulge with all of her strength, but it will not move.

"Allow me," says Temple. "Stand well back."

Temple pulls hard enough to shatter the rust, and tears the door from the rotten brickwork.

When the dust clears, three humanoids stare back at them. Temple whips the axe up. Venalia recoils, tripping, and clamps her hand over her mouth to avoid screaming. Once her heart and breath have calmed, she gets up from the floor and peers closer. Temple puts a hand up, telling her to stop.

Once it is clear that the shapes are dead bodies, he allows her in.

Venalia has seen bodies before. Autopsy and funeral, cremation and anatomy, medicine and surgery; all require dead bodies, donated to the temples, for practice. Those cadavers had their faces covered out of respect, and now she sees why.

Time has not been kind to this trio, but the cold, sealed room has preserved them. Mostly skeletal. No eyes left, skin pulled tight like wax paper over their bones. Like old leather.

They rest amongst a few boxes of food, broken open, now empty. These people starved, and the door kept the vermin from them.

“Door wouldn't open from inside,” says Temple, examining the handle and lock.

It strikes her with feeling of suffocation, immediate and violent, and she shakes her head.

“Why would you lock yourself in?”

“Starving to death was better than whatever was on the other side,” says Temple. “Maybe they hoped for rescue.”

“This was a refrigeration room,” she says. “They would have had enough food – but with no water... it probably took them days to die. They look about my age.”

Two boys, one girl. They are wrapped together for warmth. She hopes that the cold put them to sleep, before thirst claimed them.

Venalia draws her shortsword, and finds her hands steady now. As a coroner might, she uses the blade to move the largest male's head to the side.

A centipede skitters from inside his mouth and she jerks away in terror, cursing. The other side of his face has not rotted nearly as much, for one good reason:

He has a patch of scaly skin, like a lizard – or a dragon.

"Aberrant dragonblood," she whispers. "I *knew* it."

"Like Gregor's ancestors?" asks Temple, stepping forward.

"Exactly."

She checks the others. The male with clasped hands is next; she pries the fingers apart with the shortsword and finds long, gnarled claws. The small girl, she pulls forward to find the rotten stubs of useless, frail wings at her back.

"Who were you?" she asks, not expecting an answer. "How many of you are related to Gregor, I wonder?"

A thought crosses her mind – that the girl may be Anabel de Llantry – but she is far too young, and shares no features with Anabel.

Venalia looks over her shoulder suddenly, startling Temple – the breeze through the shattered windows is making strange, groaning sounds, unnerving her.

"Just the wind, Priestess," he says, raising his axe. "Fear not."

She shakes it off. "Sorry. I'm a bit of a mess today. Common rooms next."

This time, Temple does not protest; he seems as curious as she is.

The common rooms are a graveyard.

No bodies this time, just bones.

"People were blown apart," she says. "By the Gods; some of these bones have ended up in the *ceiling*."

Venalia closes her eyes and whispers a prayer to the Open Door, black-veiled Goddess of death and journeys. She will not hear Venalia, but she hopes that these souls made it across the Black Sands, to wherever and whoever they sought. When she opens her eyes again, Temple is crouched by a ribcage, watching it.

"Ever seen anything like this before?" she asks Temple.

He nods, walking among the bodies in silence. “Aftermath of a battle. A Magister can do this kind of thing, in a fight. This was violence.”

“What do you think?”

“Orphans of Magisterial shame,” he grimaces. “One of them murdered everyone? This place wasn't meant to be found. That's what I think. You?”

“Agree. A fireball, or similar spell. It would have be extremely powerful though, cast from a staff or a crystal, definitely.”

“So a young Magister,” he says. “Aberrant. Sent away. Gave in to the dragon.” Temple claps his hands together. “Well. That's something to look into after we kill the Choir. Speaking of -”

“Just a little longer Temple,” she says. “Something important happened here. It's my job to unearth these things.”

He purses his lips and gives a stern nod, and they return to the atrium.

The children's rooms remain, and the *research basement.*

She tries the children's rooms.

Every door is gone. The rooms have been upended, beds tipped and drawers torn open, as though somebody has searched through them looking for something.

“Wonder if they found whatever they were looking for?” she asks herself out loud. The rooms each look to have slept six people. Three rooms; population of eighteen orphans, roughly. Families from across Altheim probably sent children here, to the far reaches of the North, where nobody would find them.

“Could have been scavengers, long after?” suggests Temple.

There are paintings that have been torn apart. Not with flame or time or nature, but with claws.

“This looks deliberate,” she notes.

In another room she finds a larger painting, ripped from the frame and scattered. Venalia messes around with it until she can rest it on the floor and spread it out, putting the unburnt pieces back together like a jigsaw within the broken frame.

"Venalia..?" begins Temple. "A search I can oblige, but a *jigsaw* -"

She can sense the light fading outside. "I know, I know," she rushes, putting the jigsaw together finally.

Sixteen people, she sees. Standing for a group portrait – before the time of crystalline image capture. Fifty years, matching her estimate. Fifteen younger looking people, and a single older one, all human – or humanoid, might be some Aelfa, she'd need to see their ears and eyes to tell.

Once they are all together, she realises that their faces have been torn from the picture. This is not random destruction. This is rage, anger, hatred; and perhaps, shame?

"What happened here?" she asks the room. Nothing answers her back.

Venalia returns to the hallway, looking into the darker hall, the last one left unexplored.

Within it is a door to the basement, and the research room. She stares at it for a while, till she realises that she is waiting for Temple to drag her home. He does not. Instead, sensing her unease, he puts a huge hand on her shoulder.

"Your call," he says.

"Damn it," she whispers, and stalks towards it, drawing her shortsword. It feels heavier, badly balanced.

She casts a spell of Light, illuminating the atrium, but something about the inky darkness will not retreat. It resists her. The temperature drops when she crosses the threshold. The wind fades, and everything seems muffled. Behind her, Temple feels miles away.

There are two doors. The first she comes upon is Research, and it has been blown off the hinges. Basement, the second, has not; though the wood has been stripped away by both fire and claw, revealing the heavy metal door beneath.

There is a single keyhole.

Venalia wonders if that is what they were looking for in the bedrooms: a key?

The room marked *Research* lies open to her.

There are no skeletons, bodies, bones, nothing. Just piles of burned papers, wet ash, cracked lead boxes that are now empty, and little else. This was an office, once.

Piles of scrolls and parchment have become piles of blackened ash. She takes the shortsword and pries it between the burned pages, splitting open a fossil of ink and paper.

Venalia sees yellow-white parchment, and cheers for herself. Little has survived – a square inch, perhaps, of a few pages near the centre – but some of it *has* survived.

"We cannot read all of it," says Temple. "We do not have time."

"I won't, I won't," she says, hushing him.

The old thrill hits her; of reading things not meant to be read, of learning secrets not meant to be learned. She takes her time despite Temple's huffing, and spreads the ten little pages out to read them. From going over them sequentially, she pieces together the key words from these research notes, and speaks them aloud.

"Blood. Aberrants. Magisterial orphans, disinherited and disowned, sent away. All to hide the shame of an Aberrant bloodline."

"So?"

"Well this confirms our theory," she announces. "This was a home for Aberrant dragonbloods, those of Magisterial families; to live away from society. It says they used something to alleviate the symptoms." She reads on, pacing around the room, whispering to herself. "... completely presents as human, it says here. As in, lost their Draconic features?"

"A cure for Aberrant dragonbloods?"

"Nothing that worked, it seems," she sighs. "Blood keeps getting mentioned – but surely Magisterial blood is the *problem?* Drawing out of the blood, perhaps? Leeches? Purification?" She reads the pages quickly again, shrugging. "There's no answer. Not written here, at least. But in the basement; the fire might not have reached there. The door seems to have held?"

"Venalia..." Temple is shaking his head. He can read her mind, she feels – he knows what she wants to do. A closed, locked door in a place like this is a red flag, and Venalia is a bull. She *needs* to see what is down there.

Children keep vanishing from Llantry, every generation. Magisterial children. Here is an orphanage for Aberrant Dragonbloods – Magisterial orphans of circumstance.

Anabel de Llantry vanished.

Evelyn de Llantry vanished.

Magisterial children, no matter how weak their bloodline.

It's connected somehow, she *knows it.*

"Priestess, it is time."

"Almost."

She looks at the basement door again, feeling it call to her. It has a story to tell. Claws, she thinks. Claws did most of the damage to the basement door. Flame and claw tried to get in, but for *what?* Surely not a coincidence. Maybe the children were experimented on, she thinks; maybe the tests were harmful or invasive, and they rebelled?

"Can you get this door open?" she asks Temple.

He tries to pry his fingers in the edges, but cannot get any grip. He shrugs, shaking his head, and she begins thinking around the problem.

A Magister would blow the door down, or melt it, transform it, or charm the lock, turn themselves ethereal and walk through it. Venalia can shine a light, shield herself, heal people, and, on a good day, hold somebody in place.

Nothing that opens doors.

"We can come back -" begins Temple.

"Temple," she silences him. "Let me think."

For a while, Venalia leans against the wall and considers the door. Whatever did the damage was obviously looking for the key first, overturning the bedrooms, and failed. She sees no reason that she would do any better. Worse still, maybe some survivors fled to the basement and locked themselves in. Maybe the key is *behind* the door. No sense looking for it, then, when time is of the essence.

A locked door problem. She smiles. Classic. This was a

question in an exam once; lateral thinking. The door is locked. There is no key. How do you get through it.

Easy answer: go around. Find another door. Dig past it. The issue is never the door, she learned – the issue is how much you *know* about the door.

Venalia kneels by the keyhole and summons a small mote of light to her finger, peering inside. It is a generously sized lock, probably with a big key.

If she could pick locks, this might be doable. Sadly, she cannot. Luckily, she has a connection to the God of Knowledge, which comes with distinct, if costly and situational, perks.

Venalia leans back on her knees, breathes deeply, closes her eyes, and says,

"Temple, protect me."

"Venalia, come on -"

"I need to pray."

She falls silent, drops out of the world, and begins to count her breaths.

Physical tension fades as her mind expands to touch the great presence that is always with her. It watches her watching herself. She falls down the rabbit hole in her mind, into the honey-sweet libraries of the Mind's Eye. Faster, this time, she thinks. Practice pays off.

Venalia stands, soul bared, before the great scholar-angels of eternity. Their thousand eyes fall upon her, see within her, and know what she seeks.

Secrets.

Knowledge.

Clues to the missing girls. Research about Aberrant dragonbloods. Magisterial scandal.

Redemption for a great sin.

And it lies behind a door.

Locked. No key.

There is a thousand years of discussion, played out as mind-shattering song, sung into her soul. Then comes an answer.

Temporary mastery of a skill, and the knowledge required to correctly use it, can be gifted to a Priestess of the Mind's Eye. The drain on her body is intense – previous attempts at this have left her semi-conscious, but she has her mixtures in her satchel.

A moment of anxiety follows her back to her body. She gasps as information crystallises in her memories, shocking her awake. She has experiences that are not hers;

Mastery.

Talent.

Her fingers twitch with new movements they were not previously capable of.

Venalia opens her eyes, and a soft Celestial light burns through them, casting a blue glow on the door. On her forehead blazes the light of her third eye, the eye of the soul, through which the locksmith now looks.

Every door looks different through these new eyes. She has an appreciation for the work, the material, the craft. It is not her. The sensation is alien and horrible, as though she is being pushed out of her own mind by somebody else; but she *knows* locks.

Venalia looks again at the lock, fervent with intention, desperate to use these new talents before they wear off. She knows about padlocks, deadbolts, lever handle locks, mortise locks, cams...

This is a door that she can unlock.

"Temple? Dagger, now."

He passes her a blade from his boot, small and thin, like a stiletto, all the while staring at her forehead. Motes of light drift from her third eye, covering her in a dancing cloud of blue fireflies.

She knows he wants to ask about it, but he is giving her the space to work.

Venalia works quickly. She jams the dagger between the door and the wall, using the flat edge to lever against the bolt, working dagger back and forward, back and forward, until she finds the catch.

The next stage requires specific tension, perfect timing and balance, and decades of experience. For the next few minutes,

Venalia has just that. Her hands move in a way that she did not know possible, carried by generations of experts, and she slides the dagger back towards her.

The blade lifts the deadlock, and she uses her free hand to rotate the handle and -

The door creaks open, and she turns to Temple, grinning, blue light flooding from her third eye.

"I'll admit that was well done," says Temple, but his pride turns to concern when he sees her eyes rolling into the back of her head.

Venalia's third eye closes shut with no warning, and she collapses the second the light fades. Temple rushes forward to catch her, cursing. Without needing to be told, Temple finds the vials of caster's mixture and rubs some of it on her parted lips.

Venalia opens her eyes. She clutches her head, groaning like a hungover drunk.

"That was intense," she mumbles, taking the rest of the mixture.

"We really need to get back now," says Temple.

"But the basement -" she begins.

"Quick, then. Do not tarry."

He helps her up. Swaying on her feet, Venalia fills her lungs and prepares herself. She drinks a full jar of one of her mixtures, leaving one for later. The sugar rush hits and she can feel her pulse in her eyeballs.

Darkness beckons on the stairwell. Cold air rushes out.

Venalia looks at the lock. She has no idea what kind of lock it is, nor how she got past it. She whispers a prayer of thanks to the Mind's Eye, and -

- hesitates.

The stairs are stone, cold and solid, but the darkness seems tangible. Venalia edges forwards, listening. No sound, save a heavy, patient silence.

This stone has not seen light in decades, and in that time it has grown lonely, and a little mad. Mortal feet have not tread these stones for too long – they have grown accustomed to the solitude. They do not welcome her. They have forgotten what they are for.

"Temple?"

He has gone pale. Venalia sees the axe in his hand is trembling. He gives her a look, and she understands: the Inverted World felt like this. This is too much for him, to descend once more into the that old, deep, dark.

"If you need me -" he begins.

She shakes her head. For all that he has done for her, she cannot force Temple to do this. The secrets below beckon to her alone.

Venalia summons the light in her hand, breathes to calm herself, and steps into the darkness.

"Be quick," he says.

Then the sound of the world fades entirely, and Venalia is alone in the darkness.

Chapter Eleven

From her hand comes soft light, searching across the basement. Venalia jumps in fright when she illuminates a skeletal body, resting in a lounge chair, grinning.

The skeleton is alone, wearing the last decayed remains of a green dress, with wild white hair exploding out of the scalp. A woman, with a note crumpled in one bony hand. Venalia groans, realising what must be done.

"Eye watch me," she whispers as she approaches. "Eye keep me."

She prepares a Shield spell in her head, and tries to snatch the note; but the skeleton does not want to part with it. Venalia grits her teeth, and pries apart the stiff fingers, taking the note at last.

There sits a single, large machine in the corner, attached to a dentist's chair. At least, that's what it looks like. It has straps, and a muzzled headguard that would fit a human.

The walls are covered in tapestry, paintings, charts. A chalkboard covered in equations, written in Draconic numerals.

"Venalia?" comes a muffled shout from above.

"I'm fine," she shouts back. "I've found a note."

"What does it say?"

Venalia eases the note open, and reads it aloud by her own Light, for Temple's ears:

I pray now, only that the Gods accept my apologies, for that is all I can offer.

Belereon de Llantry has began calling himself the Red Terror, after his ultimate progenitor. We should never have tried the transfusions. He has developed a taste for it.

The blood reversed the Aberrant mutation for awhile, but it seems that it ultimately strengthens the Draconic mutation, and with it, the Draconic identity.

The method is a failure. The mansion is aflame. Gods preserve me. Gods forgive me. I never meant for this.

The children tried to stop him.

Now I hear him clawing at the door, screaming my name.

I thought myself a pioneer of the arcane medicines, like my father; but time has proven me a coward again. The Red Terror knows that I am a Magistress. He wants to use me for my blood. For another transfusion.

I deny him this, even though it means my death. I will wait for him, on the Black Sands, until he has been held to account.

This is my dying promise.

Magistress Catherine De Witt, 6th of Heimalkaa, 2181pD

"Gods above," whispers Venalia, looking again at the skeleton of Catherine De Witt. "Belereon de Llantry. Gregor's family."

She hasn't considered the date in a few days now, but by her own estimation it is the 2nd of Heimalkaa, the last month of the year, the first month of winter, in the year 2221pD; post-Dragonfall.

"Forty years ago, almost to the day," she shouts to Temple. "That means that Belereon de Llantry was born perhaps sixty years ago. Gregor's grandfather, or a great uncle perhaps. Sent away at a young age. Gregor probably never met him. I have to ask him."

"All the more reason to head back then," says Temple.

Venalia knows that he is correct – but she cannot shake the feeling that she is missing something. She talks herself through her findings to stall Temple, searching the room with her eyes for more clues.

"This woman is a Magistress, she was trying to find a way to reverse the physical mutations that Aberrant dragonbloods experience, via some kind of blood transfusion." Venalia regards the obvious machine by the chair, with its empty bags, pumps and needles. "Magisterial blood. This is where the transfusions happened, I imagine."

The note says that the transfusions strengthened the Draconic personality; *the dragon comes out.*

"He's calling himself the Red Terror," she whispers, reading from the note again. "Whoever did this, that's the name that he chose."

The Red Terror. Emperor. Warlord.

Karak, the Red King of Dragonkind.

Emperor of Altheim, a very long time ago.

The most feared of all dragonkind were the children of Karak.

Red dragons. Fire-breathers.

They said that Karak's flames could melt stone in seconds. It was he who led the Draconic invasion of Altheim. He who ruled for thousands of years.

He whose fallen body became Brokenscale Keep, where the Magistry erected their palace on his indestructible bones.

Through this lens, the scenes upstairs make sense. The other children tried to stop him. The explosions were the breath of this *Red Terror*.

She has her answers.

She knows what happened here.

And yet, nothing has been answered at all.

An Aberrant dragonblooded child wiped out the orphanage, the treatment failed.

So what became of Anabel de Llantry? Where is Evelyn? What does this have to do with Gregor's family? What of the Choir? Is *any* of this linked?

Venalia has all the pieces, but she cannot see how they connect.

The skeleton of Catherine De Witt watches her wander the tomb.

"Priestess," begins Temple, and she holds her hands up.

"I'm done." Nothing else to see. She turns to the skeleton and addresses it. "I'll be back when this is over. You'll all be buried. Then I'll find out what happened to this boy, to the Red Terror – I'll bring him to justice if he lives still. You have my word, as a Priestess of the Mind's Eye."

She takes one last look at the skeleton before she leaves. It stares back, eyeless, grinning, as though it knows something Venalia does not.

She walks out into the freezing snowfall again, and Temple helps her onto Pretzia's back.

"I hope that was worth it," he says. "We have one, maybe two hours before nightfall. I hope they found the lance."

"Let us make haste," she says as he climbs atop the saddle.

"Finally."

Temple spurs the horse on, and Pretzia rushes at the treeline.

Llantry looms through the snowfall, and Venalia breathes a sigh of relief. The chimneys are smoking, the windows are warmly lit. Temple says nothing as Pretzia carries them to the palisade, and gradually comes to a stop.

The gates remain closed. No guard meets them.

No watchmen.

“Guards?” she shouts.

No response. Temple draws his axe.

“Where is everyone?” she asks.

Temple leaps from Pretzia's back without a word. Venalia's heart stops cold.

Temple charges the gates shoulder first and bursts through like a battering ram. The wood clatters, the gates open, and Venalia leaps to the snow.

“No, no, no,” she mutters as she rushes across the frozen mud to the village centre, ignoring Temple as he shouts after her. “Gregor?” she shouts. “Bell?”

Doors lie open, fires still burning in their hearths. Tools lay where they were dropped. Snowfall coats the village in a blanket of silence.

Nobody.

“But it doesn't -” she begins. “It doesn't attack during the day.”

Temple curses, leaning on his knees. He looks up at the sky. The sun is not shining. The snowfall is thick enough to block it.

He dashes to the forge first, and Venalia hears him overturning chests and tables. He slams through doors, searching, before stumbling back on to the square.

Across his shoulders, he carries the twenty foot lance, a sparkling star of silver atop its point.

“Is that it?” she whispers.

“There's nothing more we can do,” he says, joining her, his shoulders heavy.

“No, I mean; is that it? Is it over? Did we lose?”

Temple says nothing, but he bows his head.

Venalia feels the weight of her failure well up in her chest, so heavy that it buckles her legs and brings her to her knees. She clutches her sigil of the Eye out of reflex, but no spark of inspiration comes to her. No tears come this time. There is too much to feel, too much to handle.

Temple appears in front of her, kneeling, hands on her

shoulders. She can see in his old, hollowed eyes that he knows this feeling well.

"I am sorry, Priestess," he says. "I am sorry. This is how it happens."

She tries to talk, and it feels like her throat is wrapped in tight metal bands. When she gets the first word out, the spell is broken and tears stream from her cheeks. Her entire body shakes as Temple holds her in an embrace. She is a child again.

"Did you know? That it would go this way?"

"Everybody asks that; I swear, I did not."

"I thought -" she tries to speak into Temple's shoulder, hanging from him on weak arms. "I really thought we were going to make it, Temple, I *really* thought we could do this."

"We did everything that we could."

"We didn't though, we didn't, this is my fault. We failed, everyone is gone, I promised I would protect them Temple, I -"

He leans back, looking her in the eye. "I know."

She shoves him back, angry now. "You *don't* know, Temple, this is my *home,* these people were depending on *me*."

"Priestess," he says, calm and cold. "Venalia. Look at me." She meets his eyes and some of the fury leaves her. "You know I'm no stranger to loss."

"I know, I know, I'm sorry, I just -"

"Apologies have no place here," he soothes her. "We lost this one. We did our best. We did everything *right*. Everything by the book. And we lost. We were lucky to survive. Sometimes that's just how these things go."

She nods, despite disagreeing down to her very soul with his words.

Every time she thinks the tears have abated, they come anew, stronger, racking her whole body. The images are coming now too, thoughts of everybody merging into the Choir, becoming a shade under the Tall Woman, screaming for help, looking for her and Temple in vain, their body consumed, their souls locked away in aching loneliness forever.

And cold.

So cold.

"What do we do?" she manages.

"We've lost Llantry," he says. "But maybe we can still save Atlan, aye? The Choir will be busy now, it'll be distracted."

"While it feeds," she says.

"Yes. It will go down below, to the Inverted World, and feed. It'll leave the road clear. We have a window, however small, to get ahead of it. We need to warn the Magistry, in Atlan. It's their problem now."

It feels like a shameful weight off of her chest – to admit defeat.

"This is too big for us now, isn't it?"

"I think that it always was, Venalia," he nods sadly. "My team couldn't beat it. Magistry's bloody mess –" he spits. "It should have been them cleaning it up from the start."

She wipes her eyes and nods, accepting what he says. "We have to go to Atlan?"

"Immediately."

Venalia breathes, but every time she tries to summon any strength or courage, it drifts away with the snow.

Llantry is dead.

Bell, who brought her here when she was orphaned, who thought her his niece, is gone.

Gregor will never show her if he is capable of being more than a petty child.

She realises now how young and petty she was when she arrived. The years at Whitehallow taught her much, but she never did let go of her childhood. They were all young, too young to know.

She will never, now, make up for what she did to Gregor's sister. She will never thank Bell for everything that he did for her.

All for nought.

Wherever Evelyn de Llantry has gone, she will remain. Buried somewhere in history along with the other unsolved mysteries of Llantry, beside Venalia's parents.

“I told Gregor I would solve this,” she whispers.

She feels, more than anything, like a liar and a fool. A part of her wants to find the Choir now, and throw herself into it. To join her people and go together to a fate worse than death. Then, at least, none of them will be alone.

Temple ties the lance to Pretzia's side, then offers Venalia his hand, but she can barely stand.

“Come on, Priestess,” he says. “The fight isn't over.”

She manages to lift a hand, and Temple heaves her to her feet. He helps her onto Pretzia. Venalia moves in a trance, dazed and only half-aware of what is happening.

They pass by empty houses, tools dropped on the road when the singing started.

The square. The Minotaur, the clock tower, the tiny shrine to the All Faith. There are still flowers for Evelyn.

Her house; her home.

Then the Southern gate, where the blackened earth of the oil-crater greets them.

Then they are gone.

The path ahead is trampled snow, hundreds of footprints leading South.

The buck and sway of Pretzia's body sends Venalia into a trance. Snow melts on her unmoving face.

As though reading her mind, Temple speaks.

“Do you feel like you should be with them?” he asks.

“I do,” she says. “I should have been there.”

“And perished alongside them.”

“Yes.”

He nods. “Anybody who survives something. We all feel that way.”

“Even you?”

"Even me," he says. "This is not my first time."

"What..." she tries to ask a question, but it takes her a while to realise what exactly she wants to say. "What do you *do?*"

"What do you mean?"

"When does it stop feeling like this?"

"When does it stop?" he asks. "It doesn't – not really. If you hit a tree with an axe, it'll always carry that wound; but the tree keeps growing. Eventually it'll grow so big, that the scar isn't visible. But it is still there."

"That's it? You just... keep going?"

"Exactly."

"How? I want to lie down in the snow and stop thinking. I'm exhausted, Temple. My chest feels like it's going to explode; like I'll never *relax* ever again."

"You need a good *why*. A reason to fight on."

"What was yours?"

"The first time? To honour them. My unit faced a battle-mage in open combat. Are you familiar with battle-mages, Venalia?"

Fourth year. Advanced tactics and warfare. Lesson one; if you find yourself against a battle-mage, reconsider how you got yourself into this situation and then, preferably, go back in time and change those decisions. If this is not possible, the lecturer had joked, then attempt extraction by any means necessary. Focus on defence.

Run.

"I am familiar," she says.

"We did not take them by surprise. We had little ranged weaponry. We were caught flat-footed. Getting close to her wiped us out. It was complete luck, Venalia, that I was not vaporised with the rest of my unit."

"Were you victorious?"

"Define victory, and I'll tell you," he scoffs. "I took her down. We lost nineteen. Everyone except me. Biggest target on the field, and she misses me alone. Fighters I had known for years;

bled with, drank with, lived with. Brothers and sisters, all of us. I don't know that I'd call that a victory. General certainly did; nineteen fighters is a cheap price to pay for one battle-mage. I was given a medal. Because I was lucky enough to survive."

"So what kept you going?"

"Spite. Their memory. Nobody gave *them* any medals."

"I don't know that this helps me any Temple," she sighs. "But thank you."

"Doesn't have to help you," he says. "Sometimes it's enough to know that you aren't the only sole survivor in Altheim. After the first time, you get... numb."

"Gods above, Temple. You've went through this... how many times?"

"Four, now. It's part of the job. Sometimes you win. Sometimes you lose. A mercenary understands this. They have to."

"So what keeps you going now?"

"Now?" he bursts into dark laughter, with no humour to it. "Curiosity."

"What?"

"I want to know what happens in the end. I am tired of this cycle; but I am almost at its end, I feel."

"That's what I have to look forward to," says Venalia. "If I become a mercenary, that'll be me. Maybe we get a team, make friends, maybe grow into this huge operation – then they all die. Oh, except for me if I'm lucky. If I'm lucky, I end up like you, for the rest of my life."

Temple shuffles and looks down at her in concern. Venalia is staring into the snow, detached and dejected, a picture of melancholy.

"At least I'll be rich," says Venalia, barking a bitter laugh. "You know, when I graduated, I wasn't sure what I wanted to do. I thought maybe I could help people somehow – but this life, being a mercenary, it's not really *for* people like me, is it?"

"I don't know," he says. "There's a reason most Priests *aren't* mercenaries. Sometimes a free company needs someone like you."

"I don't know if somebody with any empathy can do this, Temple."

"I have empathy," he shrugs. "Otherwise I'd become a bandit and rob people. Money isn't *all* there is. You get to make a difference. Some of the time."

"And sometimes, you bury all your friends."

Temple nods, and the pair fall silent again.

Venalia thinks about Marius; a life spent helping a tiny village to be better people. Marius had been a mercenary for a short while; travelling, performing, getting a taste of the high life. Venalia wonders if maybe this is her taste, her one little experience with the horrors of the world, before she retreats to a library somewhere and spends the rest of her days studying old scrolls.

Maybe this is what Marius wanted her to see – to walk his path for a little while, and see the joys of being a small village's Priestess. Would it be such a bad life? She felt *good* when she was healing people, teaching them, leading them through hard times. It felt fulfilling. Does she need anything more than to serve her God, teach her people, and keep a village safe?

It is her watcher, the eye within her mind, that answers her.

First, it tells her that she knows fine well that she would be bored after a couple of months. It is not adventure that she craves, but knowledge and secrets. She wants to *see* Altheim, to learn everything about it.

It also reminds her that her chance to be a small village Priestess vanished along with the *village she would have worked in*.

She becomes acutely aware of the life before her. It seems so clear to her now, as though the Mind's Eye has allowed her a glimpse of the future. There are roads in front of her, each different in subtle ways, the same to an untrained eye. She has been taught not to disregard these moments, but to embrace them. She wonders if this is how Temple sees the world. As potential futures, fading as he passes by the choices that would make them.

Down one path, she sees herself living as a mercenary. She sees herself losing people, hurting people, losing herself. She dies a meaningless death in a ditch somewhere with a knife in her stomach, her magic exhausted. She realises, as she dies, that she has chosen the wrong path. She has done nothing – made the world worse, if anything. When she crosses the Black Sands with Marius at her side, he is awkward and silent, trying to hide his disappointment, and she walks on alone, for she barely remembers him.

Down another path, she finds work as a scholar and delves into ancient ruins with her team, studies the Giants and their civilisation, publishes papers that get her requested for lectures across Altheim. She uses her money and status to travel and see the world, and she cannot rest. Llantry haunts her forever. She cannot stop working, because when she does, the memories come back. She never really moves on, never leaves Llantry. She spends the rest of her life fostering a troubling alcohol habit to quiet her mind, people whisper their concern for her, and she gradually fades away. On her deathbed, with a handful of people around her, she realises too late that her life has been an attempt to forget this one event.

Venalia falls into a deep silence, caught between a dozen awful futures.

"Time to be silent," says Temple, snapping her out of it. "We're close."

"To what?" she looks up, around at the forest.

"The entryway to the Inverted World."

"Oh," she whispers. "Do you think it'll be nearby?"

"I doubt it. We'd hear the singing."

Her eyes track the ground, the trees that press in upon the pathway. A glint in the snowfall catches Venalia's eye, and as they trot past it, she sees what it is.

Her heart jumps from her chest.

"Temple, stop, stop, let me down -"

"Venalia -"

He protests, but Venalia leaps from Pretzia's back and tumbles to the ground, rolling, righting herself and sprinting to the tree line.

"Venalia!" he hisses after her, leaping down from Pretzia and giving chase.

When he catches up, she is standing knee deep in the snow, looking at the haft of a weapon sticking from the snow.

The handle is inlaid with crystalline, dull neon, out of charge.

She wraps her hands around it as he shouts,

"Venalia, *no* -"

Too late. She lifts the handle and reveals Gregor's symbolic warhammer, *Minotaur,* the Hammer of Llantry. Snow falls off as she raises it, eyes wide.

Venalia recalls the experience of being under the thrall of the Choir. She remembers the sporadic returns to consciousness, the realisation that she was being controlled. There are brief windows of self awareness, she remembers, when she was able to exert control.

What would she do, she thinks, if she were Gregor?

Leave a trail. Let the Priestess find it.

Temple closes his eyes. He knows this scene, he has watched it before. Venalia realises it herself when she sees his face.

"Oh," she whispers, holding the warhammer below the pine trees, as snow falls upon her. A break in the clouds bathes them in daylight, however briefly. "Oh no."

"This is how it happens," Temple says, deflating.

"This is how it happens," she echoes.

Suddenly there is another path before her, and it is too terrifying to look directly at, but it *feels right.* In each of her futures, she forgoes her duty, she leaves her people to die. She breaks the first rule.

What if she didn't?

What if she settled this matter now, for better or worse? What if she took her vows seriously, and greeted whatever ending came to her with open arms?

"I have to go after them," she whispers, looking up at Temple.

"No," he says. "You don't have to. You can come with me right now. We can ride away."

"Temple, they were alive, right here," she whispers. "It's taken them below, hasn't it? It won't feed up here – it needs to feel safe before it can feed."

He looks at the ground, pinching the bridge of his nose. Temple does not share in her joy. His face drops. "I think so, yes."

"What?" she asks. "What's wrong?"

"This is the last dream I've ever had. The visions end here. You go to certain death. I never have another dream. Which means it comes for Atlan. Which means that you don't succeed, Venalia, you go down into the earth and you don't come back out. Thousands die, me among them. Who knows how far it spreads."

"You don't know that."

He holds up a hand and stops her. "Venalia, we lost. The Choir has won. We cannot – *cannot* – beat it down there. The Inverted World is its home. Where it's strongest."

"Why not? We have the lance, I have the Hold spell, I can cast Light, I have some mixture, Temple we *can* do this! Come on, we don't have a lot of time."

"We don't have *any* time, Venalia," he shouts, finally snapping. "The Inverted World shifts constantly! *Even if* we could, somehow, manage to track it down there; even if we *somehow* survive the wild magic, the Scarlings, the other dangers, and *somehow* manage to confront it?" He takes a breath. "It'll be too late. If it absorbs even a few of your people, then it's too big for us to beat. The Magistry is our *only* hope now. Come on. We can make it to Atlan. We can get out of here alive. Please."

He is begging, she realises. He is begging her not to do this.

"Temple, if there's a chance -"

"*There isn't!*" he shouts, rushing her and grabbing her by the shoulders. "Look at me! This sliver of hope will kill you, Venalia. It will kill you stone dead. I've been there. I've been to the very depths of that place. You *will not* survive it. Gods above, Venalia, it's a miracle that I made it out of there alive. It's a second miracle that you've survived alongside me. We skirted a fate worse than death. Now we have a window to get *out,* to live! *That's* how a mercenary gets old. They have to know when to admit defeat, when *not* to fight. Do you understand? We have *lost.*"

She hears him. She does; but what she hears him say is the truth, hidden underneath his desperate plea.

"You're afraid."

"I have a pulse and two eyes, Venalia – I'm *terrified.* As should you be. That thing is worse than death. Worse than a sword through the heart. I am not going in there again. Neither are you."

She breaks away from him, removing his hands from her shoulders.

"Venalia," he begins, warning her. "Come on now, lass."

"You aren't my captain," she tells him. "There's a chance that Llantry survives this yet."

"I can't bear to hear your voice amongst the Choir. I cannot let you go in there."

"You can't stop me."

"Venalia -"

"I'd rather die trying, than live knowing that I didn't. I know what the future holds when I give up on this. Those people need my help, or they deserve vengeance. Either way, I have to go in."

"You don't know how to navigate the Inverted World. You're going to get lost and starve, afraid and alone."

"I know," she says, and despite everything she hears, she feels her courage swell in her chest. This is it. This is how it happens. "I *know.* And I'm going anyway, Temple."

She turns and leaves, trudging towards the cliffs through the trees, following the trampled snow. Temple dashes after her, still shouting.

"Venalia, this isn't your responsibility!"

"How can you say that?" she spins around. "I'm a Priestess -"

"- of the Mind's Eye! You are a *scholar.* A student of mystery, a researcher, an investigator. The world below asks for a warrior, a Priestess of the Champion; of the Light Within. There will *be* vengeance for those people, Venalia," he begs her. "It need not be you who enact it."

"I am sick of people saying that. *Oh, if only we had a Priestess of the White Wrath, if only we had a War Priest...* well they don't, Temple! The cavalry isn't coming. It's just me."

"And you can still help to stop this. The Magistry need information, they need to know what you've learned, what you've found. Think, Venalia!"

She feels the blood rushing to her face, but she refuses to be shamed for this decision. Her grip tightens on the warhammer.

"Do you know the rules of the Priesthood?" she asks him, her nerves fraying as she rants. "Do you?"

"Venalia, don't -"

"The big three," she shouts. "Rule three, right? Everybody knows that one, Priests talk about it all the time. It's the subject of a bunch of jokes: *do not lie.* Because if we start messing about with the truth, people will not trust us. People should always be able to trust a Priestess. It's awkward to keep up and it costs you friends, but its the easiest rule to stick to. Rule two is lesser known, but harder to enforce. *Never let evil take root.* Simple to say, right? Ultimately, the rule is mostly for *us*; if we let evil take root within our own ranks, then *everyone* is in trouble."

She takes a breath, wiping the tears from her eyes. "But it's the first rule that kills us."

Temple finishes it for her. "You can never give up on your people."

"Never."

He has nothing to say. Venalia feels confident in her decision. This is the right thing to do. It will kill her, but when she meets Marius on the Black Sands she can do it with honour, with her head held high.

Maybe this was what she trained for all these years – so that when the time came, she could make one good call.

This is what she wants to do with her life.

Temple shakes his head. "You're a short sighted fool."

"I'm a Priestess."

"I can't go with you. One of us has to reach Atlan, otherwise the Choir will eventually destroy it. The Magistry need to be warned."

"So go warn them," she says, and she feels the tears come afresh. "Live another day, get paid, keep working alone and burying everybody who joins you."

"Fine," says Temple, walking back to Pretzia. "I've watched enough young soldiers die for someone else's ideals; for Gods who don't know their name."

"I'm not a soldier. I could never be a mercenary. Just like you could never be a Priest, because a Priest doesn't *run from a fight*."

He snaps around. "You're damn right I'll run. That's why I'm alive. That's why I'll continue to survive."

"Survive, aye? You dream of the fights you'll win, and you flee from everything else. How can you be brave if you know you won't die? No, no, I *see* you now, Temple. You're a survivor, not by skill or by bravery, but by virtue of your gift alone. Now you see a fight that you don't know the outcome of. Your visions have run out and what do you have to show for it?"

"I've lived a long life," he says. "Survival is all that matters. Go and ask the villagers of Llantry if they'd rather die with honour or live as cowards, I know what they'd say."

"Well I'd rather die for something, than live for nothing."

Temple had almost forgotten the last request of his friend Ungren, in the Inverted World.

Let me die for something, Ungren had said.

Temple looks away, then at the ground. She has shamed him.

Without another word, Temple takes his belt, and a torch, and tosses them onto the ground in front of her.

"There are medicines and fire starters in this belt. Flame and silver are your friends down there. At least you'll have the hammer. It's silvered."

"Aye."

He searches for the words, unable to meet her eyes. "I hope that when the end comes, it comes quick."

He turns and stalks towards the trees, pulling his cloak

over his shoulders. She picks up the belt, and gives Temple a bittersweet look.

He stops and turns as he considers his parting words. "I knew it would go this way. I just didn't know how. I'm sorry for what you've gone through, Venalia. If I could have prevented it, I would have."

"Don't be sorry," she says. "I didn't go through it alone, eh?"

He nods. "I did tell you exactly how this would end, did I not?"

She laughs – but he shoots her a heart breaking smile; she sees respect there, and a deep, aged sorrow.

"I understand your decision," he says. "I don't like it, but I understand it. I'll see to it that Atlan knows what you did. If this is all there is to your story, Venalia; if this is goodbye, then consider this. You found out who you truly are. You were tested, and you were not found wanting. People will remember the Priestess of Llantry. I shall tell them."

"You should return to Llantry afterwards," she holds up the belt, far too big for her, and wears it like a sash. "So that I can give you this back."

"If I look North from Atlan," he says, "and I see the smoke of chimneys, then I will return."

"You'd better," she says, thinking it final – but Temple wants to say something, she can see it.

"I wish that you did not have to do this part alone."

"I know," she says. "But I think that I have to."

He nods, sadly, to himself. "Gods keep you, Venalia."

"And you, Temple."

He disappears into the trees. She hears Pretzia whinny, and longs to run and join them. To flee from certain death.

She looks away before her nerve breaks.

Venalia stands alone, in the snowfall. The warhammer is heavy and cold, but the weight is satisfying, a reminder that it is real. She shoulders it and hikes up through the snow.

Amongst the hillside there is a cliff face rising into mist. Venalia whispers a prayer under her breath as she approaches. There lies, between two rocks, a path of trodden snow.

The shattered rocks lean upon one another, forming an angular doorway that beckons her forth.

Venalia peers into the darkness. The snow stops about a metre in. The way is narrow. It must have taken a while to get all of Llantry through it. That might buy her time.

She remembers her education on the Inverted World. The entry points are few and far between, with many more suspected to be undocumented and well hidden. Specially trained rangers and researchers keep tabs on the entry points, fortifying and studying them where they can. The classic indicator is a shift in the direction of gravity.

One does not descend into the Inverted World; it is a climb, always upwards, into the depths of the earth. A long way to fall, should you slip. Sometimes those who are in a rush to escape lose their footing, tripping and tumbling and smashing themselves against the rock, or landing in the myriad nets and webs of the creatures that dwell there.

Venalia tosses a rock into the entrance, and it hovers for a moment, as though unsure of which way to fall. It does not hit the ground. Rather, it drifts to the ceiling of the tunnel and back down, bobbing there until it settles on a direction and drops upwards with a clatter.

"Eye watch me," she whispers. "Eye keep me."

Venalia shifts forward, weightless and floating, until her feet hit the ceiling. Her stomach lurches and turns as

the

ceiling

becomes

the

floor

and

up

becomes

down.

She lands in a heap of her own limbs and struggles to stand in the inky darkness of the Inverted World.

She feels a chill run across her skin. Worse than the basement, or the forest, this place does not want her. The air is coarse to breathe, her skin is cracking from the icy dryness in the air. It ages her; she can feel the wild magic seeping into her bones and changing her; there is a faint tingling in her lungs, as though she is breathing in fumes.

Venalia readies the warhammer, and casts a spell of Light to illuminate the climb.

The tunnel is perfectly round, clean stone, like the gullet of some great creature allowing her in. Teeth and tonsils would not surprise her. She walks into the darkness and the tunnel repeats itself. Every inch looks the same as the last. No distinguishing features. She looks back and finds that she cannot see the entranceway any longer.

For the first time, she does not have Temple to remind her that it will turn out fine – she is through the other side of his visions, and still alive.

To certain death.

Venalia finds that her hands are not shaking.

"To certain death," she says.

Her light falters and ebbs as the dark swallows it, viscous, alive, swirling with monsters and tendrils at the edge of her vision.

The silence, the darkness, feel like the rising waters of the ocean. She strains against the fearful tension in her own muscles.

A wind comes through the tunnel, and she flinches – but more importantly, she smells something: the familiar scent of the herds, the mud, of *Llantry*. There's a surge of adrenaline, and the sudden conviction that she knows exactly what is required of her.

Venalia pauses – a sound, ahead in the gloom.

The chill of cold air on her face, as the cavern in front of her opens up. The wet sucking of something porous, moving, covered in a thousand tiny mouths; not the Choir. Not yet.

Venalia braces herself.

This is the Inverted World that Temple warned her of; the one that wiped out his squad.

With Minotaur in her hands, and a Shield spell prepared, Venalia presses forward.

Chapter Twelve

Something moves in the shade ahead. She denies herself the option of retreat, and forces herself to stand still, whispering a prayer to steady her nerves.

Whatever lies before her, it certainly *moves* in the physical realm, for it makes noise. Which means it can be hurt with the hammer – though she lacks the room to swing it properly.

She can hear wet suckling noises and thinks of creatures with suctions pads; mostly sea creatures that use them to catch prey.

A few steps further, and she catches sight of it. It stops moving, as though it knows, and it takes on the colour of the wall. Camouflage, she thinks. Excellent. Camouflage, suction pads; all the hallmarks of an ambush predator.

Best to not be the thing that it ambushes.

She takes an empty bottle from her pack and tosses it into the darkness. As soon as it hits the ground, several clammy appendages uncoil out of the tunnel ceiling.

Venalia recoils in horror.

Arms. Pale, humanoid arms, covered in small, wheezing mouths, like the tentacles of an octopus. Lips, tongues, teeth. The arms are long, multi-jointed, hanging from a lumpy body attached to the ceiling.

It grabs the bottle and turns it over in six hands, analysing it. The mouths open, licking the bottle's surface, grimacing. They find nothing, and the hands toss it aside.

The arms slither back into the darkness, leaving her in silence.

Her Light flickers out.

She is frozen. In her mind she is facing the Choir again, running into the darkness to confront it. She is driving a shortsword through a scarling's neck as acid bursts out like pus from a wound.

Her heart is pounding, her ears ringing with a high pitched whining. She is on the very edge of panic, she can feel it. Her legs want her to run. It feels like a nightmare, as though her legs have lost all feeling.

She takes another breath. Though Temple is not here, his lessons remain. Three seconds in, three seconds out.

Venalia is terrified.

Three seconds in, three seconds out.

Too scared to cast. Too scared to fight.

Three seconds in, three seconds out.

Without Temple, she is but a girl with a little training.

Three seconds in, three seconds out.

No; not a girl. A Priestess.

The same woman who faced the Choir without fear.

It is she that takes control, forms the shapes of the Light spell, and narrows it to a beam. With a finger, she points down the tunnel, and traps the creature in a spotlight beam.

It recoils with its numerous hands raised, and she feels sorry for it. In the light, it is more curious than horrifying. The little mouths are huffing, panting.

It is afraid.

Her wonder is cut short when its many mouths unleash a horrid screeching sound, and it detaches from the ceiling. It lands with a wet *slap* and scurries into the tunnel.

“Goodbye,” she whispers, laughing nervously. She hopes

– prays – that it has not left to summon help.

Venalia keeps Minotaur in her hands for good measure, and stays that way until she can no longer hear the sound of its numerous hands slapping on the wet ground.

Silence.

She casts a Light ahead of her and pushes forwards, deeper into the gloom.

Venalia feels her legs burning from the constant climb; it must have been fifteen minutes so far – or maybe an hour. Time feels elastic. She clutches the edge of panic, saved only by the firm grip on her mind. Thoughts of fear, of doubt, are cast down by the grim-faced determination of the Priestess, set upon her journey into certain death.

Her light finds a fork in the path. The tunnel shifts from smooth rock face to craggy, bony stonework on either side. Handmade.

“Ah, hells,” she whispers. She remembers Temple warning her; you'll get lost, and that'll be the end of you. “Coin flip?”

No, says the watcher in her mind. Do not bet the fate of Llantry on a coin toss.

“Right. Which way do I go, then?”

Her voice echoes back from both tunnels. She stays still and lets her ears attune to the silence. She stills her thoughts, letting her brain settle like a lake till the ripples of her thoughts calm, at last.

After a moment, things start to *tremble*. The air has a texture to it, a faint current; wind upon her face one second, and blowing against her back the next. It changes direction every...

She counts.

... seven seconds.

In, and out. Inhale. Exhale. As though meditating; or asleep.

It brings a scent to her, the faintest trace.

Cow shit. Silage. Feed, grain, *mud.*

Llantry.

She steps towards the tunnel from which it comes, and opens her eyes, surprised to find them welling with tears.

“I'm coming,” she says, and chooses that tunnel.

The tunnel opens up into a void so deep that it has a sound, a rush of white noise that she realises is the flow of blood in her ears. So silent is this cavern, so large, that it eats sound. Venalia feels the pressure and temperature drop.

It seems that she is standing at the edge of the ocean in the dark of night, no stars in the sky. A sense of scale overcomes her, and she is struck by the urge to hide. She is nothing. An ant on the edge of a canyon.

Her Light reveals the ground, flat and even. Stalactites dot the landscape, breaking the monotony.

She focuses her light into a beam and finds only a vast floor – floor, she thinks, because this feels like a *room* – with no wall, no ceiling that her Light can find.

The Choir could have gone anywhere. There are no footprints, no clues; the entire cavern seems devoid of life.

Venalia remembers the other tunnel, and wonders if she trusted her senses too willingly.

“There has to be something,” she mutters, and the void swallows her words. No echo.

She lifts a loose rock from the ground, after testing it with her hammer, and casts her Light upon the rock itself. It will glow brightly for a few minutes like this, turning any item into a small lamp.

The rock glows bright, and she throws it as hard as she can into the gloom.

It illuminates the floor, the rocks, as it sails through the air, hits the ground, bounces, and -

Splashes.

Water.

The light vanishes beneath the surface, as though snuffed out.

Venalia keeps her eyes pinned where it fell, casts her Light spell again, and stumbles across the rocky surface towards it. As she gets closer, she stops, tapping the ground with her hammer as she goes, until -

Splash.

The rocks ripple under her touch. The *rocks are rippling*.

"Well this is new," she whispers. She taps again, watching intently.

It keeps happening. She is not imagining this.

The ground looks like a normal, rocky cavern floor – but it is not there. It is an illusion upon the surface of the water.

She could easily have stepped right into this, into – is it water? Ancient, stagnant water?

Venalia takes another rock and drops it in. It shimmers through the rocky floor and sinks beneath the water.

"Like a trap," she sighs.

This is a complication, but also perhaps an answer.

The Choir could not have come this way. Not with the population of Llantry in tow; most of them have never seen a body of water larger than a river. Swimming is unheard of.

Unless the Choir knows a way around.

She grabs a handful of rocks from the base of the stalactite formations and begins to test the edges of the illusion.

A rock to the left.

Splash.

To the right.

Splash.

Sighing, she turns and uses a focused light beam to find her tunnel, so that she can return to the entrance and chart this place properly.

Splash.

She freezes.

Splash.

Behind her.

Venalia whips around, Light blossoming into a wide radius.

A humanoid shape drags itself out of the water. She sees no skin, only the white pearl of bone, the grinning teeth of someone long dead, creaking and groaning as they move, clad in badly rusted scraps of armour. Within empty eye sockets are little pinpricks of red fire.

Undead.

The armour is ancient, rusted, bears no resemblance to anything from Llantry. Even as she stumbles backwards, tripping over a stalactite, her brain is conducting an investigation.

Human, judging by its size. It drags a large, rusted sword behind it, held in hands covered by rusted chainmail. The two red pinpricks of fire focus on her, and it opens its jaw. Had it any vocal chords, it would be screaming a war cry. Instead, she hears only a strained crackling sound.

Venalia climbs to her feet, trying to think as it advances. The main issue facing her is that the undead do not respond to pain, or force. To stop them, one must remove the spirit or magic animating the body.

Had she time to bind it down and pray over it, she could exorcise the spirit and banish it from this plane. Were she a better Priestess, she could blast it apart with divine fire.

The skeleton's sword rattles and screeches as the rusted steel is dragged across rock.

Her back hits the cavern wall.

The skeleton swings the sword two handed, coming in sideways towards her rib cage. A sword does horrible things to a mortal body.

Instinct kicks in, and just before the blow lands, she throws out her Shield – which means dropping her Light.

Blind, she feels the blow hits her Shield, throwing her to

the ground, winded but alive. In the darkness, she sees its red eyes find and fixate upon her.

It can see in the dark.

She casts her Light to see, and finds it raising its greatsword overhead, a killing blow against an enemy on their back. It brings the blade down.

At the last second, Venalia summons her strength, drops the Light, closes her eyes, and forces out the strongest Shield that she can manage. The sword isn't just deflected, it *bounces* backwards with enough force to leave the skeleton's slippery hands.

The sword lands with a clank on the ground, and the skeleton reels backwards from the force, leaving it open. Venalia rolls to her feet, screams her fury and swings the hammer in a wide arc at the space where those red eyes are.

Her hammer smashes through its rib cage with a sound like shattering pottery.

Blind, she cannot see its arms, and she screams as they latch onto her wrists. The stench of wet death fills her nostrils. She fights down the urge to vomit, and in the darkness, she focuses another Shield out. This one blows the skeleton backwards, and Venalia takes a moment to cast another Light, finding her bearings.

She is running out of energy, and has no mixtures left.

The skeleton has found its sword upon the ground, and drags it up with surprising strength. It darts forward, taking her by surprise.

The sword comes in fast and hits her torso.

It clatters off her breastplate, the one that Bell fashioned for her, but still it knocks the wind from her and drives her to the ground. Her Light spell drops, and she scrambles to her feet and keeps her distance as the skeleton advances, swinging its blade in a figure eight.

There is one spell in her arsenal that she has not yet cast.

Hold.

The skeleton darts forward, greatsword raised.

Venalia forms the shapes in her mind; shapes of binding

and solidity, a rock in the ocean, a frozen moment when the rain stops falling.

It takes form, rippling with energy. Never before has she cast something of such power. It trembles with anticipation, coiled like a serpent.

With it, she reaches outside of her body and finds the undead spirit, bound to a body against its will. The soul is furious, thrashing, trapped. Venalia wraps the spell around it, and the steel bands of her will bind it, *Holding* it.

It stops dead, paralysed, in the pitch black. The flaming red eyes do not move, fixed in place.

Venalia's heart is pounding, her head is swimming. The spell is powerful and complex, draining her energy – but worse, it is a constant battle to dominate the mind of another creature. It throws itself again and again against her Hold, testing for cracks, straining, screaming into her mind.

She manages to get one eye half-open, walking the tightrope between concentration and intention. For long enough, she can balance the tightrope.

She steps forward, focused on the red eyes burning in the dark, and raises the hammer above her head.

It feels *good.*

It strains and screams and struggles against her Hold, but it cannot break free.

Venalia brings the hammer down with all of her strength, shattering its body. Dust and shrapnel explode from the hammer blow, and the *CRACK* echoes through the cavern.

The pins of red light flare and dissipate. With nothing to anchor them to this plane, they will be dragged into the ethereal plane. Let the Open Door, Goddess of Death, deal with it.

Venalia's heart pounds, and her mother's barbarian spirit flares in her veins. She lets out a roar of victory that turns to laughter, giddy on adrenaline.

You are not truly a Priestess, she was once told, until you have returned something undead to the Black Sands by force.

Triumph turns to exhaustion as the adrenaline wears off. Hold is a powerful spell, and now the crash hits her. Venalia needs a Light, but she barely the energy to think.

She fumbles for the jars in her satchel and knows from sound alone that they are all empty.

There is no time to rest.

With a deep breath, she shakes some life into her limbs, and casts Light. Staggering like a drunk, she takes the greatsword from the pile of bones and uses it to test the ground in front of her, leaning on it for support.

Tracing the edge of the water, Venalia is shook out of her anxious stupor by another *splash* that stops her heart.

She looks down and finds a puddle.

A simple puddle;

with footsteps leading out of it.

Fresh footsteps, with the markings of the cattle boots that are common in Llantry.

Venalia almost screams in joy. The footsteps are fresh. Without thinking, Venalia kneels down and touches her finger to the footprint. A man's shoe, a cattle herder probably – the *faintest* smell of mud and grass, the hills, the cattle. She breathes deep and pushes on.

Soon after, her light finds walls in the darkness.

Stone walls. Constructed by people, *planned and built* by someone.

There, built in a semi circle into the very rock, is the tower of a fortress. It seems as though a part of a castle has been teleported into a space too small.

Upon it is a single stone door about twice as wide as it needs to be. This is where Temple and his team found the Choir. A fortification, built by the Magistry.

"I know what you are," she whispers as she approaches.

Karak the Red Terror and his dragons invaded over two thousand years ago. Froze the Celestial membrane solid, stopping the Old Gods, the spirits of the world, from intervening. Karak won a very brief war, and settled in to rule the ash heap.

Alas, only mortals really know how to rule mortals. The

dragons pulled the Kappi out of their mountains and mines, the Aelfa out of their holy forests, the smallfolk out of the hidden spaces in the world, and forced all of the mortals together in cities, where they could be watched. Strife and war followed. Mortals could not coexist. They required leaders.

Thus came the Magistry, given Draconic blood for their loyal service, and allowed to rule through the power of their magic.

Centuries later, in order to plan the genocide of the Dragonfall, the Magistry would meet here, deep within the Inverted World, where no eyes magical nor mundane can see.

Venalia lights the torch that Temple gave her from her pack. The skeleton caught her unable to see and fight at the same time, and she will not fall for that trick again.

Venalia readies Minotaur, assembles the shapes of her Shield, and steps into the darkness of the old Magisterial fort from which the Choir first emerged.

Chapter Thirteen

The air inside is damp, lush with the scent of rotten vegetation. Venalia's torch casts flickering orange light across the ruined interior; piece by piece, she builds a mental picture from the snapshots.

A circular room with four doors. At the far end, her light finds a humanoid figure, standing in the shade, and she jumps in fright, dropping the torch and swinging Minotaur up into her hands. When the figure does not react, she approaches.

Under the glow of the torch it is but a simple statue of an armoured figure wielding a greatsword half his size in two hands, head bowed, resting his sword point-first on the ground as though in prayer. Just a statue; though knowing the Magistry, it will come to life and kill her when her back is turned.

She check the four doors; two doors on each side of the circular chamber.

The wet footprints from outside lead here, but they do not go anywhere. They stop, disappearing halfway into the chamber.

"Hundreds of people," she whispers to herself. "Teleportation circle? No, not with so many..." She curses under her breath, and kneels down, running a hand over the spot where they stop. There are half foot-prints, cut off suddenly. Something is not right.

Her hand runs along smooth stone on the floor, but there is no edge to find. To be sure, Venalia takes the hammer and gently taps the floor in several spots. Here, it gives a thinner, hollow thud.

It is empty.

"Hidden staircase," she concludes.

Which means there must be a mechanism to open it. Venalia's heart leaps at the thought of a puzzle, but if lives are on the line, then overwhelming force is her quickest way through.

Venalia takes a breath, and raises the warhammer overhead. She brings it down with all of her strength, just like she did to the skeleton, and grunts as it smashes on the ground.

It barely chips the stone, and causes an ear-shattering ringing that carries through the tunnels of the Inverted World. She winces, and looks around. The doors do not burst open. Undead do not swarm over her. The statue stands perfectly still.

She has neither the strength nor the tools to get through the floor here – but if this is where the Choir led them, then there must be *some* way of getting down there. She just has to figure out how.

In her mind, an hourglass is running down the sand – but she doesn't need to be fast, she just needs to get this right.

Magisters are famously lazy – they would automate eating and drinking, if they could. Some actually do, she is certain. If she were a Magister, designing a fortress with a secret staircase, she would want it to be as convenient as possible.

She runs her hands over the smooth wall, pressing every couple of inches. Nothing. No secret wall panel, no secret switch within arms reach. She does the same with the other wall, and the floor below her. The ceiling is over ten feet above her – even the tallest Aelfa couldn't manage that.

The Tall Woman could, she thinks, and shudders at the thought.

She runs her hands through her hair and tries to come at the problem from several angles.

It could be a magical switch, she reasons, but why would the Magistry take that risk? The Inverted World is teeming with wild magic, which interferes with *everything*. If one had to cast a spell to enter, their arcane magic could potentially trigger a wild magic cascade. Obvious oversight.

"Come on," she whispers. "It's just a puzzle like any

other."

Without any obvious keyhole, the other option is a password. Something has to *receive* the password. She sees no such thing.

Unless it is the statue. A statue in a Magisterial ruin can either be security, or decoration. This place does not look like decoration was a factor. It has been built for secrecy and safety.

She approaches the statue and clears her throat. Any password is going to be in the Draconic tongue, and her Draconic is terrible. She can swear in Draconic, recognise a few symbols, say a few phrases, but not much else.

Venalia coughs out a word. In Draconic, it sounds like she is loudly cracking her jaw. It means:

"Password."

Nothing. She rolls her eyes.

"Passage," she tries. She only knows so many Draconic words, and they come out with the sound of brick breaking. "Stair. Stairs. Down."

Nothing.

Time to start looking for clues.

The doors remain closed.

Venalia picks the first door on her left for no particular reason. She eases it open with the torch. The door itself is thick lead, designed to block magic.

It is a study, long defunct. A bed that has been devoured by insects and spiderwebs. Desk, covered in cobwebs, a stack of scrolls, and a tome laying open. Venalia uses the handle of the hammer to shuffle the scrolls around – they disintegrate into dust as soon as she touches them, and she curses.

The tome. Mouldy quill in a dried inkwell. Someone was writing something. She dare not touch the book, lest it turn to dust as well. Instead, she reads what remains on the paper, brushing away webs.

It is written not in Draconic, but in an older, readable version of the common tongue.

It reads:

...Vance continues his studies on combined neural awareness in the Lady's Elbow.

Another spate of transfers, asking to work on his project. They have all been rebuked.

Apparently I am here to play with insane theories, whilst Vance takes the credit for the entire Dragonfall. Father will be spinning in his grave.

I see their doubt in every interaction. They do not understand neuroharmonics. Maybe I should have asked for musicians, people who understand waveform, vibration. It's a simple concept, once you stop using shapes and start seeing it all as a symphony.

Given the harmonic geometries of magic, why are all Magisters not musicians?

We are decades yet from the Dragonfall, if it ever happens at all. The co-ordination of hundreds of Magisters across a continent the size of Altheim - the preparation takes too long. Parameters keep changing. How many times have we ***nearly*** *started the uprising, only to realise that half of our plans and orders are outdated.*

It's been called the Hard Problem of the Dragonfall for good reason. We need a way to act together, as one mind. Whilst I know that my nit-picking is seen as bitterness, I genuinely hope that Vance's research into combined awareness bears fruit. My solution is, I think, better; but how else to prove it?

I want to perform a test. Once they hear the song, they'll all realise what has happened. Proof of concept. Then, after everything, they will know that I was right.

There finishes the writing. Something must have pulled her attention away from it.

Venalia knows that the Dragonfall was a monumental undertaking, but in a way, that's all *anybody* knows. The specifics of so much of it were lost – many Magisters died that day too, taking their secrets with them.

How do you coordinate hundreds – thousands – of Magisters in tandem? Neural awareness, minds sharing the same experience; it would be one way of doing it.

It is also what being with the Choir felt like.

It says it right there, on the page.

Once they hear the song.

The Choir welcomed her into a mass of other minds, to share her thoughts and be one with them. A neural link.

Venalia tries the other rooms, still no closer to opening the stairwell below.

In one room is a workshop with copper and gold tools, designed for working with crystalline, the best medium for storing arcane energy. The same material imbedded in Minotaur's handle.

The third room has only a few beds. She has a quick search around in the beds and the open lockers at the bottom of each; nothing. Mostly packs of rations that are long rotten, and mixtures similar to her own that are full of glowing fungus.

The fourth room, then - she stops as she tries the door.

The statue's head was bowed before, and now it is raised to reveal curious eyes of crystalline, fixed upon the far end of the room.

"Oh no you don't," she whispers, and throws the torch on the ground, gripping her hammer in both hands. "No. I am *not* playing this game. Explain yourself!"

She says it with authority, no matter how ridiculous it sounds. What comes to her is not a voice – but a thought, spoken directly into her brain with the clipped, proper accent of an educated young man.

You are a Magister, it says.

"I'm a Priestess," she corrects him. "Of the Mind's Eye. My name is Venalia. Who are you?"

I am a watcher-construct. If I am to have a name, it is 'Security'.

"Hello, Security."

You have the blood of a Magister.

"I..." she stops. Does she? Her mother was a Steppe woman, she knows that, but her father? Bell never told her anything specific, only that her parents were burned to ash. "Right. Let's say that I do."

My previous masters are no longer fit to command this outpost.

"What happened to them?"

An arcane experiment. Unforeseen complications.

"Are they dead?"

No.

Because those in the Choir are not quite dead, she thinks.

"They came through here recently, right?"

Yes.

"With a few hundred people?"

Yes.

Her heart is pounding out of her chest. She's close, she can feel it.

"Down the secret staircase here?"

Yes.

"How do I open it?"

I cannot disclose this information.

Though it is only an arcane artifice, Venalia can sense the frustration in Security's thought-voice. It has a purpose that is going unfulfilled. She walks closer to the statue.

"You want to help me, don't you? You want to help me stop the Choir?"

I do not feel desire. I am simply a security construct.

"Quite a rudimentary one, then. A more basic model than the automata that we use today. Pre-Dragonfall. You're over two thousand years old, yes?"

Yes.

"You have a writ in your head, like our automata do? A

scroll of instructions, written in Draconic, that outlines the parameters of your behaviour?"

Yes.

"Then it stands to reason that there is something binary, a yes or no condition, that instructs you to open the staircase. Yes?"

Yes.

"You control the stairs, don't you?" she guesses.

Yes.

"Let me see... the first condition to opening the stairs, is that I have Draconic blood. Yes?"

Yes.

"How many conditions are there?"

Two.

"So there must be another parameter, something that the Choir can still do, that any Magister could do..."

Silence from the statue. She has not asked a question, she realises. Other clues begin to bubble up in her brain. Things that do not fit. She needs more information.

"How did you know that I had Draconic blood?"

There is an advanced sensor array in the walls of this fortification. I see much.

"Do you have other arcane measuring devices built into you?"

Yes.

"Tell me about them."

I cannot disclose that information.

How does the Choir get in, she wonders. It dawns upon Venalia that they were researching neural arcana here. The study of thoughts, of thinking.

She looks at the statue, keeps her mouth closed, and thinks at it:

Can you hear me? she asks it. Can you hear me think?

Yes.

Fantastic. Incredible. Is there a password?

Yes.

And it must be thought, rather than spoken, right?

I cannot disclose that information.

Which means that I'm right.

Which also means that it could be anything. The first thing that you see when you walk in the door? Statue. Stairs. Stairwell. Password. Passage. Magistry. Password. Password One?

"Nothing," she grumbles aloud. "Do I have to think it in Draconic?"

Nothing.

Venalia looks around, and finds one door that remains unopened. Within is a meeting room with a single table, and a board upon which is pinned a selection of papers and drawings that have stayed largely intact.

At the top of the board is written a title that she reads aloud:

"The Hard Problem of the Dragonfall – Neuroharmonics and Crystalline Conductivity."

The names of those taking part are listed below, and the leader of the project is Magistress Ceylandwelle Finduilye.

"Kay-land-well Find-Will-Yay," she whispers to herself, rolling her eyes. "Well that's an Aelven name if I've ever heard one."

The rest of the writing is mostly postulation and question marks, with equations scrawled around sketches of arcane geometries. No other clues. Maybe the password is a shape she thinks, like a spell, that she has to hold in her mind.

If the project leader, *Ceylandwelle,* was Aelven, perhaps she set a password in Aelven. Venalia's Aelven is limited to rude words.

'Neuroharmonics' keeps appearing. Her brain won't leave it alone.

Harmonics, she knows; that is when the soundwaves

interact in a certain way. Venalia knows music – she has to foster a decent singing voice to speak Celestial properly. The Gods communicate in a language of music.

She walks back outside.

"Security, what *are* neuroharmonics?"

I cannot disclose that information.

Well, she thinks to herself. Time to try it out then.

She closes her eyes, and thinks of her childhood with Marius. She remembers him teaching her to sing – to match a note that he played on the lute. To ascend a step at a time, to descend without sliding one note into the next, to distinguish her notes and to sing with power, from her stomach. She feels her body tense and flex as though she were singing.

In her mind, she matches Marius.

Harmonises.

Stone grinds on stone behind her.

Harmony was the password – not the word itself, but the very thought of harmony.

She spins around to see the stone fall step by step, revealing the staircase that leads into the thick shadow below. The torch flickers across the stone, where the footprints now continue downwards.

"Thank you," she whispers to the statue, hesitating a moment. "How, uh... how *much* of a Magister am I? Like, entirely? Or half? Or..."

Impossible to tell.

"But I'm definitely partly of Draconic blood?"

I sense arcane energy in your blood. This is a classic signature of Draconic heritage.

Her mother is of the Steppe – everybody tells her that. The hair, the height, it all says so. Magisters do not often hail from the Steppe, where magic is drawn from bonds with the ancient spirits of the land. Draconic blood does not run thick amongst barbarians. It is also frowned upon for a Magister to bear children with somebody who is not, also, a Magister. Diluting the bloodlines is a great – though often breached - taboo.

Her father must have been the Magister.

It nags at her, but she shelves it amongst her mind's library for now. There are more important things at stake.

Venalia finally has a clear path in front of her. She raises the torch and descends into the darkness, Minotaur in hand.

Chapter Fourteen

Venalia hears singing in her head.

Her. The Tall Woman.

In only a day, Venalia has forgotten how insidious the Choir is, indistinguishable from her own voice.

There is a depth to the song now, layered voices all singing in harmony. *Neuro*harmony.

The chant is that of a gifted choir, like the ones that she joined in Whitehallow. To join others in song, without needing to be taught the melody or notes, is a decidedly mortal thing. Music is a part of the soul. A part of creation that somehow contains all of creation.

It almost has her again, hypnotising her into a lull, charming her like a Solar mystic with a serpentine flute; but this Priestess is not the fledgeling that first faced the Choir. This Priestess is a veteran of the Inverted World, slayer of crawlers and undead.

She sings her own song out of defiance, the hymn that she sings at funerals.

Then comes Gregor's voice, and others, Magisters and soldiers, mercenaries; Temple's team.

Venalia holds her torch high and walks down the stone corridor until it opens into a large chamber, the walls decorated with lines of copper and gold, lead and crystalline. There are low red lights, crystalline, ever-burning.

Before the Priestess forms a corridor of people; the population of Llantry. They create an aisle for her to walk down.

At the furthest end of this arcane cathedral kneels the Tall Woman, tiny white eyes fixed upon Venalia.

All of us

it says

All together at last.

The people of Llantry are assembled to watch something beautiful, slack jawed, singing with their minds, eyes blank. They turn, staring, as one. Venalia sees her torch reflected as a red dot in their pupils.

Their singing takes on a tone of celebration in her head, a rejoicing.

We have been waiting on you.

We are cold, Priestess.

Cold.

Afraid.

Lonely.

Among them stalk the many shades of the Choir, caressing the faces of Llantry's people. The Tall Woman opens her mouth and croons like a mother bird singing to its chicks, soothing and calm.

With one long arm, the Tall Woman plucks a man from the crowd and leads him out like a dazed child, to stand in the centre of the aisle.

Gregor. He gazes, lost, into space.

The Tall Woman places an elongated hand on his head and he kneels. As Gregor takes to his knee, the rest of Llantry follow suit.

Venalia stands alone before the Tall Woman.

With her long fingers, the Tall Woman begins pulling his eyelids back. Venalia sees Gregor's pupils blow out, and his eyes fill with inky shadow. The Tall Woman looks poised to drag him into the mass of shadows behind her. As one, the Choir shout the command into her head:

APPROACH

She is as ready as she can be.

Venalia stands before her as a child stands before their parents; the Tall Woman is trying to pull something out of Venalia, raiding her mind, reading her down to her bones.

The shades have taken a position, surrounding her, hiding between the kneeling people of Llantry.

Venalia feels herself trembling, and cannot make it stop. She stares into its face, determined to show no fear. She looks for some ounce of awareness, of mortality in the Tall Woman, but finds only the slightest outline of something, with the delicate long ears of an Aelfa.

There are you, she thinks: the Tall Woman has a name. Magistress Ceylandwelle Finduilye. Her triumph is cut short by the hundred voices:

Priestess

Keeper of Secrets

She hears Gregor's voice among them, though he is right in front of her, and does not move. His eyes have rolled into the back of his head; they are spheres of black.

“I wish to address Magistress Ceylandwelle Finduilye,”

she says, standing as tall as she can manage, speaking as loudly and clearly as she can. "You speak to a Priestess of the Mind's Eye. I ask that you release these people, and allow them to leave your domain, lest you be destroyed."

The Tall Woman does not move, but the Choir of shades bristles, folding and rumbling with strange ripples of music that unsettle her stomach. Her muscles cramp, threatening to snap with tension. She repeats the hymn in her mind, defiant still.

The Tall Woman leans over her, swelling in size as the music rises.

"Let them go," she says.

I cannot.

"Why not?"

We are saving them.

They are safe here.

There's a feeling, surface thoughts that she can make out through singing in her mind.

You serve the Mind's Eye.

We have a use for you.

"Is that what you seek? Knowledge? Then perhaps we can make a deal," she offers. "For I have a theoretically infinite pool of knowledge; why, I have access to the God of Knowledge himself."

We know.

She has but one chip with which to negotiate; her own life. It wants knowledge, for some reason – and if it devours her, it can have it.

"If you try to take all of us," she lifts the jagged spike on the warhammer, one horn of the bull's head, and rests the point against her neck. "Then I will ensure that all of my knowledge dies with me. You can't absorb the knowledge of a dead thing, can you? It has to be alive."

You lack the mettle for suicide.

"I'm a Priestess," she shouts. "I *cannot* lie. It's the third rule of the Priesthood, everybody knows that. I almost died protecting Llantry from you once. I'll do it again."

The Tall Woman leans over her, as one might an insect, and Venalia feels that alien presence in her brain again. She is being read – and by the change in the song, she knows that it is unhappy with what it finds.

She tells the truth.

She came here to die.

"We can make a deal," she holds up her sigil, keeping the hammer spike pressed against her neck. "Look. I'm a Priestess of Knowledge. You want me. Not these people; Gods above, these people?" She motions to Llantry's villagers. "They have knowledge of, of... cattle herding. When to plant potatoes. How important the rain is. What mushrooms to avoid eating. They have nothing of use to you, they know nothing that you do not already know. Most of them are illiterate. What do you want with morsels like this, when you can have me?"

Why not both?

"You cannot have both," she says. Nothing is working; she has a plan, and she has to try. One throw of the dice. "I have deep knowledge of neuroharmonics, and its applications. I know that this was an experiment gone wrong. I believe that I can help you."

The reply is instant. Her guess was correct.

Neuroharmonics?

"Yes. But you have to let the villagers go."

This is a wild, desperate play, but if her rudimentary understanding of the science is accurate, if her guess is correct, then she may yet be able to break the spell that binds these people together into a monstrosity.

Nor is she, strictly speaking, lying.

Venalia has a plan, or rather the shape of a plan. The song is what binds everything together, and if she can end the song, the Choir will dissipate. It is a theory, based upon what she has found, read, and felt herself.

The problem is that if she is wrong, she is condemning herself to thousands of years of psychological torture.

Certain death; or a fate worse.

"If we have a deal," she says, "then release these people from your spell."

The Tall Woman stands up, removing its hand from Gregor's head, and Gregor pitches forward, groaning. Behind her, the crowd shuffles, and a spell lifts from them all.

The song is diminished, quieter; not gone.

She hears voices, spoken out loud; children asking where they are. Confused people, voices trembling, turning to one another. There are panicked shouts when they see the Tall Woman, cries of mercy and pleas for help from the Gods.

Then she hears her name.

"Venalia is here," someone whispers. "The Priestess has come for us."

"I can't hear the singing, ma, it's gone -"

"Priestess? Where are we? What do we do?"

Gregor's head lifts, rubbing his eyes, groaning as he gets to his knees. He looks up and around, at the Tall Woman, and then at Venalia, confused.

“Venalia?” he manages, his face falling. “Did it get you?”

“The Hells it did,” she says. “I have an oath to keep.”

He stands up and runs to her, throwing his arms around her. “Gods above,” he cries, “you came for us.”

The honest gratitude in his voice is enough for her. All of this would be worthwhile to hear him speak like this.

“Burroughmaster,” she says, and allows him the briefest of an embrace before she holds him at arm's length. She pitches her voice perfectly; firm without shouting, confidence without arrogance. “I need you to lead the people out of here. Back to the surface. Do not stop for anything. Do you understand?”

“The surface?” he stutters. “Where are we?”

“The Inverted World. An old Magisterial fortress.”

“Oh Gods,” he whispers, and she can hear the fear in his voice. He's close to breaking, just as she was.

“Gregor,” she whispers, taking his face in her hands. His eyes are wild, darting around the room. He's shaking. “Gregor, look at me.” He looks, and is still. “Gregor, this is it. This is your moment, like we spoke about, aye? I've got Minotaur, your weapon, you can take it with you. You are the *only* other person here that can lead. I have to do something here, and you have a job to do on the surface, and neither of us succeeds if the other fails. Do you trust me?”

“I do,” he whispers. “What are you going to do?”

“I'm going to try and save everyone,” she says, passing him the warhammer. She keeps her voice low. The Choir cannot know what she is saying.

He looks confused. “But, you already -”

“There are innocent people trapped inside that thing,” she whispers. “I have to try.”

“Venalia, are you –“ he sees what she intends to do. “You're going to let it take you, aren't you? Venalia that's *insane* -”

“Temple's team are still in there, Gregor. I can't leave them. You have to get to the surface, understand? Far enough away that if I fail, you all survive. Temple has gone to alert the Magistry – they'll be coming soon. One way or another, you just have to survive."

Gregor understands. He sees the finality in her conviction, and he cannot argue with her. He pats her on the shoulder, nods, and stands up. Gregor picks up Minotaur, and takes a flickering torch from the nearest villager. In that one moment, he looks like a leader.

"Everybody listen," he shouts, trying not to look at the Choir. "You are in the Inverted World, far below the surface. We are leaving. Follow me, stay close, and take the hands of your children and elderly. We do not slow down until we reach the surface. If you stumble or falter, Gods help you."

A rabble erupts amongst the crowd as people try to organise, and Gregor puts a hand on her shoulder.

"Priestess? The way?"

"Go out of here, stick to the left wall, be careful for water that looks like rock. There's a tunnel leading upwards, it'll take you up a long descent. No other turns. Just get up there as fast as you can."

He nods, and the two of them look at one another across the crowd. Venalia does her best to say it with her eyes:

I forgive you; and goodbye.

Gregor turns, and marches into the darkness with his torch. The crowd filters out, one person at a time. As the villagers pass by her, they put their hands upon her, thanking her, whispering prayers to her. Gregor raises a hand, and disappears.

She is alone, watching Llantry's people – her people – head for safety.

Never give up on your people.

She turns to the mass of shadow behind her, writhing in anticipation. The Tall Woman towers over her.

Priestess of Knowledge.

Keeper of Secrets.

Tell us what you know of Neuroharmonics.

She has to buy them time now.

"The last time that we met, I told you that I'd send you to the Nine Hells," she says, and tosses the torch down. She grasps her sigil, no other weapon to hand. "If nothing else, I'm a woman of her word."

She has never been a good actor, but her plan depends upon her losing this fight convincingly.

You do not know of Neuroharmonics?

"No more than you do."

LIAR

The shades reach around from behind and pull her to the floor, clawing at her hair, frozen hands pinning her down. More shades pour out of the Tall Woman's body, scrabbling for her, singing all the while. The song is a deafening crescendo in her head, a psychic scream threatening to burst her skull open.

Venalia screams.

The shades get their hands upon her skin and her body freezes with the shock of it. The song is driving her into madness. Her mind breaks into separate pieces, driven apart.

Panic.

Thoughts of her plan, of resistance, are swept away, and there is no Venalia left to think.

Whilst she is pinned, the Tall Woman touches her, and Venalia's body tenses, solid, paralysed as the handprint is burned into the skin of her arm. She opens her mouth to scream, but her body will not obey.

Ice water floods her veins. Black tendrils spread across her body.

She watches from the inside of her own head, from the last bastions of her mental fortress where her spirit dwells, as she loses any remaining ground.

Her arms are useless, and now foreign hands grip her torso. Venalia is pulled, limp, into the Tall Woman's silhouette as it fills the cavern. The shades pile in, forming a dark mass of limbs.

Silence.

Darkness.

Only the flickering torch remains on the floor.

Venalia is gone.

There is only the Choir.

Sense of awareness.

Discomfort.

Hungry.

Alone.

Cold.

Gods, it is so cold.

And if

I

can feel cold

then there must be

somebody

here

to be feeling it.

Venalia's pulls the tendrils of her self together, the different patterns and identities that make up her ego and her mind. It feels like prayer, only in the opposite direction, a binding rather than a freeing from the ego.

She coalesces together, holding herself like mist around the core of her soul.

Venalia senses that she is entombed somewhere away from her physical form. She can feel her hands and her face and her body but they are burning away, dissolving.

Something is digesting her, and though the pain is unbearable, she is far from it. She is being soothed. Sang to sleep. She is within the great shadow, somewhere else.

Part of the Choir.

Panic, in her body; her plan has not worked, for her plan requires her body, and she is separate from it.

Useless without it.

Something huge, a towering presence that dwarves all others, is staring her down. The mountain of the Tall Woman surrounds her.

LIAR

comes its judgement

LIAR

LIAR

LIAR

LIAR

Venalia would cover her ears if she had any, but her mind cannot shelter itself from the onslaught. The Tall Woman has pulled apart her thoughts and memories, and has found nothing about neuroharmonics.

She tries to reach out to her, to communicate her intention, to *help,* but the Tall Woman is lost to madness, rampaging in their shared headspace, pouring waves of scorn and anger upon Venalia. She is an insect being stood upon over and over again, unable to die.

Rather than pull her apart over and over again, the Tall Woman instead turns her senses to the hundred beating hearts trying to flee. Venalia can feel the pull of the villagers, the scent of their memories and minds, drawing the Choir towards them.

They are on the hunt.

Not the villagers, she thinks. *Stop.*

She cannot exert any control over what it does, and the Tall Woman will not relent for a second to allow her to breathe. She has double-crossed the Choir, and now she must watch as the rest of Llantry is pulled in here with her to suffer for an eternity.

This is how she fails.

Then there are others here with her, other minds without bodies. They wrap themselves around her, and the next time that the Tall Woman brings her heel down upon Venalia's mind, they shelter her with what strength they have.

Venalia cowers whilst they protect her, trying to crawl away to hide, to find safety somewhere and recuperate – but all is the Choir, and there is no reprieve outwith the comfort of these others.

All the while, she is aware of her body disintegrating.

She is sobbing, for her heart is breaking, and the weight is more than she can bear. Venalia wants, more than anything else, to be close to somebody. The loneliness is too much to bear. It is cold.

She wants to feel their presence and let it soothe her, to remember what it feels like to have a body, to have sensations and weight. She wants to sing with them.

"No, you don't," comes a voice, that of a man she does not recognise. It sounds like a *Kappi,* a dwarf.

I don't?

"No. You came here with a plan."

He is right. Her theory. She remembers her theory.

Neuroharmonics. Arcane geometry. Music. The shapes of a spell. The Aelfa in charge – the Tall Woman.

Several minds bound together in a spell, a spell that was *sung.*

A spell of binding.

And now they cannot stop singing the spell. Millennia have passed, and nobody that they have consumed has any idea how to stop it.

But Venalia might.

Stop the song, stop the spell.

That *was* her plan; to drive the Choir apart, to stop them from singing together. The pain, the loneliness, the hunger and the cold – it drives them to huddle together, to stay as one unit. To drive them apart, she must make it *worse.*

The others begin to drift towards her in the darkness, protecting her, shielding her. She feels the Tall Woman's hatred, like a twisted child standing on a cat's tail for the joy of hearing it scream. The kind of monster that would burn a child's bow, and let a girl stay missing.

Venalia feels her way to the hard-hearted minds clustering together nearby. They are in formation, it seems, a defensive stance, to protect her. They feel regimented, organised, serious – but familiar. They feel like Temple.

The leader is a fighter, and a dwarf; she can feel the steel in his bones, the earth in his mind; one of the stonefolk. A dwarf, the one who spoke to her.

"Ungren?" she tries. "Temple's friend?"

The unit turn as one protective shell. It strikes Venalia that Temple's unit have stuck together, even in this psychic hellscape.

"You know Temple," says Ungren.

"I do."

"He made it out. The Magistry are on their way?"

"They are."

"Then the job is complete," he says, and a wave of relief gives them all a moment of respite.

"No rest yet," she says. "I think I have a plan to end this."

"Easy there, girl," says Ungren. "There's no ending this. Our bodies are gone. We're already dead. As will you be soon."

"What?"

"You're being digested. Becoming part of the whole. No, once the Magistry destroys this thing, we'll be free to move on to the Black Sands."

"What if it doesn't return to the surface?"

"Then we remain. There is little greater an insult than denying a warrior a good death. Magisters should have cleaned up their own mess in the first place."

She's heard Temple say that before, she thinks. She can

hear so much of him in this dwarf.

"There is truly no saving you?" she asks.

"Nothing to save, lass."

"I can still save Llantry. I thought I could win this. I had a theory. A plan."

"What plan?"

"To force all the minds of the Choir to separate, by making it so painful to stay together that they break harmony, ending the spell that binds them together."

"How are you going to separate them?"

"With Light."

Clamouring voices talk over Ungren. They remember the Light in the forest. They remember how it burned.

This might work, she thinks.

Before they can act, the Tall Woman slams her presence down upon them again, scattering them. Ungren is thrown far from her, and Venalia is drifting alone again. Venalia is assaulted with deafening, intrusive thoughts that stop her from forming any coherent response.

Then comes the single note of a song that does not match the Tall Woman's. She hears, in the darkness, the first notes of a dwarven battle-hymn. Then comes another voice, and another, joining in harmony. The Tall Woman is distracted, however briefly, and Venalia knows that if she is to act, then she must act now.

Her connection to her body, the innate sense of *being* that she has, is starting to drift away. She can feel her mind bending to the song. More and more she finds her thoughts aligning with the greater whole.

She feels cold.

She is hungry.

She wants to be safe, she wants to be near others.

Everybody should join her here.

High above, she can feel the chase, the hunt, the excitement as the Choir closes in on the people of Llantry. Gregor is shouting orders, somewhere. Children scream, people jam themselves into a narrow tunnel.

They are not going to make it.

Gregor pushes them all past him, telling them to make for the surface. He stands in the tunnel and blocks it, warhammer in two hands, a torch at his feet.

Venalia has to act now.

"Magistress Ceylandwelle Finduilye!" she shouts into the void.

An old, decrepit soul meets her with surprise, withered by two thousand years of *cold* and *lonely* and *hungry*. There is little left of what Ceylandwelle once was. Without pause, the Tall Woman's face is pressed against Venalia, and she is loud enough that Venalia feels she might be blown apart.

LIAR

LIAR

LIAR

"I didn't lie," says Venalia. "You're trapped in a binding enchantment, your minds are locked in harmony – I need to force you all apart whilst my body can still produce Light."

There is no

apart

not

help me

any more

Venalia hears the tiny voice of a weary, beaten woman, hiding under the anger. She hears it beg for help, for an ending to this suffering.

But the Tall Woman says otherwise.

You will pay a dear price
liar
We will consume Llantry
and take them deep
to the peaks
of the
lowest
undermountains
the deepest depths
of the trenches
of the
underocean
where no light has ever shone
and none will ever find us
and we will pick apart your soul
until we are satisfied
that you have suffered
enough

She feels her body disintegrating.

Outside, Gregor is swinging the hammer and the torch in desperation, fighting for time. He has been knocked to the ground, and the massed shades of the Choir swarm over him. His legs are caught in many hands, his head is surrounded by singing mouths. He is being dragged into the Tall Woman's silhouette just like she was.

His eyes glaze over.

The Choir almost has him.

"Then you cannot be saved," says Venalia. "May the Gods forgive you – and may they forgive me."

Returning to her body feels like returning home – but her home is aflame. Her body is being absorbed, melted down – her skin is burning, she's in *agony* – but there is no way to do this from outwith the physical.

The pain makes it difficult to focus on the spell, but after years of practice, casting a Light spell comes to her as naturally as walking.

Her clothes are burned away, exposing every inch of her skin.

She takes the pain and pours it into a war cry as she casts the spell.

First, she lets the Light flow from her skin. It blooms from her body. Then, both Venalia and the Light *scream.*

There is a new sun born, deep below the earth.

The tunnels of the Inverted World turn white, filled with starlight that burns the Choir from the inside out.

The shades writhe and scream, beg and plead, breaking the singing -

breaking the spell.

Her energy is fading. She pushes with everything that she has, burning as bright as she can bear, and then brighter still.

Light bursts through the shadow of the Tall Woman as the Choir starts to split. No matter how cold they feel, how little they want to be alone, the blazing pain drives them apart. They repel one another, clawing and climbing, stretching to a near break.

The songs are all separate. The voices are becoming individuals again, almost,

almost -

Venalia feels her energy sputter and fade. She has nothing left to give. Her body is empty. Then she feels the presence of Ungren – and of his men, and the other, ancient Magisters.

They throw themselves upon her as though she were a

funeral pyre, burning with her, giving her everything they have left.

Light.

Pain.

Like the cracking of a glacier, the minds finally begin to separate – and as soon as they bend just a little out of shape, the Choir snaps, and breaks apart.

The spell is shattered.

The song stops.

The music is gone.

The shadowy mass of the Choir disintegrates, blown apart in a supernova of Celestial light.

Tell Temple what happened here, lass.

Comes a voice to her mind.

Tell him that his debt is paid.

And then from the blinding light, from the brightest of endings, comes darkness.

Venalia goes into it gratefully, at peace.

To certain death.

Chapter Fifteen

When she opens her eyes, she feels a hunger like she has never experienced. Gregor is kneeling over her, eyes full of concern. He shouts for something. She is aching all over – a dull, burning pain.

Daylight is streaming in the window. Only now does she recognise her childhood home. She is in her own bed, in her own house.

She tries to speak, and finds her throat too dry. Gregor reaches over with a sponge and motions for her to open her mouth. He squeezes some moisture in, and she starts to cough immediately. It burns – not with heat, she realises, but with strong alcohol. The tavern keepers best mixture.

Awful though it is, she can feel it returning her strength to her.

"What happened?" she manages at a croak.

"You were absorbed by the Choir," says Gregor. "Then, seconds before it consumed me, I believe you blew it to pieces with a spell of some kind."

It comes back to her like the sour aftertaste of a nightmare.

"I don't think I saved any of them," she sighs. "They were already dead."

"We shall not speak like that, Priestess," he gives her a

stern command. “You saved the very village of Llantry and her people. You saved me.”

Venalia does not feel particularly victorious – but she'll take it. She shuffles up in her bed, pillow against her back. Somebody – hopefully one of the women – has had the grace to put her in fresh nightclothes. She is otherwise covered in some kind of ointment.

She can see that her skin is... *fresh*. She has healed quickly, but she can only imagine the state she was in after the Choir took her. She could feel her flesh dissolving. In fright, she raises her hands to her eyebrows, her hair.

Still there, she sighs with relief. The weight of everything begins to come back to her.

“How many?” she asks.

“How many what?”

“How many did we lose?”

He looks away. “To the Choir? Would you believe me if I said 'none'?”

Venalia looks away, unable to meet his eyes, for a great victory has been won here, and yet;

“Gregor, when I was part of it; I never sensed Evelyn. She was not there.”

“I know,” he says. “I was a part of it too, for a while.”

“Your sisters -” she begins.

“Whatever happened to them, Venalia; it wasn't the Choir.” He gives the tired smile of a survivor. “There is hope yet.”

He is taking this well, she thinks. Seeing it as a positive. She wishes she could say the same.

“Gregor, I swear I will find them.”

“I have no doubt,” he says. “For now, you must rest.”

“I don't want to rest,” she grumbles, reaching for the mixture in his hands, and begrudgingly drinking more of it. “I want to... I want to eat, and sit by a fire and feel its warmth. I want to talk to people, and I want to tell them the truth, I want everybody to know exactly what happened, and *why,* and - Gregor, I found an orphanage for Aberrant dragonblooded children, and-"

She feels herself getting light headed.

"Relax, Priestess," he says, pushing her gently back to her pillow. "There will be time."

"Is Temple here? The Magistry?"

"No. Why would they be?"

"Temple went to get them."

"To fortify Atlan, surely? They must assume that Llantry is gone?"

She deflates. "You're probably right. Temple said that he would return if our chimneys blew smoke again."

"Well, they're doing just that."

"How long was I out? How bad was I?"

"I could see muscle in places, when I dragged you out. It's only been a day. You heal faster than anybody I've ever seen."

"It's a Priestess thing, a divine blessing. Our bodies heal quickly."

"Most of your skin was burned off. I did not recognise you, except by your hair."

"Thank the Gods for that," she sighs.

A heavy silence comes between them. It is clear that both of them have something to say, but neither has the courage.

It is Gregor that finds it first.

"Venalia, there is something I wish to say." He reaches out and takes her hand. She can see a long overdue apology coming and, strangely, she does not want it.

"No," she puts her hand over his, like a doctor breaking bad news. "No, I'm doing this first. I owe you an apology."

"What?" It catches him off guard, and he nearly laughs. Then he sees the tears welling in her eyes, and his face drops. "Venalia, why?"

"For Anabel," she whispers, and the weight is gone from her soul. "I was young. I was stupid. I never wanted for anything bad to happen, but I was so angry, and -"

He shushes her, patting her hand. "Given what you have done for Llantry," he says, squeezing her hand. "Given what you were *prepared* to do for our people? Given what we put you through in our youth. I think we are best served by putting this entire thing behind us, and moving forward."

"I would like that very much," she nods. She feels it in her heart; a sin put right. Redemption. "Then I have one last thing to do here."

"What's that?"

"I will stay in Llantry until I find Evelyn. I owe you that much."

"You owe me nothing," he says. "Any help that you can offer, I gratefully accept."

"She wasn't taken by the Choir, so we can score that lead out."

"Do we have any other leads?"

"Well - it gives me something to work with. If the Choir didn't take her, I *can* find her. I'm a Priestess of the Mind's Eye, this is what I do. One way or another."

"And then?"

"What do you mean?"

"Well, you came to Llantry unsure of what to do with your Priesthood. Have you decided?"

"I think so," she smiles. "I think so."

"And what is that?"

"Travel the continent. Help people like us, help villages like Llantry to keep their fires burning in the dark of winter. Learn a bit along the way, stoke the fire of learning in others, you know?"

"Like a knight errant."

"I suppose so. I don't know that I was ever meant for a normal life."

"I know the feeling," he laughs. "Will you join a free company?"

“Maybe – if it makes living easier. I'll need money. Maybe I can do weddings, or teach, give lectures, that kind of thing.”

Gregor laughs. “I'm sure you'll make it work.”

“You know, I think I'll be fine wherever I end up.”

“Until then, Llantry has a Priestess that it can rely on.”

“Gregor,” she laughs. “It always will. You ever need me, I'll come running. This is my home.”

“Then you'll need this,” he says, and hefts a warhammer onto the bed. “You know *Minotaur,* I'm sure?”

“Oh Gregor, that's yours -”

“All I ask is that you do not change the name. This weapon should remain the Hammer of Llantry. Bell can make you a proper belt for it, I'm sure, if you'll accept the title that goes with it?”

“Accept the..?” she takes a moment to understand what he's saying.

“The title, Venalia – I am the Burroughmaster of Llantry – it is within my power to grant titles.”

“Gregor,” she whispers, though her heart is racing.

“The paperwork has been written. I didn't expect you to resist the offer, though...”

“No, no,” she laughs. “I accept! I accept with honour and gratitude, I just didn't expect it.”

“You have earned this,” he says. “Twice over.”

Gregor stands, takes the hammer, and holds it in two hands. As is the custom in the Herdsman's Moot, he takes to one knee and offers it to her, head bowed.

“Priestess. Venalia. Do you accept the burden of Llantry and her people, its well-being and protection?”

“I do,” she whispers, sitting up in bed. This feels like it isn't really happening to her. Like she is watching it happen to someone else.

“And do you accept the rights of a knight, to a seat at the Moot, the right to an audience, to a steed, and to a night's rest?”

“I do,” she says, breathless.

“And do you accept the name of Venalia de Aria, as the heir of Marius de Aria?”

A surname.

She has never had a surname before.

“I do.”

“And do you accept the title: Champion of Llantry?”

“I do.”

“Then take this hammer, dubbed *Minotaur* for our ancestry, the Hammer of Llantry.” He passes it to her. “May you think of home when you are far from it. May it crush the shields and the bones of those who would do you harm.”

She rests the hammer down and puts her hand to her mouth. “Gregor, thank you.”

He laughs, waving her away. “Days ago, you would have hit me with that very hammer, quite gladly.”

“Well, a lot has changed in a few days.”

“Indeed it has,” he smiles, and brushes down his cloak. “I shall let you rest, Priestess. It's good to see you doing well.”

“And you,” she says.

Gregor leaves the room, and then the house. She waits until absolutely nobody is looking, and then allows herself a brief, few tears of joy, laughing all the while.

Venalia enjoys a long, well earned bath next to a roaring fire, sipping on Sarantja Orange and singing to herself. It takes a while to brush the last few days out of her hair, to scrub clean her newly healed skin, to rest and push her own healing energy through her body. The windows stay open, letting a breeze in to keep her cool. Winter wraps itself around Llantry, throwing a soft blanket of snow over it. It was always her favourite season.

When the sun is at its highest, Venalia dries and dresses. The Choir's digestive process seems to have removed some scars from a rough bout of acne when she was fourteen. The natural healing that she is gifted has restored her anew.

Some of the villagers have repaired her Priestess robes. It takes her a few tries to decide which she prefers; between the robes and cloak, or the shirt and riding breeches. To look like a Priestess in full regalia, or a wandering mercenary with a warhammer on her hip?

Unwilling to compromise, Venalia sits down with a needle and thread, and combines the two together. When she leaves the house, it is in her riding breeches, boots for comfort, and her shirt, covered by the flowing cloak and hood bearing the symbols of the All-Faith. Around her neck hangs the sigil of the Mind's Eye, cold metal against bare skin.

This is what she always thought a Priestess *should* look like. The breastplate, inscribed with the sigil of her God, is the piece that ties it all together. She leaves the armour for now; the fight is over.

As soon as she gets the chance, she needs to pray. The Mind's Eye will want to know everything that she learned – and if she has performed well, then she will be rewarded with new miracles, new spells, new blessings.

Before the mild trauma of prayer, however, there are things that she needs to do. Details and investigations, planning and preparation.

Evelyn de Llantry is still missing.

Venalia sits down at her desk and pulls her parchment and ink over, and starts at the beginning.

She vanished delivering the lance. During an attack by the Choir, no less. Who would take her? Why? Ransom, perhaps? Revenge? Did the de Llantry family do something to somebody? She must speak to Gregor about the enemies his family may have made. The De Witt orphanage was suspicious, but she cannot tie it directly to Evelyn.

Who had the means, the motive and the opportunity?

There must be *something* she is missing.

She establishes a plan of questioning for the people who last saw Evelyn, a plan for the guard to help her search and interview everybody in Llantry. Any minor inconsistencies in somebody's answers or story might point them to the truth.

She feels alive, wrapped in the mysteries and puzzles of a real investigation. It takes her an hour, and then Venalia checks that the ink is dry, rolls the scroll, and checks herself in the mirror one last time. Minotaur hangs with its head in her belt – awkward, but it will do for now. She ties her hair into a warrior's braid, wrapped around her head like a circlet, and smiles.

This is what she wants to do with her life. Find missing people. Solve murders. Answer questions. Unearth secrets.

Ready to face the world, Venalia leaves her house, and steps into Llantry.

Villagers are gathered near her door. When they see her, they light up, greet her, ask her how she's feeling. She stops to talk to them, to learn names. These are her people, after all.

As she passes the guards, she orders them to follow her. When she reaches the guardhouse, she brings with her a gaggle of them following like ducklings. They make her tea and sit patiently whilst she pins her scroll to their briefing board, and when she starts talking, they listen.

No need to demand respect; not when it is given freely.

Venalia assigns them their tasks, the legwork of questioning and searching that goes into a missing person, and watches them leave. When the last guard has left, she flops into a chair, and counts her breaths. She focuses, meditating, *praying*.

She is not ready to face the Mind's Eye. Not yet. When she next sees her God, she wants to have answers for him. The solved mystery of the Choir, the case of Neuroharmonics and its part in the Dragonfall; these are valuable secrets that she will be rewarded for. She is eager to find out what spells, what boons, she will receive.

But not yet.

The case isn't *done* yet.

She needs to speak to Bell again, and get a sense of Evelyn's mindset going into the night the Choir attacked. She sets out for his forge.

Her hammer hangs heavy on her belt as she makes the short hike to Bell's house. She feels the faintest of butterflies as she approaches. The forge is unlit. Bell must be taking some time off – and she cannot fault him.

She wants to ask him about her parents, about what he might have noticed when he found her, though without his sight she expects it will be little. She wonders if he knows anything about her Magisterial bloodline.

Venalia knocks the door to his shop, and waits. When no answer comes, she lets herself in.

Inside is still and quiet – just the counter, where Bell would consult with richer customers, and the show rack, filled with cheaper models. Behind a curtained doorway is Bell's actual home – off limits to her for most of her life. There is a smell that seems familiar, that she cannot quite place.

"Hello?" she shouts. "Bell? It's Venalia!"

There's a cheerful ring to her voice, but it strikes hollow as it echoes around the forge. She feels an immediate sense of dread – this reminds her of something.

Marius. It reminds her of walking into Marius' house, when all that remained was his body. The silence.

"Oh no," she whispers. Bell is old, half-aelven or not. Perhaps the stress and fear finally got too much for his old heart. "Bell?" she shouts, walking to the counter. The door clicks shut behind her, and she lifts Minotaur from her belt. "Bell, are you home?"

She freezes, certain that she heard something. "Bell?"

thud

Venalia can hear it through the wall. More of a feeling than a sound.

thud-thud

Venalia moves around the counter. "Hello?"

thud

The forge is quiet. The counter is empty. There is nobody here, but -

thud

It's on the other side of the curtain, in his home. It dawns on Venalia that Bell was not with the villagers in the Choir's fortress. Perhaps he protected himself by locking himself in a basement, or chaining himself to something.

"Eye guide me," she whispers a blessing upon herself, preparing a Shield spell, unsure of what to expect. Her run in with the undead creature has taught her not to relax. "Eye keep me."

thud

She pushes through the curtain – new territory, unexplored.

There is a single large room, with a door at the back of it – the privy, she guesses. A bed, huge by Llantry's standards, and of exquisite design. Expensive – but then, she remembers, Bell is richer than Gregor. Decadent rugs and animal furs are draped across the walls, paintings that she has seen in Whitehallow galleries. The candlesticks and lanterns are *crystalline*. Gold inlay on everything, even the water by his bedside is in a diamond bottle.

She wonders exactly how rich Bell is.

thud

Under the floor.

"Who's there?" she asks, readying the hammer. "Bell? Is that you? Are you trapped?"

thud-thud

In the corner there lies a rug made from the skin of a dead timber wolf. Venalia crosses to it and leans down -

THUD

The floor shakes, and she jumps back in fright. She can *hear* something.

Sobbing.

Venalia drops to the floor and tears the rug away. Beneath, there is a wooden hatch with a thick steel padlock on it.

THUDTHUDTHUDTHUD

Someone is below her, screaming, and she can barely hear them.

A young woman.

"Evelyn?" she shouts.

THUDTHUDTHUDTHUD

"Evelyn!"

Did she lock herself here when the Choir came?

Where *is* Bell?

Who put the padlock on, Priestess? comes a pestering little voice in her head. She pushes it aside for now. She plants her feet, straightens her back, and grunts as she lifts the hammer overhead. Venalia brings it down on the padlock -

It cracks, but does not break.

"Damn it," she whispers. "Hold on, I'll get you out!"

She slams the sledgehammer into the padlock again. It rattles and jangles, but nothing.

Summoning her strength, whispering a prayer for guidance, Venalia raises the warhammer one last time. With an almighty roar, Venalia delivers a blow that shakes the very house, and she shatters the lock.

Throwing the hatch open takes even more effort – it's heavy. Floorboards over stone over metal.

Not just metal, her senses tell her.

Lead. Enough lead to block any magical sensor, any spell of detection. This looks less like a bunker, thinks Venalia, and more like a prison.

She heaves the trapdoor aside.

Evelyn de Llantry looks up at her, bloodied and bruised, curled and shaking. Evelyn reaches for her like a child, and Venalia grabs her .

Evelyn's wrists are bloody, slick. Venalia sees wires and tubes hanging from her arms, medical tools. Blood transfusion equipment, like the ones in Catherine De Witt's basement.

As Venalia lifts Evelyn out of the hatch, she sees the tiny crawlspace where she has been held prisoner. Bones peek from the dirt, like plants sprouting from a garden.

“It's Anabel,” whispers Evelyn, pointing back into the crawlspace at the bones. “He did it to Anabel too.”

She has been lying on the bones of her sister.

The skeleton of Anabel de Llantry is under the floorboards, only a stone's throw from where Venalia found her ribbon.

Venalia stumbles back as though she has been struck, and feels a sweat break across her face.

It was here this whole time.

Bell.

Belereon.

As Evelyn curls into her arms, shaking and crying, Venalia's mind assembles the puzzle. The transfusions, the De Llantry bloodline, the De Witt home for Aberrant dragon-blooded children, the *picture in the manor* with the faces torn out in hatred.

Bell was the Aberrant who burned down the orphanage. It was he who was pumped full of Draconic blood, he who traced his lineage back to Karak, the Red Terror. It was he who killed the other Aberrant children - and the more Draconic blood he consumed, the worse his Draconic aspect became.

Suddenly Evelyn is screaming, pulling away from Venalia, hiding behind her. When Venalia turns around, heart in her mouth, she sees the silhouette of Bell through the curtains. He is standing by the open door. Waiting. Listening.

She thought him a tormented artisan, passing on his wisdom in place of his bloodline. She cannot reconcile that image with the predator in the doorway.

Children, thinks Venalia. Young women, just like her, who thought the best of him, *trusted him.*

“Evelyn, whatever happens,” she whispers. “Stay close to me.”

Venalia stands up, and readies her warhammer in both hands.

Bell pulls the curtains aside. He looks younger. Stronger. Larger. Just like Catherine De Witt wrote, he is strengthened by

Evelyn's blood. His blindfolded head is staring at the ground, a matter of habit.

She can hear him breathing, and when he exhales she can smell something like the lamp oil, a heady mixture of chemicals, obviously flammable. She stays completely silent, and prays that he truly is blind.

Bell closes the door, and gradually de-robes from the waist up. He drops the old tattered rags and hood, revealing a body swollen with knotted, mutated muscle. His arms are three jointed, his hands tipped by vicious claws. In some places the growth has been too severe, and his skin has burst to reveal red scales.

He lifts the blindfold, and for the first time in her life Venalia sees his eyes. They are the eyes of a reptile, yellow and black, slit down the middle. His *face* – she can see the malice on his very features. His eyes are fixed on the floor.

Bell breathes in deeply, and sighs.

Then his eyes dart upwards, and fix upon her. His pupils narrow, and Venalia feels like a mouse before a lion, a plaything of no consequence.

He was never blind.

He had to hide his eyes; a predator's eyes.

"Bell," she takes a guard stance. "Short for *Belereon de Llantry*. You've been hiding in Llantry for an age, haven't you? Preying on anybody with Draconic blood – to *strengthen* yourself."

Behind her, Evelyn is whimpering, covering her eyes. She cannot bear to look.

Bell says nothing. He sways, listening, watching Venalia intently. His eyes say *rage,* and *hunger*. Every fibre of her being tells her to run – but run to where? The only way that she gets out of here is *through him.*

"You were sent away, weren't you?" she asks. "Is that it? You must be..." she's guessing now, remembering the book that Gregor showed her. "...Evelyn's great uncle? Belereon de Llantry. Sent away for your Aberrant bloodline. The blood of Karak the Red Terror, lord of all dragons."

Bell shuffles – *bristles* – when she says the name; but he says nothing still.

"That's what you called yourself." She tries to engage him, get him talking. "Before you burned down Catherine De Witt's orphanage? Before you killed all of your classmates. For their blood. You wanted their blood."

Still, Bell says nothing. Come on, she thinks. Come on, anybody – Gregor, guardsmen, *somebody*.

"I bet you wandered for a while, feeding on people – moving from town to town to avoid notice. People like Anabel de Llantry, people that wouldn't be missed. Then you groomed Evelyn to fulfil that same purpose."

A realisation dawns upon Venalia – that it was Bell who brought her to Llantry. The final piece falls into place.

"You were raising me for the same thing, weren't you? Did you know that I have Draconic blood too, Bell? When you found me?"

Bell shifts his head, narrowing his eyes, and she realises that the details aren't correct. He *disapproves*. So what does she have wrong?

"You didn't just find me, did you? My parents were burned to ash. You can breathe fire, can't you? Just like your forefather. You consumed them. You burned them. Then you took me, to raise me and harvest me when I was of age. Like cattle."

Bell smiles, and she sees sharp white teeth amidst bleeding red gums. His teeth have grown too big for his mouth. He seems to enjoy hearing the story – hearing his name – but Venalia is running out of things to say.

"What were you going to do, vanish again after the Choir took Llantry? Leave Evelyn in a ditch somewhere, once you'd taken everything that she could give? Reappear somewhere else weeks from now, with a different name, right? Do it all again."

Bell says nothing.

"You weren't counting on us *winning*. Well we did – and when Temple left, he left to alert the Magistry. The best battle-mages in Caladan are on their way here, *right now*. If you start running, you might be able to vanish into the forest before the airships arrive."

Bell takes a step forward and Venalia leaps back, hammer raised to strike. He stops, chuckling, playing with her. His laughter is low, crackling, filled with a wet, burning heat.

"Bell, if you kill us now, our blood dies too. Take me instead. I have Draconic blood. Let Evelyn go, and I won't even resist. She's given all she can, look at her, she's the colour of chalk."

Evelyn needs medical treatment, and quickly. Bell breaks his silence, and his voice carries the low, crackling flames of an orphanage ablaze, the hiss and pop of bubbling skin. He sounds nothing like his old self.

"The Priestess has solved the mystery," he grins, "and before she can tell her masters, she will burn just like her mother and father."

"You don't want my blood?" she tries – anything to stall him, anything to distract him.

"I will have it anyway," he says. "I tire of this act – this miserable town, human cattle tending to hoofed cattle. I tire of hiding my majesty. I could set Llantry ablaze with a word."

"The dragons of old had worshippers," she says. "If you wipe out Llantry, you'll remain a mystery, none will ever know of your conquests, your strength."

"Karak failed, because he needed to be worshipped. He made mortals into slaves and sycophants," breathes Bell. "I will do what my forefather should have done in the first place."

He rears his head back and his jaw unhinges, slack. Pilot lights burst from his throat, his chest glows a dull red with the rising eruption, and wet flame vomit in a heavy stream from his mouth.

Venalia grabs Evelyn and stands between her and the flame, summoning the strongest Shield that she can. Torrents of heavy flame cover the Shield, viscous, thick, driving her back. Sweat bursts from her forehead. Her skin prickles red as Evelyn howls and clings to her.

Already her energy is fading. Her Shield is giving.

Bell stops. The room is ablaze, smoke chokes the ceiling. Through the smoke she sees his silhouette step forward. Blind and gasping, Venalia stumbles backwards, trying to protect Evelyn with her body. The wooden walls burst into flame on their own.

Bell takes another step forward, and Venalia manages to

hold her hammer up. He takes it between two clawed fingers and holds it aside.

"Did you see Anabel's bones down there, child?" he grins, holding her hammer at bay. "Do you remember sneaking her bow past me? Throwing it in the crucible? Did you know that she was only a few feet away, bleeding into a bag? Do you know that I saw you do it? Such a hateful, spiteful little child."

"Who *are* you?" she screams.

There is little she can do – there is no way she can wrench the hammer from his grip. He raises his scaled hand to slap Venalia unconscious – but she throws up another Shield and is, instead, thrown against the burning wall. She slumps, struggling to stand. She needs a mixture, sugar, anything, before she passes out.

She needs to get Evelyn out of here; the girl lies semi-unconscious from the smoke.

Time is up.

"Your magic is borrowed," shouts Bell, over the roaring flames that silhouette him. "You exchange favours for tricks – but this fire is *my* domain. I do not tire. My blood *is flame*." He stands over her, the same man that watched her play as a child, unrecognisable. "Stand up again, and I will kill you."

"You'll kill me anyway," she grits her teeth, picking up the warhammer from where Bell dropped it, and trying to stand. "How could you do this?"

Nothing in her legs but pain. Her Shield spells have drained her already, she has no potion or mixtures to recharge with, and Evelyn is dying from the smoke. She has enough energy for one last try at something.

Venalia wonders where her wit has gone – her ability to improvise, to plan on the fly – where is the woman who defeated the Choir?

Bell is an Aberrant dragonblood - that must bring with it some weakness?

The eyes.

His eyes are that of a dragon – similar to a cat or a lizard. Aberrant dragonbloods can see well in the dark. Just like the Kappi and Aelfa, their senses let them live in places where humans cannot.

It makes him over-sensitive to Light.

Bell pins her to the wall with one hand, and with the other curls his clawed fingers under her breastplate to pierce the soft flesh of her stomach. He meets her eyes with a grin, and Venalia jams her hand over his eyes and blasts them with Light, enough to turn midnight into day, if only for a second. Bell roars and belches liquid fire upon her in his fury, clamping his claws over his face.

But Venalia has already moved. She ducks aside, plants her feet, and swings the hammer at the side of his head. It connects, delivering a blow that would shatter the skull of a mortal man. The hammer cracks the skin, but the scales underneath hold his skull intact. The blow throws him to the floor. He grunts and drops to all fours, clutching at the bloody skin – stalled, but not stopped.

Venalia throws the hammer aside as she shakes Evelyn.

"Come on, lass, we have to move, we have to go *right now* -"

Evelyn's eyes flutter open – and as soon as her brain catches up, she springs to life. The two of them stumble out of the forge and make for the door as flame consumes it.

A roar from behind them – Bell, jaw unhinged, screaming after them. With his words comes a gout of fire, blazing napalm that will burn to the bone.

There is no way to dodge it. Venalia throws a Shield around her and Evelyn, at the exact moment the flame hits – and then she's airborne.

Everything is red.

Then blue.

Venalia comes to a rest under the open sky.

It takes her a moment to process the explosion - the third one in three days that has knocked her on her arse – that has blown them clear of Bell.

Evelyn lies beside her in the mud, breathing hard, groaning in pain, patting out flames on her clothes. Venalia's throat is clogged with smoke.

The forge is blown to the heavens. Venalia lets her head drop back in the wet mud, and breathes. Her head is spinning. She can hear bells.

Curious villagers descend upon them, and her throat is too dry to voice the danger. She rasps at them, waving them away, but they run to her instead.

Gregor leads the guard, throwing himself down beside Evelyn and embracing her, shouting for water, for medics, for help. The villagers help Venalia to her feet, filled with questions.

Venalia can barely croak a reply, and so she can only point in horror, and tell them with her face.

From the flames appears the silhouette of a monstrosity; an aberration, his skin burned away to reveal shining red scales.

Belereon de Llantry. Son of Karak.

The Red Terror.

Chapter Sixteen

"Gregor," croaks Venalia – he sees the look in her eyes, and the mood shifts. "Gregor, evacuate the town. Get everyone out. It's Bell. It's all him."

Gregor does not hesitate to pick up Evelyn, passing her to the waiting crowd as they start to flee, and begins shouting orders to the guards to evacuate.

Bell is watching them. He isn't moving – not yet. In each of his hands he carries a battleaxe, and around his waist is the fireproof apron of a blacksmith.

He resembles a butcher.

"Venalia, come on, we're leaving," says Gregor, taking her by the shoulder.

She shakes him off. "I have to make sure he doesn't follow you."

"Not this time, Venalia, not again."

Bell watches them from afar.

"So come back for me!" she hisses. "But get the people to safety first."

"Do you have any magic left?"

"A little," she says, shaking.

"Enough?"

"Probably not," she admits.

"Guards!" shouts Gregor – four of his men run towards him, breaking from the crowd whilst the others herd people out of Llantry.

There comes a sudden roar, splitting the sky. Bell has decided that time is up. He makes a sound like no mortal man, a loud screech like a bird of prey, of a register far lower, the sound of a mountain breaking.

Bell paces towards them, clanging the axes together in anticipation, laughing to himself all the while, his fanged jaws set in a permanent grin.

They have seconds in which to act.

"Go recharge," Gregor pushes Venalia away and draws his own sword. "We will hold him. Get to the tavern and recharge!"

She sees in him the same resolve that took her into the Inverted World. There is no argument to be had – nothing but the knowing nod with which they say goodbye.

Venalia turns, and runs for the tavern.

Gregor is trained by knights, by warriors. He is trained to fight other soldiers, with similar weapons, similar armour. What he faces now is a berserker who breathes wet flame. Gregor has no armour, and an ornamental bastard sword last used to open a wine bottle.

Bell cackles, globs of fire and blood dripping from between his teeth, savouring the fight. He comes at Gregor with his axes low, leaving his guard wide open. Gregor spreads his weight out in a practised stance: uses Bell's momentum against him. He deflects the first axe and pivots aside, slashing at Bell's torso.

The sword fails to break through, and Bell is already countering.

An axe comes in low, towards Gregor's ribs, and Gregor moves to parry before he sees the feint. The real killing blow comes from overhead. Gregor rolls his shoulders to back, feels the axe-blade whisper past his face.

A momentary opening as Bell recovers. With all his strength, Gregor drives the blade into Bell's ribs, but the blade cannot pierce his scales.

Bell drops an axe and grabs Gregor's blade. He grimaces, locking eyes with Gregor.

"Brave boy," he breathes, and inhales. "If your blood were any thicker, I'd spare you."

Gregor can drop his sword and run, or stay here and be incinerated. A glow lights in Bell's throat, his jaw unhinges;

This is Gregor's only chance.

He drops the sword, grabs Bell's axe from the ground, and swings it high. It shatters Bell's jaw, snapping it aside. The blow would have removed any man's head from his body, but Bell is far too strong for such an easy death.

His flames choke in his throat, sputtering out in molten drips. Gregor can feel their heat.

Bell regards it as a minor inconvenience, rubbing his broken jaw, his teeth misaligned and bloodied. Gregor steps back, gripping the axe, watching Bell as he clears his throat, belching smoke and sparks.

Gregor's guards assemble behind him, crossbows aimed at Bell.

"What are you waiting for?" he shouts to his guards. "Shoot him!"

In unison, the guards all loose their crossbows. The bolts land dead on, but strike so shallow that they appear to bounce off. Bell looks up, and in those yellow reptile eyes Gregor sees no trace of the kindly old blacksmith.

Broken-jawed, Bell throws his head back in laughter, molten flame dripping from his throat. Behind him, the flames of the forge are spreading to other buildings whilst a symphony of screaming and alarm bells plays Llantry's last moments.

Bell puts his head down and charges, too fast for Gregor to dodge. Gregor is thrown aside like a doll, and Bell crashes through the guards, scattering them like bowling pins. As Guardsman Corryn falls, Bell grabs his leg and throws him into the blazing forge.

They hear his scream cut short. Agnir rises to his knees and scrambles to escape. Bell plants his foot upon his head and crushes it into the mud. Bell twists his heel, and something pops. Agnir falls limp.

Gregor rises to his feet, winded, and charges Bell. His axe clatters off of Bell's scales, and Gregor is hit with an open-handed slap that throws him to the ground.

He tries to call for the others to flee, but his ribs are tightening around his lungs.

Two of his guards remain, young men who swore him an oath, expected an easy life. They cling to one another on the ground as Bell bathes them in flame.

Their screams are cut short, and Gregor can only watch.

Bell tosses his last axe aside and savours the walk towards Gregor, who can stand no longer. Bell unfurls his long shining claws, freshly grown from his hands, dripping with his own blood.

Before he can descend upon Gregor, Venalia's voice comes from across the road.

"Belereon!" she challenges him, emerging from the tavern, no weapon in her hands, crackling with energy, sparks of Celestial light spilling from her eyes. She sees Gregor, sees the destruction, the deaths, and in her eyes Gregor sees a divine fury ignite.

"Gregor," she spares him a glance. "Run."

Slipping and scrambling on the mud, Gregor backs away, breaking into a sprint.

Only the Priestess remains.

Venalia is ablaze, eyes fixed on Bell's. He grins through his broken jaw, his new needle-point teeth cracked and broken.

There are no more words or challenges to be exchanged; just a reckoning for unspeakable crimes.

Venalia trembles; not with fear, but with fury.

Having drank everything that she could get her hands on in a half-minute, she has to expend this energy soon.

Bell sprints the distance and raises his claws overhead, and this time she directs her Shield with efficiency, focusing it only upon the small area in front of her hands.

She turns the blow aside and dances back, keeping her distance. Bell circles her, and stares Venalia down. He tests her again, first with the flame, then with the claws, and every time Venalia blocks him with her Shield.

She just needs *time.*

"So much for the Red Terror," she laughs. "If you can't take me, how will you handle the Magistry?"

"Look around you, child," he slurs through his broken jaw.

Venalia has to concede the point. The main street of Llantry is ablaze. Other houses are aflame, and it is only spreading faster.

Bell circles around her, till his back is near the square, where her home is.

Home.

He looks over his shoulder, and grins, inhales deeply, fire bubbling in his gullet.

Venalia screams, desperate; she cannot stop him, but she has the Hold spell.

Venalia reaches into her mind, searching for the unfamiliar shape of the spell. She barely knows these shapes, ideals expressed as geometric patterns in a higher dimension.

Rigidity. Cessation. Binding.

She feels the spell click together, and reaches for Bell, one hand on her head. Her mind touches his, and all at once she is aflood with horror, enough to break her casting attempt.

Screaming children drained into blood bags, drank dry in a fit of mad lust. The bones of young Magisters. A red haired woman of the Steppe and her love, protecting their newborn daughter with their bodies as the flames turn them to ash.

To feel Bell's mind is to walk into flame. Rage, malice, domination. Venalia cannot reconcile what she finds, for there is nothing in him left of the man she once knew. It is all a mask; Bell never existed.

The shock is too great.

The spell fails, and with a cry of frustration Venalia drops to one knee. Her head throbs with effort.

There is nothing that she can do to stop him.

Venalia watches, helpless, as Bell incinerates her childhood home. Every little memory of Marius raising her, all of her books, everything that she held dear, a pain far deeper than any burn.

Bell turns, silhouetted by the flames of her youth. He clicks his jaw back into place, wincing at the pain. Those with Draconic blood heal fast. Just like her.

"You can't keep this up much longer, Priestess," he cackles. "No weapon of yours can hurt me."

She needs *time*.

"Evelyn never left your forge did she? You stashed the lance away, hoping that the Choir would overpower us."

Bell laughs. "No use figuring it out now. They really should have sent a Priest of the Champion."

"They would never have seen you for what you are," she shakes her head. "No. Llantry survived the Titans, the Old Gods and the Dragonfall – it survived the War of Storms, and the Age of Fear, the Scar and the Devourer. It survived the Choir. It will survive you."

"Why die for this place?" he asks her as Llantry burns. "For these people?"

"I'm a Priestess," she answers. "It's what we do."

"Then die you shall."

The time for words is over. Bell advances, mouth open, and a wash of flames spills over Venalia.

She casts her Shield, keeping it in front of her. Flames lick around the edge. They would ignite the hems of her robes, were she wearing them instead of her breeches.

Bell keeps coming, flames like heavy sludge, and she is pushed back step by step. Shield is draining her quickly.

Her vision goes first, blurry and hazy. Her legs go weak. Her breath is coming in short bursts.

Still come the flames.

She lets her Shield drop and rolls aside. Blinded by his own flames, Bell misses her roll, and she ears a few seconds on her knees. Bell rounds on her, the flames stopped for a second.

Only alarm bells now; no more screaming. Llantry is empty but for the remaining guards, who Gregor leads in now. Gregor orders a volley, and a half-dozen bolts stick in Bell's back.

He cares not. Bell rushes her and kicks her onto her back, pouring the flame upon her. Venalia holds her Shield as the weight of the fire presses her into a casket of mud. She hears herself screaming.

The flames keep coming until, without fanfare, they stop.

Venalia lets out a breath, lying in a small crater surrounded by burning mud. She takes her chance and scurries onto all fours, stumbling upright. The sky itself is black, filled with such smoke that it appears like night.

Bell is looking down the long main street of Llantry.

There at the gates, saddled atop Pretzia, is Temple. In his hand he holds aloft a silver tipped lance that shines in the flame.

Her heart swells.

"Temple," she whispers.

Temple looks not at Bell, but at Venalia. Across the distance, she sees the message in his eyes: a greeting, and a farewell. She remembers that Temple's dreams ended after they left; that his visions have stopped. He has never gone into a fight without knowing the outcome, until today.

This, then, is how it happens.

Temple gives her a nod – one warrior to another. Neither can do this alone. Neither would allow it.

Pretzia scuffs her hooves on the cobbles. Bell growls and readies himself, walking out into the road to meet Temple, his throat and lungs glowing.

Temple and Pretzia lower their head together, and as one, they *charge*. Pretzia pulls herself to full speed in a heartbeat. The air shatters before her, dirt and rock flying, a wake of swirling snow and smoke behind her. She bears down upon the road like an avalanche, a drumbeat of clattering hooves.

Temple does not blink. He lowers the lance, breathes deep, and from his massive lungs comes war cry.

Bell screams a dragon's roar, and opens his mouth, fire spilling out to meet Temple.

Not like this.

As he inhales, Venalia finds the shape of the spell, and reaches for Bell's mind. Her casting is messy, inefficient, an amateur using raw force to make up for technique;

but it works.

Divine light bursts from her eyes, her third eye breaking open upon her forehead, pulsing a bright blue.

Venalia's mind is stone and water, the safe walls of a temple fortress, a place of solitude and peace, a place of rest.

Bell's mind shocked her before, but now she sees that Bell's fury is his weakness. He will lash out instinctively.

If ever she doubted that she can overcome Bell's will, she only need remember the Choir's destruction at her hand.

She touches Bell's mind, and feels that same fire and fury from before, but this time she lets him attack and mentally steps aside like a bullfighter.

Venalia surrounds Bell's mind with her own; not with malice, but with love, a mother swaddling a child to protect it from the flames. It takes him by surprise, and in that moment, Venalia forms herself into a solid prison of stone, steel bands of will holding Bell in place.

Hold.

She holds her breath, and stops.

Bell is frozen to the spot.

He rages against her, straining the bands that Hold him. He burns her, guts her, rips her in two and scatters her organs to the wind, but nothing that he does can disturb the peace that she keeps here. Bell is a firestorm, burning her to death, skin melting from her bones.

Still she Holds him.

Then comes the storm, borne from Pretzia's hooves, two tonnes of muscle focused into a singular sharp point. Temple strikes Bell like a shining meteor, blowing him off his feet and shattering the lance in one. The silver tip finds its mark, and Pretzia thunders past Venalia like a lightning strike.

Venalia feels Bell vanish. His mind is no longer there.

With a deep sigh, she drops the spell and collapses to the ground. She lets her head fall back into the mud. When she opens her eyes, she finds Bell to her side, a pile of limbs on the ground, tangled and broken.

But it is not Bell. There is no Bell. Never was.

It was all an act.

She hears heavy footsteps as Temple runs to her side.

"Venalia?" he lifts her from the ground and into his arms. "You're alive?"

She has never seen him so happy. There are tears in his eyes. Without a word she embraces him.

"So are you," she laughs. "I thought this was how it happened – I thought you ran out of visions?"

"I did."

"But you came back?"

"I saw the smoke," he laughs. "I saw the smoke from the chimneys, and I had to know if you had made it."

"What if you'd died?"

"Better to die for something than to live for nothing."

Temple puts her down with great care. Llantry is swarmed now by villagers with buckets of water, rescuing what they can from the flames as their homes collapse.

It takes her a while to realise that she is crying. She looks at her house – her *home* – in flames, and puts her hands on her head.

"God's above, if this hasn't been the worst day of my life..."

"It's still morning, Venalia," he pats her back, and leads her away as the villagers rush in to battle the flames. Venalia cannot help the bleak laughter that consumes her, tears rolling down her cheeks as she is led away.

Venalia is finally allowed to sleep whilst the fires are put out. Gregor orders a bed to be made for her in his home, and she gratefully accepts. She awakens a few times to find Temple watching over her. From time to time she overhears him in conversation with Gregor, discussing their rescue from the Inverted World, the death of the Choir.

When eventually she wakes, it is to the smell of food. Temple sits by a roaring fire in her room, in his shirt and kilt, eating four loaves of bread and a bucket of soup. Next to him is the blackened, but intact, *Minotaur,* the Hammer of Llantry, recovered from the blaze. Temple is cleaning it. He looks over as she shuffles upright.

"Priestess."

"You came back," she says. Her voice is still a little hoarse.

"There's water beside you," he says. "Soup here too. Hungry?"

"Ravenous." She shuffles out of bed and pulls a chair beside him at the fire, helping herself to a bowl. "Temple?"

He looks up. "Hm?"

"You *came back."*

Temple stares into the fire for longer than she expects. He is thinking. Eventually he looks her in the eye.

"Got halfway to Atlan. At last light I saw smoke coming from Llantry. I said I'd come back. I assumed that today was my last day. I thought that perhaps I owed it to you."

She reaches out and pats him on the back. "You saved my life – and likely a hundred others."

"Then we are even."

"Fine by me," she says. "Does Gregor have a bath?"

"He does. There are ladies waiting to assist you, he said. Told them to treat you like royalty."

She laughs. “Fantastic. I can still smell the smoke.”

“Dragonfire. Very distinct smell.” He puts down his bowl and leans back, cracking his knuckles. “So you beat the Choir?”

“Aye. Evelyn, too; solved that one. Though that was mostly by accident, granted.”

Temple smiles. “I heard. A victory is a victory.”

“I feel like I was robbed of a good mystery, I just stumbled right into it.”

“Just be glad the girl survived.”

“She's alright?”

“She's up and walking. The fires are out. People are rebuilding. Getting ready for winter.”

“She's alright,” she sighs, and feels the cool water of relief upon her soul.

They stare into the fire awhile.

Venalia can still hear Bell, taunting her, cornering her. The fire only reminds her of how close she was to death.

“Venalia?” asks Temple. She looks up from the fire in response. “You good?”

“Bell was never blind,” she tells the fire. “He saw me throw Anabel's bow into his forge. She was right there under his floor the whole time, being drained of her blood.”

“He was a monster,” says Temple. “Had me fooled.”

“Had everybody fooled,” she says. “I think he killed my parents. Took me to Llantry so he could raise me, and drain me one day.”

“A patient predator,” says Temple.

She wrestles with the words until they fit. “How does a person do that, Temple? How does someone keep up an act so convincing for all that time?”

“There are many whose entire lives are lies, Priestess,” he says. “More than you'd expect.”

She understands; for her entire adult life thus far, she had kept a secret hidden so deep that none would ever guess it. That secret had a weight to it, a burden that she did not realise was weighing upon her until she released herself of it.

They sit together in silence, staring into the flames, eating without pause. Her stomach is groaning from emptiness, but she has to force the food down.

To her surprise, Temple breaks the silence.

"I've always known I'd survive a battle," he says. "Today, I was sure that I would die. It is a very different experience, riding into combat whilst... *uncertain*."

"You went to certain death," she says. "And lived."

"I understand," he says, locking eyes with her. "Our argument weighed heavily upon me. I wondered if you were right. I think, now, that you were."

"I said some horrible things," she whispers.

"But true," he says. "Certainly true.

"You proved me wrong, in the end," she says. "You're no coward. You rode to certain death without hesitation."

He gives an introspective nod. "I surprised myself with that one."

"Do you think the visions will ever return?" she asks him.

"I don't know. Perhaps this was my gift's way of saying goodbye. Perhaps I die in my sleep tonight? Perhaps I just don't get any more visions. Perhaps I have one in a decade and that's my last. I am no longer *certain* of anything."

"This is how the rest of us live every day," she laughs and leans back in her chair.

He gives her a moment, and she stretches and cracks most of the joints in her body. Everything is aching, but it feels good; it feels earned.

"How do you feel?" he asks, and she hears his curiosity and his concern in equal measure.

She gives a pause, trying to voice it. "It doesn't feel real."

"You want my advice?"

"Of course."

"Write it down. Memorialise it. Then, in times to come, remind yourself that it happened. Not the heroic stories that you'll hear. Not the songs and the legends, and there *will* be songs, I've already heard one. Remember the reality of it. You must never forget the reality."

She gives him a long sideways look. Temple is not one for poetic speeches, but she hears the experience and wisdom in his words.

"What is the reality of it, then?" she asks him.

"You walked into certain death. Alone. To save your people – people who mistreated you. You did it out of duty. You faced a monster that my expedition fell to, and you won. You gave life to people who would have been otherwise denied it. You were tested to your core, and found that your core is indestructible."

She nods, unsure of what to say.

"Have you prayed yet?" he asks.

"I'm building up to it. I've got a *lot* of stuff to tell the big guy."

"Shall I leave you to it?"

Venalia takes a while to decide. She has time, finally.

"Can you stay awhile?" she asks.

"Of course."

She stares into the fire; reliving the day, and Temple returns to cleaning Minotaur, revealing the veins of crystalline. Venalia makes a mental note to charge it, when she has the time.

"I've been thinking," he begins, working himself at a problem out loud. "About what to do now that I'm, you know -"

"Now you're what?"

"Free."

"Free? Were you under a bond to the Free Company?"

"Free from my visions," he sighs. "The future is no longer decided for me, it seems. I do not know what I do next."

"Oh look, you've turned into me from three days ago," she laughs. "Shall we do this together? One last time?"

"Sure," he laughs. "Tell me. What are you going to do now?"

She smiles, because this time she has an answer. "Well. Llantry is safe. I told them I'd stay till I found their missing girls. I have. Now, it's time to move on. I want to keep doing this. I want to help people, travel the continent serving my God. More than anything, I want to find out about my mother, my father. There are questions that needs answering."

"Funny you say that," he says.

Temple reaches into his kilt, and pulls out a flame-blackened ram's skull. He holds it up to the light, and she sees sigils engraved into the side. Druidic symbols, unfamiliar to her.

"I've been polishing this while you slept. You know what this is?"

"Druidic artefact of some kind?"

"Steppe-folk use them. They engrave them with the sigils of their clan. When they leave their home, they take one with them. It's like a badge of office. It identifies them to other clans. It tells people who you are."

"And that one is yours?" she guesses. "Your mother left it with you?"

"No, Venalia," he looks long at the ram's skull, at the runes. "The guards found it in the ruins of Bell's forge, protected inside a safe." He looks up at Venalia. "It was blackened with soot, but otherwise unharmed. I believe that this belonged to your mother."

He passes it to her. Venalia turns it over in her hand. The engravings, strange sigils of ravens and stags. Her mother once held this. Even without Temple telling her, she would know. Holding it, she feels the same call of the Steppe, the smell of grass and rain beneath the open sky. The wind calls her name.

"Do you know what the sigils mean?" she asks. "Do you know this clan?"

"No," says Temple. "Don't read Druidic. Nor does anybody in Llantry. But I think that maybe you should find out what these symbols mean."

Venalia again considers the ram skull, a link to her

mother, and wonders if there are others out there on the Steppe, living wild with the wind in their red hair, who look a little like her.

"Where would I start?" she asks.

"Atlan," he says. "Ask around for Vigo, he'll be able to decipher this. Perhaps he can tell you who your mother was."

"Who's Vigo?"

"Chieftain of the Stitched Banner. If he won't see you, show him that skull."

Venalia runs her hand over it again. Her mother scribed these runes. This is her mother's handwriting.

"Thank you," she says. "Bell had this the entire time?"

"Seems so."

Venalia places it on the floor, away from anything that she might drop.

"And what about you?" she asks.

"I'm going North. Into the wild."

Venalia sits up. "Alone?"

"I'm going to Sunstone, to find my people." He leans back, and she hears the sadness in his voice. "Venalia, I *know* that were I to ask, you would accompany me in a second -"

"Of course!"

"- but this is a journey that must be undertaken alone."

Venalia wants to argue, but she senses that the decision is final. "Like a pilgrimage?"

"Exactly. It may take me a long time. You have your own journey to see to."

"I would have joined you in a second," she says, smiling.

"I know," he laughs.

She sighs, turning over the ram's skull in her hands. "Well, I can't say that I'm not sad to lose you, Temple. I quite liked having a half-Giant to fight my battles for me."

He laughs. "I do not know if the life of a fighter is for me. Not any more. I'm not assured of my survival, after all. Problem is,

I'm no good at anything else."

"I know the feeling," she says. "You'll find your path. I'm sure of it. Certain I can't come with you?"

"I am certain."

"Fine," she sighs. "Could you teach me some things before you go?"

"I can try," he raises his eyebrows in surprise. "What do you think I can teach you?"

"How to fight?" she suggests. "But if you need to re-learn that yourself..."

"Not the best teacher for that, am I?"

"What about leadership?" she asks. "I've never led people in combat before. You could teach me tactics and strategy?"

Temple takes a breath. She knows that he is not a man used to expressing his feelings. She is not entirely sure that he even has that many of them. Yet here he is, brow creased, trying to put something complex into words.

"Here is all that I can teach you about leadership, Venalia: I can count on one hand the number of people that I would willingly take orders from. I would only serve under the command of somebody in whom I have absolute trust," he says, staring into the flames. "The highest compliment that I can give you, is that you earned that trust the moment that I met you. I have no doubt that if you lead, people will follow."

Venalia feels her stomach flutter with pride. "Can I have a half-Giant bodyguard until I leave Llantry, then?"

He smiles. "I think you've earned that too. What are my orders?"

"Get me a bath," she says, standing up. "I smell like a battlefield."

"You've never been on a battlefield."

"That's fair," she says with a chuckle.

Marius once told her that sometimes all one can do is laugh, especially when things are at their worst. It helped her through many a dark night; and it helps her now.

Venalia has come to a greater appreciation of baths since leaving Whitehallow, where she took the showers for granted. She washes, dries, and for the first time in a while, takes her time to dress.

Hair dried and down. Riding boots and breeches, belt, shirt, long cloak of dark green and hood. Her breastplate is polished to a shine, her sigil around her neck. Minotaur hangs from her belt, polished but still uncharged.

She steps out of Gregor's house, and finds Temple waiting by the front door; keeping guard. Motioning for him to follow, she leads them down Llantry's main street. Snow hides the scarred ground, allowing it to heal.

People are leaving Llantry, making for the grassy copse on the outskirts, where Venalia set the pyre for Marius. She considers the way that they look at her now, compared to how they looked at her then. She takes all of those feelings, the insecurity and the uncertainty and the anxiety, and she tosses them upon the pyre in her heart, burning them away. She was a child then still, and she forgives that child for their petulance.

A Priestess has no need for grudges and jealousy.

The crowd are gathered around five funeral pyres. Gregor stands beside Evelyn, in their thickest furs, as snow gathers in their dark hair. It sizzles on the bonfire as it falls. Evelyn is looking better by the day, the colour returning to her face.

"Priestess," he surprises her with an embrace which she returns after getting over the shock. He pats her arm, and shakes Temple's gigantic hand. "Mr. Temple. We're burning the fallen guards. Jonsi. Alain. Corryn. Agnir."

"I count five pyres," says Venalia.

"One for Anabel," he says.

Venalia stares at the fifth pyre, unlit. The last time Anabel was cast into flame, it was her hand that did it. Gregor sees her face, and puts a hand on her shoulder.

"Will you sing for them?" he asks.

"Of course," she says, without hesitation.

Venalia sings a soft aria as the snow falls upon the pyre flames, her voice one with the wind. She watches Gregor hold the crowd in a way that seems new to him. He eases their fears, acknowledges the sacrifices made, the nightmares that will stay with them all.

He speaks like his father once did, about the spirit of Llantry, about the traitor and murderer in their midst this entire time. Admissions of his own weaknesses, a pledge to learn the lessons, to grow from the horrors and outlast them.

Gregor has changed much in just a few days, she thinks. They all have. The shepherds watch Gregor talk, nodding along with him, and right then Venalia knows that Llantry will survive. She has done what she first thought impossible, and repaired not just Gregor's reputation, but the fabric of Llantry as a whole.

To the guards, she sings the hymns of the Champion, God of War. For those who have fallen in combat, in the line of duty, who have died as warriors with honour, protecting the innocent. They will be honoured in Llantry's songs forever.

And as she tosses the bones of Anabel de Llantry upon the blazing pyre, she sings a hymn of the Light Within, Goddess of Redemption. She sings for Anabel; for she forgives her any hatred, any wrongdoing, any grudge. She sings for her own penance.

As they honour their fallen, Venalia locks eyes with Evelyn across the flames, and feels the warmth of forgiveness wash away the stains upon her soul.

When the sermon is finished, Venalia says her farewells to the people of Llantry as they pass her, laying their hands on hers. Temple allows her the spotlight, though a number touch him as they pass by.

At Venalia's side, Evelyn and Gregor wait until they are alone.

"Until we meet again, Priestess." Gregor gives a brief bow, and places a sack of coins in her hand. "And I hope that we shall."

"Burroughmaster." She returns to bow, does not mention the money, and watches as Gregor leaves.

Evelyn remains, hands clasped, nervous. Venalia breaks the moment to pull her into an embrace. She has not seen her since the rescue, since she pulled her out of a concrete grave with the bones of her older sister.

They stay in the embrace for a while, as Evelyn whispers thanks in her ear. Venalia dries Evelyn's cheeks.

"He didn't get us, eh?" she tells Evelyn. "We beat him. It isn't going to happen to anybody else. Never again."

Evelyn nods, and Venalia walks her to the fire, to the warmth. It reminds them both of the forge, of Bell. Venalia points Evelyn towards the flames.

"You look long into those flames, lass," she says. "Don't be afraid of the memory. Face it head on, and you'll find it can't hurt you. These things; they only have power because we give them power."

Evelyn looks long into the flame, and in her eyes Venalia sees the reflection of Bell. Flame, hot enough to scar.

"Evelyn?" she asks, after a time.

Evelyn finally looks away from the fire, but something is lit in her eyes. "He can't hurt me any more," she says. "Can he?"

"He can't hurt anybody any more."

Evelyn smiles, though Venalia can see the pain, the wounds that have been left by Bell. They both trusted him, both thought they knew him.

"Can I ask a question?" asks Evelyn.

"Of course," beams Venalia.

"I don't know what to do now. Gregor tells me that I could go to Yorostadt. Become a proper Magistress. Or I could go to Whitehallow, take the trials, serve the Faith."

Venalia laughs to herself. "If you want my advice, I think you'd be great at whatever you choose."

"Well that's not an answer. What do *you* think I should do?"

Venalia consider the question. Not so long ago, she had no idea what to do with her own life. She is not so sure that she is qualified to give this advice.

“A while ago,” she tells Evelyn, “I thought that I wanted to do something that I *enjoy*. And do you know, Evelyn, that's bad advice.”

“Why?”

“Because I enjoy...” she waves her hands. “Books. Reading, and singing, and crosswords and puzzles and riddles, and quizzes. Try getting paid to solve crosswords,” she laughs. “It's hard to make a life out of the things that you enjoy - and if that was all that I did with my days, I'd be bored. Unchallenged.”

“So what path do I choose?”

“What path? Well. We aren't so different to the forests, Evelyn; we are not truly alive unless we're growing. You understand?”

“I think so.”

“Choose the hardest path that you can walk. Seek growth. Seek purpose.”

“Seek purpose,” says Evelyn. “Very wise, Priestess.”

“Oh shush,” laughs Venalia.

Evelyn gives her one last embrace, before bidding her a pleasant journey, and leaving to join Gregor at the base of the hill.

Temple watches Venalia, silent. The two of them stand, arms folded, looking out over Llantry as the snow falls.

Temple looks to the horizon in quiet contemplation.

“Do you remember when we stepped out of Bell's forge, and we both felt the Steppe call to us?” he asks.

“I do,” she smiles, following his eyes to that same horizon, to the distant snow-capped mountains under a never-ending sky.

“I've been meaning to ask you, waiting for a good moment.” He is struggling, and she can see it. “When you faced the Choir -”

He turns to her, his eyes misted and red, and for the first time she hears his voice break a little.

"I met them, aye," she says, sparing him the rest of his question. "I met the rest of your team. Ungren, specifically."

"And were they – did they say, or communicate -"

"Ungren said that you should consider your debt paid. I would have died without them, Temple. They poured their energy into me, so that I could force the Choir apart. In the end, they beat her after all."

Temple breaks into a grim smile, a stubborn tear wetting his cheek. "A good death," he says. "A warrior should never be robbed of a good death. Thank you, Priestess."

Venalia walks to his side, and this time it is she that pats him on the back. "They made it to the Black Sands together."

"And I'll see them again one day."

"Yes," she says. "Just not today."

Temple nods, and the two walk through the snow together.

"If you are to travel South," says Temple, "you'll need money – how much do you have?"

"I have no idea," she cheerfully admits. "Enough, I'll wager. I can count it on the road."

"Count this too," says Temple, and passes her a coin purse of his own. "Gold buys little in the North. I'll need what's on my back, and Pretzia. This will make sure that you eat whilst you find work."

She peeks inside the coin purse and sees the glint of gold. "Temple! Where did this come from?"

"It was an advance payment from the contract – the Choir mission was worth a lot of money. Most of it will go to widows and children. The rest – well, I want you to have it."

She presses the bag to her breastplate. "Thank you, Temple. For everything."

He says nothing, just gives her a look of pride and pulls his cloak around himself, meeting Pretzia at the fence post she is tied to. He begins to prepare her saddle for the journey.

"Is there anything else?"

"Last thing, I promise – will you watch over me whilst I pray?"

"Oh I suppose." He folds his arms and makes a show of checking they are alone before giving her the go-ahead.

She leads him to the village square.

Amidst the still smouldering ruins stands the statue of the Minotaur, and across from it, the shrine of the All-Faith. People watch her until Temple folds his arms and makes it clear that this is a private moment. When she feels ready, Venalia drops to her knees in the snow, before the shrine.

It has been too long since she has returned to her source, to her God. With the weight of her guilt gone, time slips past her like the snowfall, and she falls backwards through her own ego, down deeper into her soul.

The watcher of watchers greets her.

She smells new books and hot ink, hears the hiss of scrolls and pages, feels the sun-beam attention of the Mind's Eye lifting her up. Venalia revels in it, head held high, having brought a tribute.

He knows what she brings: information, secrets, knowledge. He knows that she has defeated not just a great enemy, but the demons that dwelt within her own mind.

Venalia cannot help but feel some pride in herself.

The Mind's Eye welcomes her into his presence, bathing her in the learned light of wisdom, and Venalia tells him a story about a Priestess, out of her element, out of her depth, trying to put right everything that she has done wrong.

When Venalia finally breathes again, the snow is falling on her shoulders. She finds that Temple has put her hood up for her, without her noticing. He prepares Pretzia, lingering as he messes with the reins, obviously unwilling to go.

This time, she vomits only a little; enough to draw Temple's attention.

"How'd the meeting with your boss, go?" he asks.

"Went well," she says. "I have some favours to call in now, should I ever need them."

"Promise me something," laughs Temple. "Have him give you a spell that you can use in a fight. *Please.*"

"I know, I know. I've not decided what to use them for yet, but I'm sure some kind of radiant fireball is overdue."

Temple points to the sky. "Hope he was happy with your performance. Especially considering that this was your first job as a Priestess."

"Yeah, it's been quite an introduction, hasn't it?"

"Oh, I imagine there's more to come."

They both realise that there is nothing more to say. Temple looks to the North, and Venalia looks to the South.

"Temple," she says, breaking the silence. "Will I ever see you again?."

He pulls her into a bear hug without warning, and holds her there for a while.

"I have no doubt," he says.

Temple then turns and leaps atop Pretzia, nodding to Venalia as he finally breaks North at a light canter. Venalia watches him disappear through the gates of Llantry, before vanishing into the snow. She could laugh and cry in equal measure.

She bids her little village farewell as she walks its only road; says her goodbyes to the snow and the herds, to the hills and the trees. Venalia turns and walks through the snowfall, into the cover of the evergreens.

Llantry fades into the distance; behind her, where it belongs.

Through the uncertain mists of the dark forest, the future beckons.

Certain death, whichever way she looks at it.

Venalia fastens her cloak, smiles, and takes her first step into the rest of her life.

From the Author

I hope you enjoyed The First Rule, and thank you as always for taking a chance on an indie book. I hope that you will follow Venalia into her next tale, **The Rain That Makes The River,** which will be out in 2023. It takes place only a week after she leaves Llantry.

If you enjoyed **The First Rule**, please leave a rating and, if possible, a review. They truly are the lifeblood of an indie author and I read every single one.

You might also enjoy the Interloper Trilogy, my post-apocalyptic sci-fi/shamanic series, which is finished and available on Amazon.

If you'd like to stay up to date with future books and news then you'll find me most reliably on Twitter (@SWHannahAuthor), where you'll find me engaging with the best self-published writer's community on the internet. I always love to hear from readers, so don't be shy.

I'll see you in the sequel, friends.

Steven William Hannah

Printed in Great Britain
by Amazon

16220954R00192